FORBIDDEN LOVE SERIES COLLECTION

OFFICE ROMANCE BUNDLE

KELLY MYERS

ALSO BY KELLY MYERS

Daddy Knows Best Series:

My Secret Daddy || Yes Daddy || Forbidden Daddy || Billionaire Daddy || Daddy's Best Friend || Pregnant with the Wrong Man || Dirty Little Secret || Holiday Daddy

Platinum Security Series:

Dark Kisses || Dark Riches || Dark Sins || Dark Secrets

Forbidden Love Series:

The Guy Next Door || Arrogant Jerk || Misunderstood || My Best Friend's Ex || Office Mischief || Tainted Goods || Brutal Love

Big Daddies of Los Angeles Series:

Daddy's Rules || Daddy's Temptation || Daddy's Fake Fiancée || Daddy's Million Dollar Proposal

Searching for Love Series:

Frenemies with Benefits || Breaking All The Rules || Fake Heartbreak || Against All Odds

Boxed Sets:

Daddy Knows Best || Happily Ever After || The Big Daddies of LA

Standalones:

Ruthless || My Possessive Ranchers

FORBIDDEN
LOVE

THE *Guy* NEXT DOOR

KELLY MYERS

BLURB

My hot neighbor is my new boss. What could possibly go wrong? How about a baby...

Getting dumped is the pits.

At least I still have my job.

Until the hot guy next door becomes my new boss and lays me off.

Thankfully, he gives me a new job as a favor and only asks one thing in return…

A date.

Only the fake date leads to something very real happening…in bed.

Zack Noble is every bit as confident between the sheets as he is in the boardroom.

I'm helpless to resist him.

I know office relationships are forbidden.

Yet the sneaking around makes what's happening between us even hotter.

Until our secret is discovered…

But I have one of my own—*a little munchkin with same blue eyes as his dad.*

When the truth finally comes out, will I lose Zack forever, or will we have our second chance at love?

1

CRYSTAL

If I opened that door, it meant my life would go on. Walking out into the world and dragging myself to work would mean that the trauma of the past few hours would be behind me. I could move on and stop feeling so miserable. I stared at the doorknob. A simple turn, I'd be outside, and I could get on with forgetting about Chase.

I took a deep breath and shoved my sunglasses onto my nose. I opened the door.

"Oh hi, Crystal." The hot new neighbor directly across from our— not our, mine, there was no 'our' anymore— apartment wrestled his bike out of his front door. He must have opened his door seconds before I opened mine. A messenger bag slung over his shoulder and a bike helmet perched, unsecured, on top of his head. Any other day and I would have appreciated the smile he gave me. Any other day and we wouldn't have opened our front doors at the same time.

"Hi." Damn, had he heard us fighting? "Biking in? New job? I thought you were a suit and tie guy."

"No, same job. The suit portion is over for a bit," he explained as he fastened his helmet. "I'm finally able to get to the real work, and into my new office." He swung a long leg over the seat and mounted the bike. "See you 'round. Have a nice day."

I should have waited. Then again, if I had I wouldn't have experienced the lovely view of his backside as he rode away in those bike shorts.

Without a ride to the commuter rail, I had to walk. The walk to the station felt longer than the walk home from it. I didn't have to wait long before a train arrived, and I was whisked away a few stops to a transfer station, where I jumped on the light rail, and eventually hiked another block to the office.

My morning commute did not magically wipe away my woes as I had hoped. I followed a few other commuters into the Shingle Click building. Grunting in thanks to the person in front of me who held the door long enough so that I could catch it; I did the same for the next person. Unlike the others who fished their ID tags from the ends of lanyards, I paused at the front desk.

"Hey, wifey!" I was greeted by a big toothy smile, a mop of orange hair, and a face that was genuinely happy to see me.

Damn, I started crying again.

Charline took one look at my face and ran around from the back of the long desk she shared; arms extended. She pulled me into a warm hug. The comfort of my best friend was much needed.

"What's the matter, Crystal? Did you hear anything about more layoffs?" Her lilting Texas drawl gave a soothing quality to her words.

I shook my head, unable to speak without sobbing. I wanted to be done with crying.

"Hey Sherryl, I'm gonna walk Crystal on back," she announced to the other receptionist as she looped her arm through mine. Using her card key, she swiped us through, and into cubicle land.

"I told you there's nothing to worry about," she said as we walked. "They always keep the receptionists and interns. They need people to answer the phones and low-paid people who will do the work to prove themselves. You and me kid, we're safe as houses."

I took a deep breath. "It's not that..." I clamped my mouth shut. I wasn't going to cry at work. I refused. "I'll tell you later, okay?"

Charline butted shoulders with me as we stopped at my cube.

"Of course, Sugar. The new head honcho already arrived today. I got a glimpse of him. He is not hard on the eyes. Too bad he's so hard on everything else. Come find me during the big meeting."

"What big meeting?"

"Check your messages. Didn't you see the stage they were setting up in the parking lot? It's all last minute. Glad I'm not paying the rush fees. I'll see ya later." With a twinkling wave of her fingers, she left me to settle in for the day.

"Good morning, Henry," I greeted my plant. After watering Henry, I put my bag in a drawer and entered my computer password.

I opened the team chat. It took up half of one monitor. A different chat program the company sent corporate-wide announcements on took up the other half of the monitor. Even though it only took seconds for those apps to calibrate and display their contents, I had already switched my focus to a larger monitor. I opened my email and the drafting program where I would spend the majority of my time.

Once everything was turned on, I typically would hit the break room to grab a quick cup of coffee before returning to my desk and start working. But not today, in both chat windows, messages were scrolling past faster than I could read. People were freaking out.

"I can't afford to get laid off!"

"Are they shutting Shingle Click down?"

"What a mess! All because Jameson couldn't keep it in his pants."

The tension at work had been palpable for weeks now. We already lost the accounting department because of the transgressions of the former CEO. People were stressed. Me included. The bullshit Chase dumped on me last night didn't help.

I scrolled back on the corporate message board to see what prompted the panic. There it was: company-wide meeting in the parking lot just after lunch. We would be introduced to our new CEO, who people already didn't like after the hatchet job he did on accounting. And we would learn about the new and exciting direction Shingle Click was headed.

I slumped back in my chair. Yep, that didn't sound good. I tried to inhale deeply, but the hitch in my breathing let me know that tears were close. I adjusted my sunglasses, still on because my eyes were red and puffy from a sleepless night of crying. I was not fit for human consumption, and being at work meant people would see.

In the washroom, the cool water on my face felt good, but I don't think it helped anything. My skin was a splotchy mess of light tan and pink spots. No amount of makeup would provide coverage to the red on my nose or the embarrassing blobs of color I got on the sides of my cheeks covering my jaw and onto my neck. The red-rimmed lids and slightly bloodshot eyes were not a good fashion look and would be staying behind glasses for the foreseeable future. The rest of me could fool anyone that I wasn't dying inside. My hair was smoothed back into a ponytail, and the jeans and tunic I wore were perfect for any Thursday at work.

Back at my desk, I scrolled through the chat for my group. I wanted to see if the manager of solar power solutions had anything to say about the widespread panic.

"We won't know anything for a few hours, and we still have solutions to provide. I feel confident that Shingle Click will not do anything drastic. Their solar power initiative was a big deal for the investors, and you know how they like to keep investors happy. Let's keep working, and we can regroup and discuss after this announcement. I've heard good things about this Noble guy, and how he's been dealing with the situation he walked into. Let's see what he has to say first, okay?" Trust Armand to be the voice of reason.

I nodded at my monitor as if he could see me agreeing. I swiveled my attention to the other monitor and got on with my task of proofreading the specs from my senior engineer.

A few hours later, the entire company stood in the parking lot. Charline approached me with two cans of pop in her hands. She handed one to me and nodded in the direction of a group by the stage. "See I told you the new CEO was good-looking."

Zack turned then and caught my eye. He gave me a little head lift in recognition.

I spit the pop in my mouth out. "Shut the front door!"

"What was that?" she asked. "Did the new CEO just smirk at you?"

I wiped at my chin. "That's the hottie neighbor guy. No way he's the new CEO."

"That's Mr. Wears-a-suit-like-he-could-seduce-you-any-time-he-wants? Are you sure?" Charline's big hazel eyes were even bigger as she gaped at me. "Zack Noble is your new neighbor? Oh, Chase is gonna love this. Weren't you saying he's acting all weird cause you smiled at Mr. Hottie?"

"Yeah, well Chase isn't a concern anymore. He left me last night." It was surprisingly easy to say, with no hint or threat of tears.

"Oh, baby." Charline wrapped an arm around me.

I gave her the details of his announcement and the fight that followed. Zack Noble started talking. We ignored his "exciting new directions," and comments about healing broken trust in the corporate environment as I told Charline about broken trust in my personal space.

Someone growled in our direction, "Would you shut up. This is important."

Chastised, we bit our lips shut and finally paid attention to my hottie neighbor, and the new boss.

"I know this wasn't the best news for all of you, that's why I wanted you to hear directly from me. Meet with your department heads. They will have more details regarding your individual situations. Shingle Click has simply hit a rough patch. As in life, progress is not always straightforward. Like an arrow that has to be pulled back to reach even farther, we step back in order to grow. Thank you." With a wave, he walked away from the mic.

"Oh, that didn't sound good, did it?" Charline asked.

I shook my head. "If I get laid off I'm screwed. I can't afford rent on my own. Chase walked out on me, leaving me to cover his half. And I'm stuck in that lease for at least another six months."

2

ZACK

I leaned into a curve and the traffic practically disappeared on the new street. With less traffic, I could think about other things as if I were on a car-free trail. My first day in the new office as CEO of Shingle Click went well. After a month of board meetings, meetings with lawyers, and fraud investigators, I was going to be allowed to do what I excelled at: bringing a tech product to a larger market. Shingle Click had a fairly decent share of the smart-home technology consumer base, but it was lagging. People wanted to control their homes remotely, not just from a main panel located in the home, or from a computer.

I hadn't realized that Crystal worked for me. Then again, I never did get to talk to her much. That loudmouth Chase always got in the way. As if I couldn't steal his woman if I wanted to. I wouldn't say no, she was a sexy eyeful. I had some standards, I wasn't going to steal a bro's woman.

"Fuck me!" I squeezed my brakes, dropping my foot to the pavement to keep from falling over as a car cut me off. "Watch it, moron!"

Letting go of all thoughts of layoffs and market share I returned my focus to the road. I adjusted my speed when I saw a car backing out of their driveway ahead. I swerved to avoid an opening door.

Car on left. Nice ass on right.

I slowed to enjoy the view. Most people walking did not catch my attention the way this backside did. Then again, it only took seconds before I recognized the woman by her clothes. If Crystal walked any slower, I was going to have to get off my bike and walk behind her. She has a boyfriend, man.

With a quick shake, I cleared my head. I pushed into the pedals and sped up. I could wave as I rolled past.

I saw the box in her arms with a plant sticking out of it. Fuck me, I definitely couldn't wave. She was going to hate me now. I knew that box. Probably snatched from the copy room, the perfect size for clearing out an office to carry home. I cut my gaze back to the road before she noticed that I was looking, or that it was even me on the bike.

I passed her. It was a business decision. It wasn't anything personal. Chase had better not be the kind of bro to come at me over something like this. I could take him, but it wouldn't be pretty.

"No!" The sounds of falling and pottery breaking followed. "Ow, damn it!"

I swiveled my head to look back. Crystal was on the ground. I grimaced and pulled at my brakes. I needed to help her. Suddenly I flew over my handlebars. There wasn't time to think, or cuss before I belly-flopped into a pile of stinking dirt. I spat bits of mulch and mud from my mouth as I sat up. Where the fuck had this trailer come from? My bike lay half in the trailer, half on the road.

"Hey, you alive back there?" A sun-worn man in a dirty green jumpsuit asked as he ran around the side of the trailer.

I looked to see what I had crashed into. I sat in an open back trailer in a pile of gardening dirt. Yard working tools surrounded me.

"Yeah, I'm good." I brushed dirt that reeked of manure from my clothes.

The guy handed me my bike. "You should be more careful," he said.

I was tempted to "be more careful my ass" at him, but the whole fucking thing was my fault.

I grabbed my bike with a "yeah, yeah, yeah," and headed back to where Crystal was still on the ground. She sat with her arms wrapped around her knee. The sunglasses that had covered her face this morning were haphazardly held between her fingers. Her head was down, and she rocked back and forth. There was a hole in her jeans, exposing the angry red skin of a scraped knee.

"Hey, you alright?" I asked.

She looked up at me. Red eyes, tears running down her cheeks, she took a minute to focus. Narrowing her gaze.

"Fuck off," she said.

Still holding my bike, I squatted down next to her.

"You're hurt. Let me help you."

"I think you've helped me enough today Zack Noble. Just... just leave me alone already."

I let my bike drop to its side and began gathering her items. I upended the box and slid her books back in, solar power technology and engineering books. Damn. No wonder she didn't want my help. To save Shingle Click, several groups that were not currently delivering, or not directly related to the product to consumer pipeline had been eliminated. That included the group developing solar power integration.

"Yeah, I probably deserve that." I reached for a plant in a broken pot. "You'll need to re-pot this."

"You killed Henry," she cried reaching for the green leaves and roots packed with dirt that I held up. "Why are you still here?"

I sighed. This woman was a mess, she didn't even know she needed help. "You're hurt, you clearly need assistance."

"Well, you're covered in shit. You are shit. Everything is shit." She pulled the plant into a hug and shook like she was crying.

Crying women were my weakness. She was beautiful and in distress. Instinctually, I reached out to wrap an arm around her. I didn't give a fuck that she had a man, or that she was pissed at me because of the layoff. She was crying. She swatted my arm away before I was remotely close.

"Let me at least call Chase to come pick you up. You shouldn't have to walk home with your knee all scraped up."

She scooted away from me with a turn. "I don't have a boyfriend anymore. And thanks to you, I don't have a job. And now I'm going to be homeless unless I can find another job in less than two weeks. Even if I do, I won't get paid in time." She sniffled for a bit and then held out her plant. "You killed Henry."

"How is it my fault you tripped?"

She spun back and glared. Even when angry she was adorable. I took a few squat walk steps back, giving her the room she needed.

She let out a dramatic sigh. "Henry would be content in a cubicle if I still had a job. But I don't. I had to pack up four months of accumulated reference material because the sexist engineers I worked with were constantly quizzing me. They said it was because I was the intern, but they never actually quizzed anyone else, no, just me. I had to be smarter than any of them, even though I was the intern. I was there to learn, not serve as some kind of human reference database. But I was killing it. I was proving that I knew my shit, and I was in line to be hired." She closed her eyes for a moment.

"I digress. The box was heavy, I tripped. The pot broke. It's your fault because if the solar panel group hadn't been dissolved, I wouldn't have been laid off today. Therefore, you killed Henry."

When she stopped talking she just stared at me as if to say point served.

I rubbed my hand over my brow, massaging away the wrinkles that formed there when I was tense. This woman was making me tense. She wasn't wrong. As crazy as her logic sounded, it was logic.

"I'm sorry I killed your plant. Let's gather your things and then we can discuss this rent situation. I'm feeling responsible."

She held her hand out to me. I stood, and then braced, as she levered herself to her cute little feet.

"You should."

She looked me up and down with a great deal of judgment, before bending over to get the rest of her things into the box. I enjoyed the view. When finished, she stood with her hands on her ample hips and looked at me and then the box, and then at me again. I took her hint and picked it up.

"How much rent money do you need?" I asked as I held her box.

She shrugged. "Chase paid half. And right now I barely have enough to cover my half."

She was eerily calm. I guess she spent all her rage yelling at me about the plant.

"Swing by my apartment when you get home. I'll transfer the rent—"

"No, you can't do that." She cut me off.

"Crystal—"

"As much as I blame you for the job, the rent is on me and Chase. So it's on me. And... and... no I can't let you."

I never noticed how big her eyes were. Or how long her lashes. The woman didn't have on any makeup that I could tell, and she was stunning. Maybe it was the way the evening light filtered through the trees and lit up her honey brown eyes. And with Chase no longer around, I was going to be helping her. She didn't have a choice in this.

"Fine, if I can't pay your rent, what can I do?"

"Give me a job."

"I can't give you your job back. What can you do? What did you do before Shingle Click?"

Her mouth formed around words and I half-listened. Distracted by thoughts of having that mouth form around other things. I heard her mention marketing, management, and graduation. What I didn't hear was any programming experience.

"Fine, be in my office Monday morning. I'll find you a job," I said.

She took the box from my hands with an excited little wiggle. Her face lit up with a genuine smile. "Really? There's an opening in quality assurance. I can do product testing and proof coding. And the pay will more than cover rent. Thank you, Zack. Or should I say, Mr. Noble?"

"Zack is fine." The way she jiggled about when she was happy sucked the blood from my brain. I cleared my throat and got on my bike before it all fully transferred to my dick.

3

CRYSTAL

My stomach roiled, I was too nervous to drink or eat anything. The first day on a new job always did that to me. It didn't matter that I had already been working there. As far as my stomach was concerned it was a new job.

"Hey stranger," I said, stopping in front of Charline's desk.

She gave a little "eep" as she looked up and saw me. "What are you doing here?"

I shrugged. "New job. There's an opening in QA, and I'm here to fill it."

"Why didn't you tell me? Never mind, who are you interviewing with?" Her smile was infectious.

"Zack told me to be in his office at eight-thirty. Can you let me in? I don't have a passkey anymore."

"You don't want to keep the big man waiting. I expect a full report later." She pressed a hidden button letting me back into the labyrinth of cubicles.

I crossed over to the elevator, and up to the second floor. It was eerily quiet there, the scene of the corporate bloodbath, the former home of accounting. I turned past empty cubes and into the hallway that led to the executive offices. The entire décor changed from a sea of gray and tan modular walls to wood paneling and the brushed gleam of stainless steel accents.

No one sat behind the executive admin's desk. I strolled past and tapped lightly on the frosted glass door to the CEO's office.

"Come in," Zack's deep voice commanded.

I found him staring out the window, a cup of coffee in his hand. I needed to stop ogling him as my hot neighbor, and remember he was my new boss. The morning light highlighted the defined plains of his face: wide strong brow, high sharp cheekbones, a strong jawline, and a squared-off chin. He was clean-shaven this morning, and his dark hair looked as if it were still damp from a morning shower. His appeal did not stop there. He had broad shoulders that tapered to slim hips. With one hand in his pocket, his slacks strained at his firm backside. Must be all that cycling.

He turned ever so slightly to see who I was.

"Hi." With a tip of his head, he indicated I should come in and over to the window.

If Shingle Click were a more lucrative business, maybe Zack would have had a more interesting view. As it was, his window overlooked the parking lot.

I stood next to him and watched as commuters began straggling into work. My stomach did one of its complaining flips. Or maybe it was an anxious flip since I was in such close proximity to him.

"Hungry?" he asked.

Crap, I had hoped the noise hadn't been loud enough for him to hear. Wrong.

"I haven't had coffee yet," I explained.

The lift of his eyebrow was question enough.

"Nerves," I confessed as I looked out the window. I couldn't look at him, not with the backflips already happening with my insides.

He glanced at me, and then he turned to look at me. In my peripheral vision, I saw him rake his gaze down my body before he returned to look out the window.

I bit my lip. If all went well, he wouldn't comment on anything. It's not like I didn't already know my hips were larger than average. It always astounded me how many men seemed to think I needed this pointed out. Would he think I was too big to have a functional brain?

"You're all dressed up this morning," he said.

I released a sigh. After a look-over like that, I expected a disparaging remark. No size commentary was good. "Wasn't sure if this was an interview, or if the job was mine. Either way, I wanted to make a good impression on my first day," I said. I risked glancing at him.

He smiled, but his attention was somewhere out in the parking lot.

"I got you something," he said.

"You did?"

He quirked his head back toward his desk without looking at me. "I figured Henry could use a new home. I hope he survived the weekend."

I turned to see what he was talking about. In the center of his desk sat a new ceramic pot. I picked it up.

"Henry's going uptown. Thank you." The pot was a combination of smooth cobalt blue glaze and red rough clay. It was hefty and seemed artisan made. With the pot in my hands, I sat in a chair facing his desk.

Zack turned, and still not really looking at me, took his own chair. "I guess it's time to discuss this job."

I sat up and was about to thank him again, when he cut me off. "I'm not giving you the QA job."

I bit my lip. I wasn't going to cry in front of him again. This was exactly why I was so nervous this morning, the job offer wasn't real. Maybe that's what the new pot for my plant was all about, a consolation prize. Congratulations, you did not get a job but you won't leave empty-handed. Have a pot.

"I looked over your records and your Linked In profile. You have a skill set I can use. Let me tell you about our newest product." He sat forward on his chair, placed his coffee down, and then clasped his hands together. His eyes bore into me. They were intense like cold blue laser beams.

I gulped. I didn't have the job I thought. But I had a job? Thank small favors for the pot to hold onto. I gripped it for all I was worth. Zack should have warned me he was going to take me on an emotional roller coaster ride this morning.

"I've pulled our leading tech developers and programmers into a small team. We are focusing on upgrading the existing operating system in the Shingle Click Home Command Center unit. As I'm sure you are aware there are only two ways to access the HCC, through the device itself, or with an IP access dashboard. The dashboard gives users computer access, but it is not user-friendly, and definitely not mobile-friendly. I don't know why they never made that happen. Fortunately, wi-fi is already integrated, but the interface to a browser on a cell phone is ten years behind where it needs to be."

I shifted in my chair. Did he want me to work on the development and programming of a phone app? I couldn't stop the smile on my face. My already messy nerves lined up into an organized conga line. This was even better than working in QA.

He sat back in his chair, running both hands through his hair, and resting them on the back of his neck.

"Exactly, you get it," he said with a satisfied smirk.

"Where do I fit in?" I asked. It was hard not to vibrate with excitement. I knew exactly where I fit in.

"Well, this is where your special talents come in handy. I saw that you were a traffic controller in a marcom agency. Engineers are notorious for losing track of time. I need you to be Project Manager on this one."

I deflated in my chair. I felt all the air leave my body. I was literally surprised I didn't continue to deflate until I was a puddle on the floor. He didn't want me to program anything. He wanted someone who could read a calendar and schedule to other people. I didn't go to night school for six years to get a degree in program engineering to remind some guy to turn in his assignment on time. I'd done that for years with designers and copy editors. The smile left my face in a blink.

"What? Don't you want the job?" Zack's entire demeanor also changed. "It has better career potential than working in QA ever will.

And you get to work directly with me," he said as if that was a major selling point. "And since you already have a few years of experience in the field, the pay rate is higher than an entry-level salary that a quality assurance tester earns."

I blinked a few times. "Did you just say I have years of experience, and that this pays better?" The QA job would pay enough to cover rent, buy food, and have some money to spend. It wasn't the best salary in the world, but it would work for me. Earning more would be a dream, and that meant I would have enough with my next check to cover rent.

He chuckled, and then stood up. "Let's go meet the team."

Clutching Henry's new home to my chest I followed Zack from the office. He paused at the now occupied admin's desk.

"Lisa, let human resources know Miss Pond is back in our employment. She'll be in their offices after our meeting to get a new ID badge. I'll email over the details regarding her responsibilities and salary."

Lisa looked down her long nose at me and breathed heavily in my direction. She could judge me on whatever she wanted to, my money woes were about to become a thing of the past.

I followed Zack down the stairs to the first-floor conference room where, just as he said, a group of engineers was waiting for him.

I recognized Tony Ramirez, solely because Charline couldn't stop talking about him. And, my stomach plummeted again— damn this roller coaster ride— Greg. I had kind of hoped he had gotten the ax with the rest of us from the solar group. I didn't like him much, and he didn't like me a lot. There was a woman I didn't yet know. It was nice that I wasn't the only one on the team.

"Oh, sorry, am I late?" Armand entered the conference room behind me. "Crystal! I'm pleased to see you again." He patted me on the back and slid into one of the chairs at the table.

I continued to hover behind Zack.

"Great, everyone's here. Let me introduce you to our new Project Manager, Crystal Pond. She is going to keep all of us on task and on schedule."

4

ZACK

"Zacky…"

I hated it when Paris called me Zacky. It meant she was cajoling and manipulating me. It meant her next approach would involve tears, and I couldn't deny Paris anything when she cried. Zacky meant 'give in now big brother, or I will cry.'

"Fine Paris, I will bring a plus one. I do not guarantee they will be anything more than a friend out for th—"

"Zack Noble you are not bringing a bro-date to my event. This is not an opportunity to get drunk and pick up women."

"You judge my friends harshly," I winced into the phone.

"I judge them accurately. Bring a woman. And one you would actually date. When I organized the Governor's Ball in Sacramento you brought mother's old friend Mrs. Dickens. That was awkward. People thought you were really dating some sixty-year-old."

"She's mother's oldest friend who actually checks on us. Not a lot of their friends did that after the accident. And no one thought we were dating. They thought she was mom. Which was worse," I muttered the last bit.

"And where do you expect me to get a date you would approve of with such short notice?"

"Get on a dating app and swipe right. And put effort into it. It's high time you started to get serious about settling down. So this needs to be a legit date."

I smiled as she berated me through the phone. I don't know when it happened, at some point, the power dynamic between the two of us changed. One minute I was the one taking care of her, helping her with homework, filling out college applications, and the next... she was the boss of me. Maybe it happened gradually, maybe it had been going on since the day she was born. As her older brother, I was going to protect her and be at her beck and call for life.

"I'll find a date for your gala."

"It's an opening, not a gala. Dress nice, but not black tie. Eat first," she delivered instructions like a to-do list.

"What? You aren't going to dinner with me and my date afterward?"

"I would never impose on your date. Love you, Zacky."

"Love..." She already hung up on me.

I tossed my cell onto the desk in front of me. My intercom buzzed.

"Yeah?"

"Miss Pond wants to see you," Lisa's voice announced.

"Send her in." I looked up to watch Crystal peek her head around my door before coming in.

She was an interesting package of commanding and timid. It was rather adorable. I liked it. I liked adorable best when it turned sexy, and the way this woman's mouth moved around words and the way her ass moved when she walked... yeah she turned adorable into fucking hot in the blink of an eye. I shifted and by sheer willpower, forced the blood rushing to my cock back to my brain.

I nodded for her to have a seat. Crystal tended to fidget. Only she didn't fidget with jerky gawky movements. She pulsed and rolled. If she stood in front of my desk undulating the way she did I was going to lose the battle of where my blood flow went.

"You said you wanted weekly status updates," she said.

"I got your email," I acknowledged. "Everything seems to be going as planned."

She bit her lip. I did not need to focus on that mouth right now.

"And you told me to let you know if there were any problems. I figured it was best for problems to be handled in person and not through email."

"Fair enough. What kinds of problems are we running into already?" I sucked at my teeth and slowed my breathing. I wanted to breathe deeply and inhale her scent.

She fidgeted, crossing and uncrossing her arms. Plumping her breasts, making a show of her cleavage.

I forced my eyes to her face. I needed her to get on with it and get out of my office so I could think about anything other than her breasts, and the way her soft body moved.

"Greg and I, no, that's nothing I can't handle. But for the record, I've had issues with him in the past. I'm a professional. I'll deal with it. We don't have any problems with the team. My issue is with HR."

"Greg? Human resources? What's the matter?" I was ready to fire Greg on the spot if she said so. But I knew that was my cock talking. It currently was in charge of my brain and blood supply. I couldn't exactly lay off the entire HR team because of Mr. Happy in my pants. That's what caused the whole fiasco at Shingle Click to begin with, someone couldn't keep their dick down. "How can I help?"

"There was a mess up with my paperwork. And I was wondering if you could possibly authorize a partial advance on my first check?" she asked.

"You didn't get paid with everyone else?"

She shook her head. Her ponytail swished side to side. "I was entered into the system as a new employee, not a continuing employee. So, as a newbie, they skip a payment on the first pay period and will play catch up on the next one. It has something to do with the auto-deposit system and standard practices." She made air quotes around 'standard practices.'

She bit her lip again. I started to reach up to pull that plump lip away from her pearly white teeth before she drew blood. I redirected my arm and picked up the closest thing to my hand, a slinky desk toy that I never played with.

The slinky made an almost musical rushing sound as I tossed the momentum of the metal spring between my hands. With something other than Crystal to focus on, my libido took a break and allowed me to think.

"Do you need me to write a check to cover your rent?"

She shook her head almost violently. "No, I don't need you to pay for my rent. My paycheck would have taken care of what I needed. But I didn't get one. HR won't issue a partial advance without authorization."

I played with the slinky some more. There was an opportunity here and I was going to leverage it to my benefit. I slammed the slinky down on the desk. Crystal bounced with startled surprise. She bounced nicely.

"I can't exactly do that without something in return."

"Excuse me?" She rapidly blinked those big honey eyes at me.

"I need a favor, you need a favor. We can help each other out."

The dubious look that danced across her face made me chuckle. "Never play poker. You do not have a poker face. This isn't that nefarious."

"You do have a poker face. I can't tell what you're thinking, and it's making me nervous," she said with a giggle.

I stood up and walked to the other side of my desk so I could be closer to her. That may have been a mistake. The way she looked up at me now gave me visions of her looking up at me with my cock in her mouth. I picked the toy back up and crossed my legs as I leaned on the desk.

"My sister is hosting a big deal gallery exhibit thing in San Francisco. She expects me to bring a date."

Crystal cleared her throat and shifted in her seat. "Okay?"

"Be my plus one, and I'll make sure you have a check cut by the end of the week, in time for rent."

"I don't have to tell you this company has a policy against employees dating, specifically subordinates and managers," she said.

"No, you don't. And this isn't dating. It's neighbors helping each other out."

I extended my hand to seal the deal. When she slipped her soft palm against mine, I couldn't think. Blood flow one hundred percent rerouted away from my brain. If her hands were this soft and warm, what did the rest of her feel like? We didn't shake, just sat there frozen in time holding each other's hands. I stared at the way her little fingers, so delicate in comparison to mine, were tipped with softly rounded nails, painted in a pink that set off the glow of her skin.

My attention was pulled back to reality as she cleared her throat. I squeezed her hand and let go. Fully ignoring that awkward moment.

"That's settled. Now, what about Greg?"

5

CRYSTAL

I reminded myself for the millionth time as I slid red lipstick over my mouth, this was not a date. Zack Noble was not taking me out in public to show me off, or because he enjoyed my company. He was taking me out to get his sister off his back.

I had no expectations and knew better than to anyway. He was my boss, and that was a huge no-no. So this wasn't a date. Then why was I so nervous?

He said to dress up, but not fancy. I chose a low-cut, basic black dress, and finished the look with a black leather harness with silver buckles. It was an edgy accessory with a touch sexy dominatrix vibe. And it showed off my breasts.

I was sliding my feet into a pair of black pumps when I heard the knock.

"Almost ready," I announced as I tossed the door open.

"Fuck me," Zack said under his breath. He let his eyes run down my body and back up. His gaze lingered on my finer assets, caged as they were in the leather harness.

My throat went dry at the hungry look in his eyes. And my pulse quickened when I saw him. The dark scruff that graced his jaw made his eyes look even bluer than they were. Also all in black, he wore a designer suit. A skin-tight silk tee covered his torso. I needed to retreat before I started counting the ripples of his abs out loud.

"Think your sister will buy it? Would you date someone like me?"

He gave the slightest nod. "Shall we? I've already called for a car. There's a great little sushi place once we get into the city, and then we can head over to the opening."

The ride to the train station was blessedly short. Zack crowded in close behind me as we boarded the train, and herded me to the second level. We sat in a row of single seats facing each other.

"You get a better view from up here," he announced.

He was right. It was a good thing I had the view to keep me occupied, otherwise, I would have spent the entire time looking at him.

At dinner, we shared our favorite sushi rolls. Everything about his smile and the way he brushed up against me felt like a date. Even the moments of awkward silence felt like a first date.

I caught a glimpse of him as he arranged for another car to take us to his sister's event. His forehead furrowed, and his dark eyebrows lifted in concentration. It was an expression I saw on him at work. Reality slapped me back into remembering this was not a date.

Zack had said the gallery opening was not supposed to be some fancy gala. Based on how everyone else was dressed, someone had their signals crossed. Zack and I were dressed for an entirely different kind of evening. It was all glamorous and red carpet quality haute couture fashion. My black dress and faux BDSM bondage boob belt did not fit the bill. Zack's style was classic, and he was handsome enough he could get away with flaunting the dress code. He didn't need to follow fashion rules, he had abs.

"Is this the right party?" I hissed in his ear.

I tried to hide behind his arm and clasped his hand hard.

"You look great Crystal, stop being so shy," he chuckled in amusement.

"Zacky!" A tall woman in a dripping column of dark silk and silver beads threw her arms around Zack's neck.

He shifted and pulled me out from behind him.

"Crystal, I'd like you to meet my sister, Paris," he introduced us.

Paris was stunning. With pixie short black hair, she had the same intense sky blue eyes. She moved with a regal grace that made me think she was comfortable at events like this.

I was not. I refused to let go of Zack's hand, as if it made my appearance acceptable.

"Hi," I said. I felt lacking.

Paris looked at me like I was the very personification of inadequacy. She tilted her jaw and pursed her lips together, "Charmed." The smile she gave me was perfectly strained.

"Zacky, did you forget what black tie means?" She chastised him with a sing-song voice.

"Paris, you definitely said this was not a black-tie event," Zack spoke through his teeth. He didn't look angry, but he sounded lethal.

She made a face, rounding her shiny red lips into an O, and placing her fingertips slightly in front of her mouth. Her lipstick and nails were a perfect match.

"Oops, did I say that? I must have been thinking of something else."

She blinked her false lashes, and glanced over at me again.

"Shoo, now take your date and go do something fun. You look cute." She waved us away with the back of her hand, dismissing us from her space.

"Paris!" Zack growled.

Her nails clicked as she waved us away before turning to leave.

"What was that?" I asked.

"Let's get out of here. I'll explain on the way." Zack twisted his hand in mine so that I no longer had a death grip on him.

On the return home, we sat on the lower level of the train, in the seats facing each other. I slipped my feet from the pumps and put them on the seat next to Zack. I had to bite my lip when one of his hands drifted over and began caressing my ankle. Each time his hand skimmed up my calf I wished it would skim higher.

"Paris," he started, his attention out the window, his hand on my skin. "Likes to bend people to her little whims. She wanted to see me, but instead of saying she's on a tight schedule, she pulled a stunt like this."

"So you knew she was going to do something like that?"

He shrugged. "There was a fifty-fifty chance it was a simple gallery opening like she said."

"So why the fake date to appease her?"

The look he gave me said everything. She was his sister. Knowing I had overstepped, I pulled my feet back to sit up, but his hand tightened on my ankle keeping me in place.

"Maybe the fake date was a lure?" With his other hand, he reached forward and fingered the leather strap at my shoulder.

My nerves danced just below the surface of my skin. His touch sent zaps of excitement through my entire body. His finger on my harness had sent a charge straight to my core. My mouth was devoid of moisture. It was all pooling between my thighs.

We said nothing on the short ride back to the apartments. Thinking the moment had passed, I fished my keys from my bag. I turned to say thank you.

The words never had a chance to leave my mouth. Zack was there, his fingers hooking under the straps of the harness. He backed me against the door.

"I've been wanting to touch this all night. Wanting to touch you." His voice was low and thick.

His breath caressed my cheek as he nuzzled against my neck.

I pressed a hand against his chest, only to fist the material of his shirt, and pull him in until his chest pressed against mine.

"Not a real date," I said, more to remind myself than him.

"Then this isn't a real kiss."

His lips descended on mine. He tickled and toyed with my mouth until my lips parted on a moan. His tongue darted in, and he seemed to lose control, deepening everything. Pressing in harder. Our tongues tangled and danced. His hand slipped under the straps and he caressed my breast with one hand. His other hand snaked up my dress, and he palmed the flesh of my ass. His fingers looped around the straps of the harness, brushing over my nipple.

I gasped into his mouth. He responded with a growl.

"I told you to put that damned video game down. We're leaving." A terse voice on the landing above us said.

We froze. Zack's hand trailed down my leg, letting go of my backside, and pressed my dress down. His fingers slid out from the tangle of leather straps that caged my breasts, and he stood back.

Feet pounded down the stairs, and off into the night. They must have parked in front of the building, and not in the big lot outback, or they would have had to walk right past us.

I think we both exhaled at the same time.

Zack took another step back and gave me a rueful grin. "I'm sorry Crystal. That was out of line. You did me a favor, and I took advantage."

I still leaned against my front door trying to catch my breath and figure out what had just happened when his front door closed.

I unlocked my apartment and slid inside. I could not get past that kiss. That kiss was the kind to remember for a lifetime. His mouth was perfect.

I kicked out of my pumps and changed into some sweats.

With a hot tea in my hands, I took my thoughts out into the night, and onto my back patio— a concrete slab with some shrubs placed around it in a pretense of creating privacy. The night was cool and soothing on my jangled nerves.

"You too, huh?"

I looked up at the familiar deep tones of Zack's voice.

Across the walkway, Zack stood on his patio, beer in hand. In the low light, I could see he had also changed. He wasn't wearing a shirt. All those abs I wanted to count earlier were out on display.

"Yeah. I had an interesting date, unexpected ending," I said with a grin.

"Mine too. Ended rather abruptly." His words made my insides swirl in delight.

"Interested in picking it back up?" I teased.

"Oh yeah. I don't think that's a good idea right now," he answered.

Damn, so much for getting the fake date to turn into a fake make-out session.

"Crystal," he started.

"Yeah?"

"I think we're both safer if I stay over here for now. You should know, you felt really good tonight."

"You did too," I sighed.

6

ZACK

All eyes were on Crystal at the head of the board room. None of them had the same hunger that I felt clawing behind mine. She was sexy as fuck talking time tables with bar graphs and flow charts. If they couldn't see the promise of passion her body offered with every graceful move, they were all blind. Their disinterest proved that the Board of Directors were all half-dead, finding comfort in their money. Good. She was mine.

She knew the status of the mobile app rollout better than anyone. Pulling her into my team may have been self-serving, but fuck me, if she hadn't proven to be the best choice I could have made.

There was a cough. The kind that indicated doubt, and a question. I turned my focus to the man who made it, the president of the Board, Uncle George. Not a real uncle, but an old family friend, my mentor, and the reason I was standing in this conference room.

"What about people without phones. I don't have a phone that can do this," his comment was an accusatory bark.

Crystal's eyes flashed to me.

I stood up from where I leaned in the back of the room and cleared my throat. Heads swiveled. I crossed to the front of the room where Crystal stood.

"Smart-home technology users are very tech-savvy. Shingle Click users who prefer accessing control from the physical Home Command Center will still be able to. However, if we are to keep up, we need to make access to the HCC mobile and secure."

My hand reached out as if on its own. I was about to place my arm around her waist. Fortunately, I rerouted that hand and placed it on her shoulder. It had only been a week since the night I tasted her and knew I was in trouble. I'd been avoiding her, the temptation too strong.

"If members of the Board have any questions, now is the time to bring them to the table."

My hand drifted down the side of her arm. Smooth silky fabric gave way to soft warm flesh. The backs of my fingers skimmed back up along her skin.

"You did good," I whispered conspiratorially.

She smiled up at me, and I wanted to kiss her again. Would have if it hadn't been for the room full of decision-makers.

With some huffing and shuffling, they decided they had no questions at this time. I nodded at Crystal. "We're done."

She smiled at the board and thanked them for their time.

"I'll come find you later," I said.

She nodded and I swear her whole body reverberated sending shock waves straight to my cock. My eyes lingered as she walked away.

A vice-like grip grabbed hold of my upper arm. Uncle George had once been a big man. He no longer looked like he had the strength to crush a grape. His grip proved me wrong.

"What are you playing at boy?" he growled at me.

I cast my gaze about the rest of the conference room to see that no one was paying any attention to us, as they gathered their things and left.

I rested my hand on top of his and looked at him pointedly. I proceeded to pry his meaty hand from my arm. Neither of us spoke until the last member shuffled out of the conference room.

"Is that the woman your sister saw you with?" he asked.

"You spoke to Paris?" George had spent years ignoring her while nurturing my foray into the business world. I didn't expect her to keep in contact with him.

"Who said anything about Paris? Your sister, what's her name, Mercedes or something French. Anyway, her. Calls me now and then. Checking to see if I'm still alive. I think she's after my money when I'm dead. You can't fuck her. You know that."

My eyebrows went up. The man never talked like that. Cussing was bad form, made a man look undignified. As a direct result of those directives, I made it a point to say 'fuck' as often as I could. I stared at him quizzically.

"Don't be stupid boy, the fat girl. She told me you got yourself a fat girl. Big titties, all squishy. I don't like big titties. Perky." He made grabbing hand gestures as if feeling up a pair of breasts.

"No," I lied. I may have told Crystal it was a fake date, but fake dates don't end with tongues in mouths and handfuls of fleshy ass.

"Good, good. You know the last CEO of this place, Jameson was boinking that little girl in accounting. Made her shuffle money around. I think she was a circus performer. It was bad enough he got caught. Damned fool pissing where he eats. Office affairs only work if you keep work out of them," he grumbled.

Circus performer? If I didn't know better I would say the man was drunk. One second he made sense, and the next he didn't.

"Jameson coerced a subordinate, who he was sleeping with, into doctoring the books. She wasn't well versed in the art of embezzlement and they got caught."

"So you know. How did you find out?" he asked.

"Uncle George,"— I placed my hand on his shoulder— "we spent practically a month with lawyers, forensic accountants, and investigators recovering the funds. Remember we submitted revised reports to the Federal Trade Commission?" I asked.

"Yes, of course. Don't you go doing the same. The Board will not tolerate flaunting policy. Nepotism will be the downfall of capitalism."

I suppressed a chuckle. Nepotism was lodged firmly up capitalism's ass. Hell, it was why I had this job, and I knew it. "Then you had better not tell anyone how you know me."

"Don't be crude, Zack. Nepotism has nothing to do with us. We aren't related, and I'm not fucking you."

I stayed in the conference room and stared at the walls after Uncle George left. George Fredrickson had stepped in as a father figure after the car crash that claimed my parents' lives. I clearly remembered the many times he told both Paris and me, we could rely on him. That our father had asked him to be our godfather, and he wasn't going to walk away when we needed him most.

I slipped my phone from my pocket.

"Dial Paris Noble," I directed voice command.

"Dialing," the computerized voice replied.

"Zack!" Paris answered with much enthusiasm. "Please tell me you aren't mad at me about last week. How was your date?"

"Did you tell Uncle George about that?" I asked.

"I might have. He wanted to know how the event went. I always talk to him about those things. Good networking."

I ran my hand back over my head.

"Did he seem okay to you? I just had a presentation, and afterward, he seemed off," I told her.

"He's old. Maybe he's getting senile. What'd he say?" she asked.

"Well, he doesn't like large breasts. That's something I didn't need to know," I chuckled.

"Speaking of, how did the date go?"

"You know it's not nice to play your games with unsuspecting victims," I commented.

"Zacky?" I could hear the enthusiasm melt from her voice. The lower lip quiver would be next, then tears.

"Hey, I'm not mad. But next time, remember it's not just me you're messing with. Love you."

"Love you more!" she yelled as she ended the call.

She was right, Uncle George was probably just showing signs of his age. He'd been old my entire life.

I needed to leave soon if I wanted to have the light on my ride. Thoughts of Crystal kept me distracted the entire commute home.

"Impressive work today," I said catching her outside on her patio.

I felt her smile in my gut.

"You think? I have this boss who I've been trying to impress," she practically giggled.

"Well, if he likes smart women, I'm sure you impressed the pants off him."

She leaned over the shrub that separated her space from the public walk. With obvious movements, she tried to look at my legs. She shrugged and sighed. Uncle George did not know what he was missing by not appreciating large breasts.

"I guess I wasn't that impressive." She bit her lower lip.

The sight of her teeth biting into that plump bit of flesh went straight to my cock. It throbbed wanting those teeth, that mouth. I stepped half over, half through the shrub that blockaded my own patio.

"Zack," she laughed. "What are you doing?"

I had more finesse stepping over the plants on her side. I stepped up to her and placed my hand on her hips.

"You're more than impressive," I said as I took my opportunity to kiss her again.

She wrapped her arms around my neck and made a low moan as she pressed her softness against me. She tasted sweet and delectable. Our lips caressed and played touch me, touch me not. My tongue traced the seam of her mouth, and she opened for me.

I moved my hand from her hip and slid it up her side. She was warm and supple. She writhed so nicely in my arms. My hand cupped the side of her breast.

She jumped like I was a fire that burned.

"We can't… I can't," she stammered.

I reached out for her.

She stepped farther away, wrapping her arms around herself.

"You like me, I like you. Why not?" I demanded.

"If we get caught, I'd lose my job. You might lose yours."

"I'm the fucking CEO, no one is going to lose their job," I growled.

"Really? Cause isn't no dating your policy? Especially with subordinates? I don't want people to think I got the job cause I'm screwing you."

"You aren't..." I stopped talking.

I threw my hands up. "You're right, you're right. Are we allowed to be friends? After all, we are neighbors."

"Yes, of course," but her smile told me she also wanted more.

7

CRYSTAL

"Give me a minute?" Zack's deep voice made my insides quiver every time I knocked on his office door. I had to remind myself that I did not have a crush on him because that would be irresponsible.

He focused on his laptop.

I focused on his face. He was as good as bosses got, giving me the autonomy to keep the programmers on task. Of course, I also kept him appraised of every step along the way. If he had a question, I had an answer. I looked away quickly as he stood. He didn't need to know that even though we agreed to be platonic, I longed for him.

He stepped toward the door and gestured that I should proceed him out. "What have you got for me today?" he asked.

Twice a week I presented the HCC mobile app updates. Zack liked to be seen as approachable. He would take several strolls through the offices every day. But he wasn't just checking up on people, he multi-tasked. As we strolled through the cubicle maze, I kept him abreast of where the programmers were, when to expect final user interface design, how soon the operating system team was going to need input from our group so they could roll out the needed updates that would integrate the mobile app with the existing system. It was a giant moving puzzle, and my job was to keep it moving.

"How's the schedule with Allison out?" Zack asked, handing one report back to me.

"We were doing great. But now that Tony's out with ankle surgery, we're slipping. It's not anything that I don't think we can make up for next week. Here's the latest user interface design." I handed him a printout of the proposed design. "Check out this controller." I handed him another page with an image of a groovy round, sound wave looking graphic.

"The design is fun, but I doubt it's functional. Look, they indicate a dual-directional rotation. But this control is for multiple linear processes." He handed it back with a shake of his head.

By the time we reached the app team's cubicles, we were done.

"Thanks, Zack," I said as I forced myself to ignore him and slide back into my chair. I expected him to saunter off the way he did. This time he leaned on the opening of my cubicle.

"Did I miss something?" I asked.

"No," he smirked, before pushing away. "I'll see you later."

I smiled. Later. After that second kiss, we learned it was safer if we each stayed on our own patios. We could chat, and we started eating our dinners together. I liked him. I liked him better than what was healthy for this working relationship. Him saying 'see you later,' meant he liked me too.

"Do you like Greek food?" Zack asked that evening from his patio.

"Yeah, is that what you're having?"

"It's what I want, but the delivery fee costs the same as a meal."

"So, order ahead, and freeze what you don't eat tonight," I suggested.

"Smart woman, I bet they love you at work," he teased. "I wonder, if you haven't already started cooking, would you like to order Greek with me?"

"That smacks of fraternization, Mr. Noble. And they tolerate me at work," I replied.

"So that's a yes then?"

He read the restaurant menu to me. We agreed that he should order a lamb dish for tonight and something called moussaka to put in his freezer. I was less adventurous and stuck with a gyro pita sandwich and some fried zucchini.

"This doesn't count as a date," I said as he handed me the to-go containers with my order.

"No date, just friends sharing a meal on our patios," he confirmed.

Between progress report strolls and evening meals with my friend, I probably got to see more of him than if we were dating. This way was better. Less stress. At least that's what I kept telling myself every evening after work as I washed my face, touched up my makeup, and made sure I looked relaxed before heading outside to see him.

Sooner than expected Tony returned to work with a big boot and a scooter.

"Hey Tony, I'm headed over to the break room. Need me to grab an ice pack or anything for you?" I asked as I paused by his cube.

"Sounds like I arrived just in time," Charline said.

"Hi wifey," I said turning to her. I ignored the grumbling I heard coming from the other side of Greg's wall.

"Wifey?" Tony asked with a smirk. He took the offered ice pack from Charline.

"She's my work wife. Don't be jealous, Sugar, it won't cut into our strictly corporate compatible non-dating relationship," Charline laughed.

"We aren't dating, Charline," Tony said in his very dry, straightforward way. I could never quite tell if he was being dead-pan, or if he just maybe didn't quite understand her humor.

"I've noticed," Charline said.

"My god, are you people serious? Get a room, and get out!" Greg yelled.

Charline rolled her eyes at us and left.

"You good?" I asked Tony. He looked a little perplexed by Charline's whirlwind presence.

Charline could have that effect on people.

I decided I really needed to have a chat with Greg before I headed off to the break room. Even with Tony back, and mostly functional, we still needed to make up for lost time. I tapped on the entrance to his cubicle.

"Hi Greg, have a minute?"

He swiveled in his chair to glare at me. "Pond," he said my name loud enough, and then followed it with a throat-clearing that sounded like 'scum.'

"Really? Is that necessary every time? This isn't middle school," I said. I had other things to discuss with him, but I was getting tired of his attitude.

"Gonna tell your boyfriend?" he sneered at me.

I blinked a few times and pasted a fake smile on my face. I was not going to get angry. At least, I was going to try my best. The man actively hated me.

"I've got a little tally sheet in my cube. I add a tick every time you say my name that way. I will take it to HR, about a hostile work environment. So, give it a rest already, would you?"

He huffed at me and crossed his arms. "Did you come here for a reason, or are you wasting my time. Gonna put me in a time-out cause I interrupted playtime? I've got real work to get done here, Crystal. I don't have time for hanging around and gabbing."

Well, he certainly thought he put me in my place. I wasn't going to inform him of the finer aspects of being friendly with your coworkers, or taking a break every now and then.

"I'm here to talk about that work you've got. Between Allison missing a week at the same time Tony was out, we fell behind schedule," I started.

"That's my problem, how? I did everything on my task list. Us being behind is not on me."

I shrugged. "No, it's not. But with Tony back, we aren't catching up as fast as I had hoped to stay on schedule. I was hoping I could get you to step up and give us an extra push to get back on track."

"Give it to Allison, not my job." He spun away from me.

"It actually is your job. With Tony's physical therapy schedule, the extra time falls in your lap. I'm not asking you for a whole lot of extra effort here Greg. As it is, you do the bare minimum of your programming requirements a day."

"Like you know anything about programming." He kept his back to me.

"I have a degree in computer programming, so yeah, I know something about it. This project needs an extra push, and Tony isn't in any shape to do it. Allison's portion of the work is complete and not as advanced as what you are working on. You're the next senior programmer after Tony."

Faster than I expected, he spun his chair and took a step at me. I retreated a few steps. He was tall and skinny. That move was a threat, even though he was hardly intimidating.

I took a step forward and shoved my finger into the space between us.

"How dare you attempt to come at me, Greg. Sit your ass down and listen up. It is literally my job to tell you when you need to step up to the plate and take some responsibility. I've put up with your petty bullshit since we were both in solar. Be grateful you have a job, I know I am. If you 'pond scum' me one more time I will go straight to HR, and to Zack Noble, because I have friends in high places, and I will show you who's the scum around here. I would rather not dangle the sword of Damocles over your head with threats, but cross me again, and I will."

He sat with a thud and stared at me wide-eyed. It felt like I crossed the line of appropriate office behavior, but I was done with him.

"I came here to give you the opportunity to be hero-of-the-week and to step up with a few extra hours of work. Instead of asking how you can help out, you argue with me. So now I'm not asking. This product needs four to six extra hours of your time. Figure out how to make it happen."

I spun on my heel and stormed off to the restroom. I thought I saw Zack out of the corner of my eye as I rushed away. I was going to be sick. Once in the stall, I started to hyperventilate. I refused to cry, and I was an angry crier. Greg was going to get me fired. I just knew it.

8

ZACK

Crystal's voice dropped low and aggressive. She did not get shrill when angry. Greg towered over her, but she did not back down. Fierce.

Suddenly, I wanted her with every fiber of my being. Watching her stand up for herself against Greg sent me over the edge. I started to follow her and then realized my intentions as my cock grew heavy in my pants. I needed to burn off this growing demand my body had for her. I needed to get out of there before I threw her over a desk and fucked her in front of everyone.

"I'm out," I announced to Lisa, as I stormed back into my office. "If there are any emergencies that will need my attention, leave a message."

I immediately stormed back out. I felt caged, needing to be out of there, away from Crystal and be somewhere where it was safe. Not sure if it was for her safety or mine. At least I had the sense of mind to grab my helmet. Beyond that, I didn't bother. I just left.

Once on my bike, I needed to eat up miles. Wind in my face, leg muscles burning, I rode. I headed toward the water and hit the trails. Without worrying about traffic I could ride until my dick went numb, and my brain could only think of breathing and pushing harder, going farther.

I didn't immediately recognize my surroundings when I finally stopped. I was somewhere mid-bay. How far had I gone? Was that the Dumbarton Bridge? In my rush to leave, I hadn't made sure I had adequate water. Fuck me. My tongue felt sticky with thirst. I got off the bike to stretch.

The GPS on my phone put me north of the bridge. I didn't remember riding that part of the trail, but I had. I hadn't ridden that hard in a long time. Good. The pain in my muscles would be a welcome relief to the pain in my balls, and ache in my chest I felt when Crystal smiled.

My clothes were ruined from sweat by the time I made it back to my apartment. I rolled past Crystal less than a block from home. The timing couldn't have been better. I had my bike hanging on its rack, downed one large bottle of water, and was working on another as I leaned against my open door waiting for her.

"Did you have a hard commute?" she asked.

"I took the long way home, through Redwood City."

"Zack, that's way out of the way. Are you okay?"

The stab in my gut from her look nailed me in place. Concern. I suppressed the groan that wanted out of my throat as she licked her lower lip. She continued to open her apartment door. I didn't want her to leave.

"I have to talk to you about work."

She stopped. I couldn't see her face, but her hand started shaking. It was my turn to ask if she was okay. When she looked at me, she was pale.

"If it's bad, would you mind saving it for the office?"

I could hear the hitch in her voice. I closed my eyes. Stupid, asshole. She thought I was going to fire her, again. Pushing sweat back through my hair, I shook my head. I wanted to reach out to her but she wouldn't want all this sweat touching her.

"No, no, nothing bad. You are gainfully employed. It's just something that's not exactly appropriate for the office."

She took air into her lungs, expanding that glorious chest of hers. "Oh, good. You want to do this now, out here?"

I looked around, and then down at myself. I needed to get clean, and change. "No, I need to have a shower so I can think clearly."

"Do you have plans for dinner? I can cook, and you can tell me while we eat. I can meet you on the patio—"

"This should be discussed with some privacy," I cut her off.

"Well, you want to come over?"

She flashed those long lashes at me. The logical answer was no. "Give me thirty minutes."

"Take your time." She smiled.

"It's a date," I said.

She blushed before stepping into her apartment.

I stared at her door. What was I doing?

Whatever it was, a cold shower was not the answer. It quelled precisely nothing. That woman had my libido roaring loud and hungry. The grumble in my gut had nothing to do with food, and everything to do with the way she looked when she answered the door thirty minutes later.

Crystal let out a small yawn as she opened the door. Slightly flush with a soft smile and hooded eyes, I knew she would look like that after she had been well-loved.

"I can't be boring you already."

She was already messing with the fight for blood between my dick and my brain.

"Sorry, today was intense, and I'm a bit worn out."

"You're tired and you still offered to cook?" I asked as I held up two beers. "I didn't have any wine. Will this work?"

She reached out and took the bottles, and placed them on a trunk in the middle of her living room. "These will suit. I'm cooking because my budget doesn't allow for take-out every night. I hope you don't mind spaghetti."

Her apartment was exactly like mine, only in mirror image. A small living area was separated from an even smaller kitchen by an open countertop. The patio, through sliding glass doors, was opposite the kitchen. A short hallway behind the kitchen led to a bathroom and then the bedroom.

"You have nicer furniture than I do," I noticed.

She shrugged. "I used to have a table and chairs, but Chase took those. We have to eat on the couch if you don't mind. He also took the nice bed frame, but left the old mattress. It's not very sophisticated. But, hey, he left me with a bed."

I stood at the counter and watched as she put long noodles and ladled sauce into two large bowls. She placed the bowls on the trunk that was serving as her coffee table. She grabbed utensils from a drawer and sat on the couch.

"Damn, do you mind? Would you grab the parmesan from the fridge?"

I found the green can of shredded cheese and joined her on the couch.

She squirmed into the corner, curling her delicate feet to the side and under her legs. Holding her bowl, she slurped a noodle between pursed lips.

I forced my gaze into my own bowl. Her mouth like that, making little sucking motions, I didn't know if I would survive the night. I should excuse myself, go home, and nut off in my fist, before facing her again, because all I could think of was sinking deep into her until she screamed.

I needed another cold shower.

"Okay, Zack. I've been fighting down rising panic for almost an hour. What did you need to talk to me about?"

She had a couch and her bowl of spaghetti between us like some kind of shield.

I set my bowl down. I reached for hers and placed it next to mine. "I overheard you talking to Greg this afternoon."

"Damn it." She looked away from me, and I could see tears forming in her eyes.

"Fuck. Crystal, what did he say to you? Why are you upset?" One little tear and my libido turned from wanting to fuck to wanting to fight.

She swiped below her eye. "I yelled at him. Threatened him, and may have called him names. He's a programmer, and I'm just a woman in tech. HR is more likely to listen to him, and ignore my list of instances against him."

"Instances?" I could hardly contain my rage.

"He calls me pond scum when he thinks no one is listening. Does it the same way as stupid cough middle school boys do. Am I in trouble?"

"You're not," I shook my head. "He is. I'll deal with him. I wanted to tell you that I saw you put him in his place, and you really shouldn't do that because of how fucking hot it was."

"What?" she laughed. "Hot? It wasn't hot. I was terrified. I went and rage cried in the bathroom."

I reached for her, cupping the side of her face with my hand. She wrapped her fingers around my wrist and leaned into my palm with a sigh.

"Oh, no. You can't do anything. He already calls you my boyfriend in a threatening kind of way. If you say anything in my defense, then we'll both get in trouble." She closed her eyes for a moment.

"You being a hellion on a mission was impressive as hell."

"Impressive huh? I could kiss you for that. It was nerve-wracking."

My hand on her face moved to grip the back of her neck. I pulled her to me, and me to her. "If I'm gonna get busted for fraternizing with you, then let's make it worthwhile."

Her mouth was as soft as I remembered. I took that lower lip that she was fond of biting, and ran my teeth over it. I eased my hold and she leaned back. I followed, pressing her into the couch. Her fingers threaded into my hair. I skimmed a hand up her leg, fisting a handful of her shirt.

Her tongue darted between my lips first. Tentatively touching mine, inviting it to tango. Her lush mouth was sweet as strawberries as she nibbled and toyed with my lips.

She bent her knee, running it along my side. My hand slipped from her clothing and I palmed her ass. She lifted her chin. My lips trailed away from her mouth along her pointed little chin and down her neck. The collar of her oversized shirt impeded my progress down to her chest. I pulled back with a grunt of frustration.

Crystal pushed me away. I wanted to protest, but her actions stopped me. She crossed her arms and pulled the shirt over her head, exposing full breasts artfully displayed in white lace.

"Touch me," she said.

9

CRYSTAL

Zack panted heavily as he knelt above me. As he said, if we were going to get into trouble, might as well make it worthwhile. Not that I was thinking clearly at the moment. I wanted him to touch me, and that's all I could focus on.

His eyes were heavily lidded as he focused on my breasts. I thought that's why he had grunted, my shirt was in the way. That's how it felt. I had on too many clothes, and so did he.

"Zack?" I whispered. "Are you okay?"

"Fuck me," he said on a long breath of air. "I don't know what to do next. I mean, damn these."

He gently trailed his fingertips across the tops of my exposed breasts. "But I also want to kiss you more." His fingers moved to touch my mouth.

I flicked my tongue out and licked his finger.

He closed his eyes with a low moan.

"What do you want?" I asked.

"To taste all of you," his voice was husky with want. His gaze trailed from my face down my entire body and paused when he got to where my legs started.

I placed a finger on my lips and dragged it down my neck and onto my chest. "Start here, and work your way down. That's what you were doing wasn't it?"

I didn't have to say more before he pressed me back with harder kisses. His lips were demanding, taking. His teeth scraped my chin, and his kisses felt more like small bites as he moved down my neck. Making up for the few precious moments of lost time since I removed my shirt.

One arm crushed me to him, while his other hand toyed with the edges of my bra. His breath was so hot as he found a nipple through the fabric of my bra and coaxed it into a tighter harder peak than it was already forming.

His arm at my back moved in a caressing stroke and I felt the release of tension as he unhooked the bra.

I fought with the straps. I wanted his mouth on me, I wanted his hands to caress and knead me. With my breasts free, Zack's hand felt stronger, more commanding. He now had both hands and his mouth teasing me to an ecstatic state.

He knew what to do with my breasts. He didn't treat them like novelty toys, but like something to be savored, not to make silly noises and slap against his face.

His hands left my breasts to trail down my middle. He grabbed and kneaded all of my flesh as if all of it were to be desired.

I was losing the fight of having coherent thought, and functional muscles. His mouth, his hands, he left me weak. I dug my fingers into his shoulders, completely at his mercy. And he had barely done anything.

I didn't suppress the startled gasp when his hand found its way inside my leggings and between my thighs.

"I should have known you were trouble from the beginning. You aren't wearing panties." He lifted his head from my breasts to smile wickedly up at me.

I shook my head. "Not with leggings. It's redundant." He made thinking difficult.

"Redundant," he chuckled. "More like brilliant." His fingers toyed with my folds as he spoke. "You are so fucking wet."

He pulled back. His actions had me slip to the side. And he slid from the couch.

"Does your pussy taste as good as your mouth, Crystal?" His eyes narrowed on mine.

All I could do was pant and whimper.

He grabbed the fabric of my leggings and yanked them down. He shifted so that he could pull them all the way off. He pressed his firm hands against my inner thighs, spreading my legs wide.

"I'm so glad you invited me over for dinner. I've never looked forward to dessert with so much anticipation before." His fingers trailed between my folds and dipped into my depths.

I moaned and lifted my hips.

He thrust two fingers in deep. Leaning forward he pressed his hand in farther.

"Is this what you want?" he asked.

He had gone from being a kid in a candy store to becoming demanding and being in control. I was now the one at his mercy.

"Yes, touch me. Touch all of me."

A keening sound ripped from my throat as his cool tongue made contact with my clit. I felt all the built-up stress in my body melt away as his tongue dragged down through my pussy before he returned it to swirl and suck at my nerve center.

I dug my fingers into his hair. Holding on for all I was worth.

He thrust fingers with one hand and grabbed my ass with the other. His mouth did wonderful and wicked things. He laved and sucked, and bit.

"Zack!" I cried when I felt teeth scrape at delicate skin.

It was a combination of too much and a need for more. I mewed and squeaked, and made noises I had no control of.

"That's it Darling, cum for me. Flood me with your honey."

My body responded to his commands. I felt the muscles of my inner walls suck at his fingers. Pulse, throb, relax, pull, all the motions happening in time with his fingers. His mouth returned to my clit and his sucking, thrusting moved in time with my own internal waves and rocking hips.

He growled against me and I counter thrust harder, faster.

I tugged on his hair. I needed more.

He responded with hard, fast movements, and I was instantly lost. I grabbed a throw pillow and bit into it. Screaming until my throat felt raw. I held on for as long as I could, reveling in the way Zack felt, the way he made me feel. But it was too much. I tried to push his head away and pull my thighs together.

He pushed back against my leg. "Okay, okay. I get it. My head's not a watermelon to crush."

He smiled up at me and wiped his chin.

"You're a screamer." He looked entirely too satisfied with himself.

I didn't care. He earned that cocky smirk. I was as limp as the noodles I had served him for dinner.

"You look done."

I replied with a weak nod.

"I'm just getting started." He stood, wiping my juices from his fingers onto the front of his tee.

He pulled me onto my feet and bundled me in against his chest. I loved the way his clothes felt rough against my sensitive skin. His lips slid across mine, and I tasted me on his tongue. It made me shiver.

"You're already naked, so asking your bed or mine is silly. Yours, because asking you to put clothes on would be a crime. Do I need to go home real quick and get condoms?"

I swallowed. I didn't want Zack to see how Chase had left me with a mattress on the floor and boxes for my clothes. "Are you sure? Your bedroom might be better. You know where your condoms are, and..."

He quieted me with a kiss. "What's wrong with your bedroom? You said your ex took the furniture. Is that all he took?"

"I don't know. Chase might have left condoms," I managed to say.

I took his hand and walked back to my bedroom. At one point it was nice, with a large sleigh bed frame, coordinating bedside tables, and contrasting dressers. The furniture had belonged to Chase's mom, so it was reasonable he took it.

Zack's gaze scanned around the room. With a nod of his head, he said, "I'll be right back. Get under the covers, I don't want you to get cold."

He was back before I had time to get comfortable. He tossed a small black and gold box onto the mattress. "That should be enough for tonight. I'll have to buy more."

He took off his shoes and pulled his shirt over his head. He was so handsome, and beautifully defined it almost hurt to look at him. I sat up and reached for the waistband of his jeans.

"My turn," I purred.

He batted my hands away. "I'm not done with my turn yet."

He sat on the bed next to me and kicked his pants off. He had the most sculpted legs and ass. I admired them in those tight biker shorts he wore often enough. But it was the beautiful throbbing cock between those glorious thighs that held my attention.

"Is that for me?" I asked with all the appreciation I was feeling.

"Come here," he growled as he slipped under the covers.

His skin felt like a full-body caress. His thick and hot cock pressed into my hip as I wrapped my arms around his neck, and pulled him to me for more kissing. He had already turned every knob on my body to full throttle, and I wanted more.

I slid a leg up his, and he shifted so his hips pressed to mine, trapping that magnificent cock of his between our bodies. I rocked my hips, stroking him. He was hot and thick. I let out little cries every time the head slid past my clit.

"Fuck Crystal," he said, rolling off me. He fumbled about searching for the box of condoms. I heard the paper board rip, and then he had a gold foil pack in his teeth and was ripping it open.

A few seconds of diverted attention, and then he was pressing against me again. His cock rubbing against me.

I whimpered again as his cock dragged down my clit. The prolonged contact was almost too much. His hips pulled back. I tilted mine back, and we thrust together. He sank deep and hard into me.

The muscles of my core, already sensitive from his talented tongue and fingers, roared back to a frenzied action. I could hardly move in a coordinated rhythm. Everything about me was in overdrive. I bucked and cried. I clutched at the arms that surrounded me and sucked on the plundering tongue in my mouth.

My second orgasm hit, and Zack continued to pound me into the mattress. I was beyond moving by the time he joined me with his own orgasmic high. He collapsed against me, panting. All of my muscles had quivered into nothing. I barely had the strength to roll over and switch off the lamp on the floor next to the bed.

He groaned and rolled away from me. "Don't do that. I'll fall asleep."

"That's the point," I said.

"Can't." He sat up with a groan. He leaned over and kissed me. "I can't risk being seen leaving here in the morning."

He walked to the bathroom to take care of the condom and picked up his pants.

"Fuck if it isn't going to be torture tomorrow at work."

I lifted my eyebrows in question.

He stepped into his pants and shorts at the same time and began pulling on his shirt.

"I know what you look like when you cum. It's gonna kill me to pretend not to."

10

CRYSTAL

I woke as Zack placed a kiss on my bare shoulder. It was becoming his habit to get half dressed before waking me to say good night. "I wish you could stay the whole night," I murmured.

"I'll be next door thinking the same thing. This way, at least, I will show up for work," he said as he pulled his clothes back on.

"How's that?" I asked.

"If I spent the night with you, I would never want to get out of bed again. This way, I force myself to go to work to see you."

He was a sexy rumpled mess. We had this conversation more often than not the past few weeks. I never went to his place, and he never stayed longer than what could be considered a late dinner date.

"Is that why you never knock on my door for coffee in the morning?" I shifted to the edge of the bed to wrap an arm around whatever part of his body I could touch. This time it was his leg.

He looked down at me. The shadows hid most of his face, but the light glinted off his teeth so I knew he was smiling.

"You know me well." He leaned over and kissed me properly.

His lips made me giddy. His entire body made me feel like I could fly.

"Go to sleep, I'll see you at work."

I waited until I heard the patio door slide close before I rolled over and went back to sleep. I dreamed of a day when he wouldn't leave, and we didn't have to hide from the world. Especially the world of work.

At work, I continued to herd my programmers toward our goals. The first full beta test of our app was coming due. I was feeling the stress.

"Hey wifey," Charline crooned at me as she walked into the break room.

I looked up from the tablet in my hands.

"You're on a break, that means no working," she reminded me.

I shrugged. "I really need this app to deliver on time. It's got my nerves in a knot," I confessed.

She reached for the tablet in my hands. I let her take it. She placed it on the table, and proceeded to rummage around in the refrigerator.

"Step one, you can't work all the time. When was the last time you ate a proper meal?" she asked. "Lordy Crystal, you haven't had breakfast today have you? Are you sleeping all right?"

She was right. I spent my morning clearing away the dishes from last night's dinner that didn't get done because Zack had been there. We had barely eaten, too eager to consume each other. So no time for breakfast.

"I had some coffee. And my sleep has been off." I shook my head. I wasn't about to tell why I had been missing sleep.

"Did you eat a real meal last night? Let me guess, a protein bar and some cold coffee? That's it, we are having lunch together so I can witness you eating."

"It's not like skipping a meal or two wouldn't hurt," I said, indicating my excessive curves.

"Healthy eating habits have nothing to do with your size, Sugar. And you know it. I don't know why you can't seem to remember you get woozy if you don't eat regularly."

"That's because you take good care of me," I chuckled. "Same reason I have to remind you to put on sunscreen."

With a yogurt in her hand, she pointed at me. "Lunch, I mean it," she said before leaving.

I picked up the tablet and returned to my cubicle. I was feeling off. She was right, bad eating habits were not going to help my stress levels.

A few hours later I met her at the food truck across the parking lot.

"I ordered tacos," she announced as I got there.

A few minutes later we each held a paper tray full of delicious tacos filled with grilled chicken, onions, cilantro, and lime juice. We each had a can of pop and a handful of napkins. I didn't know what the secret ingredient was but I could never match the taste at home.

"It's been long enough since the layoffs that you would think some of the engineering jobs would open back up," Charline complained about her lack of job prospects.

"Any luck looking outside of Shingle Click?" I asked.

She shrugged.

"Yeah, but you could finally date Tony," I said.

"Tony would have no clue that I want to date him." She crumbled up her napkins and stood to take her garbage to the nearby trash can.

I stood. And then I wasn't standing.

"Crystal?" Charline looked like she had seen a ghost. Her hands kept patting my forehead and cheeks. "You are not okay. So don't tell me you are. I saw that. You went all weak-kneed and sat back down in a big hurry. I've seen my sister pass out like that during her pregnancy. You aren't pregnant, are you? Tell me to shut up, you would have said something if you were sleeping with someone."

"Give me a minute." I grabbed her wrists to still her hands. I wanted to put a hand over her mouth to stop her prattling on. I hadn't told her about Zack, and I was having a hard time breathing around the concept of being pregnant. Why had she said that? "I stood up too fast. That's all."

"But you're clammy. Do me a favor?"

"Another one? I just had lunch with you," I joked.

"I know there's a drug store with one of those minute clinics near your apartment. Stop in it on your way home. Please."

I couldn't say no to her concern, and I wouldn't lie to her. Besides, I was definitely stopping there on the way home to pick up a pregnancy test. Now that Charline said it out loud, what else could it be?

After work, I stopped at the clinic. I sat on the paper-covered exam table while a nurse practitioner took my blood pressure. It was low.

"I don't pass out regularly," I said.

She continued the examination. "Is there a chance you are pregnant?"

I gulped. Where there was sex there was a chance. "We used condoms, and I'm on the pill."

She shined a light in my eyes, up my nose, and in my ears. "Well, it looks like you have an ear infection, that would explain the vertigo. Let's do a pregnancy test just to rule that out."

Zack wasn't outside when I got home later than usual. I knocked on his apartment door. No answer.

I wanted to text him, but we agreed that wasn't the smartest of ideas. There was no reason someone in my position would have to text the CEO. And so I didn't. I carried my bag and my new prescription for antibiotics into my apartment and scrounged a sticky note from my kitchen junk drawer.

"Sorry, missed dinner tonight. Ear infection." I drew a frowny face on the note before sticking it to his door. I knocked one last time just to be sure he wasn't home.

We had made no promises to each other. No commitment regarding seeing other people, and no expectations regarding being each other's dinner companion. I missed him, and I wanted his comfort while I felt like crap.

It was as if as soon as the infection was identified, I began feeling worse. Fortunately, all I had was an ear infection. I failed the pregnancy with glorious, not even possible, results.

I put a pot of water on to boil. I tossed in an egg and let it cook before I started the boiling water process all over again to cook a pack of cheap instant ramen noodles. I added some zucchini and sliced roast beef. I assembled my budget Pho soup creation and sent a picture to Charline, just to prove I was eating dinner.

I stared at the wall in front of me. How close was that pregnancy scare? No one knew about me and Zack. No one would know there was the potential that I could be pregnant if something happened to me.

I picked up the phone to call Charline. I didn't have to tell her I was seeing Zack. But I should tell her I was sleeping with someone regularly. And that her little pregnancy comment scared the crap out of me.

"Wifey!" she exclaimed as she answered the phone. "You're timing is outstanding."

"Why, what happened?" I asked.

"Wait, no, first how are you? You sent a picture of your dinner, good. But what did they say at the clinic?"

"I have an ear infection. Nothing life-threatening. They put me on an antibiotic and a diuretic to help drain fluid from my ear. But what were you going to say? I know you aren't that happy because I called. What's up?"

"Well, remember how I said there just aren't the opportunities for me here?" Charline had been struggling to get her foot in the door into a tech job. She didn't have the option to take a low-paying internship like I had. She took the receptionist route, hoping to work her way up from there.

"Did Shingle Click come through with an offer?" I asked.

"Not Shingle Click. I just got off the phone with a company in Austin that does similar work."

"Austin?" I practically yelled.

"Yeah wifey, I'm moving back home. Everything is so much more affordable there. And it's a real engineering position."

11

ZACK

We were less than a week from hitting the first beta version of the Home Command Center mobile app. The operating systems group was very intense that integration went smoothly. They did not want to issue a system update again, and their department head was vocal in his opinion of my 'little mobile project.'

My 'little mobile project' was going to finally get Shingle Click back in the black after Jameson's failed attempt to defraud investors and steal money. I wasn't sorry that it was putting extra pressure on the operating systems group.

Everyone involved was tense. A few more days, we would get some real results from testing, and everyone could breathe a sigh of relief before moving into the next phase. I would be able to stop having to handhold the Board and investors through dinner meetings and presentations. At least that's what it felt like. The closer we got, the less time I had for what was truly important: the nightly seduction of my neighbor.

People were overreacting to every little thing at work. This wasn't even the product-to-consumer rollout, and everyone was holding their breath.

Crystal looked exhausted as she sat across from me in yet another meeting. It was crunch time. We didn't have time for this, even though it was important for us to know what to expect. Tony fidgeted, he wanted to make sure we were all aware of the potential road hazards.

"We need to get started. I have other meetings. Do we need Greg for this?" I asked.

Crystal rolled her eyes. She was still having issues with the man, but wouldn't tell me. Wouldn't let me deal with him.

"We can get started. I'll catch Greg up, after all, it's gonna end up in his lap," she said.

With an audible exhale of air, Tony began. "There are three areas we anticipate problems. We've done everything right, we are just aware there are factors we haven't taken into account in these areas of the app," Tony explained to the majority of our team where the expected hiccups and glitches would occur.

"Why were those factors not taken into account?" I asked. My attention was on Crystal. This was not the kind of thing she would have let slip through her fingers.

She shrugged.

"Not knowing is not an acceptable answer," I sounded harsh to my own ears. I couldn't have anyone at work think I was giving her special treatment, even though that's all I wanted to give her.

She rubbed her fingers of one hand over an eyebrow. Did anyone else notice she was picking up one of my habits?

"It's not that we don't know. It's more a case of not knowing what we don't know. This first factor"— she leaned over the flow chart full of sticky notes and tapped on one of the instances Tony indicated— "involves the human element. We have a ton of data from marketing research, but once people are involved there will always be an unknown."

I sat back and crossed my arms. That was my girl, she knew what was going on.

"We can only predict so many scenarios. Same for these other points," Crystal responded.

"We're already compiling shells so we can dump the new factors into once test results start returning. We've got the A-team on it, Allison and Armand," Tony laughed at his humor.

"Basically, we know and are prepared for these problem areas. If all goes well, there won't be any surprises along the way," Crystal said.

I nodded. "Good, let's keep at it."

I waited for everyone to clear the room before walking around the table to where Crystal sat. I stood close and she leaned in. My hand trailed across her back. I couldn't help but touch her.

"You still feeling bad?" I asked.

"The stress isn't helping. This medication has really wiped me out. At least I'm no longer all woozy."

"You've been working hard. How about we play hooky from work once this thing delivers? We could take a few days and go to Monterey."

"Why would the two of you be going to Monterey? Huh? I knew there was something going on between you guys. No way someone like her goes from intern to a cushy project management position."

Crystal jumped. "Shut up, Greg."

Greg let out a low chuckle as if he were some evil genius with a dastardly plan. "I bet my buddy George Fredrickson would be interested in hearing about you making plans for a trip to Monterey."

Crystal thrust to her feet. "For heaven's sake Greg. I doubt Mr. Fredrickson would consider you his buddy. And why can't we make plans for a trip to Monterey? It's a great location for a team retreat." She slapped her fingers over her mouth and looked at me wide-eyed.

I had no idea she was such a talented little actress. Even I almost bought into her charade.

She turned to me with a look of embarrassment. "I'm sorry, that was supposed to be your surprise. I shouldn't have said anything. Don't tell anyone Greg. I'm supposed to be pulling together the details for Zack before he lets everyone know."

I crossed my arms and nodded. She was saving our collective asses.

"A retreat?" The look on Greg's face indicated he wasn't sure if he believed us or not. I think he wanted to catch us in flagrante delicto.

That wasn't going to happen, not with Crystal being as smart as she was.

"Meetings over, Greg," she pointed out.

"Yeah, I figured why waste time on something that could have just as easily been an email," he grumbled.

"Because an email would have been open to miscommunication. This way we could all be present, get the questions, and be done with it, instead of having a constant back and forth with email," Crystal pursed her lips and quirked her pretty mouth to the side. "We've had email issues before. This was supposed to help make your job easier, not make mine harder. You want me to go over everything you missed now, or should I come by your cube later?" She herded Greg out of the conference room in front of her. "I'll get those details for you later, Zack," she said as she left.

I nodded. How much was an overnight in Monterey for six people going to bite into my budget? Crystal would know, maybe we could change the location someplace that didn't require an overnight. As long as I had an offsite retreat for the team Greg would never know. I should still take Crystal somewhere nice for a getaway.

I took my time returning to my office. I liked checking-in in person. Eventually, email, while efficient, felt too disconnected. After all, it was people that made this business work, and people that needed to know their work was valued.

Later in my office, my eyes kept crossing after a few hours of staring at spreadsheets. And these were the results of market analysis, not the raw data. I needed more coffee if I was going to be any good for the rest of the afternoon.

"George Fredrickson is on the line for you," Lisa announced through the intercom. "Are you in?"

I sighed, wanting to say no. I needed coffee to deal with Uncle George at the moment, but the man did not always respond well to being called back. When Uncle George called, I was expected to take the call.

I stretched and yawned before answering. "Yeah, put him through."

I picked up my office phone on the first ring.

"What is this I hear you're taking that chubby girl to Monterey? I thought we discussed this, you are not allowed to date anyone at that company. I will not have it," his voice was loud and reverberated through the speakerphone.

Fuck me. Maybe Greg really did know Uncle George?

"I'm going to stop you right there. I'm taking my entire team to Monterey, not just one person. And I've said it before I'm not dating her." I wasn't dating her. I was fucking her and enjoying every second of it. But we did not go out in public together. I would have preferred the option of taking her out and showing her off instead of hiding her away behind take-out dinners and being neighbors.

"That's what Craig told me. He said he didn't believe it because no one else on your team seems to know anything about it," Uncle George blustered.

Craig? He meant Greg. Uncle George's retention of names was definitely slipping.

"Craig says there's something up between you and that fat girl. I told him to keep an eye open for anything."

I seethed. Greg was not going to have fun crossing me. I wanted to string him up for how he treated Crystal, but she kept stopping me from dealing with the situation.

"Uncle George, how exactly do you know Greg?"

"I play golf with his father. How do you think he got the job?

12

CRYSTAL

No thanks to Greg, my romantic reward for getting the app into testing on schedule was turned into an overnight team-building trip. I even coordinated the rental of a super van, so we could all drive down in one vehicle.

I leaned against the window of the van and watched the sky turn from perfect blue to a blanket of gray. It seemed fitting for my gloomy mood.

In addition to my regular job, I had less than a week to schedule a surprise trip. And surprise, I did it. Transportation, hotel rooms, a conference room, some team building games, and tickets to the Monterey Bay Aquarium were all brought together in record time. I did not manage to get event T-shirts made, then again that would have put me over the budget on an event that was never accounted for in the beginning.

Zack pulled the van into the hotel lot, and Greg immediately complained that we were nowhere near all the tourist activities.

"Lunch and team building activities are scheduled first. We have a small break before dinner. Reservations have been made at a restaurant at Fisherman's Wharf, and after that, we can all head over to Cannery Row." I reviewed the basic schedule with him again.

It was as if he purposefully was forgetting this was a team-building focused retreat. He just wanted to hit the tourist spots and go drinking. Well, I wanted alone time with Zack. It looked like neither of us was getting what we wanted.

We ate our gourmet boxed lunches of calamari tacos while Zack gave his first presentation. He presented awards to each member of the team. Each one was personalized. Tony received a trophy that was a gold crutch for most accurate programming under the influence of painkillers. Allison received a shoebox-sized diorama of a seedy-looking basement with old furniture and tons of old computers and video game systems. She laughed her butt off at her award for 'out of the box thinking.' She was always talking about how her mother thought she would never do anything more than play video games in their basement.

In my opinion, Greg did not deserve an award for stepping in as a pinch hitter. But that's what the little baseball trophy Zack handed him said. Armand's award was a sizable chunk of granite that had been engraved for being the stability that supported the group.

"Last but not least, Crystal. I have something for you." Zack's smile made my toes want to curl. I read more into his words than I was receiving an award.

With a nervous giggle— a real one and not like any of the fake laughing I had done all afternoon— I stepped up to Zack.

He took my hand. I gave him a panicked glance. He didn't seem phased by his actions, so I tried to calm my pounding heart. What was he doing?

"This trip is all thanks to Crystal. She felt that as a team we pulled together and met near-impossible deadlines. She has kept all of us on task, and found ways to increase our productivity when we hit a block in our path, or in Tony's case, a hole in his backyard."

We all chuckled at the jab at Tony and his broken ankle.

Zack looked at me. "Close your eyes."

I did as I was told. I shivered as his hands tickled the fine hairs on my neck. And then something was on my head. I reached up.

"Our queen bee, keeping our hive running smoothly," Zack

announced as he kissed me on the cheek. It was fast and congratulatory.

My fingers traced over lumps and bumps, smooth planes, and sharp points. Zack had given me a crown.

Allison stood and applauded. "The woman in charge."

"She got an award for being bossy." Greg glowered as he gave me a slow clap.

Zack cut his own glare at Greg. "And she's going to be bossier as we get closer to the delivery dates. So get used to it."

I could have kissed him for real at that point. I knew he wanted to do more than shoot a few curt words at Greg. I was glad when Zack left it at that.

Decked out in my new crown, I slipped back into my pretense of having fun. If I had to play another game with Greg I was going to be sick. I know I coordinated the retreat. I had to make it look good, so I put in a real effort. I was not happy, and faking it was wearing on my nerves. All I could think of was not being alone with Zack.

"I'm feeling off. I think that lunch may not have been my friend," I announced.

"Are you okay?" Zack asked. "Are you going to want dinner?"

"Maybe I'll feel better after I get a chance to rest."

I left the conference room, expecting that I would be by myself for the rest of the evening, never once getting a moment to say anything to Zack without an audience present. I wanted to pout in privacy.

"Just a sec," I called out when I heard the knock on my door a few hours later.

Zack leaned against the door frame. He looked all long-limbed with stretched-out muscles, strong and dangerous. I blinked a few times before I realized he had changed out of work clothes and the faded jeans and cable knit sweater he wore changed my whole perception of him.

I stepped back, inviting him in without a word.

Kicking the door shut behind him, he wrapped his arms around me and pulled me to his chest before claiming my lips. His kiss was full of all of the promises I felt that I was missing being in this place with all of my coworkers, and not alone with him.

I toyed with the hem of his sweater before I slid my hand underneath to find the hard planes of his defined pecs. He felt so warm and solid. He grounded me to the present when I wanted to hide from it all. But I wanted to hide with him. His hands pulled my tunic up until his hands could run along my hips and backside.

"It's been making me crazy knowing you don't have panties on underneath these leggings," He growled into my mouth. His hands slipped past the waistband, and fingers slipped between my legs.

I pulled him back toward the bed. This is what I wanted him for, needed from him. Touching, kissing.

"Won't the team be looking for you?" I asked with a moan. His fingers stroking my clit made focusing difficult.

He pressed me back into the bed and pulled my leggings off.

"We're taking a break. Meeting in the lobby at twenty after. If I can't touch you I'll go mad."

"You are touching me," I gasped.

He dipped two fingers into my heat.

"Fuck me, you are so wet." He undid the fly of his jeans. His beautiful cock sprang forth, erect and pulsing with anticipation.

He placed one knee on the bed and slid up my body until our hips met. I hitched a leg over his and pulled him in closer.

"I want you," I let out a needy whine.

He palmed my breast through my clothes. And kissed me hard. His tip teased my entrance.

"Why do you feel so good?" he murmured.

He slid in. I sighed as my body welcomed him home, wrapping him in my need. His withdrawal was fast, unexpected.

"Condom!" he barked. "Fuck, I didn't pack any. Didn't think we'd have a second alone. You?"

I shook my head. "I'm on the pill." I reached up to pull him back to my body. "We'll be fine. The condoms were mostly for diseases. We don't have to worry about those, do we?"

"No we don't," he said with a smirk.

I didn't cry out as much as I wanted when he slid back into me, just in case someone was listening at the door. That didn't stop him from moaning.

"Fuck, you feel so good Crystal. So much better with your skin around me."

I thrust my hips up, and he drove into me harder.

I pushed my hands underneath his sweater and teased his nipples with my thumbs as he continued to pound. His arms braced on either side of my head. I was trapped beneath him. Pinned to the bed by his glorious cock.

"Oh fuck!" he practically roared. His face contorted in that expression that looked like pain, but was really the 'oh so good' of an orgasm.

I wanted to laugh with delight because my body did that to him. The smile was wiped from my face as my body responded to his as I joined him in ecstatic spasms.

I wanted to stay weighed down by his body. I wanted to wrap him around me and sleep together until morning.

With a groan, he rolled to the side. "That was intense."

A buzzing sound came from his jeans somewhere around his knees.

"I've got to go." He kissed me quickly and pulled his pants back up as he stood. "Are you coming or staying?"

"Staying. Have fun."

He kissed me again before leaving me alone.

13

ZACK

I left Crystal depleted on the bed. Her limbs hung as if she had no muscular control, half-naked and utterly spent. I loved shattering her that way. Always so responsive to my touch, she stirred something primordial inside me. The mere thought of getting her hot and bothered was enough to redirect all blood flow straight to my cock.

I needed to watch it or my dick would spring back up, ready for action. Not the preferred choice for an evening out with a bunch of programmers from work. If I had a choice, I would be taking the rest of her clothes off, and stripping myself down to the skin. Instead, I was walking down the hotel hallway shoving my hands into my pockets pretending that I hadn't just had one of the best damned quickies in all of my life.

"Hi, Zack," Allison greeted me with a reserved smile. "I came to check on Crystal. Her room is up this way."

Allison pointed. I twisted to follow the direction of her gesture.

"Yeah, I was just checking on her. She's gonna stay in for tonight. I thought maybe we should pick a little surprise up for her." I continued to stride away from Crystal's room.

I swallowed the 'oh shit almost busted' lump in my throat. Not quite gone, I coughed to clear it away. I covered my mouth and smelled Crystal on my fingers. I closed my eyes and inhaled her heady musk.

If I didn't stay focused, thoughts of her would have me hard and miserable all evening. I coughed again. Maybe I could pretend to not feel well and go back to her room?

"We should call a car or two. I feel like drinking tonight. I shouldn't be driving," I announced. If I couldn't have Crystal, I'd have whiskey.

"Ooh, the boss gets wild and crazy," Allison chuckled.

When we reached the lobby I excused myself to the restroom. I needed to wash Crystal from my fingers. I didn't want to, but I was not going to share any of her, even accidentally. She was mine.

My hair was a disheveled mess. Sex hair. Had Allison even noticed? I smoothed my hair back and started washing. With hands full of soap, I awkwardly wiped at my eye. My arm came close to my nose, and I smelled Crystal. I finished washing my hands and began sniffing my sweater. Her scent was on me. I didn't bother to hide the cocky smile that took up residence on my face.

Two cars ferried us into the middle of the touristy area of Fisherman's Wharf. I kept my eyes open for a gift, something I could get Crystal that wouldn't be out of character for an appreciative boss to give an employee.

Allison pointed out a fudge shop. "Let's get Crystal some fudge."

"Does she like chocolate?" I pretended to not know. She liked her chocolate dark and bitter. Her favorite came with a swirl of orange zest, and a dash of salt. If it wasn't dark, she preferred her chocolate to have fruit in it.

"Are you buying fudge for the rest of us?" The sneer in Greg's voice set the small hair on the back of my neck on end.

"Get your own fudge Greg," Allison said.

We ignored him, and with the help of the teenager behind the counter, we bought Crystal a modest collection of flavors.

I ignored Greg's more asshole oriented comments through dinner. There were brief moments when he wasn't being a complete dick.

There were not enough of those to provide a counterbalance for the rest of his attitude.

After a few glasses of wine with dinner, and a few rounds of shots at some bar on Cannery Row, my tongue was feeling a little loose and I was feeling a little dangerous. I picked up my chair and sauntered to the other end of the table where Greg sat. The expressions around me made it clear that my move was unexpected. The panicked expression on Greg's face made me want to cackle maniacally.

The sound of scraping chairs needled in my brain, a reminder of unpleasant things and I needed to tread very carefully. I placed my chair down, sat, and draped an arm over Greg's shoulder. I squeezed hard. It was intended to intimidate.

"Greg, are you having a good day?" I asked.

The expression he gave me was one of confusion. What was I doing? Did he need to be concerned? How drunk was I, and could he leverage this behavior with my fucking, self-proclaimed uncle?

"Yeah, Zack. Today has been good," he answered with noticeable hesitation.

"I have had a fucking brilliant day," I said with a laugh. I may have jerked my arm a little tighter around his shoulder. It slid so the hold was more like a neck lock.

"You know who hasn't had a good day, Greg?"

He shrugged.

"Crystal has not had a good day. She should be here having fun, but she's not."

"She wasn't feeling good," he said. "Said lunch wasn't agreeing with her."

"Uh-huh, I suspect what isn't agreeing with her is you, Greg. You know what microaggressions are Greg? Do you?"

"Yeah, what's your point, Zack?" he stammered.

"You are not subtle, Greg. I'm tired of your blatant microaggression toward a very valuable member of this team." I squeezed tighter, dragging his ear closer to my mouth. I whispered in his ear. "Stop fucking doing it, or I can guarantee George Fredrickson won't be able to save your job."

I released my arm and he sat away from me with a lurch.

"That wasn't exactly subtle yourself there Zack." He tried to puff his scrawny chest up. Sure he had height on me, but I had muscle and strength.

I stood and wiped down the front of my sweater as if it were covered in crumbs. "It wasn't supposed to be Greg. You need to cut that shit out."

I went to the bar and ordered another shot before taking a car back to the hotel alone.

Crystal didn't answer her door when I knocked. She must have been asleep.

The next day passed in a haze of looking at fish and driving the van back to the Shingle Click offices. The headache that lurked behind my eyes was not helped by the suspicious glares Greg shot in my direction. At least he was leaving Crystal alone.

Unfortunately, so was I.

"Crystal," I said as I walked into her cube the next day. Her new crown hung at an angle on the corner of one of her monitors.

The smile she gave me made my already stellar morning even better. Her eyes sparkled, and I wanted to kiss her. I wanted her to jump up and press those warm soft breasts against my chest, and continue to wiggle the way she did when she was happy.

She was going to be happy, but there would be no hugs or kisses.

"I got the first round of results in. All those roadblocks Tony had pointed out," I shook my head. "Practically nonexistent."

I smiled as she started to squirm in her chair. Damn, she was sexy.

"Are you serious?"

"I'll forward you the reports to share. If everything continues this way, we shift tracks to the next phase. Can we do any clean-up as we go if any of those issues pop up?"

She bit her lip. Her eyes darted about as she thought. "If Allison and Armand don't have to reinvent the wheel on those unknown factors, I should be able to pull one of them for cleaning up code." She gave a little nod. "Yeah, I mean, I haven't seen the numbers, but by the look on your face, they are better than expected. If everything lines up, we could enter phase two in a couple of weeks."

"Could we push up the deadline?" I asked with a wink.

She laughed, "You're cute, but you're not that cute. The deadline has been established. It's just meant to change the rules in the middle of the game."

I shrugged. Deadlines changed all the time. We could revisit that discussion after we have all the results.

"Speaking of games," I leaned in close, cutting my gaze toward Greg's cube and back. "Have you noticed any changes in anyone's attitude?"

She tilted her head in the direction I had been looking. "He's not in today. Seems to have caught something on our little trip. Why?"

"I think he may have caught a case of 'the boss told him off,'" I said.

"Zack, what did you do?" she whispered.

"Nothing to worry over. His attitude was on full display, I told him to check it at the door. He wasn't being clever, and I was sick of hearing it. No possible retaliation issues."

She sighed. I could watch her do that all day long.

"Hey, Zack," Tony said as he walked past. "I just heard in QA that the results coming in look fantastic."

"I heard that too. It's all wait and see at this point."

"Hopefully the results stay steady. I know after this weekend I'm feeling ready to hit the ground running with this. That was a lot of fun. Thank you." He nodded at Crystal. "You should wear your crown today, you earned it."

With a happy undulation and giggle, she placed it on her head. Everything about her was dazzling.

14

CRYSTAL

I slipped my crown on my head and dove into the onslaught of emails. Its weight not only reminded me to keep my back straight, and posture corrected, it reminded me that there was a time this product rollout was moving smoothly and we all had hope and a positive outlook. We hit a hard brick wall in the integration process. As Zack said when he first took over at Shingle Click, like an arrow we had to pull back to go even farther.

The pull-back fell squarely on my team's shoulders. We were the victims of our own good work. There was no convincing the bosses what they were asking was not going to happen. It was impossible. There were physically not enough hours in the day. I stood next to Zack in a presentation where the damned President of the Board told us to find a way. I wanted to hand him a rock and ask him to squeeze blood from it.

Every other cubicle in this building had a variation of the same Venn diagram. The basic image was three overlapping circles, one labeled as 'quality,' another as 'fast,' and the third labeled as 'cheap.' The center, where the circles would overlap always said, 'no,' 'not possible,' 'pick two,' or some combination of words indicating that the three: good, fast, and cheap, never happened together.

And yet, here we were, expected to up the pre-established deadline, and deliver a quality product. All without giving me another programmer. Even with one more, we would still not be able to meet the new timetable.

My fingers flew across my keyboard, typing away with pent-up rage. I forwarded the weekly status report to Zack. I missed our twice-weekly strolls through the office where we would take our time to review what was going on, and what was coming up next. Those days were gone. There was no time. We were perpetually behind schedule.

"Make It Happen."

I fantasized about what would happen if we didn't. There were the good fantasies where Zack would sweep in and defend me against George Fredrickson. There were the gruesome ones that made me shudder as I imagined bad horror movie graphics of heads exploding. Unfortunately, there were the reality-based ones too: we all got fired.

It didn't help that our initial success changed the nature of Zack's job. Suddenly he was traveling all over, and barely ever in the office. He met venture capitalists to secure funding. He met vendors who could streamline our direct-to-consumer distribution. He was off having meetings with everyone but me.

Email sent, I stood. The next thing I knew I was back in my chair. I placed a hand on my forehead and against my cheeks. I couldn't tell if I felt hot or clammy. That spell had felt just like the stupid ear infection I had a month ago. I didn't have time to get sick.

By the time I got off the train, I was too tired to walk the extra block to the minute clinic. I just wanted to get home. I hadn't heard from Zack, and I wanted to see him.

Once home I knocked on his door to see if he was home. He answered the door and waved me in. I trudged into his sparsely furnished apartment. He needed better furniture, he certainly could afford it. I slumped onto the couch as he paced back and forth having a conversation with someone on the phone.

It was business. I could tell by his choice of words. I didn't want to know. I didn't want to hear about how the HCC mobile app was the linchpin in the future success of the company. If the work my team did was so vital, why did they suddenly start treating us like indentured servants instead of valuable employees?

He pulled the earpiece out and tossed it onto the kitchen counter before falling onto the couch next to me.

I sighed as he leaned against me, finding comfort in his presence.

"How come the more success we have, the harder we have to work?" he asked.

I shrugged. "That sounds like some kind of philosophical question they make you write essays about in business school."

He thrust a pointed finger straight up into the air as if he were making a proclamation. "Discuss the cornerstone principle of growth vectors in contrast to economic evidence of enterprise markers," he chuckled.

"I don't know what any of that means, but I swear that's what half of your conversations sound like," I lifted my hand to stroke his hair.

He lay his head in my lap and looked up at me. "Fancy words for saying prove how this thing will make money. I got today's figures."

"Oh please, can we not talk about work?" I whined.

"I haven't seen you for days. It's my first chance to ask questions," he kept talking about work.

"Exactly, we haven't seen each other for days." I leaned forward and kissed his forehead.

"That's a much better idea." He rolled around until he was over me, pressing me back into the cushions.

His lips slid over mine, and I stopped thinking about anything other than the feel of him. His tongue caressed the seam of my mouth and I darted my tongue out to tease his. I captured his lower lip in my teeth, and he let out a primal growl that had my entire body light up with want and need.

Pressing against his chest, I backed him away from me far enough so that I could wiggle out of the shirt I had on. My fingers located and began methodically undoing the buttons of his shirt. I then clawed at his back, pulling the white under tee off over his head. My bra came off somehow, and we were gloriously skin to skin.

I ran my fingers over his chest, and down his arms. He was so strong and thick muscled. He was built like an athlete and fucked like a porn star. I reached for the fastener of his slacks, wanting access to his porn star skills.

An old-fashioned telephone ringer sounded. Zack stopped kissing me and groaned. He sat up and grabbed his phone from his pocket.

"Fuck me. I have to take this." He got up and crossed to the kitchen.

Popping the earpiece in, he started having another intense conversation. He was throwing around the same words we had joked about earlier.

I felt abandoned, all hot and bothered, and half nude waiting for him to cut the call short and return to me. When I realized that wasn't going to happen any time soon, I pulled my shirt back on and picked my bra up from the floor. I tapped him on the shoulder to get his attention. When he turned I waved, and then let myself out the door.

I had enough time to start making dinner before Zack knocked on my door, and then let himself in.

"Why did you run away?" he asked.

I looked at him and blinked a few times. Really? "You abandoned me naked on your couch for a business call. I got cold and hungry."

He sighed and held his hands out. "It's business. It's important to maintain a level of progress and sometimes that means working after hours."

"No Zack. It's business. It's important to have a work-life balance, or work becomes all-encompassing. You have to hide your relationships, you aren't allowed to enjoy the things that keep you sane. It's a business, it won't keep you warm at night, or hold you when you are hurt and lonely."

"Are you saying I don't hold you?"

"You weren't there when I needed you. You certainly have to hide me." My voice dropped low with anger. "When was the last time you rode your bike?"

He threw his hands up. "Fuck, Crystal, you aren't still mad about

Monterey are you? I would have much rather been fucking you than drinking with Greg and the team."

"That's all it is, isn't it? It's just fucking. We aren't allowed to go out, we can't be seen. We can't even leave the damned peninsula together." I felt used.

"Crystal."

I crossed my arms and glared. I was done talking to him.

"What do you want from me? I'm stuck in the same position."

I said nothing.

"Oh come on! Talk to me," he pleaded.

I wasn't going to give in. I wasn't going to cry. He needed to cross the space between us and pull me into his arms and tell me we were more than just fuck buddies. I certainly thought there was more going on between us.

"Fine!" He threw his hands up again. "I have an early flight. If you feel like talking to me again at some point, you know where I live."

The door closed with the loudest click I had ever heard.

My microwave beeped. I spun toward it. Somehow I ended up on my ass in the middle of my kitchen. I started to cry. Zack was gone, and I was dizzy again.

The next morning I sat on the same paper-covered exam table at the clinic.

"I don't see an ear infection," the physician's assistant said. "How's work?" She asked as she felt the glands in my neck.

"Stressful, super stressful."

"Periods regular?"

I bit my lips together, thinking.

She looked at me quizzically. "When was the first day of your last period?"

I felt my eyes go wide. It should have been a week ago, but with everything at work… "Can stress make you miss your period?"

She nodded. "Let's run a pregnancy test just in case. You've been on antibiotics, and you're on the pill."

"So?" I asked.

"Antibiotics make the pill not work," she said.

"Oh."

I couldn't go to work. I couldn't face the world. I took my positive pregnancy test and went home. I felt more alone and abandoned at that moment than I had when Zack walked out my door the night before. I emailed the team, letting them know I wasn't feeling well. And crawled into bed. How the hell was I going to tell Zack that I was pregnant?

15

ZACK

I knocked on Crystal's door. It had been two days since I walked out of it. The only message I had from her was the group text where she mentioned she wasn't well. She was hurt, and not feeling well, and I wasn't there for her.

She was right, I had to hide her away, and that now meant I had no texts from her, no personal emails, no voice mails. I had no way of knowing if she was all right. When I checked in with the team via email, she hadn't responded. And when Allison asked if I knew how Crystal was doing, my stomach sank.

Things needed to change. I needed to change them.

I gave her a few minutes, knocked again, and then let myself in with my key. She trusted me with a key to her apartment. She needed to know I could be trusted with more.

"Crystal, I brought you some Pho," I said as I crossed to her kitchen. "Crystal?"

I put the soup and extras on the counter before heading into her bedroom.

"You in here?" I saw her bundled up under her blankets.

Sitting next to her on the bed, I peeled a blanket away to reveal her face. Her eyes looked swollen closed. My heart lurched in my chest.

She didn't look well, ashen and blotchy. Like she had been crying, like she was really sick.

I placed my hand against her cheek, and she leaned into me and opened her eyes.

"Hi," she said in the smallest voice.

I pulled her to my chest and wrapped my arms around her. She trembled in my arms. Crying, she was crying. I was prepared to slay dragons for her. I needed to do better by her and see them for myself, and not expect her to have to point them out. She had told me what she needed, and I had walked away.

"Crystal, Darling, what is it? You said you weren't well. Please tell me this isn't because of our fight."

I heard the gulp in her throat, her voice was raspy, dry. "Not the fight. But that certainly didn't help any."

"I'm such an asshole. You told me exactly what you needed, my arms around you, and I left. I can be dumb."

She nodded.

"I'm here now. Forgive me for being a dumbass?"

"I'll try if you try to not be one."

"Deal." I brushed a stray hair back from her face. "When was the last time you had something to eat or drink?"

She shrugged.

"I got your favorite Pho. Let me help you sit up, and I'll go get it ready for you." I went into her small bathroom and returned with a damp washcloth to wipe her face.

She gave me a weak smile. I felt pain in my gut. Something was wrong, I could tell.

In the kitchen, I poured the now tepid soup into a microwave bowl and hit the buttons.

"Hi." She walked so carefully, holding on to the wall, and then the counter as she moved.

"Do you have another bad ear infection? You aren't looking too stable there."

"I'm having dizzy spells, but it's not an ear infection. I thought I'd come out here. I don't want to spill soup in my bed. That would be miserable to clean up."

I crossed out of the kitchen and helped her to the couch. Crystal, so solid and strong in my arms a few days ago now felt so frail and fragile. If I held her too tightly she would break.

"If it's not an ear infection, can you tell me what's the matter?" I asked. "Did the doctor know?"

"Oh yeah, they knew. I'm still wrapping my head around it."

The microwave beeped. With her safely on the couch, I returned to the kitchen. "Do you want me to put everything in here, or do you want the Pho experience?"

She dragged her hand across her face and rubbed her eyes.

"I'll put everything together for you," I said.

She looked like she was too tired to even talk. I brought an oversized bowl of noodles in broth, thinly sliced roast beef, and hard-boiled egg— cut in half— and placed it on the trunk in front of her. I remembered exactly how she liked to order it. I returned to the kitchen and grabbed a bottle of Sriracha pepper sauce.

"Are you going to eat?" she asked.

"My bowl is in the microwave." On cue, it beeped, and I carried my soup to the trunk so I could sit next to her on the couch.

I couldn't eat. I had never done this before, been with someone who had gotten ill. Seriously ill. My parents had died before they got old, my sister was always healthy. I felt my insides twist uncomfortably.

"Will you tell me? I mean, I can help. Please, let me help you," I started talking. I wasn't exactly sure of the words that fell from my mouth.

She took a deep breath and put down her bowl. "I will tell you. I just can't yet. I haven't been able to tell anyone."

"Not even your mom, or your friend Charline?"

She shook her head.

That sinking feeling in my gut kept going lower and lower. She returned to eating her soup with slow deliberate movements. I could see the way she held the spoon she didn't seem to have much strength.

What could do this? I kept scanning my eyes over her as if I could see what was wrong. As if I suddenly possessed x-ray vision and could identify cancer tumors, or could see the lesions on her spine from multiple sclerosis.

I ran a list of autoimmune diseases through my head. I knew it couldn't be HIV, we had both been tested, a precaution we agreed upon after we got together. But it could be so many other things, things that could take her from me. I balled my fist, felt my nails bite into my palm. That caged feeling that pushed me to find an escape roared to life in my chest.

I needed to fight, to scream, to pound the fear and anger I felt in my blood out through the pedals of my bike. When she looked at me, I gave her a tight concerned smile. When she focused on her soup I breathed in hard through my nose, out through my mouth.

"Would you calm down Zack?" She reached over and stroked my thigh. "You are making me nervous."

"I'm sorry, I wasn't there with you. I should have been here to go with you to the doctor. You shouldn't have had to find out whatever you've got alone." I shoved down the panic that tried the shove its way into my brain.

"It's not life-threatening if that's what you're worried about."

I felt the fight or flight tension dissipate from my spine.

"You're really worried aren't you?" She laced her fingers through mine.

I gave her a slight nod.

"It's going to change everything, how I live, what I do. It will take some adjusting, that's all. Right now I just need some time."

She squeezed my hand, and I pulled her to me.

My arms wrapped around her and I held her. Whether she needed it or not, I did. I stroked her hair and enjoyed the feel of her pressed to me. I didn't need her to be naked and fucking to want to be with her. I just wanted to be with her. I felt frozen with that thought. I wanted her. It took her getting sick for me to realize it. In sickness and in health, I wanted her.

I relaxed into her warmth, and let it spread through me.

"Zack?"

"Yes, Darling?"

She bounced with a chuckle. "I like that, you calling me darling. I suddenly have the urge for dill pickle potato chips."

"They make those?" I asked

"Yes, you can get them at the grocery store. What I really want are fried pickles, but I don't know anyone around here who delivers."

"I haven't had those since the last time I went to the state fair. Seriously?" I didn't expect this to be the first dragon she needed slaying, but I was here for her. I sat up, easing her from my embrace. "If I can't find fried pickles, would the potato chips do?"

She nodded. "It's comfort food, deep-fried and tangy."

I could tell she wanted to move with more enthusiasm, but she didn't have the strength.

I pulled my phone from my pocket and began the search.

16

CRYSTAL

A folded letter-sized piece of paper was taped to my front door. I glanced around and noticed the unit in front of mine also had a letter taped to theirs. The apartments on Zack's side of the walkway didn't. I snatched the letter. The tape stuck to the door and tore a little crescent moon-shaped bit from the paper.

What was it now? I had already received the email, and the pestering follow-up emails requesting an acknowledging response, informing me that my lease would not be renewed when it expired. The property had been sold and the new owners were turning half the units into rotating B-N-B extended stay apartments and selling the other half as condos. No more apartment living here.

I finally had a job that paid enough that I could afford to continue to stay here, and they were kicking me out. It sucked.

I had a neighbor I was falling in love with. I was going to have his baby. Not that I liked my commute, but it was easy enough. I doubted I could find an equally nice area for the same money. I liked my apartment.

With work taking so much of my focus, I had the mental bandwidth for one extra thing in my life. I was still trying to figure out my relationship with Zack. I didn't have the time to find a new place to live. I didn't have time to figure out this pregnancy thing. I still hadn't found a baby doctor for checkups. Oh damn, I was such a mess.

"Now what?" I said as I struggled to unfold the paper while I unlocked my front door.

I stopped inside the front door and stared at the page. This was complete and utter bull shit. I let my bags slide from my shoulder and fall to the floor. I turned and stared at Zack's door, he didn't have the note. He was out of town, so I knew he hadn't already gotten it.

I stepped out and looked at the front unit on his building. They didn't have a note either. As I tried to figure out what was going on their door opened.

"Hi," I said, maybe a little too loud.

I held out my note and walked toward them. "Did you get a notice of eviction because of termites, or just the lease non-renewal?" I asked.

My neighbor met me halfway. His hand outstretched to take the note from me. I tried to remember his name. I could not think of it.

"Yeah, I got the lease thing, but nothing like this." He handed the notice back. He looked up. "I would think if you had termites we would, but the overhang doesn't really connect does it?"

I followed his gaze up. I lived in a single-story four-unit building. The building that I shared a walkway with had two stories and eight units. The roof that covered the stairs extended slightly over the edge of my building, keeping the walkway protected from direct rainfall.

"That's tough luck. I have to start looking soon myself. My lease is up in three months." He handed the note back to me with a shrug.

"Good luck. I think we're all going to need it. How many units are they taking off the market?"

He groaned. "Three hundred units. That's going to impact the cost of rent in all of this part of town." With a shake of his head, he waved and continued on his way.

I was screwed.

Extensive termite damage had been found in several of the buildings. Where possible the buildings would be tented and fumigated. Residents of those buildings would need to vacate the premises for seventy-two hours. There was an empty check box next to this option, along with a section for dates to be out of the apartment, not filled in. The other option, the one with the ugly red X in the check box, was what I had to deal with. My building would be demolished. Great, I was living in a building with severe enough termite damage that when I moved out, they were going to knock it over.

I had five weeks to find a new place to live and move. I had to find a baby doctor and get the situation with my womb figured out. I still hadn't told anyone. My mother would be so disappointed, and probably disown me. I wanted to know what the situation with Zack was before I told her. She didn't even know about Zack.

No one knew about Zack. He was the most amazing person to have come into my life and I hadn't told anyone. Not even Charline, and she was safely away from work gossip in Texas.

I had a moment to myself a few days later at work. I squirmed in my chair, not able to get comfortable. My undies had felt uncomfortable this morning. I changed my entire outfit so that I wore leggings under a dress instead, and they were binding. My focus was torn between the app rollout and finding a place to rent. I pulled a rental website up on my monitor. I wanted to stay in Sunnyvale. I wanted to stay on the north side so I could be near Zack, and so that my commute routine didn't have to change.

One train stop farther north, the next town up, and rents were another couple of hundred dollars higher. Enough of a difference that I wouldn't be able to afford rent. It was hard to care about QA testing results on a product the rich used in their homes when I was going to not have a home soon.

I needed to talk to Zack. He was supposed to be back in the office today. Hopefully, that meant he would be home tonight. I missed him.

"Are you house hunting on company time?" Greg's voice crawled up my neck like a slimy thing.

I spun my chair to face him. "I am allowed to take a break. You know legally it's required." I did not have time to deal with anything Greg had to say to me that wasn't directly related to the app.

He thrust a fat stack of printed pages at me. "There is an error in the code."

I shrugged. "So fix it."

"I don't know what it is. Allison can't identify it but says it's there. Tony says it's impeding one of the command sequences."

I blinked up at him. This was the kind of thing that, had upper management stood behind us over this whole "Make It Happen" directive, we could have avoided. We would have had the time to locate the error and get the code cleaned up. If they had given me the budget to hire another programmer, we could have had them go over this stuff with a fine-toothed comb.

We were behind, and I had nowhere to pull the extra hours from. I didn't have a magic hat or a time machine.

"What do you want me to do about it?" I leveled a dead stare at him. His whining wasn't helping anything.

He rustled the papers at me.

I refused to reach out for them.

"You need to proof this. You said you had programming experience. Well, prove it." He slammed the documents onto my desk.

I stood and picked up the stack of code. I tried to hand it back to him. "This is still your job." I shook the pages at him.

He lifted his hands in a 'won't touch that' gesture and took a step back.

"It's out of my hands now," he sneered at me and walked away. "I have other command structures to clean up."

"Greg!" I stormed after him. "How do you know it's in this block of code and not the OS? How long have you known about this?"

"Ask Tony, he's the one who gave it to Allison. I'm done talking to you about this Queen Crystal. Get another one of your flunkies to work on it."

I stopped chasing after him. If this came from Tony via Allison, that meant they had known about it for a day or two, a week maybe. "You are so childish. This is not how you ask for help."

I stood there seething. This team, which had hit it out of the park on the first phase of the application, was starting to cave under the pressure.

I caught a glimpse of Zack as he and several important-looking people in suits walked past the cubicles on the other side of the room.

"Look up," I willed at him. I could really use a hug and support right now. I'd take a nod, a half-smile.

I needed something to drink before I dealt with this code issue. Returning to my cube, I attempted to take a drink. My stupid water bottle was empty. I dropped the stack of code onto my desk and headed to the break room for a refill.

"I totally think your skin looks better," one of the women seated at the small break room table was saying. "My hormones hated me. I had zits like a teenager."

"Oh, I hope not. I'm already showing, that's bad enough. I don't want to look like some pregnant teenager," a different woman said.

I cast quick glances at the one who said she was already showing. Did she mean she was pregnant?

"I wore my husband's shirts over my baby bump. It was months before anyone realized I was expecting," the first woman chirped.

"Lucky. I'm already in maternity jeans and I'm not even three months along."

I tried to walk calmly out of the break room, and then I dashed to the bathroom. I stood in front of the big mirror. Did I look any different? Has my skin changed? I smoothed my dress over my belly and my hips. I was already round everywhere. At what point would my pudge become a baby bump?

17

ZACK

I felt like announcing my entrance into Crystal's apartment with a cheesy, "Honey, I'm home." The thought didn't slam into me like a sledgehammer but brought with it an all-encompassing feeling of rightness. Home and Crystal, yeah, that was good.

I had bags of aromatic spicy take-out for dinner. I unloaded our dinner onto the kitchen counter. I had to shove aside a bag of the dill pickle-flavored chips she had been constantly munching on recently.

"Crystal, I got dinner. You like Thai right?"

She staggered out from the back of her apartment, fingers pressed to her lips.

"Darling, are you okay? You look gray around the edges." I was by her side and guiding her to the couch.

"Sick again? Are you sure it's not those chips?"

Her eyes would have blazed at me if she had the energy. Instead, she looked defeated.

"You need to slow down at work. It's taking a toll." I sat next to her.

She shook her head.

"No, listen to me," I started.

"You have just as much experience with any of this as I do," she talked over me. "Zack, I don't know how I'm supposed to handle all of this," she sounded like she was going to cry.

"I can help. Let me."

"I'm just going to get more tired." She leaned into my shoulder.

I stroked her arm. I didn't know how to soothe her, how to make it better. "I'm here for you."

She sighed. "Yeah, but are you going to be here when…" she swallowed.

I hated that this was hard for her. I hated there was nothing I could do but hold her.

"Are you going to still be here when I'm not sleeping through the night? You already don't stay with me. And what happens when everything starts to swell up? Are you going to stay with me when I get fat and bloated?" She sniffed.

I leaned over and kissed the tears from her cheeks. I wanted to give her so much. "I'm here now, and I plan on sticking around."

Her hands flopped up and fell back to her lap. "What am I supposed to do when I have to take time off?"

"If you could at least tell HR. They could make accommodations for your illness."

She held up her hand in a stop gesture. "Can we stop calling it an illness?"

I sighed, "Your situation. Crystal, if you don't tell me what's wrong I won't know what exactly is going with you, and what I need you to help with. All I know is on the nights I do get to see you, you are so worn out from work you can barely stay awake through dinner. And half the time you don't finish eating, and the other half you're running off to puke."

"That's a fun side effect." The sarcasm was thick in her tone.

"I got some lemongrass soup and satay sticks. You think you'll be okay eating those?"

I returned to the kitchen to finish assembling our dinner, and pour her soup into a bowl.

"They sold this property," I mentioned.

"I know. I have to find a new place to live." She sounded dejected.

"I was thinking, we could look for a place together."

She snorted. "Like that's going to fly with company policy."

"I've been thinking," I said as I brought over the tableware we would need. "I want to take care of you. No matter what this thing is that you have. We can figure it out together. You don't have to be alone. We can get a bigger place, two bedrooms. There are some great townhouses out there with two master suites, each with their own bathroom. We could officially be roommates."

"Officially roommates, with our own bedrooms if anyone decided they needed to come to check up on us? Will I need a fake boyfriend? How do you want me to act around any of your fake dates?" she asked tersely.

"No more fake dates for me. But, yeah, we can have our own space if that's what you want. We could set up a home office." With a home office, she could work when she felt well enough. She could move in with me, and I would help her find a new position at another company. One that would work better for her new limitations, whatever those might be. Even if I could get the board to back off the whole dating a coworker mandate, Shingle Click wasn't a work environment conducive to supporting employees with chronic illness. Working from home was an exception, not a rule.

Crystal needed a situation where she could work from home. I could support us both, but she wasn't the kind of woman to let me coddle her. She was a tenacious fighter.

I set dinner down before joining her on the couch. I watched as she nibbled on a skewered chicken piece. I opened my mouth to fill her in on all my thoughts.

"I have to move before you do," she announced.

"When is your lease up?" I knew she had been here longer than I had. I expected her to need to be out a month or two before my lease was up.

She made a 'stay put' gesture and got up. She moved slowly and my heart lurched. I wanted her to not get hurt. She shuffled through a stack of papers on the bookshelf next to the door. She held out a folded sheet of paper to me as she sat back down.

In the middle of the page was an angry red X indicating that her lease was being terminated early. She needed to be out so the new owners could begin demolition.

"They're going to level this building because of extensive termite damage. I have until the end of next month."

"Next month is two days away," I said like a moron.

"Exactly."

"Fuck me." I rubbed my thumb into my eyebrow. If I helped her to find a new apartment, then I would see even less of her. If she moved in with me, there was no ploy of fake roommates.

I didn't want to be fake roommates with her. I wanted to have her in my arms, in my bed, and to be able to spend the entire night together. She was going to need me.

I pulled her to me and pressed kisses to the top of her head. I wished she would tell me. But I understood not wanting to announce anything until she was certain.

"Do you have specialists lined up yet?" I asked.

"Not yet."

"Will you tell me after that? I could take you to those appointments so you don't have to go alone."

She pushed out of my embrace and swiped at a tear on her cheek. "When it gets to that point Zack, I would really like for you to come with me. And I will tell you. Right now I have to focus on finding a new place to live. And moving, and all the crap with work."

I lifted my brows at her. She was the one who said no work talk. She usually brought her work concerns directly to me, but I hadn't been at the office very often lately.

"Right, I know, no work talk. It's the stress. And stress isn't good—"

"Stress isn't good for you. I can't help the way you would like regarding work. I know it's tough right now. But I can take one worry off your plate. You are going to move in with me. Fuck work. I can ask Mike to help move your furniture across the hall."

"Mike! That's his name," she practically laughed.

"What?"

"Mike, in the front unit. I could not think of his name the other day. Oh, I feel so stupid." She smiled at me. It was the kind of smile that was more pity than happy.

"I can't live with you, Zack. Work. Our jobs will be at risk. I can't ask you to do that for me."

"You aren't asking. Let me handle work. I'm not worried about my job. If it makes you feel any better, we can tell people it's a temporary measure while you look for a new place. You are stuck between a rock and a hard place. I'm your friendly neighbor coming to the rescue."

"Really?" She blinked back more tears.

This woman was trying to gut me. I reached out and trailed my thumb under her eye. "Don't cry, Darling. I will take care of you."

Her arms were around me and her sweet lips crushed to mine. Her lips fluttered over my face like butterflies. I eased back. I brushed her hair from her face and held her. Her honey gold eyes searched my face. Tendrils of her brown hair twisted between my fingers. I loved her.

Our lips found each other. If this was how she needed my support at the moment, who was I to argue?

18

CRYSTAL

In a few weeks, Zack was going to move me into his apartment. I needed to tell him. I couldn't live with him and not let him know. He would notice when I didn't have a period. I needed to tell him so he would stop treating me like I was dying. I wasn't dying. I was pregnant and scared.

I needed to tell him before he moved my furniture.

Thoughts ping-ponged through my brain as I made my way into work. I still needed to find that specialist that Zack knew I needed. He just didn't know what kind of specialist I needed. How the hell did I find a baby doctor?

My stomach sank when I saw Greg sitting at my desk, waiting for me.

I girded my mental loins. "Morning Greg, can I come find you after I get a moment to get settled?"

"Oh no," he templed his fingers together. "I found out a little secret, Crystal Queen."

He had replaced 'scum' with 'queen.' Of course, how could that word ever be misconstrued as an insult. He was safe from my pond scum tally list.

I leveled the flattest dead stare at him as I could muster. My insides were dancing around. I had a few too many secrets, was there any way he had found out any of them?

"What?"

He leaned forward menacingly. "Wouldn't you like to know? Have you gained weight? Stress getting to you?"

"Greg," I growled.

"I'm only concerned about your health. Wouldn't want you to have a stroke or choke on a sandwich because of stress."

He thrust to his feet and loomed over me before stepping out of my cube.

What the hell was wrong with that man? Why was he talking about my weight? I wasn't showing yet. I know my clothes were feeling snug, but they still looked okay.

That was it. The last straw, I couldn't work with him anymore. If I quit working at Shingle Click then I could openly date Zack, and I would remove myself from the temptation of putting superglue all over Greg's chair.

"Morning Crystal," Tony grunted as he passed my cube.

Damn, I couldn't leave the team in the lurch just because I didn't like Greg. Of course, I could map out everything they needed to implement and when. I was a glorified calendar minder. I could simply provide a very detailed calendar, and they could get someone else to read it for them.

I could. I bit my lip.

Zack was out on business trips enough that I could take that home as a project and work on it on the nights I knew I would be alone.

Zack had connections, and with his reference, he could help me find a job even if I was pregnant. I was barely pregnant. There was time I could give to a new job before going on maternity leave.

This could work. Zack said he wanted to help, well this would help. Now that I didn't have to focus on finding a new apartment.

I tucked my bag into its drawer, pulled up the team chat, the corporate messenger, and my master spreadsheet. I could catch up on all the messages once I had coffee in hand. I stopped by Tony's cubicle on my way to the break room. I needed to cut back on the caffeine.

"Hi Tony," I said. "What's the problem child got up his sleeve?"

Tony started to choke on his coffee. "Are you okay?"

"I can't believe you called Greg that. I mean we all know you must hate him, but you are always so professional."

"I see you knew exactly who I meant."

"He thinks you used your feminine wiles on Zack to get us some extra time," he said.

"But we aren't getting any extra time. I keep getting turned down. What makes him think that?"

"Last night, Zack sent out a message after you left. We have an extra week. It's not much. But it will help."

"Damn. I should thank him." Anything for an excuse to see Zack during the workday.

I got a cup of decaf. I can't say I was impressed, but it was hot and it tasted mostly the same. I returned to my desk and began catching up on all the messages.

My eyes dragged over the words on Zack's message. I read, and re-read it. Tony was right. We had an extra week for "Make It Happen."

I could almost do that. The next several hours were spent reworking the schedule for the next few days. I needed more time to revise the whole thing based on the new deadline. There was the potential that this could happen without working the programmers to death.

I shot an email to the operating system group. We were in the middle of integration on a new product. The extra week helped them out as well. New product first, and then the integration through a system upgrade for existing units. Using the excuse of having to rebuild the schedule with the new deadline, I spent extra time and built out a more comprehensive plan.

An extra week did not solve all of my problems, I was still secretly seeing the CEO of this company and I wanted that to no longer be a secret. I was quitting, but I wasn't going to leave Tony, Allison, or Armand in the lurch. Greg could slow roast on a spit for all I cared.

It was dark out when I looked up from my work. I had been so focused, I hadn't realized how fast the hours flew by.

On my way out, I decided to check and see if Zack was around. It was a shot in the dark, but he had been working late a lot. There was nothing wrong with us leaving the building at the same time. We could even walk to the same train stop without any judgment. Besides, I wanted to tell him my plan about the job. And then, if I was feeling brave enough, I could let it slip he was going to be a father.

The second floor was mostly dark. Lights came from the executive offices. Odds were good one of those offices was Zack's. My heart skipped a beat when I noticed his office door slightly open and the lights on.

A booming voice I recognized as belonging to George Fredrickson, President of the Board, came from the office. My stomach sank. I did not like that man. I turned to leave. I could tell Zack my brilliant idea later. I did not want to see Mr. Fredrickson and feel forced to smile at any of his platitudes.

"Uncle George." Zack's voice was clear and sharp and calling that man 'Uncle.'

I had to hide my affection for Zack because of some stupid rule about fraternization and nepotism, and his uncle was President of the Board? My blood started to simmer with the heat of indignation. I leaned against the wall just past the door to listen. How deep did this hypocrisy go?

"Who on staff are you fucking? Craig told me something is going on between you and that woman," Mr. Fredrickson said.

Craig? I didn't know any Craigs at work, but I didn't know everyone who worked here. Could he possibly mean Greg?

"I'm not fucking anyone I work with," Zack said. Damn, his lie was smooth as silk. Even I believed him, and I was fucking him. Then again he was good at lying, wasn't he? Nephew of the President of the Board, wonder how you got this job, Zack?

"I told you to stay away from that fat girl with the big titties."

Did he mean me? I noticed Zack wasn't saying anything.

"You know your job is on the line if you are."

"We both know it wouldn't be me getting fired if that were the case. Look, Uncle George, the dating coworkers' thing—"

"No, no, I'm sorry. I know you wouldn't stick your prick in a fatty. Never stick your prick in a fatty, you can never tell when they get pregnant." The man went on a rambling rant. He was hyper-focused on me being fat as if he wasn't. The simmer in my veins reached the boiling point.

"She's not pregnant, is she? Fat girls like that always look pregnant. Fire her anyway. Craig doesn't like her. Says she's stupid. Why are you fucking a stupid fat girl?"

I couldn't listen anymore. If this was how Zack let people talk about me now, what would it be like once I started showing? Or did everyone already know about us, and I was just the one in the dark?

Zack just let his uncle say horrible things about me. So what if I had extra curves? None of that hadn't seemed to bother Zack at any point in time. As a matter of fact, he seemed to like my 'big titties.' How in the hell did Greg have the ear of the President of the Board?

This was not good. Tears blurred my vision as I ran from the second floor. I needed to get out of there. I needed to get away from Zack and every messed up policy at Shingle Click. I needed to go now, it would only get worse once I was obviously pregnant.

I returned to my cube to grab my purse. I looked at Henry, and then at my monitors. I slid my fat ass into my chair and powered up my system. As I waited, I reached over and pulled Henry next to me. There was nothing else in this office that I wanted.

I wrote an email to the team, hit send, and picked Henry up. Out in the parking lot, I glanced up and saw the light in Zack's office still on. I called for a car, I couldn't face a train commute home tonight.

I punched more numbers into my phone.

"Wifey!" Charline answered with enthusiasm.

"Charline," I sobbed. "Could I really get a job at that place you work?"

"Of course Crystal. What's the matter?"

"Do you think I could come and stay with you in that big house you got in Texas?"

19

ZACK

One Year Later

The sound of white noise dampened all the noises that should have been echoing through the cavernous waiting room. Footsteps, the wheels of push trollies, the whispered conversations of people should have made noise. The ambient din was all sucked into the masking shush. The lack of sound in hospitals always set my nerves on alert.

Paris leaned against my shoulder, focused on her own distraction with a game on her phone. Did she remember the last time we sat together in a hospital? We didn't have phones to distract us back then. Was that something that could ever be forgotten? Uncle George had been with us then. In a way, he was now too.

"You're thinking of mom and dad, aren't you?" Paris asked.

"And you're not?" I bumped her with my shoulder.

"Yeah," she sighed. "Hard not to. You know, I can't remember it as clearly as I used to. But the smell of hospitals always brings back the tickle of that memory."

"Uh-huh, only I get more than a tickle."

"Does it make you sad, Zack?" she asked

"Are you trying to be my therapist now?" I responded. I didn't need therapy regarding my parent's death. I had already spent years working on that particular issue. "Not anymore. You?"

She twisted so that she could lean her head against my shoulder. "I miss them, but never so much as when I'm in a hospital. It always reminds me of the night that they died. I suddenly feel lost."

I leaned my head against hers. "Yeah, me too."

I couldn't help but think of that night seventeen years ago. It had been an accident. Both drivers had driven through the four-way stop, not stopping, both had been speeding. Reports after the fact showed that everyone had blood alcohol levels exceeding legal limits for driving. One person died at the scene. The other two died several hours later in the hospital. Mom had been killed instantly. We sat in the hospital for hours waiting for news on our father.

The waiting now felt entirely too familiar. We weren't waiting to learn of recovery, we were simply waiting for the end. This time we weren't here because of an accident, but the eventual giving out of the body through age and disease.

I hadn't been thinking of my parents, or even Uncle George, the reason we were here. Like so many quiet moments over the past year, I thought of Crystal. What had happened to her? Why had she left the way she did? Had she gone to a hospital to get better? Had she gotten better? Why hadn't she told me, or contacted me since? I had told her I wanted to take care of her, go to doctor appointments with her, be there for her. I refused to consider worst-case scenarios. I wanted her alive and well. I wanted her back.

I pulled my phone from my pocket and scrolled back through my emails. Almost a full year. I didn't have any pictures of her, only emails from work. Her last message had been so concise, not her typical email style. She had to go. She didn't want to leave us in the lurch but the decision really wasn't hers. She left small notes of positive advice for each member of the team. Even Greg. Well, she really told him to fuck himself. I was left off the list. What could she say? There were too many missed words between us.

The detailed schedule she provided made my chest burn with

despair. With her ability to predict forks in the road ahead for the rollout she provided alternative task schedules that all returned back to the master schedule and met the final deadline. She had taken care of the team, even when not there, and I couldn't take care of her the way she needed me to.

It was a flow chart of exceptional detail, the kind of detail with thought and effort put into it. It was the level of work that I had come to expect from her, but she had worked so far in advance which made me think she knew she wouldn't be there. She mapped out what needed to happen, and she did it in such a way that even the other teams that were involved further in the process knew what timelines needed to be kept. Her work laid a foundation that supported the success of the team and the product, even in her absence. She had known something would take her away from the project, from me, and she still cared for the work.

I wish I could tell her how valuable her contributions to our success had been. And it had been a huge success. Shingle Click had record sales increased from word of mouth promotion only, all because we added a mobile control app that worked as promised and delivered as promised. My business success could do nothing to lessen the dull ache that I now associated with her loss.

Putting the phone down, I closed my eyes. The memories and pain I felt had nothing to do with losing my parents, but with losing the love of my life. And I had never told her. I had hidden her away, not letting anyone know about her. Not letting her know what she meant to me. No wonder she didn't trust me enough to tell me what was wrong.

Fuck me. I pressed my fist against my chest. It hurt.

Paris, thinking my actions and my pain were for other people, rubbed my shoulders.

"It's okay. It hits me like that sometimes too."

We sat in silence until a nurse approached us. "Zack, Paris? You might want to come on back now."

I didn't want to go back. I hadn't seen my father after he passed. I didn't particularly want to see Uncle George. The nurse followed us into the room. None of the monitors were beeping, the machine that had kept him breathing no longer made the same rhythmic hiss and sucking sounds. Everything was eerily quiet.

"I'm sorry. We're pretty sure he was already gone before we removed him from the ventilator," she said. "Take your time." Then she left us.

I stood with an arm around Paris's shoulders. She wiped at tears, but I felt apathetic, empty.

"He was an odd one," she started.

"How? Odd isn't a word I would have used for him."

"I so desperately needed a father figure. You were doing your best to take care of me. It was too much for a college student to also suddenly have to be a teen parent to another teen. I foisted myself on him. I called him all the time," she spoke quietly. "It was only in the last five years or so he started listening to me and having conversations. And then, you know it wasn't until you pointed out that he was acting differently than I can say he was acting differently. Like, paranoid."

"That was the dementia. When he started cussing like a drunk frat boy I knew something was up." I couldn't take my eyes from his face. I thought he would look asleep, but he didn't. He looked like a figure from a wax museum, a pretense of being human, there was no life there.

"You aren't sad are you?" she asked.

"Not really. Numb. He wasn't our dad. I think he wanted that from me. You know, for me to see him as a father figure. I appreciated his mentorship. He got me started in business. Made things happen for me. But he also made certain things not happen."

"What's that even supposed to mean? Made certain things not happen?" a bitter chuckle in her tone.

"His paranoid rules toward the end made me have to treat someone very important to me in a way she didn't deserve. I couldn't be the man she needed me to be because I was just another flunky dancing around his temper tantrums." I dropped my arm from Paris's shoulder.

"You're talking about that woman? I knew you liked her. You never got mad at me when I inconvenienced you before."

"You know you're doing it? Then why do you do it?"

"I love messing with you, Zack. It's the only time I see you get riled up, and even then you contain that temper of yours. I think that's the closest you've ever come to actually yelling at me," she smirked.

I loved my sister, but damn, she was manipulative.

"So whatever happened with her? How did Uncle George get in the way?"

I shook my head. I didn't want to remember the words he used or be reminded that I never shut him down when he spoke that way.

"He was insulting and crude. Had he been anyone else, I would have punched him for speaking that way about a woman. Then there was that antiquated policy about dating subordinates." The more I thought about it, the angrier I got. Uncle George could burn in hell, especially if I ever found out if Crystal had been alone and scared at the end.

"I don't know what happened to her. She got sick and left," I sighed. "I think I was in love with her."

"Oh, Zacky. I'm so sorry." She gestured, indicating the dead man in the bed before us. "Look at this as the ending to that chapter of your life. Take this opportunity to get over the loss of Uncle George as a chance to get over the woman."

I shrugged off her suggestion. I didn't need to grieve Uncle George, and I refused to grieve Crystal. Grieving would mean she had lost her fight.

"We should go, so they can do whatever they need to. I should call his lawyer. Can you make arrangements? I guess we need to schedule a funeral?"

"I can handle that. It should be a somber affair, huh? I think a festive thank you party for the man who just left me millions of dollars would be rather inappropriate, wouldn't it?"

I shrugged. "I guess all those years of turning him into your father figure were not lost on him."

"Does this mean I'm your boss now? I own more shares of Shingle Click than you do, don't I?" she mused.

It was something I needed to consider, Paris now held a controlling block of shares. She needed to be introduced to the board. Hopefully, she wouldn't take an interest.

20

CRYSTAL

The climb to the second-floor apartment would get easier, I reminded myself. I would get stronger. I would gain strength. I had to. I had the best reason ever. I gazed lovingly at the tiny face of my baby boy, all tucked up in his car seat infant carrier.

I carried the portable seat into my new apartment. And set him down gently, not wanting to disturb his sleep.

A small study table and two mismatched wood chairs already occupied one side of my new living room. It was smaller than my last apartment. I shook my head to clear those thoughts away. Regret lay in the past. I had a bright future to look toward with no time for regrets.

"Stop pushing, this is heavy," a cranky voice said just outside.

I stepped over to the door to hold it out of the way. Walking backward, in stepped a tall lanky redhead, Hunter, Charline's brother.

"Well move faster," Charline demanded as she followed him in. Shorter by several inches, and all-around smaller, she didn't complain about the couch being heavy.

"I can't believe you made me pick this up off the side of the road," Hunter continued to complain.

"You're the one with a truck," she sniped back.

"I can't thank you enough," I gushed. I was still full of all kinds of over-the-top emotions. The doctor said it was leftover baby making hormones that would work their way out of my system, eventually. I only needed to be worried if the depression became all-encompassing. Crying at TV commercials and crying from being so very happy were all within the realm of 'perfectly normal.'

They placed the couch in the empty space along the wall.

Charline put her hands on her hips. "See, I knew it would be perfect. And it's in good shape."

"It's ugly," Hunter mumbled.

"It really is. But it is in good shape. I've got some fabric cleaner, and I'll give it a good scrub this evening." I reached my arms out to hug Charline. "I can't thank you enough."

The tears started again, this time they were the good kind. I had cried more than my share of the bad kind over the past year. I was done with those.

"Are you sure you want to move out now? You could have stayed," Charline said.

"I know. I had meant to only stay a few months. You let me live in your mom's bonus room far too long."

"Hardly," Charline said.

Hunter shuffled and grunted. He stared down at Adam, but he acted like the baby was a scary monster. "I'll be glad to finally be able to play video games on the big TV again."

Charline swatted him on his upper arm. She would have hit him on the back of the head, but he was so much taller than her and leaning away from her reach.

"It's okay, I know what he means," I said. "It's not like you're getting rid of me, I'll still see you at work. And your mom said I'd have a babysitter any time I needed one."

"Of course, like I'd say no to quality time with my boyfriend." She clapped her hands together. "We still have to go pick up your mattresses. Come on Hunter."

He grumbled.

"Shut up boy, you are being paid for this. Crystal, do not raise Adam to be an ingrate like this thing."

"I'm not a thing," Hunter protested.

"Are you sure? Have you smelled yourself?" Charline razzed her brother as they left.

Another well of tears blurred my vision. Would my Adam ever have a sibling to love and annoy the way their family did? Charline had one older sister and two younger brothers. Hunter was the baby of the bunch and the only other redhead. They had a special bond.

I closed the door behind my friends and sat with a heavy sigh on one of my chairs to look at the new-to-me couch. The arms were a little worn, and the front corners had been scratched by a cat or two, but the rest of it was perfectly fine. Maybe not my preferred color choice, in a muddy brown color, but all the superficial things wrong with it could be hidden with a slipcover.

Adam smacked his perfect little mouth in his sleep. He would wake up hungry in a minute. Getting up, I unbuckled and lifted him from the car seat infant carrier.

My instinct was to snuggle into the corner of the couch, but as comfortable as it looked, I didn't want my baby near it until I could get it properly cleaned. I returned to the wooden chair, another side-of-the-road find. I adjusted my clothing and placed him to my breast. With an excited squirm, he latched on and began nursing.

My perfect baby boy. He had so much of his father in his face. The feathery wisps of hair indicated he would have his father's dark hair. Adam's eyes already settled into the same sky blue that Zack Noble had. Adam would grow up to be a handsome man. I was going to do my best to make sure that he was beautiful on the inside, unlike his father.

Maybe starting completely over again had been a mistake. But I couldn't have stayed. I had to leave that job. I was being forced out of the apartment. I blinked away those tears, those were the not-so-good kind. Thoughts of Zack always did that to me. He thought I was fat and stupid. I was an easy fuck, and I had let him use me. That was my fault. He may have been a predator, but I walked straight into his snare and dared him to catch me.

Maybe he was right, I had been so stupid. Zack should never have been more than a quick rebound fling after Chase. He wasn't supposed to be anything permanent.

A wave of love washed over me as I gazed at Adam. So much for not being permanent. This little man certainly was lifelong commitment material.

Adam detached on his own, and fell right back to sleep. He was going to have one hell of a wet diaper when he woke up.

I had him back in his infant carrier, it was the easiest way to manage him while I unpacked and cleaned. Yellow plastic cleaning gloves covered me from fingertip to elbow. I cleaned out the crevasse behind the cushions after I put the gloves on. I wasn't sticking an unprotected hand down in there. I found a pencil that looked chewed on, a few pennies, and lots of dust and cat hair. I scrubbed fabric cleaner into the sides and back of the couch when I heard Hunter's unmistakable grumbles of complaint. I hurried to move my cleaning supplies out of the way, open the door wider, and made sure Adam was safely tucked off to the side where I could see him.

Hunter, walking backward again, a plastic-wrapped mattress, and Charline came in.

"Don't stop, keep going on into the back," Charline directed him.

Without stopping to say hi they walked through my living room with my new bed. They crossed the living room in and out several times with the mattresses and the frame.

"You want me to put this together now?" Hunter asked.

"Yes idiot, she wants you to put it together now," Charline quipped at him.

Hunter shrugged back toward the single bedroom, and Adam began fussing.

"Oh, my boyfriend is waking up," she cooed at the baby. "I've got him."

She lifted him and made happy burbling noises at him. He responded with a large toothless baby grin.

"Oh boy, someone is wet. He's soaked through. Crystal, where's his changing stuff?"

I pointed back to the bedroom and then started to pull the gloves off.

Charline held him closer. "I've got him. Don't I Adam, yes I do, yes I do," she was no longer talking to me.

I don't know who would miss living with her the most, me or Adam? Or maybe Charline would miss him the most.

I dumped the bucket of now dirty water down the sink and refilled it with cleaning fluid and water. I returned to scrubbing the couch. I unzipped the covers from the cushions, I would toss those into the laundry. This apartment was small, but it had laundry hookups in the kitchen, and I decided that paying the extra for a washer and dryer was worth it. Especially with an infant who needed clean clothes constantly.

Charline bounced around with a now awake Adam.

Hunter appeared from the back. "I've got the bed all set. You have a crib you need us to pick up too?"

I shook my head.

He grunted. "Oh okay. Where are the sheets? I'll make your bed."

I pointed to a red suitcase that held my sheets and towels. For all the complaining he did, he was a good guy.

"He's going to expect extra pizza for doing that," Charline said.

"It's worth it. I'm going to be too tired to make my bed tonight. I was probably just going to sleep directly on the mattress, so it can't be any worse than that."

"He'll probably get it all wrong. You know he's just trying to show off," she said. "He wants to butter you up to use as a reference on some job applications."

"Me? I'm a receptionist, how is that helpful?" I asked.

"You aren't related," she answered. "And you won't be a receptionist forever. Unlike that other place we worked, Rollins Tech actually hires from within its ranks. You know I have my ear to the ground for a position for you. And Rolly likes you. He keeps employees he likes."

I sat back on my butt. “Thanks, I mean it. You’ve been a total lifesaver. You gave me a place to stay, you found me a job, and the help with the move”— I nodded at her as she kept my baby boy occupied while I worked— “and the help with Adam. How can I ever repay you.”

“You can start with pizza and a beer,” Hunter said, coming back into the living room.

“Pizza, you’re too young for beer,” Charline corrected him.

“How about pizza and a side of cash?” I asked.

“Cash always works,” Hunter said.

21

ZACK

Another Year Later

I faced down the President of the Board across the polished conference table. Shingle Click needed to expand its product base by offering more products, hiring more workforce.

"Expansion not acquisition," I said through my teeth.

Paris focused her attention on her perfectly manicured nails. "It's faster to just buy what we need. Why reinvent the wheel?"

"It's not reinventing, it's building systems perfectly integrated from the ground up. Integrating another company's product involves retrofit programming. Those solutions always have problems."

"Why can't you just wipe their programs and install new operating software that runs both systems?"

I controlled my breathing through my nose. No amount of ranting and all attempts at educating her on how Shingle Click's smart-home technology worked were lost on her. In a way, she was worse than George Fredrickson had been toward the end of his life. He literally did not have the mental capacity to understand the limitations he wanted to disregard. Paris just disregarded them, thinking that money changed how things worked.

"Look we have been holding steady financially. No growth. That's not good. Financial growth will happen by raising the base price of our product, and by offering more products." She tapped her fingers on a tablet.

I knew she had notes on that tablet. She was repeating what a consultant had told her. She didn't have the business background to do what she was doing. What she had was the money, and she decided that her money talked.

I don't know what possessed Uncle George to leave her the bulk of his financial estate, but he had. I had a hefty share of Shingle Click, almost the same as she did. Almost. She still had the majority, and as long as she stayed out of my business, figuratively and literally, everything went smoothly.

For some reason, Paris decided it was time to play business. Fine, if she had done some studying beforehand, then I would welcome her insights. A few internet videos were not the same as an MBA, or years of boots-on-ground work. She had been a flighty artist, a party planner.

I ground my thumb into my eyebrow. I inhaled deeply.

"Paris, when I was brought in for damage control, Shingle Click had several products in development. It would be a smarter move and in the long run more financially responsible to unearth those projects and get them back into development than it would be to start to hunt for similar businesses, and begin negotiations regarding partnerships and buy-outs."

She lifted her brows at my words. "You used to be more cutthroat, Zack. Did you get complacent after one successful product launch? You're only as good as your last success. And it's been years. It's time. You've had the opportunity to stabilize Shingle Click's market position. And you did. But 'did' is done, and that's in the past. What are you going to do now?"

"We need market research. Projections, what is the next smart appliance everyone will need? What is it that clients would like to have the product do next? How is the smart-home market evolving? That's the next logical step here."

Paris, already relaxed in her chair, seemed to settle even further in. She shook her head.

"The Board has already discussed this. We feel that you are no longer the proper person to continue determining the growth vector of Shingle Click."

I didn't let her announcement change my expression. I wasn't surprised. I fixed what they needed me to fix. And without Uncle George's bizarre directives keeping everyone just doing their best to keep the status quo functioning, the board now wanted revenue growth. So did I. Only I disagreed with how to achieve it.

"We want to restructure your position. You've been effectively CEO and COO for the past two and half years. We are going to bring in a full-time operations officer."

Fuck me, it had better not be Paris giving herself the job. It was bad enough she adopted Uncle George's position on the board after six months. She should have stayed playing at rich trust-fund brat with no real direction in life. It suited her better.

"What does that mean for me?" I asked.

"I know you are aware that you're reasonably attractive. Now, I want you to be equally charming, and go out there as the face of Shingle Click."

I closed my eyes. My thumb ground harder into my eyebrow. "I'm not going to be some kind of spokesmodel for smart-home technologies, Paris."

She laughed. I used to like it when my sister laughed, it meant she was happy. I did not like the sound that emanated from her. "Spokesmodel, you're funny Zacky. No, we need you to be the point person for growth and acquisitions. I want your smiling face to be the one our competition sees walking in the door to discuss purchasing options. We want them to think of us as being personable and reasonable."

"And when they aren't open to selling or partnering?" I asked.

"Be tenacious. Be charming and convincing, especially with the privately held companies. Publicly traded companies can be bent to seeing the benefit of being absorbed into the HomeWorks Technology Group."

"The what?" I asked.

"Shingle Click is a cute name, great play on words for marketing. With a Shingle Click monitor your home from any mobile device. Cute, shingle sounds enough like single, the wordplay is subtle. But it's too limiting. The Board feels we need a broader name to encompass the expanded product base. HomeWorks Technology Group is now the governing entity. Shingle Click is our first technical acquisition, and will serve as our home base to expand from."

"Any questions?" She blinked at me over steepled fingers.

When the hell had Paris turned into a shark? "I liked you better when you were some bohemian wandering artist," I said. I gave her half a smile, let her decide if I was teasing or not. "Are we done? I believe I need to clarify the new parameters of my position."

"I emailed those to you as soon as we started this meeting. You'll need to start building the list of other companies that we can begin assimilating."

I stood to leave. I was done with the Board. I didn't care if they were done with me or not. "I'm done."

I couldn't believe what they were letting my sister get away with. Was it sound? I had no idea. It wasn't the path I would have taken for this company. But hey, it wasn't my company, and I probably wasn't going to even be CEO in name by the time I got back to my office.

"Zacky," Paris had followed me from the conference room.

I stopped, keeping my back to her. Now what?

"Why are you upset?" she asked.

I slowly turned to face her. Was she seriously asking why I was upset? I tilted my head and considered her for a long moment. I gestured holding my hand out, the words still didn't come yet. I closed that hand into a fist.

"You completely disregarded my years of experience in this industry, with this company, in business. You ignore all of my recommendations. Why did I bother to get an MBA, when all it took for you was to inherit a lonely old man's money to make you so knowledgeable about business? Are you living out some office porn fantasy, Paris?"

I took a step in her direction and paused.

"Why am I upset? You told me in that conference room, that all I am good for is my good looks. So now the entire board thinks I'm a face without the brains and skills to competently run this company anymore. You took away my job, Paris. Why do you think I'm upset?"

"You've been working constantly since Uncle George died. At first, I thought you were trying to prove something to yourself, to his memory. You never give yourself a break. When was the last time you took a vacation, Zack? I think these changes will be good, you'll get a chance to do some travel, get out of the office. Have time to start dating again. When was the last time you got laid?"

I glared at my sister.

"My god, you need to get over that woman and get over yourself. I'm doing you a favor, Zacky. You are attractive, but the whole tortured brooding thing is not a good look on you. Take the trips, screw the secretaries. Find your sense of humor again."

I took another step closer to her.

"You don't know what you're talking about," I growled.

"Stop mourning her, she left you, she didn't die."

The knife Paris had stabbed in my proverbial business back now twisted in my heart. Even after all this time, I still had no idea where Crystal was out there. There were nights the pain wouldn't let me sleep.

I took another step closer, close enough that my breath ruffled her hair.

"Don't ever call me Zacky again. It stopped being cute when you stopped being nice. You can only be the boss of me in one, business or our private lives, and you have clearly chosen business over being my sister." I turned and walked away. I needed to get on my bike and ride all of this frustration out.

22

CRYSTAL

Another Two Years Later

The schematic on my monitor looked fine, but there was a problem in the details somewhere. If it wasn't here, then it was in the programming, and I was the one who had to find it. The QA team found that a problem existed, got the issue to repeat with consistency, and handed it back to me.

I had narrowed down the error to either physical relays that were not functioning properly or to a piece of code that would trip the sequences those relays were needed for. I was running out of time to solve this problem, and I needed to solve it to prove that I deserved this job. I ran the simulation sequence again. Everything worked as it should.

I picked up my phone and pressed to be connected to the QA department.

"Huan," the voice on the other end of the line said.

"Hi, it's me again," I said. I heard Huan groan, I had been calling him every fifteen minutes.

"I just cannot duplicate the error, and Ellen is getting antsy. Will you please go over it again?"

"I'll call you back." He hung up on me.

I ran the simulation again. It should be fine, it should pass QA without incident.

My phone rang, I hit the speaker. "Crystal," I said.

"It's still a no-go," Huan's voice on the other end said.

"Okay, that's it. I have to see this for myself. I just ran the simulation again, and it should work." I ended the call and got up. QA was on the other side of the factory floor, tucked away like mad scientists testing all the products that Rollins Tech built.

I looked down at my shoes and cursed. I had sandals on. That meant I was going to have to walk the long way around. Factory floor rules were closed-toed shoes, safety glasses, and in some areas hard hats. I would not be going into any of the actual manufacturing zones but safety rules were in place for a reason. I think that's why the QA department set up shop where they had, to prevent designers and engineers from dropping in on them at random.

"Look Crystal," Huan started when I showed up in their workroom. "None of these work. The signal goes in at the start of the command sequence, and nothing comes out the other end." He pointed to six units that matched the schematic back on my computer.

"Show me," I said with a sigh.

Everything ran perfectly and then the command sequence stopped doing anything as if it never existed.

"It does that every time?"

Huan sounded so aggravated with me. "Yes, every time."

I picked up one of the units and stared at it. I willed it to cough up its secrets, why wouldn't it work? "Can I take this?"

He shrugged. "Don't break it."

"It's already broken, Huan. I need to find out why, and how to fix it."

Walking back to my desk I flipped the unit back and forth in the sunlight as if that would provide some illumination.

"Where were you?" Ellen, my team lead, asked.

"I headed to QA to see if I could watch the testing. I can't figure out why Huan keeps breaking the sequence while I can't."

"You really should have told me you were leaving. What if I needed something? Crystal, I shouldn't need to remind you that you have responsibilities to the team. It's not just you working here. You can't take off on a whim every time you feel like it."

I held up the offending unit. I hated how she was on the attack every time she spoke to me recently. She had micromanagement down to an art form. I hadn't taken off on a whim. I was doing my job.

"Your job is to input the data from QA and locate the where's and the why's they are having problems with. Your job isn't to play in their department."

Her eyes bore into me, making me feel like I was a small child who did something wrong.

"I thought I was doing..." I trailed off. It didn't matter, she didn't want me to think.

"I don't think you were, thinking that is. I don't have to remind you, we have a deadline, and the longer this troubleshooting takes, the more likely we are to be off schedule. Your work impacts the entire job flow."

I bit the inside of my lip. I fully comprehended the concept of workflow and the importance of sticking to schedules. I wasn't dumb, and I hated being spoken down to this way.

"I'm going to let you get back to work. Once this is off your plate, I think we need to have a chat regarding your future in this department." She smiled at me as if that was helpful. I was game for getting out of her department, especially if she thought threatening my job was the best way to get me to perform better.

I placed the faulty unit on my desk in front of my monitor, so I could visually compare the schematic to the manufactured piece. I clicked the button to rerun the simulation every so often so that if Ellen came back she couldn't say I wasn't doing anything as I studied the unit. Something was off.

I picked up the phone again. I didn't give Huan a chance to say anything on the other end.

"Something's off," I started.

"Crystal." I could practically hear him rolling his eyes.

"No, not a proverbial something, a physical something. Pull up the schematics." I waited until he grunted that he had.

"Look at the spacing of the relays. They don't match what the guys fabricated."

"Yeah so?"

"So? The sequence timing of the program is very specific, this throws the whole thing off."

He grunted again.

"Can you send me calibrated measurements of the fabricated units?" I asked.

"You're looking at millimeter differences, Crystal."

"We're looking at a measurable difference that is outside of acceptable tolerances," I countered.

"They might not be able to match your required tolerances in manufacturing," he said. "That's going to push back your schedule."

"No, but I can adjust the line of code to speed up or slow down the sequence. And boom it's fixed. But I don't know what the adjustment needs to be until I have a measurement to start with."

He said he would get on it, and I started to locate the lines of code that related to that part of the command sequence.

I had a spreadsheet open and was cranking through numbers to determine what formulas I would need to help me to revise the timing in the program. The alarm on my phone went off. Timing! I was so close, but if I did not leave now I would be late getting Adam, and his daycare charged for late pick-ups.

I contemplated stopping by Ellen's cube and thought better of it. Then again, I could follow up with malicious compliance and start telling her every time I had to go to the bathroom if she needed to know where I was every second of the day.

Pleased that a solution was in sight, I left the building. I hurried down the block to the local daycare. I couldn't remember ever seeing a daycare in an office park before and thought— not for the first time

— how smart to have the daycare near work, and not near home. This way if something happened, I could be there within minutes.

Once in the foyer, I rang the doorbell. The security they had in place seemed a bit over the top, but I was grateful for it. Everyone entered a secure foyer and then had to be buzzed into another inner office. They brought the children to the front office. Parents were only ever allowed inside for special events, and when touring the facility. The playground wasn't even visible from the street or the parking lot. It meant they kept my baby safe.

I couldn't help but smile when I saw my boy being carried out. My baby boy wasn't going to be a baby much longer. He was long-limbed for his age. Most people thought he looked like he was going on five, he was barely three. If they looked at his face, they would see his big blue eyes, and the chubby pink cheeks under a mop of almost black curls, they would see he was just a baby.

I had my arms extended and pulled Adam into my embrace before his caregiver finished saying hi.

"He's had a quiet day today," Sue said. "He's been a very good listener, but he didn't want to use any big kid words."

Adam wrapped his arms around my neck and squeezed.

"Thanks, Sue," I said. I picked up his day pack and carried him back to my car in the office parking lot.

"Did you have a good day today?"

He gave me a small nod. No words. That meant my usually talkative guy had a hard day. I had a hard day too.

"Should we stop and get french fries and chocolate shake for dinner? Was it that kind of day?"

When he rested his head on my shoulder, I knew it had been a bit harder than he could tell me. It was a chicken nuggets and cuddles kind of night.

23

ZACK

I followed the throng of passengers down the concourse, and out to baggage claim. My bag rolled behind me. I had the necessities for two nights. I never stayed for longer than two nights anymore. When the parameters of my job changed and I was on the road almost full time, my admin, Lisa devised a time-saving plan. A week's worth of clothes and incidentals would be packed in a box and left at the office that she could ship as soon as I called her. That way I didn't need to carry around more than what was necessary, and fresh clothes were twenty-four hours away.

The box sat in my office, ready to be shipped to any given location, for at least five months at this point. Maybe longer. I didn't even remember what was in it, generic slacks, dress shirts, boxers, socks, the usual. After this purchase, I would get to unpack that box. I was done being on the road. Paris had finally agreed, it was time for me to return to the big picture projects. Shingle Click was finally heading back to solar power for maintaining our smart-home technologies. Rollins Tech would be my last purchase, and my next integration project. They had the know how I needed to plug into Shingle Click's Home Command Center.

As I made my way out of the airport I saw the big man, just as he described himself. Stacey Rollins said he'd be a good head taller than most, in plaid, with a cowboy hat on. He wasn't the only one dressed that way. The sign with 'Noble' scrawled on it was the real giveaway.

"Mr. Rollins." I stopped and held out my hand.

He engulfed it in his thick-fingered grasp. "Zack Noble, welcome to Austin. Call me Rolly."

"I didn't expect you to pick me up in person. I don't think I've had that happen in all my years of business travel. It's always been a car service, or finding my own way."

I followed him out through sliding glass doors, and eventually, I was climbing into an SUV larger than my first apartment.

"I thought we could get a jump start on getting to know each other before we got mired in the details."

"I'm pretty much here to make a sales pitch, Rolly. Details come later."

He scoffed. "It's all details, Noble. Now which ones you focus on determines your path in life."

Hate fate intervened on my behalf? Was I going to be subjected to this man's philosophies? It would certainly save me time. My plans for the evening consisted of food, if I remembered to eat, drinking probably too much, and researching everything I could find out about Stacey "Rolly" Rollins. If he wanted to hand me the information I needed, I would accept it. Would he give me the secret insight that I would be able to leverage for a purchase?

"Tell me, Noble, what got you into smart-home technology? Did you see one of those movies with the talking house as a kid?" he chuckled.

I had seen those movies, and they had not inspired me. Something about this man told me he would not be impressed with my answer.

"What got you into it?" I turned the question on him.

"That's easy, love."

I shifted in my seat to look over at the man. Love wasn't anywhere near the kind of answer I expected. "Love?" He didn't strike me as the type to be obsessed with technology. His hands looked too rough to be a programmer.

"Love makes the world go around Noble. I love my late wife, and I love the land. Having smart appliances made her life easier. Anything I could do to make things easier for her I did. And I believe we are stewards of the earth. I adapted solar and kinetic wind power early. I had the means. So, I did. I have wind turbines on my land. Seemed like a smart business decision."

I nodded. Love, an interesting driving force. My driving forces were nothing so virtuous. Market share, product development, money, I was told it was in my best interests to take the job. As far as I was concerned love had nothing to do with smart-home technology. It was all money. I was interested in the money, certainly not the technology itself. I could talk a good game, but I had no need for lights that turned themselves off and on. And the thought of a refrigerator that could order my groceries made me nervous. I was the kind of tech industry leader who put black-out tape over the camera on my laptop. The only reason the GPS was turned on in my phone was for when I needed to call a car to my location.

"I can see how all of that might get you into smart-home tech. But what I'm wondering is how exactly does love for your wife turn into solar-powered smart-home tech for the RV and tiny home industries?" I asked.

"My Marta loved to camp."

Seeing him smile over memories of his late wife felt like an intrusion. I turned my attention out the car window.

He pulled the vehicle into the parking lot of a low single-story brick-fronted building with a large steel warehouse at the back.

"I have to pick something up. You want to come in? I'll show you around a bit while it's empty and we won't get interrupted with questions."

"Sure," I shrugged. I had nothing better to do, and I didn't feel like waiting around in his SUV.

The reception area had furniture that had to come from a catalog, I had seen the same pieces in a hundred other office buildings. I waited while he punched a security code into a keypad that let us into the back. The inside of Rollins Tech looked as cookie-cutter generic as any other office building with modular cubicle furniture and filing cabinets.

"Sales and marketing are up front here," Rolly indicated.

We strode past cubes that looked like every other cube in America. Some were stark and efficient. While others were over the top expressions of the personality of the worker who claimed that space, photos, toys, posters.

"This is my solar department," Rolly announced with a wave of his arm.

There wasn't any visible distinction between departments that I could see. More cubes with more pictures and plants. Not that I was a plant aficionado, but something about a plant in one of the cubes seemed very familiar, especially the pot. I needed a closer look.

"May I?" I asked with a jerk of my head.

"Sure, go ahead. I'm sure she won't mind."

The company logo floated across and down, then bumped up and crossed the monitor again like some kind of early video game. I stepped into the cube and wiggled the mouse, grateful I had an excuse to further explore this particular cube. I expected a password prompt, instead, a large schematic appeared on the monitor.

"That's one of our newer relays. I think it's for maximizing storage. Crystal here is troubleshooting something."

I froze at the name. My eyes locked onto the planter. It looked familiar because I had given it to a woman in another place at another time. My throat felt like it was swelling shut, and I couldn't hear anything beyond the deafening rush of blood in my ears. Rolly kept talking but I did nothing. I gasped, my body forced me to breathe. I coughed to cover my inability to function. I looked at the blue glaze and red clay. I reached out and rotated it in place. Henry seemed to be thriving in this office environment.

"I'm sorry, what were you saying?"

"Crystal's one of my newer engineers and programmers. Talented young woman. Worked her way up from receptionist."

I couldn't fall apart now. Crystal worked here. At the very least I needed to pretend I knew what I was doing. I nodded at the schematic. “Aren’t you concerned that I’m looking at proprietary tech?”

“If you convince me to sell, that proprietary tech will belong to you. Besides, that schematic doesn’t do you any good without the corresponding programming.”

As he spoke I scanned the cube for photos, anything to confirm that his Crystal was the same woman. Henry should have been the conclusive evidence that I needed, but I wanted more. I needed to see her.

There, peeking out from behind Henry, the corner of a photo.

“My office is right up this way,” Rolly said, motioning me to go with him so he could continue with his tour.

I pushed some papers and books from her desk. “Oops. Let me get these, I’ll catch up,” I said as I knelt to gather the items.

“I’ll be right up ahead,” Rolly said and stepped away.

Moving quickly I placed the items back on her desk, moved the plant, and for the second time in so many minutes, I stopped breathing again.

My heart pounded, and I gulped in air. She was more beautiful than I remembered. In the first photo, she smiled at the camera, a child in her arms. He was entirely too big for her to have had him since I last saw her. Maybe he was a nephew or a friend’s child. I scanned the rest of her photos. They were all of the same child at different ages. He had large blue eyes rimmed with dark lashes. His hair was the fine texture that I associated with babies. If it weren’t for the distinct boy style of the clothes, his pretty looks could easily be mistaken for a girl’s. Realization slammed into my very core.

That child could very well be mine. What if she hadn’t been sick but pregnant? Fuck me.

I slipped my phone from my pocket and snapped a few pictures. I confirmed that I saved the images and left the cube to catch up with Rolly.

“Oh good, you want to see the shop floor? Or want to wait until tomorrow?”

I couldn't keep my hand from my phone and its contents. "Tomorrow," I said, distracted.

"Manufacturing floors are always more fun when something is going on." He said, clapping his big hands and rubbing them together. "Did you get the corporate secrets you needed for a hostile takeover?" he said with a laugh.

I smiled around the lump of uncomfortable emotion that lodged in my throat. "You'd have to be a publicly held company for me to force a hostile takeover. Besides, I'm getting the distinct feeling you are trying to hold yourself back on just handing me the deed."

He clapped me on the back. "Of course, I'm gonna make you work for it."

Back in the SUV on our way to a 'properly sized steak' dinner, I pulled out my phone and sent Paris a series of quick texts.

"Who does this look like?" I asked as I sent over the photos.

"Why are you sending me baby pictures, Zack?"

"Who?" I prompted.

"That's you. Why?"

I laughed at something Rolly said. I had no idea if that was the proper reaction or not. He laughed too, so maybe it was. I heard nothing he said. The loud roar of blood in my ears returned.

Those weren't baby pictures of me, but they could have been.

24

CRYSTAL

"Do you know what this is all about?" Charline asked as we stood in the employee parking lot.

I shrugged. Rolly liked to make proclamations, typically followed by barbecue with lots of smoked meat and all the fixin's. The grills were smoking, and my mouth was already watering in anticipation. If he interrupted our work time, he certainly made up for it. He was the kind of man who inspired loyalty by taking care of us. Fully tummies made happy employees.

Rolly was busy talking to a few different people. He was already positioned next to his platform of choice, an open bed pickup, so we would know soon enough.

Ellen stopped next to me. My insides cringed away from her. I had turned in my findings the day before, and Huan had been able to get the unit to run the revised command sequence. The code had been handed over to a more senior-level programmer to refine.

"I wanted to say well done on figuring that out, Crystal," she said.

I looked at her and tried to keep the surprise from my expression. She had been ready to fire me less than two days ago.

"Not only did you come at that problem from a different angle, but your solution is also going to save us a chunk of time and a bigger chunk of money. Um…" she hesitated.

I waited, maybe she was still going to give me the ax. If she did, maybe Rolly could find me a job on the factory floor sorting nuts and bolts. I wanted to keep working for him. I was definitely motivated by good barbecue.

"I was stressed and spoke harshly. I'm glad you're on my team." With that, she gave me a nod and walked off to join another group of employees.

I released a deep sigh. That was one stressor off my shoulders.

"Did Ellen just apologize?" Charline asked.

"Yeah, is it just me, or was that weird?"

"From Ellen? That woman is never wrong, so definitely weird. You didn't hear this from me, but apparently she tried to take credit for your brainchild of fixing the code instead of having the manufacturing recalibrated. Huan was there and said it was you who had been pestering him for days, not her. That's all I know," Charline nodded at me as if to say 'so there.'

Someone had gotten into trouble, and it wasn't me. My ego needed that extra boost. I needed a good day at work after the hell trouble shooting that pesky unit and its corresponding programming had been.

Rolly jumped up into the bed of the pickup truck. His voice was loud enough he never needed a bull horn or a mic. A man with dark curly hair leaned against the side of the truck, facing the other direction. My heart tripped and righted itself. For a panicked moment, I thought he was Zack.

I focused on my shoes trying to get my nerves to calm down. I hated it when I thought I saw him, and my body went zing into panic. That guy wasn't Zack, just another businessman. Lots of them have dark hair and broad shoulders. Besides, Zack had kept his hair super short when I had known him. This guy did not have that tight fade with long hair on top. This guy's hair was thick and wavy down to his collar.

Rolly started speaking. "I haven't said anything to any of y'all until

I knew exactly what was going to happen. I didn't want anyone to worry. So I'm gonna start with I am healthy as a horse, so don't go thinking I'm doing this for any other reason. Okay?"

"Crystal." Charline bumped me in the shoulder a few times. I mumbled something with the rest of the crowd, but kept my focus on a pebble I kicked around.

"Crystal," she bit out my name again.

"What?" annoyance laced my voice. I was still fighting down the fear and anxiety over my split second of thinking that man was Zack.

She grabbed my arm and shook. "Look," she said.

My gaze followed her pointed finger back to the man by the truck. Back to… my knees felt weak, my tongue numb. Breathing required focused effort to suck in air. My stomach vanished in a poof. My skin pricked with uncomfortable tingles seconds before sweat dotted the surface.

His hair was longer and his sharp jawline was covered with the shadow of a beard. He looked thinner. A little harder around the edges. But it was Zack Noble. I had recognized him from the set of his shoulders.

I was rooted in place by fear. And something more, curiosity?

"Shut the front door. Why the fuck is Zack Noble here?" I whispered.

Rolly kept talking. "I decided last year it's high time I retired. I've got grandchildren to teach fishing to. I've got camping to do. And for those of you who knew my Marta, you know she wouldn't want me working myself into an early grave. I've been looking for a buyer who will continue to take care of this company as the family it has become. Zack, get on up here."

My focus tunnel-visioned in on Rolly's outstretched hand. Zack's long fingers, elegant and strong, wrapped around Rolly. Cords of tendons strained in Zack's arm as Rolly hoisted him up onto the bed of the truck.

"Not exactly like the stage show we got when he took over at Shingle Click, huh?" Charline said.

My gut twisted. My focus shifted from Zack's hands back up to his face. I wasn't sure I was able to function at the moment. "Yeah, but it feels familiar, doesn't it? Zack's talking to us in a parking lot. How come I can't help but think everything is about to change, and not necessarily for the best."

She let out a derisive laugh. "Seriously. At least we get fed this time." She sighed. "Are you going to be okay with him here? I know you've got your reasons, but is he in any way behind your secrets for leaving California the way you did?"

I shrugged. I already was not okay, and there wasn't anything I could do about him being here. I couldn't run away, not after Ellen had apologized. If I pulled a runner, she would think I was as flighty and thoughtless as she had accused me of being. If I did anything but looked shocked, annoyed, or surprised, then Charline might put two and two together. I had never told her.

As far as Charline was concerned, my reasons for leaving were that I was getting evicted, the job was not paying me enough for rent, and definitely not enough for putting up with Greg. Adam's father had been one night of fun, and he had no idea about the baby. None of these were exactly lies. They weren't the complete truth either.

Besides, I wanted to see Zack. I wanted to know if he remembered me at all. Had I been as big of an impact on his life as he had on mine?

"He's got hair a lot like Adam's. You sure he's not the father you won't tell me about?" she laughed.

I winced.

Rolly kept on talking. Zack stood there with his hands in his pockets, his expression hidden behind dark sunglasses. From where I stood I could tell he was still biking, still had those powerful thighs. But he looked thinner. Leaner. Meaner.

And then he smiled. Even his business smile had been stunning, and I was painfully reminded of that. Emotions that I hadn't felt for years stirred up in my body, and tears threatened. I looked up and blinked hard. I refused to cry. I didn't have sunglasses to hide behind.

"Ain't no better way to get to know someone than over a good brisket." With a thunderous sound, Rolly clapped his big hands together. "Let's eat."

I didn't move as the rest of the people made their way to line up in front of the tent where the caterers were serving. It was like a reception line with Rolly introducing Zack to everyone as they walked past with plates piled high with lunch.

"What are you waiting for?" Charline asked as she started to head over. "Crystal, come on."

I wasn't ready to meet Zack again. But the food smelled so good, and I was hungry. My stomach rumbled. The desire for the food won out over my panicked thoughts of running away. I fell in line. The closer I got to the head of the line the more nervous I got. My hands could hardly hold on to my plate of food.

"Crystal, I want you to meet Zack Noble. This is the young lady I was telling you about, Zack."

I met his eyes for the first time in almost four years. All strength left my body.

25

ZACK

I barely registered the baked beans and the potato salad that slid down my shirt and globbed onto my slacks, and then onto my shoes. Crystal stood in front of me, alive, vibrant, and full of health.

A deep red flush colored her cheeks in the seconds our eyes met before she went pale, and then dropped her lunch all over me. If she hadn't reacted that way, looking like she had seen a ghost, I probably would have.

"Whoa there, Crystal, are you all right?" Rolly's big voice cut through the haze that clouded my brain and stunned my reaction.

"Crystal!" A woman behind her cried out.

I stood, frozen in shock. Shock at seeing her, shock at being attacked by barbecue. I reached out to steady her, my eyes on her face. A flurry of activity happened as a chair and a bottle of water were brought for her. I was ignored in the very obvious concern for her well-being. Maybe she still wasn't healthy, maybe she came here for treatment. Maybe…

"I'm so sorry Mr. Noble, I don't know what happened," she said.

Mr. Noble? Was she pretending not to know me? My gut tightened as emotions I needed to sort through fought for dominance: anger, surprise, shock, relief.

"Hey, Mr. Noble. I doubt you remember me, I'm Charline." The redhead, who had been behind Crystal in line, gave me a nod and a smile as she fussed about. If she remembered me, what was Crystal's game? "I used to be a receptionist for Shingle Click. Came back here cause Rolly gave me an engineering job."

I nodded. "I remember you. You too, Crystal. You both used to work for me. Or have you forgotten, Miss Pond?"

She looked shaken. Her eyes darted around, but would not meet mine again. Someone handed me a handful of napkins and I began brushing the food from my clothes.

"Somebody get Noble here a clean shirt. Sorry, I can't help you with the pants, maybe we have some work boots you can borrow," Rolly said.

I was grateful he wasn't paying attention to the conversation I was having with the women. Instead his focus was on handling the mess.

"I don't think boots will be necessary," I said, giving him less than half of my attention. It was difficult not to give my full attention to Crystal. After all, I was surrounded by people eager to meet me, and covered in food. But she was here, breathing, alive.

"I… I remember." Crystal's voice was so tentative, nervous. "I wasn't sure if you would remember me."

My gut coiled in and my chest squeezed. How the fuck could she think I would have forgotten anything about her? A derisive chuckle left my lips.

"Your work ethic was something to be commended. I was perplexed that you never contacted HR regarding references. Your team spoke highly of you."

That got her attention, and her eyes snapped to my face. "Most of them at least," I smirked. Maybe I should tell her that I fired Greg after one off-color remark about her after she vanished.

Someone handed me a Rollins Tech tee. I unbuttoned my shirt. Crystal's gaze followed my hands before returning to my face. I held her gaze, daring her to look away. Did she want to drink me in the same way I was fighting my instinct to look at her? I wadded up the soiled shirt and tossed it in the garbage. It was too stained to even bother with. I pulled the tee on over my head and returned to wiping my shoes clean. Small mercies, the food had not made its way into my shoes, and it wasn't puke.

"I hope you're feeling better." I left her with a curt nod and followed Rolly to meet more employees.

My focus was completely shot. All I could hear were her soft gasps of shock. All I could see was the flush across her face, the way her breasts strained at her blouse as she gulped for breath.

She was as shaken up as I was. Only everyone could see her reactions. I hid my own reactions well, I should go play a round of poker. I was so cold and shut down I might as well have been dead. But I didn't feel dead. I felt like the human equivalent of a thousand swarming bees, all movement, and buzz. I wanted nothing more than to follow my queen around now that I had found her.

I smiled and shook hands, and forgot names the second they were told to me. Excusing myself, I phoned Lisa. "It looks like I'm going to need that box of clothes sooner than expected," I said.

"Rollins Tech has potential?" she asked.

"He's motivated. My real problem is someone just dumped their lunch all over me. I have enough clothes for tomorrow and that's it."

"I'll get your clothes out to you immediately. Will you need help locating a dry cleaner, or can the hotel concierge handle that for you?" she asked.

"The concierge should be able to handle that. Thank you, Lisa."

As I ended the call, an image of the little boy flashed on my phone with a text from Paris.

"Looking at this again. You sure it's not you? Secret love child? How many mystery spawn do you have out there?"

I did not appreciate her humor and shoved the phone into my pocket. I was not an irresponsible lover. I didn't lose control like that.

The familiar swish and wiggle of Crystal's hips in my peripheral vision caught my full attention. Fuck me. My body instantly reacted to that woman's walk. She was the only one who could ever drive me so wild I could lose that level of control. I followed her, needing answers.

I slammed into the building and staggered at my sudden blindness. The interior of the office space was darker than expected, coming in from the bright of outside.

"If you close your eyes just before you walk inside it's not so bad. Your eyes will adjust faster."

I turned to the sound of her sweet voice. "Crystal."

"Hi, Zack."

"So, you do remember me? What was that out there?" I didn't hide the bitter resentment in my voice.

I heard her swallow. "I'm sorry. I didn't expect to be overwhelmed. I didn't know if you would want people to know we knew each other. I thought I was over everything."

"Over?" I growled. My vision was still impaired with purple spots, but I could see her outline. I stepped closer, crowding her. I slammed my hands against the wall on either side of her head, boxing her in.

"What is there to get over? Did you have to get over me, or some illness? I thought you were sick. What was it, Crystal? What did you have?"

Her breasts lifted with heavy breaths, brushing my chest. I was no longer in control, my body remembered every soft curve of her and wanted her back. I dipped my nose to her neck and inhaled.

"Why did you leave me?" I hurt for so long, and she had been here the whole time.

Her hands pressed into my chest, and I relaxed against her touch. More. I needed more.

She smelled so good. I trailed my nose along her neck and into her hair. I wanted to taste her skin. Her ear was soft under my mouth.

Her hands rested for a moment. "I didn't have a choice." Her voice was small as she breathed hard. She swallowed again and then shoved me away.

"I heard you talking to your uncle, Zack. You were going to fire me. You let him say those horrible things about me, and you did nothing. I had to leave. I couldn't be your fake roommate once I realized what you really thought of me. I couldn't stay."

"Crystal," I rubbed at the spot on my chest where she shoved. I didn't need to remember the exact words of Uncle George, whatever he had said wasn't complimentary or nice.

"Your uncle, Zack? You couldn't date me, but your uncle is President of the Board?" Anger fueled her now. She shoved me again.

I stepped back before she could push me one more time. "Let me take you out to dinner, give me a chance to explain," I said. I reached for her. I wanted her in my arms again.

She scoffed. "Is that allowed? Looks like I work for you again."

"You don't work for me yet. But Rolly is certainly throwing this sale at me."

"I can't go out with you, Zack." She wrung her hands together. I didn't see the flash of a ring on her finger. As much hope as that gave me, I realized that no ring didn't mean there wasn't a man in her life.

"Look, I'm going to be here, number-crunching for a few days, maybe a week. Can we go out while I'm in town? I owe you," I didn't want to beg, but for this woman, I would crawl across broken glass for another chance.

"I'll think about it."

26

CRYSTAL

I wanted to avoid him while he was at Rollins Tech. Maybe if I didn't talk to him, I wouldn't have to face all these emotions he stirred up. There was no reason for me to be walking past the conference room, but there I was. I stared at Zack through the plate glass window.

He ran his thumb over his eyebrow like he always did when he was thinking. His focus divided between an open binder full of papers, and his laptop. The sleeves of his dress shirt were rolled up and I had a clear view of the muscles of his forearms at play.

He looked up and our eyes met. My stomach flipped.

He waved me in. "You might as well come in, or would you rather stand there staring at me all day."

I felt a blush burn my cheeks. "Busted, huh?"

I slid into a chair across from him. I didn't know where to focus. I picked up a pen that had rolled away and was on my side of the table. I put the pen back. I adjusted in my seat.

He leaned back and braced his hands on the back of his neck. The movement strained his biceps against the fabric of his shirt. I was losing the battle of being physically attracted to him again, still. Had I ever stopped?

"Stop fidgeting, you're making me nervous," he said.

"You nervous? What do you have to be nervous about?" He wasn't the one who had a massive walking talking secret to tell.

"I'm not going to be here too much longer. Rolly's books are exceptionally organized. He's already had the business evaluated by an outside source to determine value. He wants to sell. He's motivated, that makes my job here easier."

I shifted, I wanted to look at his face, but I still couldn't look him in the eyes. "What exactly is your job here, Zack? I'm surprised you're the one here. I thought you were the 'talk to investors and make sure things got done' guy."

He cleared his throat and sat up. He reached across the table and picked up the pen I discarded. I forgot how long his arms were. I had forgotten so much about him, and I thought I had committed every word, every breath, everything about him to memory.

"Go out with me and I'll tell you everything. A lot has changed since you left."

"Did the HCC app rollout end up going smoothly? I…" I couldn't finish. I had abandoned everyone in a selfish fit.

Zack chuckled. "Everything went perfectly. You really made sure your team was taken care of when you vanished. How long did it take you to work out that revised schedule?" He shook his head. "No, let me take you to dinner. You can tell me everything then."

I twisted my fingers in my lap. I needed to tell him everything, and more. I finally looked up and our gazes locked. The sadness I saw in his eyes brought tears to my own.

I nodded. "Dinner."

It was a scramble to find a sitter at the last minute. Fortunately, Sue from the daycare was available. I know I could have asked Charline, but I would have had to explain everything to her, and I didn't have it in me for two major confrontations in one day.

"I don't know where to take you, do you mind suggesting a place? I'll pay. A place where we can sit and talk and not feel rushed."

"I know just the place."

He gave me his hotel information, and I told him I'd pick him up at seven. That would give me enough time to make sure Adam had dinner and was ready for bed before I left.

I couldn't focus on anything for the rest of the day. Fortunately, I wasn't in the middle of anything pressing, or Ellen would have had a fit.

Nerves I thought were long dead danced in my belly as I pulled up to Zack's hotel a few hours later. He had to have been waiting in the lobby since he walked out the doors mere seconds after I texted him.

"Hi," he said as he slid into my small Prius. "I should have known you would have an electric car."

I was too nervous to say anything. Would he notice the car seat under the blanket in the back? He was inches away. I could smell his skin and the hotel soap. His chin still sported the scruff. I itched to reach out and scratch my fingernails along his jaw.

"This is a mom-and-pop kind of place. I think you'll like it." I bit my lips closed before I could say that Adam liked the sparkly red vinyl booths. I wasn't ready to dive right into Adam, just yet.

I closed the car door and my phone started going crazy.

"Give me a sec, I need to take this," I said to Zack. I turned around as if my back to him magically made him not hear anything I said. "Sue, what's up?" Sue never called when she babysat. She never had any problems with Adam. I had to fight to keep panic from my voice. The babysitter calling was never a good sign.

"Crystal, I'm so sorry. Adam's fine, but can you come home?"

"What happened?" I swallowed bile and began fishing for my damned car keys. How had they wormed their way into the depths of my bag so fast? I had just tossed them in.

"I'm really sorry, but my mother called. My dad fell off a ladder. She needs me to come home so she can take him to the hospital. She doesn't know how long that's going to take, and she doesn't want my little sisters home all by themselves for too long."

"I'm about thirty minutes away, will that be okay?" I asked.

"Yeah, that will be great. Thank you. I'm so sorry."

I disconnected the call and breathed out a heavy sigh. I hoped her father was all right, but I couldn't hide my relief that nothing was wrong with my baby.

"Hey, Zack. Something has come up and I have to get home. Would you like to come over, and I can cook? I'm really sorry. Um..." I started shaking, the keys jangled in my grasp.

"Sure, are you okay?" He turned around and put a hand on the car door.

I clicked the unlock, and got into the car. "Yeah, I don't know. The sitter's father had an accident. So I have to get back."

Oh damn. That wasn't supposed to have come out that way. I drove the entire way home in silence, my eyes on the road ahead.

Zack didn't say anything either. He followed me up to my second-floor apartment without a word.

I paused at the door. "It's going to be messy. I'm just warning you," I said as I turned the key and opened the front door.

Brightly colored plastic toys were everywhere in the chaos that I called a living room.

"I'm gonna get you," she said as she sat on the floor and reached out for Adam.

Adam squealed and ran in circles around her.

I snatched him up. "I've got you," I declared.

"Oh Crystal"— she glanced at the clock in the kitchen— "that was fast." She jumped to her feet and went quiet for a second when she took a look at Zack. "I'm so sorry. I've got to go."

She grabbed her bag.

I shrugged. "Things happen. I hope your dad is okay."

"Thanks! Bye, Adam," she called as she closed the door behind her.

Adam reached out toward the door and made a sad mewing sound.

"She'll be at daycare tomorrow." I gave him a sloppy kiss on the cheek.

"Zack, this is Adam. Say hi." I directed the last to Adam, but Zack was the one to say hi first.

I put Adam on the floor, put my purse on the small table by the front door, and ignored the looks Zack was giving me.

"Adam, why don't you show Zack your blocks? Zack, if you sit on the floor, it's easier to play together. I hope spaghetti is okay, that's all I have right now that I can put together quickly."

"Sure, you always made good spaghetti." He cut his gaze between me and Adam.

Within a few seconds, Adam was holding out a block. "Blue," Adam said. It sounded more like bleh, but I understood him clearly.

Zack hunkered down and sat on the floor. He picked up a different colored block. "What color is this one?"

"Lello," Adam said. A big smile on his face.

Zack returned his smile.

I turned away before either of them saw me tear up.

27

ZACK

It was like watching old videos of me. The curl of his hair, the color of his eyes, the child I sat in front of could have been me. Until he smiled, that smile was one-hundred percent Crystal. I cast my gaze to her, she was busy putting our unexpected home-cooked meal together.

Adam waved a red toy truck in front of me. "Reh," he said.

"Red," I repeated.

The smile he gave me melted my heart. He was either speech delayed or not as old as I thought he was. "How old is he?" I asked.

"Adam." Crystal turned to face where the boy and I were on the floor. "Can you tell Zack how old you are?"

He nodded and approached me. He picked up one of my hands and tapped my index finger with his tiny one.

I dropped my other fingers and held up the single digit.

He proceeded to pick up my other hand and did the same thing, this time touching two fingers instead. He then brought my hands together.

"Tree," Adam said proudly.

"Show off," Crystal said before returning to her cooking.

"Did you just do math? Did he just do math?" I asked.

"Yep. He likes numbers. And colors. If he can count it on his fingers he can do the addition. He hasn't figured out subtraction yet."

"He's not very talkative, I mean, he's not..." I wasn't sure how to even ask this.

"He's not speech delayed if that's what you're asking. He's got talking days, and not talking days. You're new to him and he's three. A lot of people expect more from him because he's tall. But for a three-year-old, he's doing great. And he likes you. He's showing off."

I kept my attention on the boy the entire time. She was right, he was tall, and because of his size, even I had assumed he was older. But he was three. I had to breathe around a knot forming in my gut.

"What do you have that's green?" I asked him.

He rummaged around the toys strewn about and finally brought over an action figure.

"Sweetie do you want noodles?"

Adam paused in his playing and looked up at his mother. He gave her an exuberant nod and then launched himself at her. Pressing into her leg and hugging her with everything he had. I understood his need to do that. I wanted to hug her too. Hold her and never let her go.

"Up, noodles," Adam said as he danced by one of the chairs.

I saw that it had a booster seat strapped to it. Crystal placed him onto the booster and buckled him in.

"Sorry I only have the two chairs. I hope you don't mind sitting on the couch. I have to sit with him to help him out sometime."

"I can feed him," I volunteered.

The look she gave me lanced through my chest. It was an expression of awe and gratitude, joy and shock. I had never seen so many emotions play across a person's face at one time.

"I don't have to feed him, he just needs some help sometimes." She brought over a small bowl of plain noodles and set it in front of Adam. She put another bowl in front of the still empty chair.

"Can I sit with you?" I asked Adam.

"You noodles?" he asked.

I laughed. From the look on his face, he loved noodles.

"I like noodles too," I answered.

"I like noodles best," he announced before shoving a handful into his mouth.

Crystal kissed him on the top of his head. "You're using big words, good job."

I could tell she was proud of him. And he was proud of himself. I felt that my ability to use big words had left me.

After helping Adam to eat, I could see why she hadn't given him any sauce. Noodles were smeared everywhere. Crystal lifted him from his booster with a groan. "You are getting so heavy. You ate two dinners tonight. Someone's gonna be taller when they wake up."

She excused herself and Adam into the back of the apartment. I heard bathroom noises and proud mommy responses. When they returned, Adam had a freshly washed face and a different set of pajamas on.

"I'm sorry, Zack, it's his bedtime. This is going to take a while. You can wait, or..."

"I'll call for a car and go back to the hotel. We can try this again later," I said.

"Thank you." Her smile was warm and genuine.

None of my regrets hit until I was back in my hotel room, and through the first travel-sized bottle of Jack from the minibar. Why hadn't I asked her right then and there? With Adam in front of me, how could she deny me being his father? She hadn't denied anything. She hadn't said anything either. I hadn't asked.

I twisted the top off a second bottle. He was a smart and beautiful boy, of course he was, his mother was smart and beautiful. The thought of her having my child filled me with a sadness I wasn't prepared for, having missed her entire pregnancy.

"Fuck you, George!" I threw the half-empty bottle across the room. That man had taken everything that mattered away from me. His policies and callous words turned Crystal away from me. No, that was my stupidity. I should have never let him speak that way about her in my presence.

My muscles burned, and I felt the need to go for a ride, to push through until I could no longer think. I changed into sweats and went to see if the hotel's executive gym had a stationary bike.

I was in the office early the next morning. I stood just outside Crystal's cubicle, not even pretending I wasn't staring at the few pictures that were barely visible behind Henry's foliage. Why didn't she have pictures of Adam's father? Her apartment had been small. She only had two chairs.

Rolly entered the area like a thunderstorm, all loud booming voice and a noticeable drop in air pressure. He clapped me on the back.

"Ready to visit some of my resellers, Noble?"

I turned to him, disoriented for a moment. All of my focus had been on Adam's face, and suddenly I needed to restructure my thinking for the purchasing of a smart-home product manufacturing company.

"Yeah, right. Is this the tiny homes or the campers today?"

Rollins Tech's systems were not direct-to-consumer products. They were sold as an aftermarket modification and retrofitted into existing campers, RVs, any mobile living situation on wheels. If the living solution involved appliances and lighting fixtures, a smart-home system could be installed.

Installation of the equipment needed to take place at trained partner facilities. Rolly had more than enough to keep in business with the few regional partnerships he had, but he recognized a larger scale need. One of Rolly's caveats for selling was that HomeWorks and Shingle Click wouldn't just take his innovations and scrap the rest, but that we would implement scaling up and getting his system to even more partner facilities. I wanted his solar technology, Paris wanted market expansion. Rollins Tech was a perfect acquisition.

I spent the day distracted, touring camper maintenance sites, and talking to installation technicians. Thoughts of Crystal and her child lurked in the shadows of my mind, making forays into my forethoughts when least expected.

I faced another evening alone in my hotel room with my negative thoughts and too many questions. I wanted Crystal in my arms, in my bed. But I also wanted our children tucked into their own beds. I wanted Adam to be mine.

28

CRYSTAL

Charline sat on my couch, twisted to the side so she could look at me. Adam sat at my feet, completely distracted by the car animation on TV. I wiped the tears running down my face. Every so often she would reach out and pat me on the knee.

"So, you're going to tell him?" Her voice was so calm. She wasn't even mad at me.

After a stressful day at work, I asked Charline to follow me home, I had something I needed to tell her. And like the best friend she was, she was there. Through hiccuping breaths, and more snot and tears than I thought possible, I confessed everything. I told her about the fake date to sneak around, and how Greg almost found us out so we ended up taking the entire team on a retreat.

"I was going to tell Zack last night. Nothing worked out, Sue had to leave early. And when we came back here, I froze up. I pretended like there was nothing to tell."

"He met Adam?"

"Yeah," I swiped at more tears. I didn't want Adam to see me crying. "They sat on the floor and played together. It was so wonderful. He has to know. I mean look at Adam, he looks like a mini Zack. He really does."

Charline released a sigh and stood. She took a few steps into the kitchen before returning with a glass of water. She handed me the glass.

"Drink. Did he say anything to you today at work?" she asked sitting back down.

"I didn't see him at all."

My phone rang. Neither of us moved, we both stared at the sound as it continued to ring.

"Well, answer it," she said.

"Hi, Zack," I said. I had to clear my throat suddenly. Why was talking about all of this so hard?

"Come have dinner with me. I think there are a few things you need to explain," he demanded. His voice sounded rough, possibly angry.

"Hold on," I said. I hit mute on my phone and looked at Charline.

"You need to tell him. I'll stay with Adam." She nodded encouragingly.

I turned the sound back on. "I can meet you in the hotel restaurant."

He told me to be there in thirty minutes and hung up.

I blinked away more tears as I looked at Charline. "I'm sorry I didn't tell you before. And now look at this mess I'm in. Everybody is angry with me."

Charline leaned over and put her arms around me. "You were trying to protect your heart. I may not agree with what you did, but I understand why you did it. Keeping Zack a secret must have been killing you, so I think you've been punished enough. Wash your face, and go tell him. I'll still be your friend when all is said and done."

I squeezed her back and did as she said. With a clean face, and a change of clothes I walked into the dark restaurant and looked for Zack. When he saw me, he stood. His poker face was in place, expression unreadable.

Dressed as he had been every day for almost a week in a dress shirt, and a suit, he looked like sex on legs. If he had given me half a smile I would have gone weak in the knees, and in my resolve. I would have confessed everything and not asked for the explanations I deserved. He didn't smile.

I was glad that I changed out of work clothes. The restaurant was slightly more upscale than anything I had been in for a long time.

"I went ahead and ordered some wine," he said as I joined him.

I nodded. "Good." I fingered the glass in front of me. This was going to take some external support. My cheeks burned with the need to smile or cry, I wasn't certain which.

I swallowed hard and started. "So..."

"Crystal, I—" Zack started talking at the same time.

I slumped into my chair, all momentum lost.

He cleared his throat and adjusted in his chair. "I'll go first then. I owe you an explanation. I owe you an apology. But I think you owe me a bit more than that, don't you?" His voice was edged in ice and bitterness.

I bit my lip and nodded.

"Who is the boy's father, and are you married to him?"

A cackle escaped my lips. How little did he think of me? "Would I have accepted a dinner date with you if I were married?"

"No, no. Sorry." He shook his head. "You weren't sick, were you? You were pregnant with Adam."

"Yeah. I was pregnant, and you are his father." As soon as those words left my lips the floodgates opened. "I wasn't allowed to be seen in public with you. I couldn't let anyone know we were together. How was I supposed to handle being pregnant on top of all the other stress? I didn't even know if there was more to us than sneaking around. I was going to tell you I just hadn't figured out how." I looked up, trying to get the tears to stop.

I felt his thumb caress my cheek, wiping tears away.

"I wanted to take care of you. And, this may be foolish, but I still do. Crystal—"

"Why did you let that man say those nasty things if you wanted to take care of me?" I cut him off.

"George Fredrickson was—"

"Your uncle. What kind of bullshit is that if he is so against fraternization and nepotism?" I spat the words out between my teeth.

Zack ground his thumb into his eyebrow. He lifted his gaze to me and we locked eyes. He stared until I shrugged and sat back. I needed to let him speak.

"George Fredrickson was my mentor. He had been a friend of my father's since before I was born. He was uncle in name only. At the time he had a form of dementia, and I didn't know it. No one did. His word choices changed, but he seemed very cognizant of everything, still aware of business proceedings. No one knew until he was well into his decline. The rude language always caught me off guard, and I was never certain how to respond. The man had never used foul language before. He didn't consider our mentorship to violate his nepotism rules. However, he was very concerned about my dating habits in regards to Shingle Click. Even after you left, he accused me of sleeping with every woman employee in the building at one point or another."

"You're talking about him in the past tense, did something happen?"

"He had a stroke."

"I'm so sorry." I covered my mouth with my fingers. Guilt poked at me for speaking ill of the dead.

"You asked why I was the one out here going over books for the purchase of Rollins Tech. He left my sister the majority of his estate. When she stepped in as President of the Board, because of her stock majority, she redefined my position within the organization. For the longest time, I thought I was angry about that. George cost me the one thing that mattered most in my life. It wasn't my position at Shingle Click. I lost you because of him."

My heart surged and felt as if it would pound out of my chest.

"I can't believe I found you because of Paris. Rollins is my last take over. I head back into the office with a focus on company growth through product development after this. I'm tired of negotiating, tired of being on the road. Paris has created a little empire to rule over, so she's happy to let me get back at what I do best."

We had both lost because of that man. We sat in silence and stared at each other.

The waitress approached us. "Would you like to place your order now?"

I wasn't feeling very hungry, but I needed to eat something. I couldn't just drink wine for dinner. I still needed to be able to drive home. "I'll just have a grilled chicken salad," I ordered.

"Same," Zack said and handed over the menus we hadn't bothered to look at.

"When you left," he started after another long silence. "I spent years terrified that you had died before I ever got a chance to tell you how I felt. I thought you were sick. It never occurred to me that you could have gotten pregnant."

"Surprise," I said with no humor.

"I have two grilled chicken salads," a different server announced as they stopped at our table. They placed the large bowls of greens and chicken in front of us. Offered freshly ground pepper and left.

I stabbed my salad. It tasted bland. "I doubt you remember, but I had an ear infection and was on antibiotics."

He ate and nodded, indicating he was listening.

"Apparently, those made the birth control I was on stop working."

A sly grin spread across his lips. "Not quite the souvenir I would have expected from Monterey," he smirked.

I was too emotionally drained to blush. I nodded.

"If I invited you up to my room for a nightcap, what would you say?"

"Are you flirting with me, Mr. Noble?" I teased.

"I'm not flirting. This is a blatant proposition." He narrowed his eyes and tipped his head to the side. The scruff on his jaw made him look dangerous and sexy ass hell.

"Ask me, and we'll see." I was flirting.

29

ZACK

Dinner tasted like nothing because it wasn't what I wanted. I wanted my mouth on Crystal. The smile she gave me redirected my blood flow straight to my cock. I hadn't felt a need that hot and demanding in years. Not since the last time I had been with her.

I was ready to throw the table aside and toss her over my shoulder. I made pen-signing motions to the waitress.

"Are you okay? You stopped eating," Crystal pointed out.

"I'm saving room for dessert," I said, draining my wine glass.

The waitress handed me the black folder with the bill. "Is this the same kitchen the hotel uses for room service?" I asked.

"Yes, it is," she answered with a smile. "Did you want to arrange a meal being sent to your room?"

"I'd like dessert to be sent up." I glanced at Crystal. "Two chocolate tortes and a bottle of cabernet sauvignon." I finished the order and signed the revised slip.

"Are we in a hurry?" Crystal chuckled.

"I want to be able to leave the second you say go." I felt like a caged beast, waiting to be set free. Crystal was my freedom.

She delicately placed her fork to the side of her plate. "Then I guess, pretending we are having a polite conversation when we both want something else is foolish."

My chair fell over with a crash. Crystal had a bemused smile on her face as she waited for me to set right the offending piece of furniture and help her with her chair.

She placed her soft hand on my arm, and I thought I would fall apart then and there. Other than the toppling chair, I pulled myself together as I guided her through the hotel lobby and to the elevators. I was a perfect gentleman until the doors slid closed and we were alone.

With my hand on her back, I swung her in a dance-like move until I could wrap my arms around her and crush her to me. I could drown in her softness and beg for more.

Her lips were soft and pliable under mine. I didn't need to demand because she kissed me with even more fervor and want. Her soft moan undid me. I pressed her against the mirrored wall, not caring cameras were monitoring us.

She dug at my shirttails, pulling them from my slacks. Her hands slid up my sides and against the skin on my back. The warmth and contact of her hands held me in place. I didn't want to move. I could have stayed like that for days, her lips on mine, her hands holding me close.

The elevator doors slid open. I would have completely missed it if the woman waiting to get on the elevator hadn't let out a surprised gasp.

I pulled away from Crystal's sweet kisses long enough to recognize this was my floor. I waggled my eyebrows at the woman as I grabbed Crystal's hand and dragged her from the elevator.

"Zack." She tugged me to a stop about halfway to my door. "Are we sure about this?"

I stepped up to her and slid my hand along the side of her waist. "I haven't been more sure of anything. I've missed you. Tell me you've missed me, that you've missed us."

She sighed against my body and kissed me again. I needed her naked in my bed. I pulled away with a regret that felt like a punch in the gut.

"Come on." This time I didn't drag her along like the barbarian I felt like. We walked arm in arm to my room.

She sat on the edge of the made bed and I kicked the door closed behind me.

"This is a nice room," she said.

I shrugged. I normally stayed in more budget-oriented hotels, ones where room service was pizza delivery. I hadn't planned on staying as long as I had. Thinking Rolly was going to play games with the sale, I had Lisa book me into a nicer place.

"It has a well-stocked minibar." I gestured at the mini-fridge and booze selection. "If you want anything."

"I'll wait for the wine you ordered." She fidgeted with her fingers.

I suppressed another moan as she began that undulating squirm that had always driven me mad. I ripped my suit jacket off and threw it. I was vaguely aware of a chair in that direction. If there wasn't one for my suit, I didn't care. I stalked to Crystal, placing a knee on the bed next to her.

She pressed a hand to my chest. Closing my eyes, I covered her hand with my own and pressed it to me. She was here and touching me.

"Condom." That one word broke the emotion that threatened to overtake me.

"Right." I pointed to the minibar. "You look over there. I'll check the bathroom."

Fuck me. There weren't any hotel-supplied condoms. I tore through my bathroom kit. There in the bottom, a strip of three black and gold foil packs. Relief rushed from my lungs with a heavy breath.

"Success," I declared holding up my findings between two fingers pinched together.

A tap on the door caught my attention. Snorting in annoyance, I yanked the door open.

"Room service," the server announced.

Stepping back, I pulled the door open. "Just put it anywhere," I said.

Quickly I dug a tip from my wallet, careful not to accidentally slip the condoms over as my tip.

Crystal crossed the room and peaked at the dessert. "Oh, this looks good."

"You look better," I said once the door was closed.

This time when I approached her, she reached for me, pulling me in close.

I lowered myself to her and pressed into her lush curves. I didn't have enough hands to touch and caress and fondle all the parts of her that deserved my attention.

She fumbled with my buttons while I kicked my shoes off and shoved my slacks away. I knelt naked in front of her. She ran her fingers in light ticklish caresses over my abs.

I pressed my hips forward as she wrapped a hand around my length. I needed her touch. This was what had been missing from my life. I about swallowed my tongue when her warm wet mouth took my cock into its depths. I dug my fingers into her hair and braced the other against the wall. She made the sexiest little humming sounds as she slid her lips and tongue over and around me. I wasn't going to last long if she kept that up.

"Fuck me," I moaned.

Finding my balance, I reached for her and tugged at the hem of her dress. I couldn't figure out how it worked. There was no zipper. It seemed to tie, but I couldn't find the fucking knot.

"Get out of this." I gasped as she released me and sat back.

She undid the tie and the dress unrolled around her. She wore a basic skin tone bra. It was the sexiest lingerie I had ever seen because underneath was Crystal.

She crawled out of the bed to finish disrobing. I flopped onto my back, watching her the entire time. I drank her in.

"What are you looking at?" she asked with a giggle.

"You are so beautiful. You haven't changed one bit."

"I've had a baby, Zack. Things have changed and shifted." She held a hand out to me and I pulled her close.

"I can't tell, you are as perfect to me as always. Maybe more so knowing that you grew my child in your belly. Come here. I want to look at you." I kept pulling her hand so that she had to either flop across my chest, or toss a leg over and straddle me.

"I'll break you," she said as she straddled my hips.

"Please, break me. If I die, I'll die happy."

From her perch over my hips she began exploring my abs and chest with her fingers. I pressed my chest into her touch, wanting, needing. With delicate soft touches she caressed my face, and scratched with her nails along my jaw, playing with the shaggy facial hair I had been too lazy to shave off.

She leaned over, and brought her lips to my skin. Satisfaction and desire escaped from me with a loud sigh. I hissed in a breath when her tongue found a nipple. She was killing me, and I loved every second of it.

My hands skimmed over her skin. Her round ass and thigh thighs were so soft, I had to resist sinking my grip into her, marking her with small bruises. My hips pressed up and I slid against her slick entrance. That's where I wanted to be. I lifted my hips and rocked, sliding my cock between the groove of her folds.

"So wet. Don't make me beg, Crystal," I murmured.

I fished around for the strip of condoms and ripped one off.

Pressing against my shoulder she lifted back to her knees. She plucked the condom from my hand and tore it open. It was the most astounding torture as she rolled it on. She lifted her hips up, shifted, and positioned her opening directly above my tip. I could feel her heat, and I wanted to be lost in her.

With a swallow, she bit her lip and sank onto me. I couldn't help the sounds I made. Relief, desire, longing, home. Her body was my refuge, and I had been lost for too long.

I couldn't help myself. My intention was to let her control the evening since she had started it off with my cock in her mouth. But I wanted her surrounding me. I thrust up into her, needing to be in deeper. She whimpered one of those noises she made that set me off, made me crazy. When she rocked her hips against mine I realized that if I died, I was already in heaven.

From the first second she welcomed me into her body I felt like I was on the verge of cumming. Each thrust felt as if I would explode on the very next stroke. I dug my fingers into the flesh of her ample hips and drove into her like some crazed pile driver. She braced her hands against my shoulders, her breasts brushed against my chest. I dipped my head to capture a nipple into my mouth. She cried out and I thrust harder, faster. The rocking of her hips stopped, but the keening sounds she made grew higher until she was gasping for air. I felt her entire body quiver, and her internal muscles clenched and milked my cock. She was undone in her orgasm. All she could manage was to clutch at me while I drove into her wetness and buried my face against her breasts.

I rolled her onto her back. Her eyes were heavily lidded, and a satisfied smile crossed her face. She looked satiated and content. But I wasn't done yet. I couldn't take my eyes from her as I continued to pound my way into her. My balls squeezed tight, and I couldn't move fast enough to meet the frenetic pace my body suddenly demanded of me. It didn't take much more before I seized with my orgasm. It felt as if my entire being was pulled through a singularity, only to burst back into bright dazzling existence. And at the end of it was Crystal's beautiful face smiling at me.

After taking care of the condom and returning to bed, I pulled her into my embrace and wrapped around her. I wasn't done with her by any means. This felt like a teaser, a mere appetizer to all the making love I had plans for. I may have been limited in some aspect with only two more condoms, but there were so many more options to explore, and I wanted them all at once.

"I need to go," she whispered.

"Stay." I tried to trap her under my arm.

"There was once a time you ignored me every time I asked you to stay," she said.

I rolled onto my back and flung my arm over my eyes. "I know. I was full of ego and stupidity. I regret so much of how I treated you. Stay, let me make it up to you."

She gave me a level stare. I read a million thoughts into that expression: could she trust me; had she made a mistake sleeping with me tonight; I would only let her down again.

She climbed from the bed. I shut my eyes not wanting to face the grief of watching her get dressed and leave. I opened them when I heard her whispering into her phone. The bed dipped and she slid her air-cooled skin against me.

"I have to be home before Adam wakes up, but I can stay."

30

CRYSTAL

The apartment was dark and quiet when I opened the door. I turned, pressed my finger to my lips, and indicated Zack should wait in the living room. He closed the door quietly.

Depositing my bag and coat, I walked quietly into the back.

Charline and Adam were curled up together in the bed. I smiled, they were both sound asleep. Leaving them I returned to the front half of the apartment.

"Still out cold," I said in an almost whisper.

Zack was in the kitchen, putting together a pot of coffee. "I figure we owe Charline breakfast at the very least. I can make pancakes."

"That sounds good."

I curled into the corner of the couch while Zack bustled about in my small kitchen. He wore slacks with a button-down. I couldn't help but remember how his clothes had looked after I dropped my lunch on him the other day.

"You want an apron?" I asked. I pointed to the drawer where I stored clean aprons.

There was something sexy about him, dressed in business clothes with the sleeves rolled up, wearing a canvas apron with the ties wrapped around his middle like that. Maybe it was just that Zack was hot and he looked good wearing anything.

"Thanks," he nodded and returned to mixing batter.

Charline stumbled out from the bedroom with a big yawn. Her hair was the definition of bed head, with strands reaching out like tendrils in all directions. "Do I smell coffee?"

She stopped and stared when Zack handed her a cup. He returned to his cooking, but she stood there and continued to stare as she sipped the coffee.

"Am I mad at him, mad at you, or am I going to ignore this and pretend everything is happy fun times?" she grumbled.

Zack turned and leaned a hip against the counter. We all looked at each other in awkward silence.

"Oh for pity's sake, I slept with Zack last night," I confessed.

A slow cocky smirk spread across his face.

"Yeah, I figured that out," Charline said, finally sitting in the only available chair.

"As far as I'm concerned it's all happy fun times," Zack said.

I gave him a pointed look.

"But we have a whole lot more talking to do. I don't even know what comes next," he said.

"You're not going to go back to work and pretend this didn't happen, only to return to your old habits are you?" Charline asked.

Zack and I looked at each other for a long time.

"I'm never hiding her again," he said in a low whisper.

I couldn't help but smile. "I don't want to hide you either."

"Mommy," a sleepy Adam ground a fist into his eyes and dragged his favorite dinosaur stuffy behind him. "Waked up," he announced in a sad voice.

I was off the couch and picking him up in a blink. "Morning baby, did you wake up?" I kissed his blanket-warmed face. "Do you remember your friend Zack?"

Adam kept the not-happy-to-be-awake frown on his face, but his eyes widened and he nodded.

"Hey big guy," Zack said as he slid an arm around my waist. He ruffled Adam's hair with his other hand.

Adam leaned hard into Zack.

"If he does that, he expects you to kiss him," Charline said.

I couldn't take my eyes from the two of them, Zack as he kissed Adam for the first time, and Adam being kissed. Zack closed his eyes. It was as if he were imprinting this moment into his memory forever. Adam simply expected everyone he liked to love on him and kiss him.

A hard lump formed in my throat, and I blinked back tears.

"Y'all are disgusting, being all lovey-dovey happy family and shit over there. Feed me already. I need to get home and change before I go to work. You are not coming in are you?" She looked at me and then at Zack.

"I don't know, are we?" Zack asked as he returned to pancake making.

I pressed another kiss to Adam's cheek. "Let me think about it while I get this guy ready."

I took Adam to the back for morning potty and getting dressed. How would he react if I suddenly announced Zack was his father? Daddy was not a concept Adam ever seemed to be worried about. He never once asked about having one, or who his was. And if I told him Zack was his father, and then Zack left, how would that make Adam feel?

Charline was giving Zack a death glare when we reentered the front of my apartment.

"Do I need to be concerned?" I asked.

"Not at all," Zack chuckled. "Charline was informing me that I am her prime target should you have your heart broken again."

She sat with her arms crossed. "I'm not going to apologize. I said what I said."

"I am so glad Crystal has a friend like you," he continued to laugh. "I fully deserve to be rung out over everything. And I will do my best to not repeat said offending actions."

"Okay," I said, slightly confused. "I was thinking that maybe taking a day off work to get us figured out might not be a bad idea. Do you think that's something you could do?"

Zack pulled his phone from his pocket and spoke to it. "Call Rolly Rollins."

"Dialing Rolly Rollins," a computerized voice responded.

"Good morning, Rolly. Do you think we could put off paperwork for a day? I wanted to poke around town a bit on my own." He paused. "Not exactly on my own, right. That's right. And Crystal Pond won't be coming in today either. She's volunteered to be my tour guide." He laughed. "Exactly, I need to get my insider trading intel from somewhere. Yes, sir, I'll have her back at her desk tomorrow."

He ended the call and looked up. "Done. Rolly said he'd tell your manager you'd be out for the day."

"Well damn," Charline stood with a stretch. "Be good today, kids. I expect a full report. I've got to get going."

She kissed Adam and left me staring open-mouthed at Zack.

He smiled at me and placed a small plate of pancakes in front of Adam's place before lifting our son into his booster seat.

"Pahcake!" Adam tried to shove an entire one into his mouth.

"Now what?" Zack asked.

"First cut up his pancakes so he doesn't choke. After that, I guess I should get dressed and tell them at the daycare Adam isn't coming in today.

This time when I re emerged from the back, I had on fresh clothes. Zack and Adam were making a mess eating pieces of pancakes and giggling. My heart squeezed, and I wanted to cry and laugh at the same time. Was it possible to be any happier?

"Should we go to the park?" I asked.

I knew Adam would be thrilled. He could run around and climb and play, and Zack and I would be able to talk without little ears hearing everything, and constantly asking 'what's that,' or 'why?'

Zack insisted on cleaning up after breakfast while I got Adam ready for a day out and about. I needed to pack snacks and juice boxes, and distractions including toy cars and crayons. Leaving for the park was never a case of 'let's go,' and being out the door within a few minutes.

With my coaching, Zack got Adam into his car seat before buckling himself into the passenger seat. Zack asked Adam about all of his favorite colors, something Adam could go on about for a while. My little guy was an artist at heart, and he loved to look at colors and scribble with crayons.

Once we made it to the park, a small neighborhood playground, Adam dragged Zack off to the swings. I followed behind, content in the moment of watching the two loves of my life together.

I put the tote bag with our things down by the swing set and stepped next to Zack. I ran my hand up his firm back. Feeling the movement of his muscles as he pushed Adam in the swing; feeling the warmth of the sun on the fabric of his shirt, I opened my mouth to tell him how I felt when he turned and kissed me. I leaned into him.

"I love you," he said. "I may have forgotten to tell you that four years ago. I didn't want to forget to tell you now."

I swallowed hard and smiled. "I was just going to say that. I love you, too. Now, what do we do?" I asked with a sigh.

"Fuck me, I love it when you do that. Sigh again."

"Language!" I chastised him.

"Sorry, he didn't hear anything. I don't think."

We both watched Adam enjoying the swing, waiting if he would parrot the bad word.

"I think we're safe," I said. "Now what, Zack? What do we do? Can I tell Adam you're his father and not have you break his heart? I mean, if you aren't going to be around, or we end up doing some long distance thing, I'd rather he not know than have to tell him why you aren't here."

"Who said I wasn't going to be around Crystal?"

I shrugged. "I live here, you're in California."

"Come home with me. There's a Project Manager position on my new solar team in need of someone with your skills."

I shook my head and crossed my arms. I didn't want that again.

"Out, out!" Adam demanded. I lifted him from the swing and set him loose to run and climb on the play structure.

Zack came up behind me and placed his hand on my hip. He turned me into his chest and wrapped his arms around me.

"I can't just work for you again Zack. I bet that stupid company policy is still in place. Adam and I have a sort of family here."

"I'll have that policy changed by tonight," his voice was thick with emotion. "I don't want you to come back just to work for me. I want you to come home and marry me. Be my wife. Let me be Adam's father. Do I have to adopt my own son?"

I swiped at tears and pushed out of his embrace. "Yes," I nodded enthusiastically.

"Yes to what, you'll marry me?"

"I'll marry you, and you're going to have to adopt Adam. I didn't put your name on the birth certificate."

Zack held my face and kissed me hard. It was a challenge to kiss him through the laughing and the tears, but I managed.

"Adam," I called out. "Come here, baby."

Adam ran over to us.

Zack knelt to be at the same level. Seeing them together, there was no denying they were a matched set.

"Adam, I want you to meet your Daddy."

He looked up at me with big confused eyes. "Daddy? Zack Daddy?"

After a moment of looking back and forth between us, Adam launched himself into Zack's arms. Zack held him tight and stood, wrapping an arm around me, bringing me into the hug.

I had been wrong earlier. I could be happier. I held them tight.

"I love you so much," I whispered to them both.

31

EPILOGUE: ZACK

"Honey, I'm home!" I would never get tired of saying that. It felt so cheesy and like a TV sitcom. It gave me the happiest feeling deep in my chest, to come home to my family.

"Deeeeee," the first part of 'dad' was lost to Adam's squeal as he ran and slammed into my legs. He held on and hugged me with everything in his tiny body.

"How's my big boy?" I asked as I hefted him up to my hip. "Where's Mommy?"

"She's in the kitchen, cooking. It smells icky."

I laughed. Everything was icky to Adam at this stage of being four. His once loved plain noodles were icky, chicken nuggets were icky. Everything was icky.

He couldn't have been more wrong. Then again I wasn't four, and as far as I was concerned, everything was wonderful. Maybe a bit messy, but wonderful. I dodged the landmines of his toys scattered throughout the living room and passed the table where Crystal had clearly been working earlier. Her laptop was open to a color coded spreadsheet, and the table had a large calendar covered with more sticky notes than I thought were necessary. Crystal had her methods and they involved all the sticky notes.

I carried him into the kitchen where my beautiful wife was surrounded by flour, open jars, and an open egg carton filled with broken egg shells. A deep fryer unit spit and sizzled on the counter. More mess, and yet, it would all be tidied away before we tucked Adam into bed for the night. She was amazing that way. It's why she was so good at her job, and at being a mother. She knew things had to get messy and expand before they could come together, refined and ready to go.

She was speaking, if I hadn't known better, I would have missed the ear piece and assumed she was talking to me. We tried to keep work at the office, otherwise, as she so wisely pointed out, it took over everything. She pressed her cheek in my direction so I could kiss her while she continued with her conversation. Her words reminded me of a time long ago when we were dating and thinking how business words made no sense. Why not just say 'this is how it makes money?'

Adam squirmed in my arms, and I set him down with a kiss to his cheek. I was going to get as many of those in before he thought kisses from Daddy were icky too. I peered over at what Crystal was busy with.

She was patting pickles dry with paper towels. In front of her she had several bowls of flour and what looked like raw scrambled eggs waiting to be scrambled.

I watched her quizzically and rubbed my thumb into my eyebrow.

"Hi, Darling," she said to me, her call finally over.

"What are you making? This hardly looks like Project Management."

"I am managing this project, so shut up." She gestured at the cooking set up in front of her. "I am allowed to cook and make phone calls. It's called multitasking."

"I see that, and what are you multitasking? Are those pickles?"

"The grocery store was out of those dill pickle potato chips. So I thought I'd try frying some pickles on my own."

"I didn't know we had a fryer. We have too many kitchen gadgets, I can't keep up with them," I teased. I leaned against the counter, and then stood quickly, thinking better of it. I didn't need my clothes to get covered in flour and who knows what else.

"Well, we didn't. I had to get one for the fried pickles. And every gadget we own is very useful," she said defiantly. "I just got a crazy craving for them. And it turns out they aren't that hard to make. At least not once you have a fryer. I'm really surprised it took me so long to get one of these."

I went silent as she spoke. The last time she wanted to eat fried pickles she had been pregnant.

"Crystal, are you feeling okay?" She seemed vibrant, super healthy. With Adam, she had been so sick at the beginning. It was possible she was just hungry. She did have a thing for kitchen gadgets, so having an excuse to buy a new toy was not out of character. Even if she did say 'craving,' and she had never once randomly purchased those dill pickle potato chips since we got married and she moved in with me, this did not mean she was pregnant.

"I feel great why?"

"You're craving fried pickles, that's why," I carefully enunciated each word.

She nodded. "Yeah, I know. It's weird like I'm pregnant or something."

"Or something," I muttered. I snuck another kiss on her cheek and turned to leave the kitchen.

"But it's not or something, Zack."

The tone of her voice stopped my feet. I turned to look at her standing there with her hands on her hips. The expression on her face made me think I had missed something, and she was judging me over it. I stared at her and rubbed at my eyebrow.

"We're going to have another baby." Her face split into a wide grin full of happiness.

I continued to stare at her, only this time I wasn't wondering what I had or hadn't done, this time I was shocked into place. We had stopped using any kind of protection with the intent of getting pregnant only a few weeks ago. I didn't think it had been a month already.

"Are you sure? So soon? That's fantastic!" I laughed and pulled her into my arms. She sighed into my embrace. I felt her head nod against my chest. "I know, that was really fast. I guess we are meant to be parents. We do make beautiful babies, look at Adam."

I tilted my head and shifted so I could see her face. "I love you."

She smiled up at me. "I love you, too."

I peppered her face with kisses before our lips met. I slid my mouth across hers. Her lips parted against mine and her mouth tasted like heaven. This is what home was meant to feel like, Crystal in my arms and her kisses on my lips.

my Best Friend's Ex

A FORBIDDEN OFFICE ROMANCE

KELLY MYERS

BLURB

Let me make this clear...

I shouldn't have let my best friend date Grayson all those years ago.

Yes, I regret it.

But there's something I regret even more.

Showing up with him to our college reunion with a ring on my finger.

A fake ring.

Well, technically the diamond was real but there was no emotion behind it.

It was a facade. It was for the optics.

And little did I know that Chloe would attend the reunion.

You can imagine my horror when I saw her face.

The drama was about to begin and I didn't want to have any part in it.

Especially since Grayson was my boss.

And speaking of bad decisions…

I handed my V-card to him and ended up with another surprise that Chloe won't like.

And this surprise might just cost me everything and everyone I care about…

1

ELLE

My phone starts ringing and when I look down and see Chloe's name on the caller ID, I almost don't answer. But a best friend doesn't ignore a call from her BFF, right? *No, she doesn't,* I tell myself, and swipe the bar over.

"Hi, Chloe," I say, trying to sound upbeat and positive, because I know Chloe is going to be anything but happy right now.

"Kill me now," Chloe exclaims in the most dramatic way possible.

I've known Chloe Charles since the fourth grade when we met and became instant best friends. We bonded over wearing the same shade of pink nail polish and having a mutual dislike of Billy Willett, the kid behind us who ate glue. Over the years, our friendship grew stronger, and I think I'm the only one who really understands Chloe and can see through what others might consider self-absorbed.

Sure, she can be a little over-dramatic and self-centered sometimes, but she's like my sister. It's not her fault that she has a strong personality and demands to be center stage at all times. The great thing is she helps bring out the fun side of me and I really appreciate that. Sometimes I can be a little too serious and quiet.

Chloe and I are like night and day yet somehow it works. While I'm more reserved and shier, she could walk up to a complete stranger and instantly start a conversation about anything and everything. Maybe it's one of the reasons Chloe and I became such good friends. We balance each other out really well.

"The wedding is going to be in June, of course, and I'm going to look like a complete fool!" Chloe laments. "She knows I want to get married in June. What a copycat."

This isn't really about you, Chloe, I think. *But how do I say that without sounding supportive?* I wonder. "Aren't you happy for Olivia? She's going to marry the love of her life."

"But she's my *little* sister, Elle! And she's getting married before me. Do you have any idea how humiliating that is?"

When I don't respond, she keeps going.

"No, of course you don't because you're an only child and never had to deal with sibling rivalry and competition. It's brutal. Now everyone is going to give me sympathy looks and think Olivia is the prettier one because she snagged a man first. Oh, God, this is awful."

As usual, I feel like Chloe is blowing this up into something far bigger than it needs to be and it's my job to talk her down off the ledge. "It's only September, Chlo. By the time June gets here-"

"You need to meet me right now. I need a shoulder to cry and a latte ASAP."

I'm kind of expecting an important call about a new job I'm starting, but I relent. Like usual. "Sure." I guess that's the great thing about cell phones. You never have to miss a call.

"B.B. in ten minutes."

Chloe hangs up and I sigh. B.B. means Barney's Beanery, our favorite local coffee shop. I grab my coat and shrug it on, mentally preparing myself for at least an hour or two of Chloe crying, whining and acting like her life is over. Good thing I'm not starting my new job for another day and can run out and meet her now.

I live on the second floor of my apartment building and jog down the steps, swinging my purse over my shoulder. New York City is home now, though I grew up in Fairview, a small town about 40 minutes upstate. My parents still live there and embrace the slower-paced life there where things get done when they get done.

Chloe and I left Fairview the moment we finished high school. We attended Boston College for four years and after graduating, we moved down here and into the city. I studied business at BC but wasn't able to figure out exactly what I wanted to do for a career until last year. I chose real estate, particularly commercial, and took the necessary classes to get my license and learn what I needed to know. The new job I'm starting is at a commercial real estate company called C.T. International. I'm so excited and I can't wait to dive in and absorb everything that I possibly can. It feels a little late starting my career at 27, but some people change careers at 40. I'm just thrilled that I finally figured out what I want to do with my life.

There's a brisk wind kicking up and I hurry down to the coffee shop. I arrive before Chloe, so I order and pay for our drinks. She always seems to show up 5 minutes after me, so I'm not surprised when she comes bustling in late.

Petite with blonde hair and big blue eyes, Chloe Charles resembles a pretty pixie. She reminds me of Tinkerbell, and she possesses the same feisty personality as the diminutive Disney character.

Chloe plops down across from me and wraps her hands around the warm drink. Instead of saying hello or thanking me, she starts in on her predicament immediately. "It's only September, right?"

I nod and take a sip of my cafe mocha.

"So that gives me ten months to find a guy and get engaged."

She says it so nonchalantly that I burst out laughing. Chloe's blue eyes narrow.

"I'm not kidding. When I go to that stupid wedding, I'm going to be bringing my fiancé."

"Sorry," I apologize and press my lips together when I see she isn't amused.

"What're you saying? I'm not pretty enough for a man to propose to me?"

"Chloe, no. Of course, not. You're beautiful. What I'm trying to say is that it just seems awfully fast."

She waves a perfectly manicured, dismissive hand through the air.

"Who cares? All I know is I refuse to show up with just a measly boyfriend."

Hell, I'd love to have a "just a measly boyfriend" right about now. As Chloe drones on about her future fiancé, I think about who I'd like my boyfriend to be. Not that I have to think very hard since it's the same man I've been pining over since junior year in college: Grayson Carter.

An image of his piercing blue-gray eyes fills my head and I sigh into my coffee. The first time I saw Gray in all of his glory, I was at a party off-campus. The initial attraction was like nothing I'd ever experienced before or since. Utterly irresistible.

Some guy with Greek letters on his sweatshirt just finished filling my red Solo cup with more beer from the keg when I feel like someone is staring at me. The house, about five minutes down the road from campus, is packed with people and I glance around. When our gazes collide, my stomach drops like I'm plunging down the first hill of a roller coaster. Holy crap. I've never seen such a good-looking guy before, and I take a sip of beer.

Shock rolls through me when he begins walking toward me and I have no idea what to do. I'm the quiet one, really reserved, and I'm not good at flirting or the social game. If it weren't for Chloe dragging me out, I wouldn't even be here tonight. I look around, my mental S.O.S. sign waving, but I don't see her anywhere. Figures.

Trying to get my stupid nerves under control, I look up into the most incredible eyes I've ever seen and a smile that nearly knocks the breath from my lungs. "Hi," he says in a deep, smooth voice. "I'm Gray."

Oh, he even has a cool name. My heart thunders in my chest and I give him a shy smile. "Hi. I'm Elle." I can't look away from his eyes. They're this arresting shade of silvery-blue and I want to take a picture so I can always look at them.

"That's a pretty name."

I clear my throat and shift. "Thanks."

"Do you go to BC?"

I nod. "I'm a junior."

"Me, too," he says. "What's your major?"

"Business."

His mouth edges up and his teeth are perfect and a dazzling white. I think about my retainer on the bathroom counter and smile without showing my teeth. I had braces for three years in high school, so I know they're straight, but I still feel like one is starting to get crooked.

"Same," Gray says. "I'm surprised I haven't had any classes with you."

Because I have rotten luck, I think. There's no way the powers that be would allow me to be in a classroom with this gorgeous eye candy for an hour every day. I'd be a drooling mess by the time class ended and would probably have no idea what the professor talked about.

"Maybe one day," I say.

"Hopefully soon," he adds.

I swear that I hear a flirty tone in his voice, and it throws me. I'm not used to men this attractive coming up and talking to me. At least not men that look like Gray. I know I'm a cute girl, maybe sometimes even pretty in the right lighting, but my self-confidence is a little shaky. Maybe it's because I'm used to everyone fawning over Chloe and I've developed Ugly Duckling Syndrome over the years.

"What classes are you taking next semester?" he asks.

I rattle off a few classes and he's listening closely, as though making mental notes. His ears perk up when I mention Business Law.

"I've been putting that one off for a while now," he says.

"Because of Professor Hindry?"

"You've heard the rumors, too?"

"That he puts you to sleep within five minutes and the entire room smells like B.O. because he doesn't wear deodorant?"

We both burst out laughing.

"It also doesn't help that it's an 8am class."

A strange boldness washes over me and I tilt my head and smile. A full-tooth grin. "Maybe we can bring caffeine and nose plugs."

Talking to Gray is so easy and he makes me laugh. He's handsome, smart and the second my cup gets low, he goes off to get me a refill from the keg. This is the beginning of my third year at Boston College and I haven't met anyone that's captured my attention like him.

When he returns and hands me the cup, it's like I'm lost in him. His eyes, his smile, his words. I can't get enough, and this new feeling is exciting.

"Do you like the Red Sox?" he asks.

"How dare you! I'm a New Yorker," I exclaim, pretending to be horrified.

"Uh-oh," he says and crosses his arms. "Damn Yankees."

"Actually, I don't really care either way," I admit with a little smile. "I'm not much of a baseball fan."

His face falls just a bit and it occurs to me that maybe he was going to invite me to a game. Ugh. I'm such an idiot.

Immediately backtracking, I say, "I've heard the games are really fun, though. Food, beer and singing Sweet Caroline until you're hoarse."

Those silver-blue eyes of his light up but before he can say anything, Chloe appears out of nowhere and throws an arm around my shoulders. It's clear she's had a few too many drinks and I put my arm around her back to steady her.

"Oh. My. God."

Gray and I just look at her and then she tugs me away. I glance back over my shoulder and give him a shrug and "sorry, be right back" look.

"What's up, Chlo?" I ask, still smiling at Gray.

"He's the guy I've been crushing on,"

My heart sinks faster than a lead weight dropped in the lake. "What?" I ask weakly, now giving her my full attention.

"Remember me telling you about the cute boy in my class? The one I wanted to ask out but was too nervous?"

Yes, I do recall her gushing about some guy in her class, but she's always doing that. Like on a daily basis and it's usually about a different guy each time.

"I'm going to ask him."

"Ask him what?"

"To go out with me, silly," she says and, before I can even respond, my best friend heads over to Gray.

For a moment, I don't know what to do. It's like my body shuts down and the idea of Chloe going with Gray makes me physically ill. But if she wants him, what can I do? Guys always love Chloe– she's pretty, outgoing and experienced.

And when Chloe wants something, she always gets her way.

"Right?"

I snap out of my reverie. "Uh, sure," I say even though I have no idea what she just said. Because when my thoughts return to Gray and our last two years in college, I'm faced with the biggest regret of my life: I didn't fight for him.

Instead, I stepped back and practically handed him over to Chloe on a silver platter. I just let it happen when I liked him so much. He and Chloe ended up dating until they broke up at graduation almost two years later.

Ever since meeting Gray, I've compared every other man to him, and no one has ever measured up. Not even close. It's the reason I haven't been able to have a relationship and why I'm still a virgin. Gray Carter is the only man I've ever wanted, and I lost him before we even had a chance to begin because I was too meek and unassertive when it came to Chloe.

Over the years, I've learned to stand up for myself more, but I still tend to put everyone else's needs before mine. I always wonder if things would've turned out differently if I'd staked my claim on Gray and hadn't given in to Chloe.

Bygones, I think, and finish my drink.

2

GRAY

Walking through the office building in lower Manhattan with the potential buyer, success is in the air. Even though nothing is definite yet, I can smell it. And it's the scent of money. More specifically, millions of dollars.

When Anthony McMann decides to purchase One Financial Center three hours later, I smile and shake his hand. Obviously, I'm not surprised, but I'm thrilled it went off without a hitch. My best friend Liam Thompson and I own C.T. International, a commercial real estate company, and this is a big win for us. Selling real estate for top dollar in New York City takes hard work, but I work with the best and only sell high-quality property.

After McMann leaves, Liam and I slap hands.

"Dude, I thought we lost him for a minute there," Liam says and swipes a hand through his dark blond hair.

"Nah., we had him the whole time," I say, completely confident.

"Carter-Thompson all the way," he says, and we bump knuckles.

"What do you think? Celebrate with some Macallan down at Sloans?"

"Fuck yeah," Liam says.

The Scottish pub isn't too far away and I'm ready to savor a glass or two of high-priced whisky. The older, the better. As we make our way to the elevator, I start thinking back to when we started C.T. International. It was nearly five years ago, straight out of college, and I wasn't in a very good place. My girlfriend had just cheated on me, and I lost the only woman I was ever really interested in.

Too bad she wasn't the same person.

Fuck. I pinch the bridge of my nose as the elevator zooms down. I don't like thinking about what an idiot I was back then. I made a huge mistake by choosing the wrong girl to date because I was blinded by her charm.

But my heart always belonged to her best friend.

Enough, I tell myself. I'm celebrating tonight. Not crying over stupid decisions I made seven years ago.

When the elevator stops and the door opens, we step out and head toward the parking garage. Several people walk through the marble-floored lobby and I'm not paying too much attention until I see *her.*

I stop dead in my tracks, stunned. It can't be Elle. But it looks just fucking like her. Long brown hair the same shade I remember with pretty caramel highlights. Tall, slim and curves in all the right places. Christ, I've dreamed about those curves, and in the waking world, my hands have itched to explore each one thoroughly.

Only in my dreams, though. In real life, I was too stupid and intimidated to go after her. So, I settled for her best friend instead.

Liam stops when he realizes I'm not walking beside him anymore and glances over his shoulder. "What's up?" He tracks my gaze over to the brunette and his mouth curves up. "See something you like?"

I ignore him, gaze caught on the woman who resembles the one who always made my heart beat a little quicker and harder. Her profile is a dead ringer for Elle, and I force myself to move closer. *Could it be?* She's talking to another woman, and they laugh. When she turns and looks my way, disappointment floods through me. *No, it's not my Elle.*

When she smiles at me, I nod coolly and keep walking. Catching back up with Liam, he shakes his head. "Why didn't you talk to her?"

I shrug a shoulder.

"She was pretty, and she smiled at you, dumbass."

"I don't have time for that," I say as we step outside and a brisk wind whip past us. It's much easier to stay parked here and walk down to the bar. Parking in lower Manhattan isn't ideal and moving my car two blocks is hardly worth the hassle.

"There's always time to get laid, pal," Liam says and punches my arm.

"I have no problems getting laid," I say with a frown. Sure, it's been a while, but if I wanted sex, I could get it. Lately, I just haven't wanted it. Or, more truthfully, I just haven't wanted to be bothered with the drama of a flesh and blood woman.

When we reach Sloans, the place is pretty quiet because it's still early. The interior resembles an authentic Scottish pub with low ceilings, snug lighting and a well-stocked bar. Wood paneling, a fireplace and stained-glass windows make up some of the details that give it a unique flair.

Liam and I sit down in a couple of overstuffed chairs near the fireplace where low flames crackle. We buy a couple glasses of 25-year-old Macallan Scotch and sip it slowly. It hits the exact right spot. *Better than sex,* I think.

I work hard but I also make sure to play hard, too. Sitting behind a desk all day isn't for me and, although I work constantly, I haven't let myself become a workaholic. Traveling, exercising, eating good food and drinking excellent alcohol are all an important part of my life. You're only young once and I like to experience things.

"She looked a lot like Elle, huh?" Liam says out of the blue.

"What?" My head snaps in his direction.

"The woman in the lobby." When I don't say anything, he takes a drink. "I don't think you ever really got over Elle Landon."

Liam couldn't be more right. No point in denying it. "She's the one who got away," I say and swirl the amber liquid in my glass.

"Whatever happened to her after graduation?"

"I have no idea. After Chloe and I broke up, we all went our separate ways."

"Man, how could you be with Chloe for almost two years and be lusting after her best friend the whole time?"

"That's not how it was," I say in an annoyed voice. "We were friends."

"Friends with benefits?"

"I never touched Elle." I let out a sigh. "You know I met her first, though, and I wanted to pursue something with her. But the moment Chloe stepped in, Elle pulled away. She completely friend-zoned me, so what was I supposed to do?"

"Did you ever love Chloe?"

I consider his question and frown. "No. That's a really strong word and Chloe was a lot to handle. Beyond high-maintenance and exhausting 90 percent of the time. I'm not sure how someone so quiet and sweet as Elle put up with her."

"You must've liked something about her."

"Well, sure. She was outgoing and fun. Chloe had a charm and vibrance about her. You know that."

"That's how she pulls people in, but once you get to know her better…man, there was a lot of drama."

"I was like 21. What the hell did I know?"

"I can't believe it's been almost five years since graduation. I just got an email about the reunion coming up," Liam adds smoothly and eyes me over the rim of his glass. "What do you think? Should we go?"

The idea of possibly seeing Elle again makes my heart rate increase. However, I have no interest in seeing Chloe. "I haven't really given it much thought." *Okay, so that's a lie*. Ever since I got the invitation I've been going back and forth, trying to decide whether or not to go.

"It could be fun. Spend the weekend in Boston, catch a Bruins game and maybe you'll see your girl."

I'm not sure what I would do or say if I saw Elle Landon again. Then it occurs to me that she could be engaged or married. My stomach curls sourly at the thought. "And when she brings her husband?"

"You think she's married?"

"I wouldn't be surprised. Elle was a damn catch."

"Or what if she's single, lonely and has been pining for you the past five years?"

"Doubtful," I say. *Although wouldn't that be nice?* "If she liked me, she wouldn't have let Chloe just sweep in and take over."

"Hmm," Liam murmurs.

I cock my head. "What's that supposed to mean?"

"Elle always let Chloe do exactly that. She was always submissive to her. Like her damn lapdog or something."

"Elle wasn't a lapdog," I say, my voice rising. My fingers tighten around the glass, and I force myself to relax. *Shit.* I'm still over-protective of her even after all these years. "She was just too loyal, and Chloe didn't deserve it."

When I think back over all the times Elle stuck up for Chloe, it's almost sad. But only because Chloe never appreciated it. No friend was ever more loyal or true than Elle was to Chloe. She should've thanked her lucky stars for Elle but, with hindsight, I know now how much she took advantage of Elle's kindness. It pisses me off. I should've said something, but I never did.

I didn't stand up for Elle and it's another regret I have regarding her. If only I could go back in time…

"Chloe isn't feeling well," Elle says.

I roll my eyes. How ironic since she seemed absolutely fine when we spoke earlier. "Great. So I wasted money on her ticket."

"Well, she suggested I go with you," Elle says carefully. "I mean, so it doesn't go to waste. Unless you want to bring someone else, of course. I totally get that."

Suddenly this is turning into a very good situation. "No, I'd like it if you came with me."

When Elle smiles, it's like the sun breaking through the clouds. I put all thoughts of Chloe from my mind and focus on Elle.

"But only if you want to. I kinda remember you saying something about not liking baseball."

"I've never been to Fenway. I think it would be fun."

"Great," I say, far more enthusiastic to be going with Elle than my own

girlfriend. If that's not a huge red flag, then I don't know what is. Jesus. I have to be the world's worst boyfriend.

I've been thinking a lot about my relationship with Chloe lately and how unhappy I am. We barely see each other and when we finally make plans, she cancels. The truth is, I don't miss her. I miss Elle. Because that's the only time I see her anymore– when she comes around with Chloe. Christ, we're a dysfunctional group.

Elle and I end up going to the Red Sox game together and it will always go down as one of my favorite days. We have so much fun and get along so well. And then there's the chemistry. It's off the fucking charts, but there's nothing either of us can do about it. It's undeniable, though. Every time we accidentally touch, or our eyes meet, there's this insane electricity.

By the end of the game, we're both well on our way to being drunk. I can't believe how much we've talked about over the last few hours, and we have so much in common. Every time I look at Elle, I smile and my heart trips in my chest. I don't think I've ever laughed so hard or had such a great time with someone before. I don't want the day to end, and I suggest we grab something to eat.

Elle agrees and we cross Lansdowne Street and find a place with burgers and fries. Almost two hours later, we're laughing so hard that tears are streaming from our eyes. I've never clicked like this with anybody. Unfortunately, my phone rings and I see Chloe's name on the caller ID.

The mood instantly subdues, and I look up at Elle. God knows, I don't want to answer it, but Elle nods her head. I guess we both know that if I ignore it then Chloe will just keep calling.

"Hi, Chloe," I say.

"Where are you?" she immediately asks.

"Umm..." I look around and then burst into laughter. I have no idea.

"What's so funny?" Chloe snaps.

"Where are we?" I ask Elle and her shoulders shake with mirth.

"I don't remember," she says, and we both start laughing again.

"You're still with Elle?"

I can hear the suspicion in her voice. "Uh, yeah. We grabbed something to eat after the game."

"Well, don't you think it's time you left? I want to see you," she adds in a whiny voice.

"I thought you were sick," I say.

"I'm feeling much better."

"That's good." I'd be willing to bet my last dollar that Chloe has been fine all day but found something better she wanted to do.

"So, drop Elle off at her place and come over."

My gaze locks on Elle and I wish I'd be going home with her tonight. "Yeah, we're leaving in a bit, but I'm tired, Chloe. I'll see you some other time."

After hanging up, I know that I need to break it off with her. The only problem is if I do that, then what will happen with Elle? Will she think I'm a huge jerk and take Chloe's side?

Of course, she will.

I sigh and finish my beer. The fun atmosphere is gone as though someone just sucked all of the happiness right out of the room. "Are you ready to head out?" I ask.

"Sure," Elle says.

I later found out that Chloe hates baseball and never had any intention of going to the game with me. Instead, she was hanging out with some other guy she'd recently met while we were at the game. The one she ended up cheating on me with right before graduation.

Whatever. It was such a long time ago and we were just kids. As I finish my glass of Macallan's, I gaze into the crackling fire and debate whether or not I should go to the reunion.

Because if there's one regret I have, it's not pursuing Elle. She slipped right through my fingers, and I stupidly began dating Chloe. *Moron,* I think.

But, what if? What if Elle goes to our reunion? What if she's single? What if I'm given a second chance?

The reward would definitely be worth the risk.

3

ELLE

When Monday morning arrives, the strangest feeling fills me. Of course, I'm nervous because I'm starting a new job, but it's more than that. There's this unexplainable fluttering in my belly. Like I'm about to do something daring. This is how I felt before I went ziplining a couple of years ago.

I guess I'll just chalk it up to the excitement of finally figuring out what I want to do with my life and knowing that my official career starts today. It took me some time to figure it out, but I finally did, and now it's time to jump in and test the waters.

Right as I'm about to leave my apartment, my phone rings and I glance down to see it's my mom. "Hey, Mom," I answer, locking my apartment door behind me.

"I'm so glad I caught you. I had to call and wish you good luck on your first day."

"Thanks. I'm actually heading down to the subway right now."

"Call me tonight and let me know how it goes," she says.

"I will," I promise and start down the stairs. "Gotta go or I'll be late."

"Okay, honey. Love you."

"Love you, too."

My mom is super supportive of everything I do and it means a lot that she called. We've always been close and, even though I live in the city, it's nice to know that she and my dad are only 40 minutes or so away. I like to go home and visit whenever I can, especially in the summer. We have poolside barbecues, light up the firepit at night and gather around it to talk and drink a couple of wine coolers.

I don't have any siblings so the three of us have always been extremely close. Maybe too close. Sometimes they can be a little too nosey and, in my business, but I know it's only because they mean well. Since I'm their only child, they tend to be overprotective. But the good thing is that they allow me to make my own choices and live my life. When I wanted to go to Boston College, they supported my decision to leave New York and paid the tuition. And when I packed my stuff up and announced that Chloe and I wanted to move into the city, they helped load our belongings up and drove us here.

When I first decided to move here, it was a decision I made all by myself. Probably the first time in my life that I only thought about myself and what I wanted. I didn't take Chloe into consideration. Truthfully, as bad as it sounds, I kind of wanted some separation. After she cheated on Gray, I think I felt worse about it than she did. Frankly, I don't think she cared and, as far as I know, she never apologized to him.

The moment I decided to put some distance between us, Chloe announced that she was moving with me. It's a big city and I didn't know anyone, so I convinced myself that it was a good thing. But I suggested we each get our own place. She threw a fit at first so I had to talk her down and remind her that she couldn't exactly bring her boyfriend over with me living there, too.

She agreed.

So here we are living in NYC together, yet separately, and it's worked well. For the most part. She's still floundering with what she wants to do and has probably worked 15 different jobs since we moved here four years ago. I think she's gone through that many boyfriends, too.

I shake my head, pushing Chloe and her drama out of my mind, and step off the subway. After walking down to the large building where I'm going to start working, I pause and look up. It's huge, well over 70 floors, and a wave of nervousness crashes through me.

Here goes nothing, I think, and push through the revolving glass doors.

C.T. International is located on floor 22 and I head straight down to the Human Resources Department where Laura, the HR Director, greets me.

"So nice to see you, Elle. We're excited to have you join the team."

"Thank you."

"C'mon, let's get you started on some paperwork and then I'll introduce you to everyone."

There's a lot to fill out and a couple of videos to watch. Typical first-day, orientation stuff. Once I'm done with the basics, Laura takes me on a tour through the office. It's big and modern with lots of light and open spaces where the employees work. I can't explain it, but right away, I feel completely comfortable.

As we walk around the corner, Laura introduces me to a few people, and everyone seems so welcoming and friendly. I have a really good feeling about working here.

"Oh, and here's one of the bosses now," Laura says and chuckles as a tall, dark-haired man walks out of the kitchen with a donut hanging out of his mouth and a mug of coffee in his hand. "Elle this is Gray Carter."

My heart drops down into my stomach as our gazes meet. Gray pulls the donut from between his lips and chokes. For a long moment, neither of us says anything. Then we both start talking at the same time.

"I had no idea-"

"Elle, I can't believe-"

Laura looks from Gray to me and then back to him. "You two know each other?"

"We went to college together," Gray says. "It's been what?"

"Almost five years," I manage to say, trying to wrap my mind around the fact that Gray Carter is standing in front of me. That Gray Carter is now my boss. I'm in complete shock and having trouble forming a complete sentence.

"It's so nice to see you, Elle," Gray says, voice low.

His silver-blue eyes draw me in just like they always used to do. *Pull yourself together,* I tell myself. I let out a breath and smile. "You, too. How have you been?"

"Busy," he says. "Liam and I started this place not long after graduating. It's been a lot of hard work but we're doing well."

"C.T.... Carter-Thompson," I say and shake my head. *God, I'm such a dumbass.* If I had done better research on the company, I would've found out Gray and Liam owned it. But I had sent out so many resumes and didn't do my due diligence like I normally do. "I just put that together."

Gray smiles and it's just as dazzling as I remember. "Laura, do you mind if I steal Elle?"

"Um, no."

I can hear the surprise in her voice and I'm a little embarrassed. The last thing I want is for everyone to hate me because I've got an in with the boss. Or, worse, what if they all assume we used to date.

"Great. I can finish giving her the tour and then I'll bring her back."

I give Laura a weak smile and Gray nods for me to follow him.

"Do you want any coffee? A donut?" he asks.

"I'm fine, thanks." I look up at his attractive profile and butterflies take flight in my stomach. Even though it's been years, Gray still has this crazy effect on me. He possesses a more mature look now and he's even hotter than he used to be. His cheekbones are more prominent and he's slimmer yet more muscular at the same time. It's clear by the way his jacket pulls that he works out. I lick my lips and imagine what he looks like under his clothes.

"We keep the kitchen stocked so don't be shy. Help yourself."

"Thanks," I say. He looks so handsome in his navy-blue suit. Almost elegant. As we walk through the office, it occurs to me that he's incredibly successful and must have millions of dollars. "So, you decided not to work for your dad?"

Gray's father owns a very successful financial services company in Newport, Rhode Island, where he's from. His parents still live there in a beautiful seaside home up on a cliff. Or so Chloe told me. I've never actually been there. I always figured he'd go work for his father after graduation.

"I briefly considered it but knew that I wanted to strike out on my own. Real estate and New York City kept calling my name, so Liam and I made the jump a few months after college."

"Congratulations," I tell him. "This place is amazing and I'm so embarrassed that I didn't know you owned it."

"How would you? We lost touch."

"Right."

"I regret that, though," Gray says.

He stops walking and I pause, looking up into his gorgeous metallic eyes.

"Don't you have any regrets?" I ask Chloe, my voice rising in angry disbelief.

"No," she says. "Because you know what, Elle? He's not a very good boyfriend. I need attention and love. Gray is cold and stand-offish. He's never affectionate and I swear, half the time it's like he's thinking about someone else. And we never have sex."

Oh, God. My stomach clenches. I don't want to hear or think about the man I have a massive crush on and my best friend in bed. It makes me physically ill. "Chloe-"

"It's true. It's like he's asexual or something. Why do you think I turned to Jarrod? Gray practically pushed me into his arms."

A part of me is happy to hear they aren't or at least haven't been intimate in a long time. It's hard when you're jealous of your best friend and wishing her boyfriend was yours. But Gray is such an amazing man, and I would die to have what Chloe has and she's throwing it all away.

I feel caught in the middle and I know it's none of my business, but Chloe needs to break it off with Gray. "When are you going to tell him?"

"Ugh, I don't know. It's not like I'm looking forward to breaking his heart."

"You're sleeping with someone else, Chloe. You need to let Gray go."

"You make it sound like it's all my fault," she says in a pouty voice.

Unbelievable. "It's certainly not Gray's fault."

"It kind of is, though. He practically pushed me into another man's arms because he was never there for me. What was I supposed to do?"

I'm starting to feel sick. We're in our caps and gowns, ready to walk across the stage and accept our diploma. But, once again, Chloe has turned the tables and made everything about her. And this time, she's going to not only ruin graduation day, but also hurt Gray.

Chloe lets out a huge sigh and flicks her tassel aside. "Maybe I should do it now. Get it over with so I don't have to worry about it anymore."

"Now? Why don't you wait until after the ceremony?"

"No, you're right. I should just rip the band aid off. I'm tired of stressing over this and I don't want to think about Gray Carter ever again."

"Chloe, I didn't mean now-"

She starts walking away and I can't believe she's going to confront Gray right before we're about to graduate. Chloe abruptly stops and turns. "You're coming with me to Jarrod's party tonight, right?"

My plan had been to go to Gray and Liam's party. "Um-"

"Great. Because I'm going to need my best friend by my side."

My shoulders sag as she heads away to find Gray. I know he's going to be upset but a part of me also thinks he'll be a little relieved. In my humble opinion, Gray and Chloe were never a good match and I'm surprised they lasted as long as they did. They never spent much time together alone and when I think about it, when they were together, I was with them.

It was always the three of us.

The moment I would leave, Gray would say he had to leave, too. He'd always walk me to my car or back home while Chloe would usually stay out and keep partying. I never thought too much of it until now. Maybe Gray and I were closer than I ever realized.

"Me, too," I say, feeling the pull of his silvery-blue gaze. "Regret losing touch, I mean."

Hell, I regret a lot when it comes to Gray. Mostly, though, I regret never letting him know how much I liked him.

"Are you seeing anyone?" he asks, completely out of the blue.

His question throws me and my stomach somersaults. "No," I answer a little breathlessly.

Oh, my God. Why in the world does Gray want to know that? *Unless...*

Unless he's interested in me.

4

GRAY

Relief floods through me. No boyfriend, no fiancé, no husband. *Thank God.*

I fucked up with Elle before but not this time. I plan on making things up to her. To us. And no one is going to get in our way.

"Would you like to have dinner with me tonight?" I ask her, wasting no time. I've wasted far too much already and this time around, I'm not going to make the same mistake twice.

I'm going after her, guns blazing.

When she hesitates, it's like a knife pierce through my heart. *Shit.* Maybe I misread the situation. It's presumptuous to think she's even given me a second thought since graduation. "To catch up," I clarify, trying to ease her reluctance. "Like you said– it's been a while."

"I'd love to, but is that okay?"

"What do you mean?"

"Technically, you're my boss now. I don't want anyone to think-"

"I am the boss which means I can do whatever I want. And I don't care what anyone thinks." I look into her pretty brown eyes and my mouth edges up. "I'd like to take you to dinner."

Elle nods. "That would be nice," she says, her face flushing.

Maybe I'm crazy or imagining things, but I swear that same spark is there between us and it feels stronger than before, if that's even possible. This time around, however, I'm not letting anything get between us and I want to explore our connection further.

"Well, I promised you a tour, so c'mon. I'll show you around."

C.T. International takes up the entire 22nd floor and I point out the different departments and introduce Elle proudly. I inform everyone how we attended Boston College together and used to go to keg parties and football games. It's almost like she's my girlfriend, not my newest employee.

Aww, fuck. I hope her working for me doesn't make things weird. *Otherwise, I'll have to fire her.* Because letting Elle walk away for a second time isn't an option. As we walk around, getting reacquainted, the conversation between us flows easily and any lingering awkwardness fades fast.

I can't stop looking at her and soaking up everything about her. That familiar tone of her voice, those sparkling brown eyes and when she throws her head back and laughs at something I say, it makes my universe tilt. Elle makes everything brighter and more alive.

We walk outside onto the patio connected to my office, and she oohs and ahhs over the view. I step up beside her and when she turns her head, I get a noseful of her soft perfume. Vanilla and flowers. My groin tightens and all I want to do is drag her into my arms and kiss her senseless.

Kissing Elle is something I've imagined countless times. My gaze dips to her glossy lips, so full and plump. Ripe for kissing. I've only tasted her in my dreams, but now there's the very real possibility that it could actually happen.

I have no idea how I'm going to make it through the rest of the day.

"Well, I'll be damned," Liam says, walking up behind us. "If it isn't Elle Landon. Bring it in."

Liam pulls her into a hug and my cheek muscle twitches. I didn't even hug her and now I'm wishing I did.

Elle smiles. "Hi, Liam. How are you?"

"I'm great," he says and grins at me. "I hear you're our newest employee."

She nods. "Gray was just showing me around."

"Oh, I bet he was."

I want to punch that smirk off Liam's face. He's highly amused by the situation and I try not to look annoyed.

"So, you two are catching up?" Liam asks.

"We're going to do that tonight," I say. "At dinner."

Liam's brows shoot up and then he nods. "Glad to hear it and welcome to the team, Elle."

"Don't you have that contract to review?" I ask, wanting to get rid of Liam before he reveals too much.

"Right. Sure do." He slaps me on the back. "Have fun tonight," he adds in a sly voice before wandering off.

"He hasn't changed," Elle says with a chuckle.

"Nope. Still the same ol' pain in the ass."

"But you love him."

"Yeah, well, somebody's gotta do it."

Eventually, I have to give Elle back to Laura, but I'm counting down the seconds until 5pm. I can't concentrate on work and Liam comes into my office and gives me so much crap, it's ridiculous.

"It's fucking kismet," he tells me. "What the hell are the chances that Elle would show up and start working here? I'll tell you– slim to none. I've never believed in Fate or Destiny, but I always believed in you two. If you don't make this work, I'm going to swoop in and steal her away."

"The fuck you are," I say, eyes narrowing.

"Chill. I'm just yanking your chain. I'd never move in on your girl."

I trust Liam implicitly so I'm hardly worried that he'd make a move on Elle. What worries me, though, is what's going to happen when I do. Will she reject me? Maybe she'll think it's weird after all this time. I'm trying not to get in my head about the situation, but it's hard.

"Where are you taking her to dinner?" Liam asks, sitting on the edge of my desk.

"Simone's."

"Fancy. What's your plan? Please tell me you're going to make a move."

"Yeah, I mean, I want to. I'm going to. I just hope she doesn't get scared off or freak out."

"Did she mention Chloe?"

I shake my head. "No."

"Maybe they aren't friends anymore."

"Guess I'll find out tonight."

"Dude, I'm so pumped for you. Everything is going to turn out nicely. Don't worry."

But when 5pm rolls around, I'm sweating bullets. The idea that Elle might not be romantically interested in me is like a weight on my chest and just the thought makes it hard to breathe. I go into my private bathroom and stare at my reflection in the mirror.

"You've got this," I tell myself and straighten my tie.

No woman has ever made me nervous before, but Elle is on a whole different level. She's always been the one. *Always.* I scrub a hand over my jaw and wonder if I should shave quickly. *Nah.* I definitely have a five o'clock shadow, but I'll leave the faint stubble. If I'm lucky, she'll like it.

I glance down at my watch for the thousandth time and then button my jacket. After running my fingers through my dark hair, I turn around and head out. Elle and I planned to meet down in the lobby at 5:15pm. I may not give a shit about what anyone thinks about the two of us leaving together, but it's her first day and I don't want any gossip to start that could possibly hurt her.

As the elevator zooms down, I pop a mint and can't wait to get Elle all alone and to myself. I have plans for her and I'm dying to see if we can finally move past the friend-zone.

I'm a few minutes early and I walk over by the large revolving door to wait for her. The moment she steps out of the elevator, my heart kicks up a notch and I feel like a smitten schoolboy. She heads right over to me, a smile lighting up her gorgeous face.

"How'd your first day go?" I ask.

"Really well," she says. "Everyone has been super nice and helpful."

"Good." I motion for her to go ahead of me, and we exit through the spinning glass door. The cool air hits my face, and it feels refreshing. "If anyone gives you any trouble, let me know."

She looks up at me, dark eyes dancing. "Will you fire them?"

"Yes," I respond instantly. She laughs, but I'm not joking. If anyone gives my Elle a hard time, I'll kick their ass to the curb without blinking.

"Where are we going?" she asks.

"Simone's. Have you ever been there?"

Her eyes widen. "The place where all the celebrities go? No. But I've heard it's delicious."

"It is," I assure her. Maybe I'm showing off a little by taking her to the hottest restaurant in the city, but so what? Somehow, after five long years, we've found our way back to each other and that's a cause for celebration.

The trendy place is packed when we get there, but I reserved a table in the back area where it's more intimate and quieter. After sitting down, I ask her if she likes wine.

"White wine," she says. "I've just started getting into wine, so I like the sweeter stuff."

I order her a glass of Riesling and myself a full-bodied Cabernet Sauvignon.

"I'm still trying to find a red wine that I like," she says.

"I'll help you. There are a lot to choose from, but some are definitely on the sweeter side."

"This place is so nice," she murmurs and takes a delicate sip of her wine, looking around at the decor.

My eyes lock on her lips and when she flicks her tongue out and licks away a drop of wine, my dick surges against my zipper. I clear my throat and try not to think about how much I want to get her in my bed. It's so hard to keep my thoughts clean, though.

Elle Landon cast a spell on me a long time ago. One I've never been able to break.

"So, how long have you lived in the city?" I ask, and adjust the way I'm sitting, trying to get comfortable.

"Almost four years. I have a little apartment in the Village."

"And you live there by yourself?" Maybe I'm being too obvious, but I don't give a shit. I'm done playing games with this woman and ready to lay it all out on the line.

She nods. "What about you? Do you live in some big, fancy place?"

"I have a loft not far away from here. It's nothing exceptional, but I like it. It's cozy."

"Are your parents still in Newport?"

"They are and they're doing well."

"I was so surprised to see you earlier. I really always thought you'd end up working with your dad."

"I briefly considered it, but finance isn't for me. I much prefer real estate. How's your family?" I only ask out of politeness because her parents never cared for me.

"They're good. Still living in Fairview."

I've put off asking about Chloe long enough and decide to just get it over with so I can gauge Elle's reaction. Try to figure out if I've got a shot in hell with her or if she wouldn't be interested in dating her friend's ex. "Do you still talk to Chloe?"

Elle nods slowly. "Every day. Which, I'm sure you know, can be a little much."

My mouth edges up. "I take it that means she hasn't changed much?"

"She may have gotten worse," Elle says and we both chuckle. "You know, I always felt terrible about what happened. Our graduation was supposed to be fun. But the way Chloe behaved and how she treated you was...very upsetting."

"It wasn't your fault." I take a sip of wine and it's interesting that Elle looks more upset now than Chloe ever did. "Can I tell you something?"

Elle nods, brown eyes shining in the candlelight.

"Our relationship, if that's what you can even call it, was over long before that—because I had feelings for someone else."

I lock gazes with Elle, and she swallows hard. "You did?"

When she doesn't ask, I set my glass down. "For you, Elle. It was always you."

5

ELLE

The moment Gray confesses his former feelings, I want to jump across the table and kiss him. But then I remember he's telling me how he used to feel. It's been a long time since we've seen each other and, for all I know, he could have someone special in his life.

I am desperate to know his current situation and blurt out, "Are you dating anyone? Right now?"

"No," he says and smiles. "But I was kind of hoping that maybe you and I could spend some more time together."

"I'd love that," I say, heart thumping so hard that it feels like it's going to burst out of my chest.

A part of me is shocked that he wants to see me and that he always liked me. But, deep down, I always knew. There's this crazy, magnetic chemistry between us and it was impossible for me to ignore. But because Gray was with Chloe, I had to do my best to pretend it didn't exist.

But now, I don't have to do that anymore. We're both two single adults and I've spent the past seven years wondering what it would be like to kiss this man. Tonight, I intend to find out.

"Good," Gray says. "Because I want to know everything about you, Elle. We have to make up for lost time."

For a moment, I toy with the edge of my napkin. There's something I need to know, but I'm scared to ask. *Ahh, hell with it.* We've lost enough time and I need to be bold. "Can I ask you something?"

"Anything."

"Did you love Chloe?"

"No," he answers immediately. "I was young, stupid and went with the wrong girl because I didn't think you were interested. Because trust me, Elle, you were always my first choice."

His words make my heart soar. "I was?"

"The night we met, I thought it was going to be you and me. But the minute Chloe turned up, you backed off. I never understood why. We had such a great connection and then you just friend-zoned me."

Is that what he thinks? "I liked you so much and then Chloe told me that you were the guy in her class that she'd been crushing on. She saw you first and I respected that even though it killed me."

Gray shakes his head. "I can't believe this. All that time, I thought..." He lets out a frustrated sound.

"I always liked you, Gray. Way more than I should have, but I let Chloe claim you and it's my biggest regret."

"I wish I'd known. Fuck, Elle." He scrapes a hand through his dark hair.

Neither of us says anything and it's suddenly clear that we're both on the same page and, for the first time, we know it. "I don't think we should dwell on the past. Just embrace the present."

"I can get onboard with that," Gray says. "Although, our 5-year reunion is coming up."

"I know. Are you going?"

"I don't know. Truthfully, the only reason I was thinking about going is because I was hoping you'd be there."

Warmth pools low in my belly. "Same."

The rest of dinner is amazing, and we spend the next two hours eating, drinking and talking. This is the first time we've been able to open up to each other without the fear of crossing that line. And right now, I am beyond ready to leap past it. Gray is everything I have always wanted, and I feel my inhibitions slipping away with each sip of wine and each sizzling smile he sends my way.

After sharing a dessert, Gray pays the bill which must be outrageous, and I thank him.

"I can give you something-" I begin to say, reaching for my purse, but he cuts me off.

"Absolutely not. Do you know how long I've wanted to take you out to dinner? It's an honor."

I don't know about that, but I appreciate it. After walking out, we stand on the sidewalk and I'm not sure what to do or say. I'm not ready for the night to end.

"Would you like to come back to my place for a drink?"

A smile curves my mouth. "I was just thinking it's still early and I didn't want to say goodnight yet."

"My place is only a couple of blocks away."

"Let's walk. It's nice out tonight." We head up the sidewalk and when Gray reaches for my hand, butterflies take flight in my stomach. His hand is large and warm and feeling it wrapped around mine is heaven.

Suddenly, I feel like the luckiest girl in the world.

The cozy loft where Gray lives turn out to be a beautiful apartment and my mouth drops open as I look around. It's masculine with tall ceilings and dark wood beams. There's a large leather couch, artwork on the walls and a spiral staircase that leads up to his bedroom perched above. One whole right side is floor-to-ceiling windows that look out over the city. The view is spectacular.

"Gray, this place is amazing." I can't help but admire the way it's decorated, too. He has good taste– classic and refined, yet modern.

"I like it," he says modestly, shrugging his suit jacket off. He walks over to a built-in wine bar, loosening his tie, and pulls a bottle out. "I've been saving this for a special occasion."

I tilt my head and toss him a flirty smile. "I'm a special occasion?"

"Yes, Elle, you certainly are." He removes the cork, pours us each a glass and hands me one.

"I feel like we should do a toast."

His mouth edges up and I can't look away from his lips. "Go ahead."

I think for a moment then lift my glass. "To second chances."

Gray's silvery eyes darken, and he taps his glass against mine. "And to whatever the future may hold."

We each take a sip and the electricity between us crackles. I am dying to kiss him, and I think the feeling is mutual. The moment I set my glass down, Gray is doing the same, and then he's right there, so close, and pulling me into his arms. He smells so good, a little woody with a hint of spice, and he briefly presses his forehead against mine, almost as if he's savoring the moment. Then, his head lowers, and he captures my mouth in the kiss that I've waited seven years to receive.

Yesss. Finally.

And, oh wow, it doesn't disappoint. Gray's lips move over mine, soft and warm, and I melt into him. My arms circle his neck and, the moment I feel the slide of his tongue against mine, desire flares hot and bright. The taste of chocolate mousse and tangy raspberries lingers from our shared dessert, and I open my mouth wider, on the verge of devouring him.

No one has ever kissed me like this before. An urgency is building up inside of me and I'm not sure how to handle it. I've never been intimate with a man before, but a fierce need overwhelms me, and I push myself closer.

Gray slides a hand through my loose hair and cups the back of my neck, holding me exactly how he wants, deepening the kiss. It's clear he's in control and knows exactly what he's doing. His other hand trails down my back and curves around my rear-end, lightly squeezing and drawing me tighter against him. There's no mistaking the hard evidence of his desire and he feels much larger than I would've guessed.

My nerves kick up and I'm not sure what to do. On the one hand, we've known each other forever. On the other hand, I barely know him at all anymore and he's my best friend's ex. Guilt threatens to ruin the moment and I try to push past it, but he must feel me tense up or something because he pulls back and looks at me.

"What's wrong?" he asks, voice husky. He tucks a strand of hair behind my ear and his metallic eyes search mine.

"Nothing," I say and slide my fingers through the hair at the edge of his collar. "This is all just happening so fast."

"Fast?" he asks, voice laced with disbelief. "Baby, I've wanted to kiss you for almost seven years. This has been the slowest-moving relationship I've ever had."

"No, I-I know. It's just..." I frown.

"Talk to me, Elle."

"I know it's silly, but a little part of me feels guilty." I drag my hand around, down his firm chest and nervously play with his tie.

"Because of Chloe?"

I nod, wishing I knew what he was thinking.

He lets out a sigh. "Elle, dating Chloe was a mistake. I wanted you from the moment I saw you. But I was young and stupid and I didn't think you liked me that way. Being with Chloe was a way to be able to spend more time with you." He picks up a lock of my hair, rubbing it between his thumb and forefinger. "I was a terrible boyfriend. Dating one friend and lusting after the other." He shakes his head. "I'm sorry. And I really want to make it up to you. If you'll let me."

"You lusted after me?"

"Still do," he says in a low, sexy voice.

His confession leaves me fumbling for words and I focus on his tie. *Dig deep and be brave,* I tell myself. *Let him know how you're feeling. This is not the time to pull back or be shy.* "I wish I would've had more self-confidence back then. That I would've been able to stand up for myself. Because I wanted you all along, too, and knowing you were with my best friend hurt. Sometimes it hurt so much that I cried myself to sleep."

"Oh, baby," he murmurs and pulls me into his arms. "It's you and me now, okay? Just the two of us. We shouldn't feel guilty about how we feel. How we've always felt."

Maybe he's right, I think. Still, I can't help but wonder how Chloe would react if she found any of this out. But no. She had her chance with Gray and she blew it. Now it's my turn and I should go for it.

"We have a lot of time to make up for it," I say.

"So, what are we waiting for?" he asks and then scoops me into his arms. With a squeal, I wrap my arms around his neck as he walks over to the couch and drops down, sitting me on his lap.

His mouth meets mine and this kiss is different. It's possessive and seductive. He traces his tongue along my bottom lip and grabs hold of my hips, urging me to straddle him. I move around, placing a thigh on either side of his legs. When I glance down, I can see his massive erection straining against his pants.

As excited as I am to finally be in this position with Gray, it's also a little nerve-wracking. While most women would probably reach for his belt and start pawing at his junk at this point, I'm so reserved. And nervous.

I'm nervous as hell.

Gray's soft lips lower to my neck, and I let my head drop to the side as his tongue and teeth explore the delicate skin there. I'm breathing hard and when he nips, a whimper escapes me.

I know I should tell him that I've never done this before, but I don't want him to judge me. Or worse, my confession could destroy the mood.

But when he sucks an earlobe into his mouth and whispers, "Stay the night with me, Elle," I know I have to let him know.

"Um, Gray?" I try not to sigh with pleasure as he kisses up my jawline.

"What, baby?"

"I need to tell you something."

He pulls back and looks into my eyes. "Okay," he says slowly and runs a hand through my hair.

"I sort of, um, have never done this."

"Done what?" he asks, brow furrowing in confusion.

"Spent the night with a man." I swallow hard. "You'd be my first."

I have no idea how he's going to respond, and I chew on my lower lip nervously.

6

GRAY

Disbelief floods me and it's quickly replaced by elation. *My sweet Elle is a virgin?* I pull back and look into her brown eyes. She quickly averts her gaze, but I snag her chin and force her to look at me. "You've never been intimate with a man?" I ask, needing complete clarification.

"No," she whispers. "I hope it doesn't change the way you feel."

Is she kidding me? "Fuck, Elle, it makes me want you more. If that's even possible." A blush stains her cheeks and it's damn adorable. "I'm sure a lot of men must have tried so why did you wait?"

"Because none of them were you," she simply says.

I didn't think she could have my heart more but the moment she says that, I'm done for.

"No one measured up to you, Gray. Not even close."

Her words touch a part of me that no woman has ever been able to reach before. "Do you have any idea how much I want you?" I trace my finger along her jaw and tuck a strand of hair behind her ear. "But I don't want to rush anything. As much as I'd love to tear your clothes off right now, if we're going to sleep together, I want to make it special for you. Assuming you want that, too?"

"Oh, yes," she declares and slides her arms back up and around my neck.

I chuckle at her enthusiasm. "I'll make it worth the wait," I promise and brush my lips across hers. She's still straddling me, and I begin dropping kisses all over her face. Between the kisses, I start telling her all the things I plan to do to her. "I'm going to worship every lovely inch of your naked body. From your forehead down to your toes. And I'm going to spend an extra long time here..."

My hand slides over her soft, full breast and I lightly squeeze, fingers pebbling the nipple. "I'm going to suck and lick until you're panting. Is that okay?"

"Mmm-hmm," she moans, pressing into my palm.

"Then I'm going to kiss my way down to your navel." I slide my hand beneath the edge of her shirt, circle my finger around her belly button and dip it in the crevice.

"Yes," she murmurs.

"And do you know what I'm going to do after that?"

"What?" she asks, voice breathy.

"I'm going to spread your legs..." I push her thighs further apart and move my hand beneath her skirt, covering her core. "And dip my head between them...and lick up your sweet pussy. I'm going to make you scream my name. I promise you're going to come so hard on my face that you see stars."

She shivers in my arms. "So wicked," she whispers.

When I start massaging my fingers over her satin panties, Elle begins breathing harder, her nails digging into my shoulders. Her wetness is soaking the thin barrier and I slide the scrap of material aside and sink a finger into her dripping center. "Fuck, you're so wet."

Elle whimpers and I pull my finger out and move it up, circling her slick juices around her clit. I increase the pressure and when I move faster, she clutches onto my arms and her hips buck against my hand. I watch her, paying close attention to how her body responds, and when she's gasping, I keep that same steady rhythm, not changing up a thing, urging her to orgasm.

"Oh, God. Gray!" she cries, and a series of tremors runs through her lower body. Elle drops forward against my chest and I pull my hand up, wrapping my arms around her.

For a long moment, I hold her. Until her breathing slows down and she pulls back to look up at me with glazed eyes. "Are you okay?" I ask.

She nods and presses her lips to mine. The kiss turns deep and sensual and I've never been so painfully hard in my life. When it finally ends, Elle looks down where my poor, aching dick is on the verge of bursting through my pants. "Are *you* okay?" she asks.

"Not really, but I'll live."

"Can I help?" she asks, trailing her fingers along my belt buckle.

I grab her hand and bring it back up, away from the danger zone. "It's probably best if you keep your hands up here for now."

Elle cups my face. "Grayson Carter..." Her voice is full of awe.

My mouth edges up. "Yes?"

"I can't believe we're here together like this. Finally."

I know exactly how she feels, and I press a kiss to her lips. "You're far too tempting and I'm going to drive you home before I fuck you right here on my couch." When I pinch her ass, she squeals, and hops off me. "I don't want to rush this."

Yeah, I'm greatly looking forward to the moment when I can sink my dick inside Elle's slick body and claim her as mine. In the meantime, though, I need to get this luscious temptress out of here before we go too far and there's no turning back.

We've waited so damn long and I'm going to make our first night together absolutely perfect in every single way.

Struggling up off the couch, I readjust myself with a low, pained groan. "C'mon, baby," I say. "Let's get you home before I change my mind."

"And where is home?" Mr. Landon asks me.

"Newport, Rhode Island," I answer and notice the look Elle's parents exchange with each other. Elle, Chloe and I are peeling corn for dinner.

"That's a nice place to have grown up," Mrs. Landon says. "Very fancy."

When Chloe and Elle invite me to the lakeside cottage her parents own, I'm filled with mixed feelings. On the one hand, I am excited to meet Elle's family. On the other hand, it only confirms the fact that I'm with the wrong girl. Impressing Mr. and Mrs. Landon is important to me, but it seems like we get off on the wrong foot from the moment we're introduced.

The look in her father's eyes speaks volumes and it's clear that he doesn't like me. But I have no idea why.

"What does your father do?" Mr. Landon asks.

"He owns a financial services company."

"So, he plays around with rich people's money all day," Mr. Landon comments.

"He invests in the stock market," I say.

"Those Wall Street types are all the same. They love to risk everyone's savings but their own."

"My dad owns a construction company," Elle jumps in to say, immediately trying to smooth things over. "So, he's not used to sitting in an office all day."

"Damn right. I'm out there with my guys, building and working with my hands."

Her parents make a few more unnecessary comments before Elle escorts me out. "I am so sorry," she says, her face bright red.

"Did I do something wrong?"

"No, it's not you."

"I think he hates me," I say. Even though I'm trying to play the whole thing off and act like it's cool, it bothers me. I really wanted her parents to like me.

"My dad tried to invest some money once and he ended up getting screwed over," she explains. "He lost it all and now he doesn't trust investors."

"My dad would never do that. He's honest and works hard."

"I'm sure he's wonderful and I'm sorry for their comments. They just don't trust anyone they perceive as wealthy and white collar. Even though my dad owns the company, it's a small business and he definitely has a more blue-collar mentality."

"Yeah," I murmur.

We're standing close to the kitchen still and I can hear her parents clearly warn Chloe about "guys like me."

What the hell does that even mean? I wonder.

"Um, maybe we should go over there," Elle suggests. When she tugs my arm, I yank it away.

"No." I want to hear exactly what they're saying about me.

"Be careful, Chloe," Mr. Landon says. "He's from a filthy rich family and boys like that are all the same. No good."

I'm waiting for Chloe to stick up for me, but she doesn't.

"It's usually true," Mrs. Landon adds.

"I hope you're not too invested, Chloe, or he'll end up breaking your heart and any other girl naïve enough to date him."

Ironically, it was the other way around—Chloe cheated on me. I'm not going to say she broke my heart because I never gave her that part of me. But it still stung.

Now, though, I have the chance to be with Elle, the one I've always wanted, and no one is going to stop us.

Absolutely no one.

7

ELLE

I'm still trying to wrap my head around the fact that Gray Carter is back in my life. Not to mention the fact that he gave me an orgasm last night and my legs are still shaky when I think about it.

Right now, his ex is on her way over with a bottle of wine. Chloe arrives at the same time the pizza delivery guy does, and as I pay, she breezes right past.

"You are not going to believe what happened today," she announces. "The sooner we get this bottle open, the better."

I couldn't agree more, I think, as I thank the guy and hand him a tip. Taking the pizzas, I close the door and head into the kitchen where Chloe is already pouring wine into two glasses.

"So, get this. My sister asked me to be a bridesmaid today. Not her Maid of Honor, just a regular, old, lousy attendant. How insulting."

"Who is going to be her Maid of Honor?" I ask. To be honest, I'm not very surprised and always thought it would be her best friend, Toni.

"Toni!" Chloe exclaims and then makes a snorting sound. She takes a sip of wine and flips a pizza box open. "How rude, right?"

I shrug and pluck a slice of cheese pizza up. "I mean, Toni is her best friend. Since like first grade."

"But I'm her *sister.* We're related by blood." She shakes her head and makes a face. "I feel totally betrayed."

Her words catch me off-guard, and I pause chewing. *Well, hell. If she feels betrayed by this, then how in the world is she going to feel about me going out with Gray?* My insides churn the moment the pizza hits my stomach. I grab my wine and take a long, much-needed sip.

Chloe vents for a while longer, but I'm barely paying attention. My thoughts are consumed by Gray, and it sucks because I'm really excited to share my news, but I don't know how she's going to react. It's not something I can hide, though, either. At least not for long.

I decide to ease her into it and casually bring him up once she stops talking. "So, I started my new job the other day."

"Oh, right," Chloe says, but without much real interest. After all, it doesn't revolve around her. "How'd it go?"

"Really well," I say. "Everyone was super nice and you're not going to believe who owns the company."

"Oh, before I forget, did I tell you that Olivia is talking about carnations for the centerpieces. Yikes, right?"

I've never minded carnations, so I shrug my shoulders. "Any particular reason why?"

"Apparently there's some silly backstory or something with her and him and carnations. I don't know. But, c'mon! So tacky."

"Don't you think it's a little sweet? Because it means something."

"It means they're cheaping out on flowers. Lilies or roses is the way to go. Or peonies or I don't know. Anything but carnations. Yuck."

"So, anyway," I say, trying to steer the conversation back to me.

"Can you even imagine what hideousness she's going to choose for bridesmaid dresses? I shudder to think. My sister never had the best fashion sense."

I suppress a frustrated sigh and sip my wine. Sometimes it's like I live in Chloe-Land. If it's not directly revolving around her then she doesn't care. Still though, I always listen and try my best to be a good friend. Occasionally, I wish it was reciprocated.

After droning on a few more minutes, she must remember I had mentioned something before she cut me off. "So, what did you say earlier? About your new job?"

"I said you're never going to believe who owns C.T. International."

"Who?"

"Gray Carter and Liam Thompson," I say carefully and then hold my breath, waiting for her reaction.

"Huh. I haven't heard those names in a while." She frowns. "You should quit. Immediately."

"Quit?"

"You don't want to work for a jerk, do you?"

"They were both very nice," I say, instantly defensive. "It's a great company and I'm lucky they hired me since I have no experience."

"Gray was a douchebag. You know that. He cheated on me."

"What?" I exclaim. *Is she kidding right now?* "Chloe, you know that's not true. You slept with Jarrod before even breaking up with Gray."

She rolls her eyes. "Don't be so naive, Elle. He was obviously getting laid somewhere and since it wasn't with me…I have to assume the worst."

"Why was that?" I ask quietly, not wanting to believe her.

"What?"

"You guys dated for almost two years. I always assumed you were hot and heavy behind closed doors."

Chloe bursts out laughing. "Oh, my God, Elle, I would've guessed the man was going to be a priest if we hadn't hooked up a few times in the beginning."

I grit my teeth, not wanting details but, at the same time, wanting to know absolutely every miniscule thing that went down between them.

"There just wasn't any spark. You know how with some men; you want to rip their clothes off and you get all hot and bothered with just a look. That was not Gray."

Yes, it is, I think. Remembering last night, I squeeze my thighs together. Gray and I had more than a spark. It was a freaking wildfire.

"Whatever. Gray was a terrible boyfriend, and I never should've wasted my time with him."

I circle the rim of my wine glass with my index finger. "You know our reunion is coming up. I was thinking about going."

Chloe scrunches her face up. "Why? Reunions are stupid. Everyone is just there to show off their spouses and brag about how wonderful their lives are going. No thanks. If I am interested in your life then I'm already friends with you. I don't need to go to some reunion and be fake all night."

"It would be nice to visit Boston for a few days. I miss that city."

Chloe gives an indifferent shrug. "New York is way better."

I struggle not to roll my eyes. Chloe and I are so different. It's a wonder she and I stayed such good friends and didn't drift apart. "Well, I might go. It could be fun."

When I look up from my glass, Chloe is eyeing me closely. "Is Gray going?"

"No," I respond instantly. I'm not sure why I lie, but for some reason, I don't want Chloe changing her mind and going. "We briefly talked about it, but he has a company to run here and not a lot of free time."

"What else did you talk about?" she asks.

"What do you mean?"

"Did you talk about me?"

I'm not sure how to answer her question and the last thing I want to do is upset her. Treading carefully, I say, "He asked if we still talked, and I said yes. That's about it."

"Really?" She arches her brow. "That's kind of insulting."

"What do you mean?"

"We dated for almost two years, and he doesn't care how I am?"

"You didn't exactly leave on the best of terms."

"Because he was cheating on me."

"Stop saying that!" I burst out. "*You* cheated on *him*!"

Chloe purses her lips and tucks a strand of blonde hair behind her ear. "I still think he was banging someone else before I cheated."

I let out a frustrated sigh and changed the subject. "How was work?" Chloe is a manager at a chic boutique over on Fifth Avenue.

"Awful. I need to get out of retail, but my resume is atrocious. Can you help me with it?"

In Chloe-Land, that means will I do it? Whatever. I just want to veer away from the current subject of Gray. "Sure," I relent and pour more wine.

For the first time in my life, I have the strangest feeling– that I can't trust Chloe. I'm not sure where it's coming from or why it's happening. But, for some inexplicable reason, a part of me thinks she would try to rekindle things with Gray if she knew that I liked him. Just out of spite. She talks shit about him and claims they had zero chemistry, so it makes no sense that she'd ever want to get back together with him.

But my gut isn't quite so certain.

Obviously, that's the last thing I'd ever want to happen. It makes my heart constrict painfully. Losing Gray once to Chloe's charms was bad enough. But twice?

Chloe had her chance and blew it. Now it's my turn.

8

GRAY

The next morning, I'm dying to see Elle. It would have been nice waking up with her warm body pressed against mine, but when she revealed she was a virgin, I knew I needed to pump the brakes. I fucked this up once before and I can't let it happen again.

Slow and steady wins the race, I remind myself. Or, in this case, wins Elle.

It's a stupid analogy, but she deserves so much, and I plan to give it to her. Starting today.

It's hard not going down and seeing her first thing this morning, but I don't want people to gossip. She's new here and if the other employees think the new girl is getting special treatment, the one who's going to get hurt is Elle. So, I bide my time, work the morning away and as soon as noon hits, I go look for her.

She's sitting with Deirdre, another employee, and they're chatting away when I walk up. "Can I see you for a moment, Miss Landon?"

"Sure," she says. "Be back in a minute."

Deirdre nods, watching us closely. She's the office gossip and seems to know everybody's business.

"Hey," I say and nudge her with my elbow.

"Hi," she murmurs and presses her arm against mine.

"How are things going?"

"Good. I really love working here and I'm learning so much already."

"Glad to hear it." I glance down at my watch. "It's lunchtime, though. Care to join me?"

"Um…"

"I know we're in a weird situation, but I can't ignore you, Elle. I need to see you, talk to you, touch you."

"Gray, shh," she warns me, glancing around.

But the temptation is too much, and I pull Elle into an empty conference room and close the door. Passion infuses me and I yank her into my arms and kiss her hard. She instantly melts, arms wrapping around my neck, kissing me back with unbridled fervor.

"You taste so good," I whisper. Her nails scratch the back of my neck, sliding through the hair above the edge of my collar and I stifle a groan. I want to bend her over the table, flip her skirt up and sink into her sweet wetness.

Get it together, Carter, I reprimand myself.

But she smells so damn good. With a low growl, I drop a kiss behind her ear and lock down my desire. *Later.*

"Are you trying to get me in trouble?" she asks in a throaty whisper.

"I'm the boss, baby. And I say it's okay to sneak off and have a stolen moment."

Elle pulls back and straightens my tie. "Well, I can't argue with the boss man."

My mouth curves and I give her another quick kiss before opening the door. "There's a deli nearby that's pretty good."

She nods and we walk over together. After we get our food, we find a table near the window and sit.

"I was thinking about our reunion coming up." I bite into my pastrami on rye.

"You're going, right?"

I nod and swallow. "Since we're both planning on going, and neither of us has a significant other, maybe we can go together."

"To avoid the poor-you looks?"

"I'm not going to lie. I hate the "why are you single?" questions."

"Me, too."

"We should just get drunk and tell everyone we're engaged." Even though I'm kidding, a part of me is dead serious.

Elle laughs. "That would be hysterical. No one would harass us about being single."

"If you want, I can RSVP a couple of hotel rooms for us. My friend is in charge of the room block. I'll make sure he hooks us up with the nicest rooms."

"Sounds great. Thank you."

Being with Elle is so easy. Truthfully, it always has been and after we finish eating, we head back to the office.

"What're you doing tonight?" I ask as we step into the elevator.

"Nothing much. Chloe mentioned coming over for a Netflix night."

"Oh," I say, disappointed.

"But I'd rather do a movie night with you."

"Are you sure? I don't want to ruin your plans."

"Chloe won't care if I switch it til tomorrow night. Why don't you come over around 7pm?"

"Perfect." I give her a swift kiss right before the doors glide open. "See you later then, Miss Landon."

Elle gives me a sultry smile before sashaying back over to her side of the office. Damn that woman is getting to me. More than ever before and that's saying a lot. Now that I've had a taste of her, all bets are off.

By the time it's 7:15, Elle and I are watching a movie on her couch and I'm doing my best to behave. But 20 minutes into the movie, she's in my arms and we're kissing. I can't help it. She's like a catnip and I want to roll around and frolic all over with her.

When I finally pull back, she's looking up at me with so much heat in her brown eyes. "I was thinking," she says and runs a finger down my arm. "Maybe when we go to Boston this weekend, we don't need two rooms. I mean, we're pretending to be engaged, right?"

All my blood heads south. "I already booked two but if you choose to stay with me, I'd be a very happy man."

She gives me a shy smile. "Just a thought. Something to look forward to, maybe."

"I am definitely looking forward to the possibility. How likely are we talking?"

"Like on a scale of one to ten?" she asks with a flirty grin.

"Yeah."

Elle tilts her head, pretending to think for a moment. "Twelve?" she says and tangles her fingers with mine.

With a growl, I squeeze her hand. "I'm not going to be able to concentrate for the rest of the week now."

"You'll manage," she teases.

At that moment, I'm honestly not sure how I'll make it to Saturday but somehow, I do. Though it isn't easy. We fly out of JFK Airport and land at Logan Airport not long after. It's a quick and easy flight. I help load our small roller suitcases into the back of an Uber and the driver takes us downtown to The Westin Copley Place.

Situated in the middle of the affluent Back Bay neighborhood, the hotel is surrounded by shopping and dining. When we check in, I slant a questioning look over at Elle and she clears her throat.

"Excuse me," she says, and the desk clerk looks up. "There was a mistake with our reservation. We only need one room."

I reach over and snake my fingers through hers. Tonight, is going to be a very good night.

Once we're in the room, I reach into my pocket and pull out the diamond eternity band that's been burning a hole there. "I have something for you," I say. "So, we look legit."

Elle walks over and I lift her hand and slide the ring onto her finger. "It's beautiful," she whispers.

I'm not sure what exactly possessed me to buy the ring. I know this is supposed to be a fun inside joke, but when I saw it, I got it. I wanted Elle to have it. Maybe it represents more than it should. We're still getting reacquainted, but I know one thing for sure.

Elle is the woman for me and I'm not playing any games when it comes to her.

9

ELLE

The night is going better than I ever could've imagined. I have so much fun with Gray and Liam who show up later in the evening. It's so fun reconnecting with old friends. We're laughing and drinking far too much, and I can't remember the last time I enjoyed myself like this.

The fact that Chloe isn't here makes me wonder. I should be missing my BFF, right? But I'm not. I've been on Gray's arm all night and we've been telling everyone that we're engaged and making up all sorts of crazy stories. By 9pm, we're both slouched over and in hysterics over some inside joke. We definitely have the giggles from too much champagne. I look down at the ring on my finger and it appears dazzling under the lights.

"I love my ring," I say. "Thank you."

Gray snags my hand, turning it this way and that way. "You're far prettier," he murmurs. We both burst out laughing again and, as I wipe a finger under my eyes, scared that my mascara is running, I catch a glimpse of Chloe.

Liam intercepts her halfway over to us and I stand up straight. "Oh, shit," I mumble. "She said she wasn't coming."

"Who?" Gray looks out over the room and his laughter fades. "Oh."

Even though Liam tries to stop her, it's too late. Chloe sees me with Gray and jerks her arm away from him, heading toward us like a missile toward its target.

I'm having such a good time and my mood deflates fast. Chloe stops in front of us, hands on her hips. "Well, if it isn't my best friend and my ex-boyfriend. You two look cozy over here in the corner."

"You said you weren't coming," I say. It comes out all wrong and I instantly regret my accusatory tone.

"I said reunions are stupid, but I changed my mind. I'm glad I did." She looks from me to Gray. "Is there something I should know?"

"I already told you that I'm working at Gray and Liam's company," I say.

Gray is looking at me, but I can't meet his gaze. "Elle fits in great over at C.T. International. We're lucky to have her," he says.

Chloe's eyes narrow slightly, but she just sniffs. "I'm going to get a drink. Elle, come with me."

Oh, God, no. I can't do this right now, right here, in front of everyone. Gray must see the desperate look on my face because he steps in and throws me a lifeline.

"We were finishing up some work stuff, so I'll bring her over in a minute."

That is not the answer Chloe wants, but she huffs out a breath and spins away on her heel.

"She hasn't changed," he mutters under his breath.

Suddenly it feels like the walls are closing in around me. "Get me out of here, Gray," I say. "*Please.*"

Without hesitation, he wraps an arm around my lower waist and turns me toward the nearest exit. Once we're in the elevator, I feel a sense of relief wash over me.

"Okay?" he asks, lightly massaging my back.

I nod. "I was having such a good time and I don't want Chloe to ruin it. Does that sound selfish?"

"No, baby," he says and presses a kiss to my forehead. "If you ask me, you're not selfish enough when it comes to Chloe."

To an extent, he's right. When I think over our friendship, I begin to see that I've given and sacrificed a lot more than she ever has and, for the first time, it's starting to really bother me.

The elevator doors open with a ding, and we walk down to our room. Gray opens the door with a key card, and I feel so much better now. Then my stomach flutters when I think about us spending the night together. My gaze drops to the bed, and I swallow hard.

Tonight, is going to be a night I will never forget and I refuse to let thoughts of Chloe interrupt or ruin it. Gray slides his suit jacket off, turns and tosses it over the back of a chair, and I can't help but admire the way his dress shirt pulls across the muscles of his back.

I want to run my hands all over his muscled back…arms… abs…thighs…

Pressing my thighs together, I bite down on my inside lower lip. Gray slides his belt off and drops it on the chair. When he catches me staring, he smirks. "Are you watching me undress, Miss Landon?"

"Maybe," I say and move closer.

"Well, keep watching then," he invites and starts unbuttoning his shirt.

"Wait," I say and cover his hands with mine. "Let me."

A muscle flexes in his cheek and he gives a sharp nod. "Be my guest." His voice is raw, full of heat, and my belly quivers.

When his hands drop away, I reach for a button and slowly take up where he left off, slowly making my way down. Releasing one after another. I've never undressed a man before. Never even came close and my hands tremble a little.

When his shirt opens, I stare at his hard chest and clench my hands into fists. I want to touch him.

"Touch me," he whispers, voice hoarse.

It's like he's in my head, able to hear my thoughts. I reach over and slide my hands over his chest. His skin is firm, warm and there's a light growth of hair spattered there that reminds me how masculine he is.

I look up and his blue-gray eyes glow with silver heat.

"Your hands are so soft," he says.

"Your chest is so hard," I automatically respond, not really thinking.

Gray smirks. "That's not the only thing hard around here."

A flush creep up my cheeks and I push the shirt back off his shoulders. Gray helps, shrugging it off, and it drops to the floor.

"Turn around," he murmurs. "So, I can unzip you."

I swallow down my nerves and slowly spin around, offering him my back. His large hand grips the zipper and slowly slides it down. I can feel his warm fingers trail down my back, hear the zipper go down, and excitement flutters through my belly. Wet heat pools between my thighs and I swear to God, this man is casting a spell over me.

I've never wanted anyone the way I want Grayson Carter.

And now he's all mine.

The thought both thrills and terrifies me at the same time. I'm nervous and I can't believe my first time is actually going to be with Gray like I always wanted. But there's something about him that calms and soothes me. I trust him completely and I know that he would never hurt me.

My dress slides down, over my hips and pools around my feet in a red silky pile. I step out of it, still in my heels, and slowly turn to face Gray in my lace lingerie.

"Christ, you're beautiful," he murmurs, eyes moving down my body like a soft caress.

I'm glad I wore my sexiest black lace bra and panties, but nerves crash through me and I lift my arms to shield myself.

Gray grabs my wrist. "Don't you dare cover any of that gorgeousness." He pulls me closer and captures my mouth in a sensual kiss that makes my toes curl. When Gray angles my head back, deepening the kiss, I melt into him and welcome the slide of his tongue against mine.

I'm buzzing a bit from the champagne I drank downstairs, but I'm so damn high on Gray right now. I don't think I ever want to come down. With a soft sigh, I slide my hands down, reach around and squeeze his ass. He groans into my mouth, and I can't help but smile.

Gray nips my bottom lip and pulls back. His hands graze down along my sides and then he lifts me up, hands cupping my lace-clad rear end. I wrap my legs around his waist, and he heads over to the bed, setting me down on the edge.

He lays a hand against my cheek, and I look up at him. The man I've longed for and dreamed of for far too long is standing in front of me and we're on the verge of spending the night together. I can't believe this moment is finally here.

"Are you sure about this?" he asks softly, tracing his finger along my jaw. "Because once we get started, I'm going to have a very difficult time stopping. But I'm going to give you everything, Elle. I'm going to bring you so much pleasure."

I nod against his hand. "I want you, Gray. So much."

"I want you, too, Elle. More than anything." He lowers me down, gently pushing me back against the bed, and kisses me thoroughly. The touch of his lips is like heaven, and I flounder in a sea of sensation. The hard bulge of his erection presses into my hip and I trace my fingers up and down his back, dipping them into the waistband of his pants.

Gray trails his tongue down along the curve of my neck and I whimper as he moves lower. His fingers slide under my bra straps, sliding them down, and he reaches behind and unclasps the hook. My breath catches in my throat as he slides it away and worships me with his gaze. Then his head drops, and he draws a tight nipple into his mouth, sucking and teasing.

My fingers rake through his hair as he moves from one breast to the other, lavishing them with attention. *God.* I can't believe he's doing this to me. That I'm nearly naked in his arms and his mouth is on me. His head lowers as he kisses his way down to my stomach and my hands fall away, dropping to the bedspread and grasping it.

His fingers hook into my panties, and he slowly drags them down then tosses them. I gasp when he pushes my thighs further apart and he pauses, looking up at me. "Remember what I said the other night?"

Oh. God. How could I forget?

"I'm going to spread your legs...And dip my head between them...and lick

up your sweet pussy. I'm going to make you scream my name. I promise you're going to come so hard on my face that you see stars."

"Mmm hmm. You said you'd make me see stars."

"That's right, Elle. Now open up for me so I can lick your sweetness."

He's got me in some kind of sensual trance, and I part my legs, watching as he lowers his face between my thighs. The touch of his soft lips on my core is jolting and my body jerks.

"Relax," he murmurs.

His hot breath against my sensitive skin has me twisting the blanket in my fists. And then his tongue gets in on the action. "Ohhh, God," I rasp, hips popping up, back arching. Gray's tongue laps and licks, sending me into spasms of pure bliss. The moment he sucks my clit into his mouth, swirling his tongue around it, I lose it. A cry tears from my throat and the orgasm leaves me panting hard.

And, yes, I see stars. A whole sky full of brilliant, white-hot, shooting stars.

10

GRAY

I lift my head, running my tongue over my lips, and lick away the glistening wetness. Elle tastes just like I always knew she would. So damn sweet. Watching her release was the best thing I've ever seen and we're only getting started.

Pulling back, I stand up and shed my pants. Elle's gaze flickers down and I grab the edges of my boxer briefs and shove them off. Her mouth drops open slightly and I smirk.

"You're not shy at all, are you?" she asks.

"Not when it comes to being naked with you," I say, and grab a condom from the nightstand and roll it on. I stretch out beside her. "Being shy makes people hold back and I refuse to hold anything back with you. Promise me you'll do the same."

"I promise," she says.

My sweet Elle. Desire washes over me as I look into her innocent brown eyes, and I position myself between her legs. I'm aching for her, but I need to make sure she's ready. My hand drops between our bodies and I slowly massage her clit then slide a finger inside her. *Fuck, she's tight. But so, so wet.*

The moment she starts whimpering in the back of her throat, I grasp my cock and line myself up. Then I begin to push inside her, and her body instantly tenses beneath me. "Relax, baby." Balancing on my elbow, I slide out then thrust deeper, feeling her body stretch around me.

And it feels like fucking heaven.

"Okay?" I ask, dying to move, but not wanting to hurt her.

"Don't stop, Gray."

That's all the invitation I need and my hips surge forward, rocking against hers, sinking deeper into her wet warmth. Elle cries out, arching beneath me, as I start a slow, steady rhythm. Her nails are tearing into my back and the husky moans coming out of her mouth are sexy as hell.

My mouth latches onto hers, kissing her with all the built-up passion that's grown over the years. I pull her leg up, wrapping it around me, and plunge deeper, faster, feeding on her panting approval.

Sliding a hand between our bodies, I tease her clit until she throws her head back and grinds her hips in unison with mine. "That's right," I encourage her. "Fuck me, Elle. Fuck me hard, baby."

"Gray!" She arches beneath me and cries out as the orgasm rips through her.

Once she comes, I drop onto both elbows and drive into her once, twice, three more times. Then the world around me explodes and I shudder hard and groan as my release hits me.

And I'll be damned. I see stars.

It feels like someone knocked the wind out of me and it takes a moment for me to get my bearings. Eventually, I slide out of her sweet body, get rid of the protection and then climb back into bed. After pulling her into my arms, I press a kiss to her temple.

Everything in the world is right.

Elle is everything I ever wanted and more. I've never been so blown away by anyone like this before and I trail my finger up and down her arm. Goosebumps surface and I drop a kiss on her shoulder.

"You're amazing," I finally manage to say, my voice low and raspy.

"So are you." She tightens her arms around me and snuggles deeper into my arms.

We both fall asleep, and my dreams are full of more sexy encounters with Elle. At some point during the night, I wake up to her soft lips kissing my chest, moving lower, tongue swirling on my abs.

My dick must've woken up before I did because it's up, aching and raring to go. When Elle's hand circles my hard length, my body jerks in awareness.

"Show me," she murmurs, looking up at me. "What do you like?"

I wrap my hand around hers and begin to slide it up and down, pumping, letting her know how fast and hard I want. *Fuck.* Being able to hold it together while Elle's working my cock like this isn't going to happen. Before I explode, I roll her over and sink deep, all the way to the hilt.

Pure, absolute heaven.

"Fuck. Condom," I hiss and pull back out. I slap a palm on the table beside the bed, grab one and tear it open with my teeth.

Elle takes it from my mouth. "Let me."

I really like when she takes initiative and somehow my dick swells even more as she slowly, carefully rolls it on. Her fingers linger and I'm on the verge of dying. I grab her hand and lock it up by her head on the mattress, my fingers lacing through hers.

"Hang on, baby," I warn her. With one powerful thrust, I sink deep into her slick body, and she cries out. I've lost all semblance of control and begin to slam hard, grunting with each slide.

No one has ever had this kind of hold on me and the fact that I almost fucked her without protection is something that would never normally happen. I'm religious about using condoms and I have never had sex without one.

But Elle is making me do and feel all sorts of things that I normally wouldn't. I let go of her hand and grip her hip, thrusting hard. I feel like I'm losing my mind. I can't get enough of this woman. Her body clenches around me and when she screams my name, I groan as my orgasm hits me hard.

Collapsing beside her, my heart is thundering and we're both panting, trying to catch our breaths. "That was a nice way to wake up," I say and pull her body against me. My lips drop kisses along the curve of her neck.

"You liked that?"

"Oh, yeah. You can wake me up like that any time, baby."

"Duly noted," she says, a teasing tone in her voice.

I hope her first time, and second, was everything she'd imagined it would be. "Are you glad you waited?" I ask her.

Elle turns in my arms and looks up. "So glad. You're everything I imagined you would be, Gray." She lays a hand against my cheek. "I'd wait forever for you."

My mouth lifts and she wraps her hand around my neck and pulls me in for a long, soul-stirring kiss. Eventually we fall back asleep, and morning comes too soon. We take a shower together, but I don't instigate anything because I know she must be sore. I should've been more gentle with her, but the passion between us was like nothing I've ever known before. I lost control a couple of different times.

We decide we're not in any rush since our flight doesn't leave until noon, so we order room service and talk. It's so incredibly nice to sit across from Elle and not worry about anyone interrupting us. Just her and me.

Like it was always meant to be.

We keep the conversation fairly light, and I have no idea what she wants moving forward. *If anything.* But God, I hope this continues. Whatever is between us is building and being with Elle...

My heart constricts.

It feels so goddamn right.

I feed her a bite of pancakes smothered in syrup and we laugh when the stickiness gets on her face. "Hold still," I murmur, dipping my napkin in my water glass and then wiping the corner of her mouth. Our gazes meet and lock. "Do you have any idea how beautiful you are?" I ask, finger tracing her full lower lip. Her brown hair is tousled and still damp and she has a very satiated look in her deep, dark eyes.

"Flattery will get you everywhere," she murmurs and flicks her tongue against my finger.

With a groan, I pop up and reach for her, pulling her up into my arms. I know I shouldn't initiate sex again so soon, but goddamn this woman is driving me insane with lust. All I want to do is rip her clothes off and-

My phone rings. *Damn.* The real world always intrudes on perfect moments like this. It might be Liam regarding work, so I drop a quick kiss on her lips and grab my cell. "One sec, okay?"

Elle nods and I look down to see it's my mom. A weird feeling fills me that I can't explain as I swipe the bar over and answer. "Hi, Mom."

"Oh, honey, I hate telling you this over the phone," her voice cracks and I can tell she's been crying.

"What's wrong, Mom?" My gut tightens as I wait for her to continue.

"Your dad had a heart attack."

My entire world tilts and I grab onto the back of the chair. "What?"

"Late last night. I called 911 and an ambulance rushed him to the hospital. He's been in surgery."

"Jesus." I run a hand through my hair. "Is he okay?"

"The doctors sound hopeful. It just all happened so fast and I'm so scared."

"I'm coming home," I say without a second thought. I glance over at Elle, her brows drawn together in concern, and she gives me a reassuring nod.

Jonathan and Amelia Carter are the best parents anyone could ask for and I'm damn lucky that they're mine. As an only child, we were close while I was growing up and we still are to this day. I'd do anything for them, and I know they love me and support me no matter what.

After college, I could've transitioned right over and started working for my father's company, but finances never interested me. Real estate and all its potential, however, did. My dad told me he'd support me whether I worked with him or started my own company.

I'm damn lucky and I need to get down to Newport fast to be there for my mom and help out however I can.

We talk for a few more minutes and then I tell her I'm going to rent a car and drive to Rhode Island. It's only about an hour and a half drive from Boston. "I'll see you soon, Mom," I tell her.

"Love you, honey," she says.

"Love you, too." I hang up and Elle touches my arm.

"What happened?" she asks quietly.

"My dad had a heart attack last night."

"Oh, God, Gray. I'm so sorry."

So much for my plans of hanging out longer with Elle. "Do you mind if I drop you off at the airport a little early? I really want to get down there."

"No, of course not. I can even take the "T" if you don't have time to swing by the airport."

I reach for Elle's hand and drag it up to my kips. "I have time for you, Elle," I say and press a kiss to her knuckles. "Now let's pack up."

Less than an hour later, I rent a car at the airport and then drive Elle to departures. I get out, pull her small suitcase out the back and then turn to her. She looks so pretty with the sun lighting up her eyes until they look like the shade of melted caramel. I cup her face. "Thank you for last night," I whisper and kiss her.

People bustle all around us, but the kiss deepens as though we're the only two left in the world. When my body begins to respond to her flowery vanilla perfume and soft lips, I pull back and suck in a sharp breath.

"I have to go." I reluctantly let her go and step away, memorizing how beautiful she looks at this moment.

"Bye, Gray. Drive safe."

I nod. "Bye." As I get back into the driver's seat, I watch her walk away and disappear into the terminal, taking a piece of my heart with her. *Hell, who am I kidding?* Elle Landon has had my entire heart since the night we met seven years ago.

Now, though, she has a sliver of my soul.

11

ELLE

Going back to New York without Gray is bittersweet. I'm happy to be returning home, but I wish he was here with me. I understand that he needs to find out what is happening with his dad, though, and take care of his mom. Plus, there's the business end of things. He's not only going to have his father's company to run, but also his, while his dad's out of commission.

As I fly back to New York, my head is in the clouds and thinking over the things Gray did to me...*ohhh, my.*

I squeeze my thighs together and bite my lip, looking out the window at the ground far below. Waiting to have sex hasn't been easy, mostly because I've felt like a lovesick fool pining over Gray, but I'm so glad I did hold out. Intimacy is a big deal to me, and I needed it to be with a man who I cared about deeply.

And I've only cared about one man deeply– Grayson Carter.

It still seems like a dream and if I didn't still feel a little sore, I'd wonder if it was. But, no, it really was Gray who held me in his arms and did all of those wonderfully, wicked things to my body.

I get back to my little apartment later that afternoon and curl up on the couch with a blanket wrapped around me, daydreaming about last night and waiting to hear from Gray. When my phone beeps with a text later that evening, a huge smile breaks out over my face and I look down, expecting to see his name.

Instead, I see it's Chloe.

With a sigh, I read it: *Where did you go last night? You completely disappeared on me.*

Yeah, I think. *Because you weren't being very nice.* My fingers tap out a response: *Sorry. I left a little early.*

With Gray?

"Obviously," I mutter, debating what to say. I'm so not in the mood to deal with Chloe right now. I'm floating on cloud nine and don't want her to bring me down.

But she texts back first: *Whatever. It doesn't matter. I wanted to know if you want to go home next weekend? I'm driving out Friday night.*

It's been a while since I've been back to see my parents so it would be nice to take a quick trip home. And with Gray out of town for a bit, I figure I may as well go now. Because if he was here, I definitely wouldn't be going anywhere. Except back in his bed.

A shiver runs through my body at the thought.

Sure, I text her. *Sounds good.*

I'm tired since I didn't get much sleep last night, so I take a shower and fall into my bed early. The fact that Gray never texted or called bothers me, but I remind myself not to get upset. He's dealing with a lot and just arrived at his parents' house earlier today. He probably went straight to the hospital to see his dad.

Still though. While I've been thinking about him all day, he probably barely spared me a thought. I squeeze my eyes shut and tell myself to be reasonable and not act like a psycho. His dad just had a heart attack, major surgery and that is his first priority. Not me.

I can justify not hearing from Gray after returning home from Boston that same day. But when he doesn't text or call Monday or the rest of the week, I'm not sure what to think. All week, it's been hard focusing at work and, by the time Friday rolls around, I'm out of excuses why he didn't reach out.

Not even a freaking hello. I gave the man my virginity last Saturday night and it's almost a week later and nothing. Not a word.

Oh, my God. The terrible thought hits me hard like a brick to the head: was I only a one-night stand? Despite the things he whispered in the heat of passion, maybe our night together meant more to me than it did to him.

If that's the case, I'm going to die. Shrivel up and absolutely die.

Suddenly I'm so grateful that I'm going home for the weekend with Chloe, or I'd drive myself absolutely crazy wondering if I mean anything at all to Gray. I leave work in the worst possible mood, full of doubts. Especially after seeing Liam and gathering up the courage to ask if he's heard from Gray.

"Yeah, we spoke earlier."

It's like a shockwave rolls through me. "Really?" I ask, taken completely off-guard.

"Sounds like his dad isn't doing that well, though, so he's going to be down there for a bit helping out. But I'm sure you already know that," he adds with a wink.

I nod my head, but no, I didn't know that. Am I being a complete baby? He took the time to call Liam but not me and it stings even though it makes sense. He and Liam have C.T. International to run so, of course, they'd talk business.

It just hurts that he hasn't reached out to me at all. It makes me start second-guessing our night together. Sadness fills me and if I don't hear from him this weekend then I guess I'll have to chalk it up as a one-night stand—that it meant more to me than him.

The trip back to Fairview with Chloe takes us well over an hour because of Friday night traffic but I don't care. I just keep my eyes on the road and do my best to drown out Chloe's incessant chatter. She mentions Gray in the beginning, but after I tell her he went back home for a while, she drops it and starts babbling about her sister's wedding.

After dropping Chole off at her parents' house, I turn my car and head for the nice brick home that belongs to my dad and mom. They've worked so hard for everything they have and believe hard work will yield results. They hate when people are handed things and have zero work ethic.

I pull into the long driveway, park near the garage and turn the car off. I'm looking forward to a weekend full of distractions. Anything that will keep my mind off Gray.

The moment I walk inside, my mom embraces me and my dad waves from his big leather chair in the family room. "Hey, kiddo," he says.

My mom and I wander into the kitchen, sit on the stools at the island and chat. It's tradition and we spend the next hour or so catching up and eating. It's getting late and around midnight, I finally slip into my childhood bed, exhausted. And, of course, thoughts of Gray consume me.

Maybe I should just text him. I've been debating back and forth whether I should reach out or not, but I always come back to the same thought: No. If he wants to check in or say hi, then he can.

The following day, my mom and I go shopping. We hit up a local bookstore, clothing store and some other cute shops on Main Street. I miss the small-town quaintness and how everyone is so friendly. Definitely not something you experience living in New York City.

While sipping a coffee, we bump into Chloe who is walking out of the nail salon. My mom chats her up a minute and then invites her over for dinner tonight. I was hoping for a quiet evening with just my parents but maybe Chloe and all of her drama will be a good distraction from my aching heart.

Later that night, we're all sitting at the dining room table, enjoying my mom's homemade lasagna, garlic bread and salad, when Chloe mentions the class reunion last weekend.

Ugh. My heartbeat quickens when she brings up Gray.

"Why does that name sound familiar?" my dad asks, biting into a big forkful of lasagna.

"Because I used to date him, Mr. L. Remember you met him that one time up at the lake?"

"Oh, right. The rich kid. Bet he's been living off his parents' wealth since graduation."

"No," I speak up, instantly defending Gray. "He actually owns the company where I just started working. He's an incredibly motivated and hard worker."

"Seems like you two have renewed your, ah, friendship," Chloe states, eyeing me over the rim of her glass. "Of course, he wanted nothing to do with me since I dumped him."

"Good for you, Chloe. Any man who cheats on a woman deserves to get dumped," my mom says.

"Gray didn't cheat on her," I say, my eyes narrowing. "Chloe, you know that."

"I know nothing of the sort," she says airily and takes a bite of bread.

It's really starting to annoy me how she's playing the victim and making Gray look like the bad guy.

"So you work for this guy now?" my dad asks.

"Yes. He and Liam, another college friend, run C.T. International together."

"Did Daddy buy it for him?"

"Dad, for your information, they built it from the ground up when he could've very easily gone and worked at his father's company. Gray's a really hard worker."

My dad gives a derisive snort and Chloe cocks an eyebrow.

"You two seemed awfully close last weekend," Chloe says. Even though she tries to make the comment sound innocent, it's far from it.

"We're friends," I say in a cool voice.

"Friends with benefits?"

"Chloe!" I snap. I can't believe she just said that in front of my parents.

"Sweetheart, please have more sense than to get involved with some rich city boy," my mom pleads. "They just use women and then break their hearts."

I let out a frustrated sigh. Their small-town mentality drives me insane sometimes, but I understand that they only have my best interests at heart. I narrow my eyes in Chloe's direction. I'm not sure why she's trying to start trouble and I don't appreciate it.

"Yeah, I remember him now," my dad says. "I didn't like that kid. Seemed a little too high and mighty. And what did we tell you, Chloe? Don't get too attached to a guy like that."

"And look what happened," my mom says, in complete agreement.

I try not to let their words bother me, but it's hard. Especially later when I'm lying in bed, staring up at the ceiling and wondering if they're right.

At this moment, I feel very used and forgotten.

And it really fucking hurts.

12

GRAY

It's been an incredibly long and hard week. I feel emotionally drained and, even though I keep thinking about Elle, I haven't had the opportunity yet to reach out. Because I want to talk to her, not just throw her a random text.

When Sunday rolls around, I realize I need to make time today. Elle knows I'm busy though, so I hope she understands. We finally get my dad home and settled so I have a moment to breathe. Between visiting him in the hospital between surgeries– he had two– and running his company and mine remotely with Liam, it's been a little hectic. Especially since I had to make sure a big client didn't leave after threatening to walk from my dad's financial services company. The market can be a volatile thing and I'm glad I decided to go into real estate.

But now I need to talk to my girl.

It's Sunday evening and I just finished washing the dishes after eating dinner with my mom. My dad's been sleeping, and we have him set up in the guest bedroom in a hospital bed that I bought and had installed. I figured it would be easier for him because it goes up and down and he can't move around a lot right now.

It's too chilly to sit outside so I drop down on the rattan couch cushioned with palm trees in the sunroom and hit Elle's number. After a couple of rings, she picks up.

"Hi," she says, voice soft.

She sounds so unsure, and I mentally kick myself. I should've called her a week ago and not let myself get swept away in everything else. "Hey, Elle. How are you?"

"Okay," she murmurs.

She doesn't sound okay. "Baby, I'm sorry I didn't call you sooner. My dad ended up needing a second surgery and work has been insane. I know that's not an excuse, but I hope you can forgive me?"

A soft little sigh comes over the line. *Of relief?* I wonder.

"I'm so glad you called," she says. "I thought you forgot all about me."

"No! Of course not. I've been thinking about you every single day. Now that things are a little more under control, I'm going to try to fly back to the city next weekend. Just a quick trip, but I want to see you."

"I'd like that."

"Good. Mark off all of next weekend for me."

"I will."

She sounds more confident and I'm so glad. The last thing I want her to think is that I don't care. Because I do. So damn much.

"It looks like I'm going to be up here indefinitely, though," I tell her. "My mom doesn't know how to function without my dad and, even though I have a nurse coming in and checking on him every day, I need to keep my mom's spirits up."

"Of course."

"And then there's his company. He only has a handful of people working there and I'm questioning how competent they actually are. No one seems to know what to do when my dad isn't there. He's the rock around here. It's just a lot right now," I add and run a hand through my hair.

"I completely understand," she says. "I miss you, though."

"I miss you, too." My heart expands at her sweet words, and I can't wait until I can see her again. Unfortunately, it isn't the following weekend and I have to cancel at the last minute when an issue arises at my dad's office. I feel bad, but Elle tells me that she understands.

To help make up for it, I send two dozen, long-stemmed red roses to her apartment. I hope she likes roses. Truthfully, I have no idea, but I should find out what her favorite flower is, so I know in the future.

We talk later that night, and she thanks me for the flowers. "I didn't know what your favorite flower is, though. I hope roses are okay."

"They're beautiful. No one ever gave me flowers before."

"Well, that's a damn shame," I say. "Just proves that there are a lot of idiots out there." She chuckles. "If you could've chosen, though, what would you have picked?"

"As long as it's from you, Gray, it's exactly what I want."

"God, I miss you," I say, voice harsh. "I miss the way you smell, the way you taste and the sounds you make when I'm deep inside you."

"Gray!" she gasps. Her voice lowers. "I miss you, too."

I'm sitting in the sunroom again and I stand up. "Are you home?"

"Yes."

"All alone?"

"No. I'm with my imaginary boyfriend."

I jog up the steps to my bedroom and shut the door. "Smart ass. You better not be with any other man, imaginary or not."

"I'm alone," she says. "Terribly alone."

I drop down on my bed. "I'm going to help with that."

"What do you mean?"

"Touch yourself, Elle," I say in a husky voice.

"What?"

"Lay back and touch that sweet pussy of yours. Stroke it until you're wet and dripping. Just for me."

She sucks in a breath.

I'm wearing loose, gray sweatpants and I slide my hand down the front of them and grasp my dick, slowly starting to pump it. "I've got my dick in my hand, Elle. And I'm pretending it's your hands moving up and down its length. Making it swell and grow."

Elle releases a soft breath and then a barely audible whimper.

"How wet are you, baby?"

"So, so wet," she says with a sigh.

I swallow hard. "Good. Keep going but tell me exactly what you're doing."

"I'm..." She hesitates.

"What, baby?"

"I'm massaging my clit."

"Does it feel good?"

"Yes," she answers, voice breathy.

"If I was there, I'd suck it between my lips. Then I'd lick and suck until you were screaming my name."

A shuddering sigh comes over the line and I start pumping harder. "I'm so fucking hard right now, baby. You're making me so huge that I'm leaking."

"Oh, God," she cries softly.

"Slide a finger inside yourself, Elle," I rasp. "Slide two inside and then say my name."

She moans and then whimpers, "Gray."

"Harder," I tell her. "Don't hold back. Because I wouldn't."

The sound of her desperate panting fills my ear and I grit my teeth, not allowing myself to come before her.

"I'm almost there," she says. "Oh, God....*Gray...*"

I'm getting just as worked up as she is and the moment she comes, I let go of my control with a guttural groan. I ground out, "*Elllle...*" as I come hard and thick, hot ropes spurt on my belly.

We both release a shaky sigh.

"Christ, baby," I hiss. "Even 200 miles away, you make me lose my mind."

"Ahhh," she moans. "I can't believe the things I do with you."

"You love it."

"I do. You bring out a side of me that I never knew existed."

"Your wild, free side?" I ask.

"Yeah."

"Definitely your sexy side."

"My passionate side. I think I was asexual before last weekend," she says with a soft chuckle.

"No. You just needed the right man. A partner you could trust." When she doesn't say anything, it worries me a little. "You trust me, don't you?"

"Of course, I do," she quickly says. "I miss you, too."

"I really want to see you. I'm so sorry it won't be this weekend. Let's try for next weekend, okay?"

"Okay."

"Dream of me tonight?"

"Always," Elle whispers.

"Goodnight, Elle."

"Night, Gray."

After I hang up, it occurs to me that she never told me what her favorite flower is so I make a mental note to find out later. Knowing my sweet Elle, it's probably something simple, innocent and lovely.

I text her and ask before it starts driving me crazy.

When Elle texts back, she writes daisies and I smile, not surprised in the least.

13

ELLE

The next morning, I couldn't be happier. Things feel back on track with Gray and my confidence soars. Maybe a little too much because when Chloe and I hang out later, I decide to tell her.

I'm bursting at the seams with excitement but, at the same time, I really want Chloe's approval. I've always given her mine and I know the situation is awkward because Gray is her ex. But I'm hoping she won't be upset or hold it against me. I need her to understand, and I really believe that she will.

I couldn't have been more wrong.

We're sitting on the couch at my place, watching a movie and drinking a glass of wine, and I'm debating how to tell her when Gray calls. We both glance at my phone and his name flashes clearly across the screen.

Chloe's eyes narrow. "Are you going to get that?"

"Um, I can call him back later," I say and hit the button to send the call to voicemail.

Chloe purses her lips, sets her glass down and stares at the two dozen red roses sitting on my end table. I was surprised when she didn't comment on them earlier because they're kind of hard to miss.

"What's going on between you and Gray?" she asks tartly, crossing her arms. "And I really hope you say nothing because best friends do *not* date each other's exes."

Oh, shit. This is not how I wanted the conversation to start. I'm not even sure what to say because I know if I don't tread lightly then this is going to turn into a massive blow-up on Chloe's end.

"I actually wanted to talk to you about that," I say carefully and pause the movie. "When I started working at C.T. International, you know Gray and I reconnected."

"Because he's your boss."

"Right."

"And I know you're smart enough to know that mixing business with pleasure is a recipe for disaster."

I swallow hard. When Chloe gets like this, it's so hard to talk to her because it's like she already has her mind made up. And it's certainly not in favor of Gray and I being together.

"Chloe, this isn't easy for me to say, but I need you to know that ever since Gray and I met, there's been some spark there between us."

Chloe holds up her hand. "Stop right there. Are you going to sit here and tell me that you were lusting after *my* boyfriend?"

"I-I met him first," I say weakly. "At that party. And we hit off and then you came over and just...claimed him."

Chloe's eyes narrow into angry slits. "I can't believe this! I'd had my eye on him for weeks because he was in my class. Then I finally got the nerve up to go say hello and you think I claimed him? Or *stole* him from you, Elle? Because you're making it sound like I'm the bad person here."

"You're not!" I quickly say, hoping to salvage this conversation fast. "The truth is we both liked the same guy and I backed down when I shouldn't have."

"Oh, gee, Elle, thank you for being such a saint and bowing out of the picture because I couldn't get Gray on my own."

"That's not what I mean."

"It sure sounds like it. I can't believe this! So, all those times we hung out together, you had the hots for *my* man. What kind of friend are you?"

Chloe is a master when it comes to spinning situations around in order to make her look like the victim. I grit my teeth and strive for control. This conversation has been a long time coming. "He's not your man anymore, Chloe, and I always respected your relationship with Gray," I remind her quietly. "But everything has changed, and we really like each other."

Chloe snorts. "You had designs on Gray for years, while he was in *my* bed, and now what? You think it's your turn or something? That's just gross, Elle. Did you make a play for him while we were in college? And don't lie to me."

"No! I swear. I never told him how I felt or ever acted on my feelings. Our friendship meant too much."

"And now?" She shrugs. "What? It doesn't mean anything to you anymore?"

"Of course, it does. But, Chloe, it's been five years since you dated Gray and you broke up with him after sleeping with someone else. Obviously, you never cared about him."

"Don't tell me how I felt!" she snaps. Suddenly, her mouth drops open. "Did Gray know that you liked him?"

"In college?" She nods and I shake my head. "I don't think so."

Something seems to be connecting in her mind and she squeezes her eyes shut. "Dammit, Elle, he must've known. And, clearly, he was harboring the same feelings for you."

"Why would you think that?"

"Because he never wanted to touch me! He was always full of excuses, and it began to give me a complex. I started doubting myself! And all along he was lusting after my best friend. Do you have any idea how hurtful that is? When I slept with Jarrod it was because Gray hadn't touched me in over a year! I didn't understand why not and was starting to wonder if something was wrong with me."

"I'm sorry, Chloe. I never wanted to hurt you."

"Did you sleep with him?" she asks.

I sigh and meet her hurt, blue eyes. "In Boston," I admit.

"Oh, my God!" she exclaims and pops up off the couch. "You are a horrible person, Elle Landon! How you could ever call me your best friend is beyond my comprehension. I have never felt so betrayed in my entire life!"

Chloe stomps over to the chair, swipes her purse up and then spins around to glare at me.

"You should've been honest and upfront with me from the beginning," she says. "But I guess that ship sailed. So, go ahead, and go out with my ex-boyfriend like I know you want to do. But know that if you do, our friendship is over!"

I bite my lip and feel tears threaten. How did all of this just explode in my face? Not trusting my voice, I watch Chloe storm out and slam the door behind her.

Well, that went even worse than I could've imagined. I grab my phone and call Gray back.

"Hi," I say after he answers. He must hear my voice waver.

"What's wrong?" he asks.

"Chloe and I just had a huge fight. She knows about us and she isn't happy." I sniff and swipe at my nose which begins to run.

"Baby, Chloe has always been jealous of you."

"Me?" I repeat, completely flabbergasted.

"Yeah, you. You're everything she's not, could never be, and I think that's always bothered her."

I consider his words with a frown. "But she's my best friend. I always believed that she'd support me no matter what."

"Is she supporting you right now?"

"No," I admit, feeling absolutely miserable. "She basically said if we date then she and I aren't friends any longer. God, Gray, she made me feel like such a jerk after telling her how much I've always liked you. I just feel terrible. It's like a no-win situation." I wipe a tear away and curl up on the couch, pulling my knees up to my chin. "Maybe she's right."

"She is not right," he says in a firm voice. "I'm going to be brutally honest here, Elle. Chloe was never a very good friend to you. She's too selfish to put anyone's needs above her own. You have to see that."

Deep down, I know he's right, but that doesn't make it any easier. "It's just hard because she's like a sister. I don't know. Maybe this is all my fault."

"Elle, please. The truth is we wanted each other from the beginning, but we were too young and naive to do anything about it. I regret letting you slip through my fingers and if I could go back, I would drag you off and never look back."

A smile lifts the corner of my mouth. He's right. Somehow, we've been given a second chance and I don't want to mess it up. But losing Chloe in order to have Gray seems so unfair. I wish she could try to see things from our point of view. At least a little.

"I really want to see you," I whisper.

He releases a soft sigh. "I know. I want to see you, too, baby."

For a long moment neither of us says anything. I just listen to him breathe.

"Fuck it," he says. "I'm going to fly down now."

"Now?" I sit up straighter. "Are you serious?"

"It's going to be the shortest trip in history, less than 24 hours, because I have to get back for a meeting. But I think we both need it."

"That would make me so happy. Can I take the day off, boss?"

"Definitely."

When Gray finally arrives, it's almost 4am and I open my door with bleary eyes. He steps in, sweeps me up into his arms and kisses me senseless.

"Holy Christ, you taste good," he murmurs and kicks the door shut.

"I just brushed my teeth," I say and smile.

"You smell good, too," he says and begins kissing the side of my neck.

With a soft laugh, I reach for his hand and guide him down the hall to my bedroom. He's half-kissing me and half-checking out my apartment.

"I like your place," he murmurs when we get to my bedroom. "It's cozy."

"Is that code word for small?"

"No," he says and drops a kiss on my forehead. "It feels welcoming and has a good energy."

"You have a good energy," I tell him, letting my robe fall open to reveal that I'm wearing nothing underneath.

Gray sucks in a swift breath. He slides his fingers beneath the material and pushes it away. The robe falls off and lands on the floor leaving me naked and vulnerable before him.

"You're so fucking beautiful, Elle." He cups my face and kisses me deeply.

When we finally come up for air, a hot need is coursing through me. "Take your clothes off," I murmur. "We don't have much time and I don't want to waste a second."

Gray chuckles. "I like how you're thinking, baby." He strips his clothes off fast and then we fall back on the bed, all over each other.

Unlike last time, a frantic feeling consumes us, driving us forward. I can't get enough of him and I'm writhing against his body, undulating my hips against his massive erection.

"You feel so good," Gray rasps and slips a hand between my thighs. "So fucking wet."

A moan rips from my throat as he teases me with those long, talented fingers of his. "Ohhh, Gray," I groan as my hips buck up.

He pulls back and I look up, on the edge of coming, wondering why he stopped. "When you come, I want to be inside you. I want to feel that sweet, wet pussy clench hard around my cock."

I watch him roll the protection on and then he's grabbing my hips and lifting them up as he thrusts inside me. It's hard and fast. *Oh. God.* My body welcomes him home and my hips rise to meet his, taking him deeper with each thrust. He angles us just right, so he's hitting all of my sweet spots, and I'm about to lose my shit.

"Gray!" I scream, nails raking down his back.

"That's right, baby," he hisses, pumping faster. "I wanna see you shatter."

It doesn't take long. A powerful climax rocks through my entire body and I swear I almost black out. I've never experienced anything like it before and a scream tears from my throat. Gray stiffens above me then releases with a hard shudder and a long, satisfied groan.

He drops down beside me and, when he pulls me into his arms, I'm still trembling. My cheek rests against his firm chest and he's breathing hard, his heart hammering.

I don't know what to make of the situation. Last time, it was sensual, slow and steamy between us. And just now, it was completely different. Hard, fast and scary-passionate. Scary because now there's no denying it.

I'm falling deeply in love with Gray and I have no idea how to navigate any of this.

14

GRAY

My body is still recovering after the most intense orgasm of my life. I drop my head down on the pillow, exhausted and more satiated than I've ever been. My nose presses into Elle's fragrant hair and I breathe deeply. Flowers and vanilla. *Mmm.*

We rest for a little bit, wrapped in each other's arms, and I love the feel of her smooth cheek pressed against my chest. It feels right. Everything about Elle Landon feels really, really right.

We don't have much time together and the temptation to take her again fills me. "Turn around, Elle," I whisper. "Lean back against my chest."

She follows my instructions and, once the condom is in place, I curl a leg over her thigh and hold her there as I slide into her from behind. "Fuck," I swear and push deeper. Elle moans, grinding her ass against me, and I nip her earlobe as I begin a slow, dragging thrust. I reach around, find her taut nub and circle it with a finger.

It doesn't take long before we're rocking together, our bodies hot and slick with need. I flip Elle all the way over, hike her hips up and she drops down on her elbows. I increase my speed, pounding into her with raw, blinding intensity. She slams back against me and the sound of our skin slapping together, our rushed, frantic mating, fills the room. Gasps, panting, whimpers.

I feel like I'm going to lose my goddamn mind to the pleasure that courses through me.

Just like before, the release is explosive, and I empty my soul into her as I come long and hard. With a grunt, I pull out and release her hips. Elle drops down onto the mattress like a rag doll.

"Are you okay?" I manage to ask, still not sure that I even am.

"That was intense," she murmurs into the bedspread.

I press a kiss to her soft back and disappear into the bathroom to dispose of the condom. No woman has ever had this kind of effect on me and it's a little rattling. All I know is that I need Elle in my life.

Always.

Saying goodbye to Elle is brutal. By the time I get back to Newport and head to my dad's office for the meeting, it's clear to me that the sooner I can get back to New York for good, the better.

Unfortunately, my dad has another massive heart attack and all my plans for returning go out the window. When I tell Elle, she drives up to visit me the following weekend and helps soothe me. Things aren't looking good and, this time around, my dad isn't bouncing back.

I've never felt more low or sad in my entire life. I know my mom is barely hanging on and I'm not sure how she's going to receive Elle. But Elle has such a beautiful spirit and calmness about her that we both really need, especially at this time.

Elle cooks dinner for us and, instead of it being a somber, depressing affair, Elle manages to lighten the mood and steer the conversation into hopeful territory. It turns out Elle is far from a chef, but you can't really mess up homemade tacos too badly, I joke. The moment my mom actually smiles, I reach over beneath the table and squeeze Elle's hand.

My mom and Elle get along so well, and it makes me beyond happy. I know my dad would love her, too. After dinner, we end up sitting together in the living room with a warm fire crackling and talking for the next couple of hours. My parents had never met Elle, only Chloe, and they weren't huge fans. *Big surprise.*

My mom starts yawning at 10 o'clock and I glance over at Elle who sits beside me. "You're staying here tonight," I say. My tone implies there will be no arguing.

Elle casts a questioning look over at my mom who smiles. "Of course, she is. We have two guest rooms and she's welcome to either."

"And you need to get some sleep," I tell my mom. We all get up and I kiss her cheek. "Night, Mom."

I take Elle's hand and tug her toward the stairs. After getting her settled in the larger guest room that overlooks the ocean, I pull her into my arms and kiss her. It's a long, lingering kiss and I can't seem to get enough of her. She soothes me on every level.

"Take your shower," I say, pulling back.

Our gazes lock, smoldering.

"I wish you could join me," she says in a throaty whisper.

"Don't tempt me," I warn her. "I'll be back, though."

I reluctantly let her go and head back down to my room. My mom pokes her head in a minute later.

"I don't know what's going on between you two, but I love her, Gray," she says in a low voice.

"She's far too easy to love," I respond without even meaning to and my mom's eyes widen. Then a huge smile lights her face.

"Hold onto her, Gray. I can tell she's going to be really good for you."

"What do you mean?" I ask.

"I saw a side of you tonight that I've never seen before. At least not in a very long time. Softer, lighter. She brings out your playful side. Life shouldn't only be about running businesses and endless responsibilities. You need to remember to play, too."

I'm not sure what to say and my mom smiles.

"Goodnight, sweetheart," she says and leaves me pondering her words.

I suppose I do work far harder than most people, but I deal with multi-million dollar deals every single day. It's a lot of hard work and constant pressure. My thoughts instantly turn to my dad who lays in a hospital bed, hooked up to monitors. Two massive heart attacks in less than two months.

We're very similar and I don't want to end up where he is right now when I'm 55 years old because I worked too damn hard. I always thought I didn't let work rule my life but maybe I was wrong.

After a quick shower, I slip on a pair of worn, plaid pajama bottoms and pad down to the guest room. Elle is dragging a comb through her long, wet hair and I move up behind her and drop a kiss on the side of her neck.

"Thank you," I whisper against her sweet-smelling skin.

"For what?"

"For coming up here today." All of a sudden, the stress and anxiety of the past couple of weeks hits me hard. I'm so fucking tired and feel like I've got the weight of the world on my shoulders.

As always, Elle must be completely in tune with me because she guides me over to the bed, pulls the covers back and motions for me to get in with her. I slip beneath the crisp, clean sheets and pull her back against my chest. She snuggles into the curve of my body and I drift off to sleep right away.

I don't think I move all night because when I wake up, we're still wrapped in each other's arms. Elle is still asleep, face resting on my chest and breathing softly. For a long time, I just watch her and soak up each lovely feature of her face. I count each beauty mark, marvel at the way her long, black lashes fan her cheeks and admire her full, soft lips. Lips that I want to kiss for the rest of my life.

When I consider what that means, it's a thought that would normally scare the hell out of me. Because I'm thinking about marriage. About making this amazing woman my wife.

Suddenly, her eyes flutter open and they're so deep and dark, like chocolate mousse. Or Black Forest cake. I get the urge to devour her, but I hold my desire in check, remembering where we are and that my mom is very close by.

"Good morning," I say and twist a lock of her hair around my finger.

She smiles and stretches against me, brushing her ass against my hardening dick. *No, no, no. Now is not the time, pal.* I sit up and toss the covers back.

"Did you sleep okay?" she asks, voice a scratchy purr.

I nod. "Yeah. Thanks to you. I'm going to get dressed. I figure we can make some breakfast before you head out."

"Sounds good," she says.

As I walk out, I realize how much I hate this long-distance bullshit. But my family needs me and it's important to be there for them. Eventually, when I return to New York, Elle and I can have a normal relationship.

Hell, we haven't even talked about it yet. To be honest, I have no idea what she wants. I'm hoping it's me, but that's still to be determined. Nothing is official between us and I'm itching to clear things up.

But one thing at a time.

Elle makes coffee while I throw together a few omelets. She watches me whip them up, adding crumbled bacon and cheese with the funniest look on her face.

"What?" I ask after flipping them.

"I never knew you were such a good cook."

"I may have some kitchen skills," I say with a smirk.

Elle moves closer and bumps me with her hip. "Those aren't the only skills you have, mister."

"Damn straight."

She leans into my shoulder and presses a kiss against my arm. Her voice drops to a sultry whisper. "You're also damn talented in the bedroom."

The moment we hear my mom walk in, we pull apart, grinning like lovestruck fools.

"I made you an omelet," I tell my mom.

"And I made the coffee," Elle announces cheekily.

"Thank you," my mom says and sits down at the table. "It smells good."

"You need to eat more, Mom," I say and set a plate in front of her.

"I will." She picks up her fork and takes a bite.

Elle and I sit down next to each other.

"Mmm. This is delicious, Gray," Elle says. She looks over at my mom and smiles. "Did you teach him how to cook?"

"I wish I could take the credit, but no. Jonathan did."

"Your dad cooks, too?" Elle asks, eyes wide. "That's awesome."

"It's one of the reasons I married him," she jokes. "And his father taught him."

"It's like a tradition," I say.

"And one day, maybe you'll have a son to teach," my mom says and looks from me to Elle, her eyes sparkling as she envisions grandchildren.

"Maybe. If I'm very lucky," I say and glance over at Elle. She can't hide the smile that tugs the corner of her mouth up.

"That would be nice," she says softly.

Breakfast passes far too fast and the next thing I know, I'm kissing Elle goodbye and watching her drive away. *Damn, this sucks.*

"Don't you dare let her go," my mom says.

"I don't plan to," I tell her.

Things get super busy really fast, and I feel like I'm being pulled in multiple directions. Dealing with my dad's company, C.T. International and my dad being sick keeps me on the go from morning until evening. Then I look forward to talking to Elle on the phone. She truly keeps me sane when everything else around me seems like it's going straight down the drain.

The weeks seem to be barreling by and my dad begins to improve, slowly but surely. He isn't out of the woods yet, but he's back home again. And that's a step in the right direction. My mom must've told him about Elle because he asks me who my new girlfriend is.

"I'm glad you're more worried about Elle than your own health," I say after catching him sneaking a jelly donut. I snatch it away and toss it in the trash. "The doctor said no junk food."

"Gray, it's become really clear to me lately that you only live once. Embrace the good shit while you can."

"Words of wisdom."

"I also think you need to take a trip down to New York and take your girl out before some other man snatches her up. From what your mom says, this Elle sounds like a real catch."

"She is," I say and can't help the silly grin that spreads across my face.

"So, get out of here for the weekend. I'm feeling better and the business will still be here on Monday."

Damn, it's tempting. "I don't know."

"She was here, what? Three weeks ago? She probably forgot what you look like."

"I sure haven't forgotten what she looks like."

"Of course, you haven't. I hear she's a beauty."

I nod, caving into the idea of heading back down to see Elle for a couple of days.

"Your mom and I will be fine. Please. Do it for your old man."

"Yeah, okay," I relent. "I could use a couple of days back in the city. Saturday and Sunday. But if you need anything-"

"I won't."

My dad can be really stubborn once he gets something in his head, but I'm grateful to escape. The moment I'm back in New York Saturday morning, I call Elle and tell her to come over.

I have plans and they mostly involve keeping her naked for the next 36 hours.

When there's a knock on the door less than ten minutes later, I'm surprised. *She couldn't have gotten here so fast from her place,* I think, and open the door.

Chloe stands there.

My stomach sinks. Not the person I want to see.

"Can we talk?" she asks.

"Um-"

"Look, I know I haven't been very receptive about you and Elle being together," she says and walks past me.

I grit my jaw. "Chloe, now isn't a good time."

"And I'm sorry."

With an annoyed sigh, I push the door and cross my arms. "Whatever you have to say, make it quick. Elle's on her way over."

"We haven't spoken in weeks. I miss my best friend," she says in a pouty voice.

"For once, can we not make the situation about you?"

Chloe sniffs. "Well, I am involved a little. You are my ex-boyfriend, and she is...was...my best friend."

"We were never right for each other, and you know it."

"Especially since you were lusting after her the entire time we went out. That can give a girl a complex, you know."

I roll my eyes. "Why are you here?"

"Because maybe I think you're wrong."

"What the hell are you talking about?"

"If it weren't for Elle always hanging around, I think you and I would've had a much better relationship. We probably never would've broken up."

What? At first, I'm not sure I even heard her right. I shake my head, cross my arms. "Are you delusional?"

"Don't talk to me like that," she snaps.

I can't miss the spark of anger, but she quickly smothers it.

"What I mean to say is that I don't think you and I are over. Not really."

Oh, for fuck's sake. She really is losing it. "You know what I think?"

She steps closer, blue eyes darkening. "What?"

"I think you're so jealous of Elle that you can't see straight. You always have been and anything that Elle ever wanted, you had to run in and steal away from her. Including me. We were in that class for weeks and you never said one word to me. You always sat next to that football player and flirted with him."

"That's not true."

"I don't believe you, Chloe. I think right now you're acting out of desperation. You've lost me, you've lost Elle and now you have no one who will listen to your never-ending bullshit and drama."

Hurt flashes through her eyes and I realize I probably went too far. But, goddammit, she's had it coming for a long-ass time. Keeping Elle and I apart on a jealous whim doesn't sit well with me.

It makes me sick.

You know what? Fuck going too far.

Hell, I'm just getting started, I think, as I lay into Chloe and call her out on her atrocious behavior.

15

ELLE

I finish doing my makeup and study my reflection in the mirror. Work is going well, Gray is flying down for a quick weekend trip to spend time with me and, as the weeks fly by, I feel myself falling more and more in love with him. It's like fate has given us another opportunity and I feel like the luckiest girl on the planet.

So, obviously, I'm waiting for something to go wrong.

Everything feels too perfect right now and I have this nagging feeling that things are about to change and not for the better.

Of course, Chloe and I still aren't speaking. It makes me sad, but at the same time, I think we needed time apart. I know I did, anyway. She's a lot to handle and right now I just want to focus on my relationship with Gray.

I give my hair a final fluff then head down the hall to the living room. My overnight bag is packed and when I reach for it, my purse slides off the chair and hits the floor. A few things roll out, including a tampon, and I freeze.

Two things occur at once: that I've been inexplicably nauseous all week and that I haven't had my period in nearly two months.

Chewing on my lower lip, I stuff my things back into my purse and mentally calculate how long it's been since Gray and I first had sex. Nearly two months. *Shit.* It's not possible, is it? We've used protection every single time. Well, except for that really brief moment in Boston, the second time when he forgot. But he pulled out so fast and-

"Oh, God," I murmur. Could I be pregnant?

I let out a shaky breath and don't want to panic until I know for sure. *There's no point in getting all crazy until it's definitely true,* I tell myself.

I need to know. Like now.

I text Gray quickly to let him know I'm running a little behind and then practically run down to the closest drug store. I swipe up the first pregnancy test I see, pay for it and then jog back to my apartment.

After reading through the instructions twice, I take the test and wait with bated breath for the results. *There's just no way,* I think. *You get pregnant the first night you spend with a man? And in like less than 5 seconds?*

No one's luck is that bad.

The idea that I could be carrying Gray's child right now is mind-blowing. I have no idea what I am going to do if this test is positive. It would change everything, and I don't think either of us is ready for that.

For God's Sake, we haven't even told each other I love you. And now I would have to tell him I'm pregnant? I cringe, sink down on the toilet lid and drop my face in my hands. This is terrible. The worst-case scenario and I hope I'm just being paranoid.

As the minutes tick by, I try to think about the outcome rationally. It's probably a million to one shot that Gray could've knocked me up in a few seconds. People struggle with fertility for years, so the chances are extremely slim. I'm making a big deal out of nothing. The stress of starting a new job and fighting with Chloe is the reason my cycle is messed up.

Make perfect sense.

I take a deep breath and flip the stick over.

Ohmygod. It's positive.

For a long moment, I can't breathe and my heart stops. *Holy shit.* I have no idea what to think, what to feel, how to process this. The stick falls from my fingers and I start breathing hard, head between my knees.

What am I going to do?

I'm totally freaking out so I can only imagine Gray's reaction. We have a long-distance thing going on and I'm not even sure I can call it a relationship. A long-distance hookup? Some steamy phone conversations and sex once a month hardly equals a serious relationship.

He never told you he loves you.

Granted, I haven't said it to him either. But I do know that I love him. I'm pretty sure I always have.

Gahhh. What should I do?

He's so busy and this couldn't have happened at a worse time. Let's not forget that he's my boss, too. How embarrassing. If the other employees find out, they're going to think the only reason I got the job is because I'm sleeping with Gray. This is the best job I have ever had, too. I'm finally doing what I love and getting paid for it. But can I stay there and reveal to everyone that I'm going to have Gray's baby?

What if he doesn't want a baby? Neither of us is in the right space to start a family. I know the easiest thing to do would be to take care of it and not ever tell anyone. A sigh escapes from between my lips and I sit back up straight and hug myself.

Even though it's the quickest solution, an easy out, I can't do it. I would never be able to destroy an innocent baby who is half Gray and half me. *No. Not a chance.*

Okay, so apparently, I'm going to have the baby. My heart thunders in my chest and I wipe my sweaty palms against my jeans as I contemplate my decision.

In approximately 7 months, I'm going to be a mom.

Even though I'm 27, I'm nowhere near ready. Well, I guess that's why they call it an unplanned pregnancy. How the hell am I going to tell Gray?

Glancing down at my watch, I realize I need to go. He's waiting for me, and he flew down here specially to see me. A part of me wonders if I should wait to tell him until after tonight. I certainly don't want to announce it first thing and destroy the mood. I'd much rather enjoy our time alone and then maybe bring it up in the morning?

Oh, hell. That doesn't seem like a good idea, either though. I don't want to drop a bomb on him right before he leaves to go back to Newport. What would I say? *Bye, Gray. Have a safe flight. And, oh, by the way, you're going to be a dad. See you next month!*

Ugh. My head hurts and I feel like I'm going to puke again. I already hurled my tea and croissant that I ate for breakfast. I know I'm getting in my head, but how can I not? Neither of us is ready to be a parent.

Then the worst thought in the world hits me. What if Gray bolts? This announcement is going to change his entire life and if he freaks out like I'm doing right now, he may decide he doesn't want to see me anymore.

Then I'll be on my own. Oh, God, just pin a scarlet A to my chest. The humiliation of working at C.T. International, carrying Gray's baby and not having his support is too much for me to think about right now.

I need to chill out and quit jumping to conclusions.

The funny thing is I'm wasting my energy worrying about all the wrong things.

When I arrive at Gray's loft, the door is ajar and I frown. Why would it be open? Is everything alright? I walk over and push it all the way open. "Gray?"

When I step inside, I spot him and Chloe not far away. His face is in Chloe's hands and she's kissing him. My heart drops into my stomach and my hand flutters over my heart. *No.* They break apart and look over at me, caught like a pair of deer in headlights.

A sick, sinking sensation fills me and I spin around and run away. Tears fill my eyes, and I don't even wait for the elevator. I blindly shove the stairwell door open and take off down the stairs.

"Elle!"

I hear Gray calling me, but I don't stop, can't stop, because my heart is breaking into a million, little pieces. The man I thought I loved and the woman who was my best friend were kissing. I couldn't be more devastated.

"Elle!"

There's no way I can talk to Gray or Chloe right now. I'm far too upset and I don't want to say something that I'll regret. I hurry out a back exit and lean against the brick building, breathing hard.

Was nothing between us real? Did I imagine our fiery connection? Was he just using me to warm his bed?

Unfortunately, I never faked anything. My feelings, though they just got trampled all over, are only too real. That's why this hurts so damn much.

I can't believe it. I blink hard as tears stream from my eyes. This is the worst thing that could've possibly happened. Gray would rather go back to Chloe than be with me.

A sob rips from my throat and I cover my mouth, trying to suppress the hurt and anger.

Well, I hope they're very happy together and I never want to see either of them ever again.

16

GRAY

When Chloe grabs my face and kisses me, I'm stunned. By the time I realize what's happening and yank away from her, Elle has already seen us and runs away.

"Fuck!" I hiss and shove Chloe back. "What the hell is wrong with you?"

Chloe shrugs a shoulder. "Just wanted to see if the ol' chemistry was still there."

"You did this on purpose. You're a bitch, Chloe."

"Oh, lighten up. It was just a kiss."

I blink in amazement at the callous words coming out of her mouth. "You just purposely hurt her. What would possess you to do that?"

"She made me mad." Chloe huffs out a breath. "Maybe I went too far, but she really pissed me off."

"I don't have time for this," I snap. "Out!"

After getting Chloe out, I slam my door and take off after Elle. I call for her, but she doesn't respond. I shove through the front lobby door and look up and down the sidewalk. She's nowhere in sight.

"Fuck," I sigh and run a frustrated hand through my hair. This was supposed to be such a perfect weekend and it just all came crashing down. When Chloe steps out of my building a minute later, I glare at her.

Chloe crosses her arms. "Don't look at me like that. Like I'm the devil or something."

I walk right up into her face, towering over her, and in a low, menacing voice, I say, "You better fucking fix this, Chloe."

Her blue eyes widen, and she takes a step back. "I'm sure if you just explain things to her-"

"No. That's what you're going to do. Right fucking now," I hiss, hands clenching into tight fists. I don't think I've ever been so angry with anyone in my entire life and I'm doing everything in my power not to snap.

"Now?" she asks and frowns in confusion.

"Call her," I thunder. I am beyond livid right now and one step away from throttling Chloe.

Chloe makes a face but pulls her cell phone out of her purse and hits Elle's number. It rings for a minute then drops into voicemail. "She's not answering."

"Then you keep fucking calling," I growl.

"Gray, you're not thinking clearly. She's upset and needs time to calm down. We should give her some space and try again later."

Panic hits me. *I can't believe this.* How could I have let Chloe just waltz right in and manipulate the entire situation like that? I'm such an idiot. I pinch the bridge of my nose and want to murder Chloe.

"Why did you do that? Why the hell did you grab my face and kiss me the moment Elle appeared? And I want the goddamn truth."

"Because..." she murmurs, voice low.

"That's not an answer."

"Because I guess I may have been a little jealous," she finally admits.

"No shit," I state in a flat voice.

Chloe narrows her eyes. "It's not like I planned to do it. I mean, well, maybe a little, but she deserved it! When she said I swooped in and claimed you and the whole time we were dating, you two were pining for each other, I got mad. How do you think that made me feel?"

"Again, this really isn't about you. It's about me and Elle. You just tried to sabotage us."

"Maybe I wanted to see if there was anything left between us?"

I cross my arms, not buying it.

"Okay, okay. I tried to sabotage you. But only because I was so mad. You guys were sneaking around behind my back. You're my ex and she's my best friend. I know this 'isn't about me' but it kind of is because I have feelings, too, you know. And you guys hurt them."

"You're resilient," I say, not feeling bad in the least. Her guilt trip isn't going to work on me.

Chloe sighs. "I think we all just need some space right now."

"No. You need to tell Elle that you purposely tried to ruin things between us. And the sooner you talk to her the better."

"Fine," she grumbles. "I'll go over to her apartment right now."

"Then text me after you talk and let me know how it goes."

Chloe rolls her eyes. "I'm sure you'll be able to salvage your romantic weekend," she says with a sniff.

"Are you even sorry at all?" I ask.

Chloe presses her lips together and doesn't say anything for a long moment. "I'll text you after I talk to Elle," she finally says and walks away.

I make a frustrated sound, spin around and stalk back into my building. This is definitely not how I planned on spending my weekend. Chloe is such a manipulative bitch, and I can't believe I ever considered her my friend. But college was a long time ago and I refuse to let her get away with her manipulative bullshit anymore. Especially when it winds up hurting Elle.

Back up in my loft, I want to call Elle so badly but I'm hoping that Chloe can clear things up first. At least a little. Then I may have to do some groveling and more explaining.

Elle Landon is the only woman I want in my life and maybe it's time I tell her. We've been having a really good time the last couple of months, but it's progressed into something so much more. At least for me.

I'm fairly certain we're both on the same page even though neither one of us has said anything. I know that I'm falling hard and fast for her. She's always enthralled me and now that I've spent time with her…now that I've tasted her and been deep inside of her…there's no turning back.

I'm ready to move forward. Whatever that means.

We need to sit down and figure it out together. I know a lot of this is on me because I've been in Newport, trying to take care of my parents and my dad's business. Maybe it's time to put Elle first.

I can't even begin to imagine what she's thinking right now, and I really hope that Chloe clears the air. Otherwise, I'm going to hunt Chloe down and there will be blood.

Wandering over to the balcony, I open the door and let the cold breeze blow in, hoping it will clear my head. I'm sweating, though. What if Elle is so angry that she doesn't want anything to do with me or Chloe ever again?

No. Not my sweet Elle. I know that even though her feelings might be hurt, once I talk to her and she knows the truth then she will handle the situation with grace. Like she always does.

Elle has a big, beautiful and forgiving heart. Hell, she'd have to in order to put up with Chloe for the last 20 some years.

God, I hate this waiting. A part of me just wants to go over to her place right now, but I have a feeling it's better to hold off. Let things play out and then head over tonight. I'm going to pull her into my arms and kiss her thoroughly after telling her that I'm falling madly in love with her.

My phone rings and I see Chloe's name pop up on the screen. I slide the bar over. "Did you talk to her?" I ask.

"She's not here," Chloe says.

"What?" I roar.

"I'm at her place and there's no sign of her."

"Where the hell is she?"

"I don't know, Gray," Chloe snaps. "I'm not a mind reader."

"You stay there until she gets back," I tell her.

"What if she doesn't come back? Am I supposed to spend the night here in her hallway?"

"I don't give a shit, Chloe," I snarl. "I need you to fucking fix this! Do you understand?"

"I understand that you're being an unreasonable jerk. I know Elle better than anyone and she needs time alone to think things through."

"Keep trying to call her, text her, sleep in the hallway outside her door. Whatever you need to do, do it! This is your fault," I coldly remind her.

To my surprise, Chloe mumbles, "I know. And I do feel bad, Gray. Jealousy got the best of me."

I shake my head, done with Chloe and this conversation. "Let me know if you talk to her," I say and hang up.

I've had enough of Chloe for the day. I pull Elle's name up and call her. It rings and rings and rings. When her voicemail clicks on, I swear and hang up. Where could she be?

Hmm. Guess it's time to find out because there's no way I can rely on Chloe to get things done. I grab my keys and decide to see if her car is parked over at her apartment. Because if it's not then she probably left the city and is heading home to hide out at her parents' house.

That's what I'm thinking, anyway.

All I know is I can't sit around here and wait, or I'll lose my damn mind. Of course, halfway over to Elle's place, my phone rings.

"Hi, Mom," I say.

"Honey, you need to come home. You're dad..."

Her voice breaks and my heart starts beating harder in my chest. I can hear it thumping in my ears. "What happened?" I ask, dreading her answer.

"He was just rushed to the emergency room," she says, and I can hear the worry in her strained voice. "It's not looking good."

Fuck. The light turns green, and I hesitate. Should I still swing by Elle's really fast or-

"I don't think he's going to make it," she says and bursts into tears.

My heart sinks. "I'm on my way, Mom."

I turn toward the airport and realize Elle is going to have to hang on a little bit longer. My dad, on the other hand, might not be able to hold on and I need to get to his bedside before anything bad happens.

The flight back is quick. When I get to the hospital, my mom is there, and her eyes are puffy and red. I hug her and ask how Dad is doing.

"Hanging in there," she says wearily. "He's still in surgery and I'm just not sure how much more of this he can take."

When she breaks, I wrap my arms around her. "It's okay. He's tough. We both know that."

"I'm sorry for ruining your weekend with Elle and making you come all the way back here when you just left this morning."

"Don't worry about it. You know this is where I want to be," I reassure her.

My mom nods and then steps back. "I love you, Grayson. You're such a good son and you've turned into a wonderful young man. Your dad and I couldn't be prouder."

After everything that's happened today, her words touch a part of me that I usually keep hidden. I've never been overly emotional or one to talk about my feelings, but my chest tightens. "Love you, too, Mom," I say and sling an arm around her shoulders. "Don't worry. Dad's going to pull through like before. I know it."

She releases a shuddering breath and leans against me. "I hope so, honey. Without him…" her voice catches and she swipes a tissue over her teary eyes. "He's the love of my life."

I squeeze her shoulder, look up at the ceiling and I hope to God my dad pulls through this. *He has to,* I think. And Elle and I have to pull through, too.

Because living life without the 'love of your life' isn't an option for me or my mom.

17

ELLE

I don't know what to do.

The man I thought I loved and the woman who was my best friend were kissing. I couldn't be more devastated.

The same thought, the one I had right before running away, keeps repeating inside my brain.

The man I thought I loved and the woman who was my best friend were kissing.

Images of Gray and Chloe kissing fills my head, torturing me. I thought things had been going well between us, but did I have blinders on? We never exchanged any promises to each other or said I love you. We never even said we'd be faithful to each other or not see other people.

Technically, Gray is allowed to kiss anyone he wants. We weren't exclusive. But I really believed we had something special. That it was the beginning of a beautiful love story.

I'm such an idiot.

I shouldn't have assumed he was feeling the same intense things that I was because all I did was set myself up for heartbreak. I've never felt like such a total and complete fool as I do now.

The man I thought I loved and the woman who was my best friend were kissing.

When Gray calls my name, running after me, I ignore him and hope he goes out the front door because I sneak out the back. Luckily, he does, and I don't have to confront him right now. Because I am falling apart, barely keeping it together. I couldn't handle dealing with him and Chloe right now.

I'm too hurt.

It's not even about just me anymore, either. Now there's a baby involved and that ratchets things up to an entirely new level. I rake my hands through my hair and suck in deep lungful's of cold air. I need to get out of here and think.

But where do I go?

Home.

Whenever things get tough, I always return home and take comfort in my parents' support. *Yes, that's the plan,* I think, and head for my car. I'm going to drive to Fairview and hide. Try to figure things out. At least come up with some answers because right now I'm floundering in a sea of what-ifs and doubts.

I certainly can't return to C.T. International. *God.* The humiliation would be too much to face every day. It makes me really sad to quit when I've loved working there the past couple of months. But I don't have an option. Especially now that I'm pregnant with Gray's baby.

It still seems surreal, and I haven't even had time to adjust to the idea. I should probably make a doctor's appointment while I'm home. The truth is…I'm terrified.

I'm not in the best state of mind to drive so after getting in my car, I sit there for a few minutes and wait until I calm down a little. Start breathing more normally again. My phone rings and I glance down and see it's Chloe.

Screw her. I have nothing to say to her and let the call drop into my voicemail.

She really has some nerve. I'm not sure what rekindled her interest in Gray, but I have a funny feeling it was me. The moment she realized I was interested and seeing him, she pounced. It proves to me that I can't trust her.

I doubt that she even really likes him. Knowing Chloe, it was more about the challenge than her actual feelings. She just wanted to one-up me.

Well, congratulations, Chloe. You stole Gray away from me. I hope you're happy.

I head onto the highway and figure that it will take me about an hour to get to Fairview. That gives me time to figure out how to break the news to my parents. The good thing is they have always supported me and helped me make things work.

I just hope that continues and they aren't too disappointed in me.

When I get home, my dad is still at work and my mom is surprised to see me.

"Elle! What're you doing here?" she asks.

I walk over and hug her. Despite my plans to play it cool, I burst into tears. "Oh, Mom," I say between sobs. "Everything is falling apart, and I don't know what to do."

"Honey..." She gives me a squeeze and then pulls back, looking at me with concerned eyes. "What's going on?"

"I'm not sure where to begin."

"C'mon," she says and motions for me to follow her into the kitchen. "I just made cookies and let's make some tea while you figure out where to start."

I'm so grateful for my mom, I think, and sit down at the marble island. Once I have a steaming mug and a plate of chocolate chip cookies in front of me, I sigh. She waits patiently for me to find the words and I figure I should go back to the beginning...when I first met Gray.

"Do you remember Gray Carter?" I ask her.

"Gray Carter?" she repeats, thinking. "Was that the boy who came up to the lake with Chloe when you guys were in college?"

I nod. "Yeah. And you and dad weren't very nice to him."

"What? Why not? What did he do?"

"He came from a wealthy family, and you know how dad gets when he thinks someone doesn't work for anything."

"Oh," my mom says. "Your father hates when people, especially young kids, are handed everything on a silver platter. But only because he's worked so hard for everything that we have."

"So has Gray, though. Instead of working at his dad's company and taking the easy road, he moved to the city and worked really hard to start his own business."

My mom nods, not quite sure where I'm going with this.

"Now I'm working for him and we, ah, reconnected." I pause and pick at the placemat. "The thing is…I always really liked Gray. Even before he and Chloe went out. For a minute, I almost thought maybe we would date. More like hoped, anyway. But then Chloe swooped in and I backed down."

"And you wish you'd never backed down?" she asks softly.

"Exactly. From the moment we met, there was a connection, but we messed up and made all the wrong choices. I figured that was it. Until we saw each other again two months ago. It's almost like we got a second chance. So, we took it."

"You're dating him?"

"We started seeing each other and went to the reunion together. It was amazing and we had such a good time. Until Chloe showed up and she wasn't happy. But we still kept spending time together and it's been mostly long distance because he's been back home in Newport taking care of his dad who had a heart attack."

"Oh, that's terrible," my mom says.

"But we talked every night and I thought everything was going so well until-" My voice cuts off and tears prick my eyes.

"Until what?"

"Gray came in this morning, and we'd planned to spend some time together. But when I got to his place, I caught him and Chloe kissing."

"What?"

"I just don't understand. I really thought he liked me and wanted to be with me."

"Did you talk to them?"

"No! I ran out and drove straight here."

"Elle, honey, you need to talk to them both and hear their side of the story."

"What's to hear? It's clear they like each other again."

"Maybe, maybe not," my mom says carefully. "Elle, I'm not sure how to say this, but Chloe hasn't always been the greatest friend to you. She's always put herself and her interests over you and everything else."

"I've started to realize that" I admit. "I just feel like such an idiot."

"Honey, I think you should talk to them both and things will work themselves out."

I squeeze my eyes shut, take a deep breath and then spill the even bigger secret. "That's not all. I just found out…" *Oh, God.* "I'm pregnant."

My mom's eyes widen, and she lets out a long, low breath. "You're sure?"

"I took a test this morning, but I haven't gone to the doctor yet."

"Well, there's a chance it could be inaccurate."

I shake my head. "I don't think so. We…I mean…it's definitely possible."

"Oh, Lord," my mom says and drops her face in her palm. "Well, this little tidbit changes everything."

"I know," I say miserably.

"Oh, wait'll your father finds out."

My dad is extremely blunt and never sugar coats anything. So, when he gets home after work and I tell him that I'm expecting Gray's baby, he looks dumbfounded for a moment. Then uncomfortable and then the anger flares up.

"Elle, I know we all make mistakes, but this has to be one of the stupidest, most preventable things in the world. But what makes me the most upset is you want to quit your job and go into hiding. What the hell is wrong with you? You said you love your new job."

"I do. But how can I stay there when Gray is my boss?"

"You should've thought about that before hooking up with him. Never mix business with pleasure."

"Hindsight," I mumble.

"That may be so, but if you go running with your tail between your legs, then you're not the daughter I thought you were. You need to take responsibility for your actions and, if you can't, then there's always an alternative."

Is my dad suggesting I get an abortion? I can't believe he would ever do that.

"He's right," my mom says. "If you aren't ready to raise a child-"

"I'm having the baby," I say, voice firm. "My mind is made up so nothing you say will change it."

"Then the last thing you should do is quit your job. Babies are expensive. And so is living in the damn city. If you don't have a job, how do you plan on buying diapers and formula and-"

"I know. I get it." I sigh. "I was thinking maybe I'd move back here for a while…"

My parents exchange a look.

"Is that really what you want to do?" my mom asks.

"No, but my choices are really limited right now."

"Elle, if you quit that job without another job to go to, you are not welcome back here," my dad says.

"What?" I can't believe those words just came out of his mouth.

"You can't run away from your problems. Why're you letting Chloe and this Gray dictate your life? Stand up to them both and do what needs to be done. Put yourself and the baby first."

"But-"

"You've never been very good at that, Elle, and it's time to change. Your wants and needs are just as important as theirs, so don't let them bully you into hiding out here for the next year or two. Look, you had sex, you got knocked up, now you gotta own it, kid."

But I can't, I think. It's too humiliating. "How am I supposed to go back to work for Gray? Everyone's going to find out and-"

"That's the way it goes. Don't throw a good-paying job away because now you're embarrassed."

"I could work for you," I say hopefully.

"I do not want you wandering around a busy construction site, pregnant and wearing a hard hat. That's stupid and dangerous and you know it."

"So, you're telling me that if, *when,* I quit C.T. International that I can't work for you or come home and live?"

My dad shakes his head. "You're better than that, Elle. Stop worrying about what everyone else thinks and do what you want."

"I want to come home!" I yell and stand up. "I want you and mom to support me and help, but I guess that's asking too much."

Hurt pours through me and, for the second time today, I feel betrayed by the ones closest to me. I don't understand why he's acting like this. I know my hormones are probably all over the place and I'm more emotional than usual, but I think I have good reason to be upset.

"Elle!" my mom calls. "Steve…"

"It's called tough love."

Their voices fade away and, once again, I run. I'm so upset that I have no words left to say to either of them. In one day, I've been betrayed by my parents, my best friend and the man I loved. I lay a hand over my flat stomach and realize there's only one soul on my side right now.

And we will figure things out.

With or without anyone else's help.

18

GRAY

I probably call Elle's cell phone 100 times a day for the next few days, but she refuses to answer. Chloe is no help, either, and then disappears on me, too. I'm so mad at myself for the way I let all of this happen.

I know I should've handled the situation differently, but when Chloe kissed me, it took me a moment to comprehend what was going on because I was in shock. When I heard Elle a moment later, I pulled away. But words eluded me. Of course, I didn't kiss Chloe back. Just stood there like a dumbass not able to believe what was happening.

And then Elle ran off.

Elle assumed the worst and I can't blame her. I never communicated with her how I was feeling or what I wanted. I've been so wrapped up in my parents, work and sneaking in stolen moments with Elle that I never made time to address our relationship.

Now all I want to do is explain what happened, even though I'm still not sure why Chloe did what she did. Sabotage and jealousy, I guess. It infuriates me that Chloe set us up because now Elle and I are losing precious time together.

I'm back in Rhode Island, pacing back and forth, about to lose my goddamn mind. I'm at my wit's end and raking my hands through my hair when my mom appears. I'm not even sure how long she's been watching me.

"Grayson," she says. "You're going to destroy the carpet with all that pacing."

I abruptly stop and look over. "How's Dad?"

"Sleeping," she says. "It's been a rough few days, but I think I'm seeing an improvement. I hope so, anyway."

I walk over and give her a quick hug. "It's okay. He's strong."

She presses a couple of fingers to her temple. "I know." She eyes me closely and touches my arm.

I raise a brow.

"What's going on with you? We've been so busy caring for your father that we haven't had a chance to talk. It's quite clear that something is wrong."

I blow out a breath and drop down into the nearest chair. My mom sits across from me on the sofa and waits while I try to organize my thoughts.

"It's Elle…" I shake my head, not able to get the words out.

"Oh, no. What happened?"

"Fucking Chloe happened," I state harshly. "Sorry," I add.

"It's okay."

"Elle was on her way over and Chloe showed up out of the blue. She set me up. The second Elle walked in, Chloe grabbed me and kissed me. Of course, Elle ran out and I haven't talked to her since. It's like she disappeared, and she won't answer my calls or Chloe's."

"Why did Chloe do that?"

"She's not happy that Elle and I are together. She planned it so that Elle would see and get upset. Now I don't know what to do."

"You need to explain to her what happened."

"I know, but she refuses to talk to me. Liam said she hasn't shown up at work. The only thing I can think of is she drove home to Fairview. I tried calling Chloe earlier to get the address, but she's dodging my calls because I'm so pissed."

"Maybe take it down a notch. You'll catch more flies with honey."

"I'm trying, Mom, but it's damn hard." I run a frustrated hand through my hair and frown. "I suppose I did send Chloe some demanding texts and she hates being told what to do."

"Chloe only does what she wants to do. But you're probably right and Elle went home for a few days. It's clear that she needed space."

"I need to clear things up with her, though."

"Honey, I think you should drive to Fairview and see if she's there. At least talk to her parents. They probably know where she is."

"But what about you guys? What if something happens to Dad and I'm not here?"

"You're only going to New York, not Alaska. We both understand and this isn't something you can put off any longer. Elle is probably upset and confused so the sooner you go, the better."

I mull over her words and it's clear that I have the best parents in the world. "As long as you're okay with it-"

"Go get your girl," she says and smiles. It's the first genuine smile I've seen in days and my heart soars.

"Love you, Mom," I say, hop up and give her a swift kiss on the cheek.

"Gray?"

I turn and look at my mom who has a strange look on her face. "Yeah?"

"Do you love Elle?"

I nod, unable to trust my voice.

"Does she know?"

"I haven't told her yet. But I plan to as soon as I track her down."

My mom absorbs my words and clasps her hands. "She's always been the one you wanted, hasn't she?"

"Always," I confirm.

"Can you picture her as your wife? As the woman you'd want to have a family with and grow old together with?"

I'm not sure why she's asking me all these questions. Maybe to open my eyes and make me realize that Elle is the only one for me. But I already know that. "Yes," I admit. "She's it for me. I know it. Can feel it in my bones. When we're together, nothing else matters and spending the rest of my life with Elle is the only option for me. I just hope she realizes that I never meant to hurt her."

My mom slowly nods her head then motions for me to follow her. "Before you go, come with me. I have something to give you."

I frown, beyond curious, and follow my mom to my parents' bedroom. She walks over to her jewelry box and opens a drawer. Then she removes a small velvet box. "This belonged to your great-grandmother. She came over here from France right after she and your great grandpa got married. You know they changed their name at Ellis Island from Cartier to Carter. No relation to the famous jeweler, but she did leave this beautiful ring to me, and I always wanted you to have the option of giving it to the woman you want to marry."

My mom hands me the box and I flip the lid open. It's stunning. A brilliant diamond solitaire set in an antique platinum band. "It's perfect."

"The story goes that they bought it in Paris, and he proposed to her on a bridge during a blizzard. I'm not sure about the blizzard part, but it must've been snowing. It was such a romantic story."

"I can see this ring on Elle's finger. It reminds me of her."

"Does it?"

I nod, turning the ring to study it. "At first glance, it looks calm, steady and beautiful. But upon closer inspection, it's so fiery. So deep and brilliant. It contains a story."

"If you want to give it to her, it's yours."

"Thanks, Mom. It's absolutely perfect and I think she'll love it." Even though I already gave her the diamond band, this means so much more. It's an engagement ring with a beautiful story behind it. It's not just an inside joke.

I close the lid and tuck the small box in my pocket.

"You're welcome, honey." We embrace. "Now go get your girl."

"Fingers crossed," I say.

After looking in on my dad who's still sleeping, I pack an

overnight back and hop in my car, determined to find Elle. I'm going to fly back to New York to save time and then drive up to Fairview. She has to be at her parents' place. I try calling Chloe a few more times to get the address and she finally picks up.

"Chloe, I need Elle's parents' address."

"She's not there. Not anymore, anyway."

"What do you mean?"

"I called and they said she showed up, all upset, and apparently, they had a big fight about something and she stormed out. They don't know where she went."

"Fuck," I hiss. "And she's not at her apartment?"

"No. I checked about 20 minutes ago."

"When did she storm off?"

"Three days ago."

Three days ago? Elle has been gone for 72 hours and no one knows where the hell she is? If I thought I was losing my mind before, I'm barely holding it together right now.

"Text me their address, okay?" I say through gritted teeth.

"Okay," she quickly says.

"If you can think of anywhere, she might have gone...*anywhere*... please tell me, Chloe."

"I'm sorry, Gray. I have no idea."

I squeeze the steering wheel so hard, my hands hurt. All I want to do is break shit and yell about how unfair this whole stupid situation is, but I need to maintain a rational train of thought or I'm going to careen off the rails.

I need to figure out where my girl is and go beg for her forgiveness.

"Chloe, I'm on my way to her parents' house now. If you think of anything, please let me know."

"I will," she whispers.

"Thanks."

"Gray?"

"What?"

"For what it's worth, I'm really sorry."

Her voice is low, but for the first time she sounds genuine. "Just help me find her," I say.

"I'll try," she promises.

After hanging up, I get to the airport and hop on the next available flight down to New York. Then, I take a taxi back to my apartment, jump into my car and head toward Fairview. It's starting to get late and by the time I arrive at Mr. and Mrs. Landon's house, it's after 7pm.

I'm not sure how they're going to receive me, but I'm here because I'm concerned about Elle. They didn't like me when we met a long time ago, but hopefully they forgot about that.

Although I sure never did.

I walk up to the front door and knock. The porch light illuminates me and after another minute, I knock again. Eventually, a face glances out the side glass pane and Elle's father opens the door.

"Yes?"

"Hi, Mr. Landon. You probably don't remember me, but I'm a friend of Elle's. From college. Grayson Carter," I say and hold out my hand.

His face instantly hardens, and he ignores my proffered hand. Confused, I clear my throat, letting my hand drop to my side.

"What do you want?" he asks in a gruff voice.

"Can I come in?"

"Not sure why you're here," he grumbles and steps aside. "I think you've done enough damage."

I step into the foyer and glance over to see Mrs. Landon standing in the hall. I've got no clue what that last comment means so I ignore it. Maybe Elle told them about kissing Chloe. I have no idea and their reaction seems harsher than it should be.

"I'm looking for Elle. Do you know where she is?"

"She was here," her mom says. "Gray, isn't it?"

I nod. "I'm not sure what she's told you-"

"Oh, quite enough," Mr. Landon says in a disgusted voice. "You were her boss, right?"

"I am her boss, yes."

"Well, not since she up and quit."

I frown. "I know she hasn't been into the office the last few days, but no one told me she quit." *She better not have quit,* I think. She loves her new job. Is she so angry at me that she'd leave C.T. International without even talking to me first? It doesn't make sense.

"I told her not to make such a rash decision when she's so upset, but Elle wasn't in a very good headspace."

My heart clenches and guilt consumes me. "I know and that's my fault. I need to talk to her and explain the situation. It's just a big misunderstanding."

"What's to explain?"

"Well, my side of things, for one," I say carefully.

"She made it pretty clear that you're not going to have time for her and the baby."

Wait, what? My head spins at his words. Did I just hear him right? I feel like I've stepped into the Twilight Zone. What is he talking about? "*Baby?*" I exclaim. "What baby?"

"Steve..." Mrs. Landon says, a warning note in her voice.

"Elle is pregnant and apparently it's your baby," Mr. Landon says.

All of the air rushes out of my lungs and my world tilts sideways. *Elle is pregnant?* But, how? We've been so careful. I'm having a hard time comprehending his words. Suddenly, I feel like I'm going to fall over.

"Gray, why don't you come in and have a seat?" Mrs. Landon says.

Yeah, I better, because I feel like I'm going to fall down on my ass in about three seconds. I swallow down the lump of disbelief caught in my throat and frantically think back through all of our encounters over the last couple of months.

When did I-

"I assumed you knew about the baby," her father says. "But since you look shell-shocked, I'm gonna go out on a limb here and guess that she didn't tell you yet."

"Um, no. She didn't," I manage to say.

"Sit before you fall down," he says gruffly.

We head into the living, and I drop down into a chair. My head is spinning faster than a merry-go-round and I'm trying to wrap my mind around the fact that Elle is pregnant with my baby.

And then it all hits me hard– she's pregnant, upset, confused and alone. I have no idea where she is and I've left endless voicemails, begging her to call me. She must be a wreck and I need to fix this fast.

"So, what're you gonna do about it?" her dad asks.

I pull in a deep breath, trying to get my bearings. "I'm going to do whatever Elle wants. But I need to figure out where she is because she won't return my calls."

"She's very upset," Mrs. Landon says.

I can only imagine. I feel like such a jerk. Like I've let her down when she needs me most. "I know. Do you have any idea where she is?"

Her parents exchange a worried look. "We figured she drove back to the city."

I shake my head. "No. She's not there."

"Well, where else would she be?" Mrs. Landon asks, starting to look worried.

"I don't know. I was hoping you could point me in the right direction because she won't talk to me or Chloe. Our calls just go straight to voicemail."

"Oh, no," Mrs. Landon exclaims, worried lines furrowing her brow. "Steve, you shouldn't have been so hard on her."

A pained expression crosses her father's face.

"She's in a really fragile state," I say. "Even more so than I knew. I have to talk to her and make sure she's okay." Desperation and worry cling to my voice and I can see her parents getting visibly upset, too.

"Oh, my God," Mrs. Landon says. "Where would she have gone?"

"I should've let her stay here," Mr. Landon says in a quiet voice.

"You told her to leave?" I ask, completely taken aback. *What the fuck?*

"I told her she'd be stupid to quit her job over you. That she needed to be able to support herself and the baby. I might've been a little harsh about it."

"Jesus," I hiss. My world seems to be caving in on itself and the answers I need are still out of my reach.

I have no idea what to do. All I know is that I need to find Elle and that's proving harder and harder to do.

19

ELLE

The days pass by and instead of feeling better, I feel worse. After leaving my parents' house, I had no idea where to go. I certainly couldn't return to the city and face Gray and Chloe.

And then it occurred to me– our old cottage up at the lake. I drove straight there, and I've been hunkered down here for over a week now. No one has been here in years so it's empty and quiet. It's also freezing cold, and I have a roaring fire going in the fireplace right now.

Curled up in front of the flames, I stare into their hot flicker and think about Gray. My poor heart breaks all over again. I came here to hide, reflect and figure things out. But my mind keeps going back to all the time we spent together. I truly believed that things would work out this time around. That we had been given a second chance.

And then all of my hopes and dreams went up in smoke.

Even though I saw Gray and Chloe kissing, I'm having such a hard time wrapping my head around it. Did I jump to conclusions? There was no denying that she had her tongue down his throat, but I never thought of Gray as someone who would cheat. Even when he was dating Chloe and we were alone together, he never made a move. Despite our mutual attraction, he was always a gentleman.

So why now all of a sudden would he do that? And with Chloe of all people? I honestly didn't think they even liked each other anymore.

"I'm so confused," I whisper.

I was so upset the way my parents, especially my dad, reacted to my pregnancy. All I asked for was a place to stay while I figured things out. And maybe a job with my dad's company. The fact that he said no hurts a lot.

All of my life, I've made it a point to put others ahead of myself. My family, my friends, even strangers. And when I finally need some support and love, everyone lets me down.

Yes, I'm super hormonal right now and my emotions feel like they're swirling around in a blender. Mostly confusion and betrayal. But what am I supposed to do? I know I should let someone know I'm safe, but I'm still angry. And so damn hurt.

My phone's voicemail is full and there are over 200 unread text messages. With a sigh, I pick it up, go into my messages and hit play.

"Elle, it's not what you think," Gray says. "I swear. Please, hear me out."

My heart tightens at the sound of his deep voice and my fingers clench around the phone.

"Elle, it's me." Chloe's melodic voice now fills the line. "I'm a jerk. Probably the worst friend in the world. Please call me."

My eyes narrow. *What exactly happened?* I wonder for the thousandth time. Did Chloe instigate that kiss? Even if she did, Gray didn't appear to pull away very fast. Maybe it was the angle, now with hindsight, because he did look a little surprised.

I play the next message. And the next and the next. Each one seems to sound a little more frantic, but they kind of deserve it. Finally, I hear my dad's voice. "Elle, honey, I'm sorry about how things went earlier. Your mom and I want you to come home. Please."

Too little, too late, I think and hit delete.

My head falls back, and I drop my phone. I'm glad everyone is so concerned about me now that I've gone and disappeared. I draw my legs up to my chest, wrap my arms around myself and press my forehead against my knees.

What am I going to do?

Yesterday, I emailed Liam and resigned. He wrote me back right away, asking if he could help and what was going on. He said Gray was frantic and trying to find me. Of course, I didn't respond, and he emailed again a little later. He must've talked to Gray because he asked where I was and said that he was worried about me.

I've never been in a situation like this where I feel like the world is against me and I have no support from the people I love. God, when did I turn into Chloe? I've never had feelings this all-consuming and desperate. Am I being melodramatic?

No. I feel like I've given everyone my all when they've needed me. Now, when the tables have turned, I'm sitting here alone on the floor, crying, in a cold, remote and lonely cottage all by myself.

I guess this is what happens when you're too nice and far too trusting. People walk all over you. If I had learned to stick up for myself and not just accept everyone else's bullshit this wouldn't be happening right now.

My dad's advice floats through my head: *Stop worrying about what everyone else thinks and do what you want.*

My father is strong and maybe if he was in my situation, he could've driven back down to New York, confronted Chloe and Gray and kept right on working at C.T. International despite a growing belly. He would've held his head high and collected his paycheck.

But I'm not like that. I'm more fragile and sensitive. I've always cared far too much what others think and maybe that's part of my downfall. Part of the reason that I'm here, curled up in a ball and crying, instead of confronting my problems head-on.

I wish I was stronger and more fearless. But I'm just not. The going got tough and I ran away.

With a sigh, I lay down, turning onto my side and tuck my arm beneath my cheek. I stare at the flames, unable to stop the tears from sliding down my cheeks.

I'm an absolute wreck.

The days continue to pass and there comes a point when I have no more tears left. I splash water on my face, stand up straight and gaze at my reflection in the mirror. *Time to buck up and face the music.* Crying and laying around here feeling sorry for myself isn't going to accomplish anything.

I send a text to my mom and let her know I'm alright and that I need some space to figure things out. While I'm making breakfast, my phone blows up with text messages, so she must've told Gray and Chloe that I contacted her.

Wishing they would just leave me alone; I flip my phone over and finish cutting up some fruit. I open a container of yogurt and sit down at the table. They all need to back off and respect my wishes for privacy. I have a lot to figure out right now with no job, no support and a baby on the way with no father in the picture.

A baby on the way. Oh, God, it's such a strange thought to have. *Me.* The good girl who waited until she was 27 years old to have sex for the first time is now pregnant. The ironic thing is, after counting the days and thinking it over, I must've gotten pregnant in Boston. The first night we slept together. Not that much sleeping happened.

But, seriously, what are the chances?

I guess pretty good even though he'd only been inside me, skin to skin, for the briefest amount of time. It kind of annoys me, actually, because if I got pregnant then, all this time we could've ditched the condoms. We could've been even closer, and I have a feeling that would've been really, really nice.

Ugh. What am I thinking? I'm supposed to be mad at Gray. Not imagining condom-less sex with him. *That's what got you in this situation in the first place,* I remind myself. Lots of wild, passionate sex with the man you fell in love with and couldn't control yourself around. I suppose I shouldn't be surprised that I'm pregnant now.

After breakfast, I'd rather die than spend another day lying around and feeling sorry for myself. So, despite the cold weather, I pull on a coat, scarf and knit hat and go for a walk. The freezing cold air feels good on my face, and I take a path we used to take as kids that goes through the woods and will lead me down to the edge of the lake.

The brisk walk feels good, even better than I thought it would and my boots crunch on the trail. I glance up through the tree limbs and the sky is very gray. It's too cold for rain so that can only mean snow. It's still only November so it would be the first snowfall of the year. Which is actually late because upstate New York is known for its record amounts of snow each year.

I pick up my pace and finally reach the lake. Memories flood through my head of all the times we used to spend here while growing up. Since I was an only child and I had no siblings to play with, I was always allowed to bring Chloe up here with me.

We used to have so much fun, I think, and press a hand to my chest. We would row across the lake or take the paddle boat around and explore every single nook and cranny. We'd go fishing and tubing. One day during one of our explorations, we discovered a secret waterway that led through a bunch of weeds.

After almost two hours, a couple of beaver dams and endless bugs, we traversed the entire length of the passage– what we later nick-named the "Secret Passage" -- and came upon a quiet, pristine lake. No one knew about the secret lake, and it was our secret. We spent the entire afternoon lazing in the rowboat, soaking up the sun and talking about our dreams and wishes.

People might wonder how Chloe and I ever became such good friends when we're so different, but it was moments like that when we were on exactly the same page.

God, I miss my best friend. It makes me sad that the special and strong connection we had at 12 years old changed over the years. As we grew older, our circle of friends grew wider and sometimes she would say or do things that would make me wonder if she really still had my back. Gray is a perfect example.

I guess people and relationships change with time. It's clear that I can't be friends with someone who tried to sabotage me. If she even did. I really don't know anything for sure. Eventually, I suppose I'll have to talk to her, but right now, I'm not interested. I'm still very raw and I need to build my strength back up and figure my damn life out.

The old tire swing still hangs from the tree, and I sit down and slowly swing back and forth, lost in my thoughts. I can't say I'm necessarily feeling better, but I'm glad I came out here and got some fresh air. Small waves roll up along the shoreline, pebbled with tiny rocks and stones, and no one is around. Most people closed their summer cottage up months ago and the peace and quiet fills me.

The summers here are hectic and the air is always filled with the sounds of kids playing, motorboats on the lake and laughter. There was always so much laughter. I can't remember the last time I laughed, but I'm sure it was with Gray.

Grayson Carter. What am I going to do about him? He's going to be a father and he has no idea. I know that I have to tell him and it's not going to be easy. Hell, if I haven't scared him off yet then that's definitely going to do it. Or, for all I know, he's back with Chloe and happily rekindling their romance.

The thought makes my stomach hurt and I lean over and suck in a deep, cleansing breathful of crisp air. I've tried to put on a brave face today and have even managed to maintain it for longer than I thought possible, but I can feel it crumbling. That's what happens when I picture my life without Gray in it.

It's dark and lonely. I know I have a baby to think about now, but it's so hard. I want our child to know his or her father. But if we're not together and he doesn't run for the hills, that means we'd co-parent.

How in the world would that work?

Well, considering I'm in love with him, probably not too well.

A shiver runs through me, and I wrap my arms around myself, trying to hold in some warmth. The sky is growing darker and it's definitely going to snow. I slip off the tire swing and decide to head back to the cottage as the first snowflakes begin to flutter down from the sky.

20

GRAY

When I hear from Chloe that Elle texted her mom and said she's safe, I sag against the couch and let out a sigh of relief. I'm back in Newport, helping my parents still, and hearing this from Chloe is the best news I could've received today.

It's been two weeks without a word, and I understand Elle was upset, but I'm pissed. The way she ran off and left us all hanging and worried was selfish. I never would've expected Elle to abandon me like that and completely ignore all of my calls and texts. I always said Chloe was the selfish one, but Elle's latest behavior indicates she learned some bad habits from her best friend.

Because Elle isn't the only one involved in this situation. So is our baby. I still can't believe she's pregnant, but I've had time to think about it and now I want to talk to her. *Did she ever plan on telling me?* I wonder. She can't hide out forever and I'm going to find her.

But where the hell is she?

I reach around and squeeze the back of my neck. Maybe this is all my fault. Yes, I'm angry that she refuses to talk to me, but it's clear that she thinks she has a good reason to shut me out. For fuck's sake, does she really believe that kiss between me and Chloe was real?

My heart sinks. She must. Suddenly I feel like the world's biggest asshole. I should've shoved Chloe away and ran my ass off to catch up with Elle. Even if I had to tackle her down and force her to hear me out.

Chloe and I are ancient history. I have zero interest in her and, the majority of the time, she drives me crazy. Even when we were dating, she had the power to drive me bonkers. It was always me-me-me and that gets old very fast. I let out a frustrated sigh and pinch the bridge of my nose.

How did this happen? Elle and I were so happy. Or so I thought. Again, I'm going to take the blame because when we first got together, she'd never had a serious relationship. She probably didn't know what to expect and the more I think about it, the more upset I get.

With myself.

I should've been there for her more. Sex and intimacy were brand new for her and I just took it for granted that everything was absolutely fine. Despite the fact that I took her virginity and never told her how much I cared about her. Hell, I still feel awful about not reaching out to her that entire week after Boston. What the hell was I thinking?

Yes, it was clear we both liked each other, but that's a far cry from love. I should've given her more reassurance and been more understanding. But I was so consumed with lust and being as close as possible with her that I never took into consideration that she might've needed more than just the physical stuff.

She needed to connect on an emotional level, too. I mean, we clearly did, but at the same time, I never expressed my feelings to her. Not knowing where I stood must have left her feeling insecure. Now I realize that she needed to hear the words.

With a low curse, I drop my face in my palm. *I'm such a damn idiot,* I think.

I was so confident that I could give Elle everything that she needed and here we are, apart and the space between us is full of miscommunications.

I need to track her down and make her listen. She has to give me a chance to explain my side because Elle Landon means the world to me. Ever since we've met, there's been an attraction. But since reconnecting, that spark has exploded into a wildfire.

It's more than just our amazing physical connection, though, and that's what I failed to tell her. The intimacy we share goes so far beyond that, so much deeper. The truth is, I love her. I love Elle so much and, honestly, I've always been half in love with her since the moment we met at that party in college.

Elle Marie Landon is my person. She brings out the best in me and there's no one else I want to spend the rest of my life with. The fact that we have a child on the way already makes it even sweeter.

Now I just need to find her and tell her all this. I dip a hand in my pocket and wrap my fingers around the ring I've been carrying since the moment my mom gave it to me.

Feeling clarity, I decide to go check in on my dad. He's been recovering well, better than anyone could have predicted. Even the doctor is surprised how quickly he's bouncing back. Truthfully, it's a miracle, but I'm so damn grateful.

I'm not really expecting him to be awake, but when I look into his room, he's sitting up and flipping the TV channel.

"Hey," I say, and he looks over. "How're you feeling? Do you need anything?"

"Feeling stronger every day," he says and motions for me to come inside.

"I can tell. You've got your color back."

"Any news on Elle?"

"Yes and no," I say carefully and sit down in the chair beside his bed. "I'm still not sure where she's hiding out, but I just had this weird moment of clarity."

"Really?"

I nod. "It dawned on me why she's so upset and won't talk to anyone, and I can't blame her. I never gave her the reassurance that she needed. I hate to admit this, but I pretty much slept with her and then took off. Communication hasn't ever been my strongpoint."

"No," he agrees. "It hasn't. I'd hardly say you ignored her, though, while you've been here helping out. Your mom mentioned that you've been flying back and forth on weekends and that you two talk every night."

"That's true but..." My voice trails off. "I realize now that she needed more than that. She needed to hear the words."

My dad raises a brow.

"I'm completely in love with her and I never told her. I can't blame her for assuming the worst when she saw Chloe kissing me."

"You love her, huh?" he asks in a gruff voice.

"I do and I'm going to marry her. There's something else, too. When I went to her parents' house, they kind of let it slip that Elle is pregnant. They thought I knew."

My dad's bushy brows shoot straight up. "You gotta be shittin' me?"

"You're going to be a grandpa. So, if that doesn't give you something to live for then I don't know what will."

"C'mere, kid," he says and gives me a big bear hug. "I can't believe it."

When I pull back, I see his eyes shimmer with emotion and a few unshed tears. "Is that okay?"

"Sure is," he says and swipes the back of his hand over his eyes. "Does your mother know yet?"

"Do I know what?" she asks and walks into the room.

I turn and smile at my mom. "Elle is expecting." Her eyes go wide. "You're going to be a grandma."

My mom's smile lights up the room. "Oh, honey," she exclaims, and I give her a big hug. "Did you talk to Elle?"

"Not yet. I found out from her mom and dad. I had to wrap my head around it first before I told you guys."

"You need to find her, honey," my mom says. "She shouldn't be all alone, especially if she's pregnant. Her emotions are probably all over the place and she's most likely scared and confused. It's not good for her to be alone right now."

"I know! I've racked my brain and harassed the hell out of Chloe to see if she could come up with anything. But we just go in circles. I don't know what to do."

"Is there a way to track her phone?" my dad asks.

"Not if she turned it off or took the battery out. And we can't report her as missing because she's texted her mom a few times now, I guess. She just won't talk to me or Chloe."

It hurts my fucking feelings, but I need to get over it and figure out where the hell she is.

The good thing is I'm going to find out sooner than I think.

21

ELLE

The weather is getting colder, and I know that I can't stay here much longer. The cottage hasn't been winterized and, other than the fireplace, there's no heat. And I'm running out of wood fast because of the recent freezing temperatures.

I've been in contact with my mom, and we text every day now. I haven't told her where I am, just that I'm safe. She told me Gray came to the house to talk to them and wants to know where I'm staying. We're going to have to talk soon and I'm trying to prepare myself for the conversation.

I'm still not sure how he'll react to the news that I'm pregnant. God knows, I was shocked so I'm assuming that he will be, too. All I do know is I'm very sad and lonely. I look like an absolute mess with shadows under my puffy eyes and heartache weighing me down. There's nothing I want more than to shake this feeling that my world has fallen apart, and no one cares.

It's hard, though. Especially since everyone who I thought I could depend on deserted me. At least that's how it feels, anyway. A couple of weeks on my own has taken its toll and I'm probably going to head back to the city and face my problems head-on sooner than later. I really don't have a choice with this cold weather and the lack of heat here.

I've never been the strongest or loudest or smartest in the room. I'm an introvert through and through. But it's become clear to me that I've spent so much time hiding in Chloe's shadow that I've missed out. Being the docile, dependable one who is too scared to share her opinion or fight for what she really wants isn't who I want to be anymore.

It's going to be hard at first, but I need to learn to stand up for myself and communicate my needs. I think it's the only way that I'm going to find happiness. And now that I'm bringing a child into the world, I have to teach him or her to go after what they want. To not be a complacent, people-pleasing wallflower like I've been my entire life.

Since I have no idea what will happen with Gray, Chloe and my other relationships, it's nice to know that I'll have someone in my life. Granted, a baby isn't a partner or a best friend, but a little one will keep me busy and not allow me time to wallow in self-pity and feel sorry for myself.

I've spent enough time pining for a man who doesn't want me and trying to please a best friend who walks all over me.

It's still early and I bundle up and go on my morning walk like I have done every day for the past week. It's become a welcome routine and the cold, crisp air clears my head. Each day I feel one step closer to being able to leave here and start living my life again.

Of course, I need to find another job since I quit C.T. International. Raising a baby in the city doesn't seem like something I want to do either and I think I should probably move back home. Back to Fairview. Hopefully, I'll find a little house to rent and a nice neighborhood to raise my child. I'll make sure I'm close to my parents so they can be in our lives, too.

Is this how I envisioned my life going three months ago? No. But things change and now I have to adjust. I'm going to dig deep and put the baby's needs above all else. Love, career and everything else will come second. Maybe eventually I'll be able to find the happiness I've always craved for myself. Deep down, though, I know only one man can give me what I need.

On my way back to the cottage, the wind picks up and I'm going to need to make sure the fire stays going. I can feel the temperature dropping fast and more snow is predicted to fall starting later today.

When I step out of the woods, I freeze. There's a car in the driveway and Chloe stands near the front door of the cottage. I knew the time to face her would be coming soon, but how did she know I was here?

Suppressing a sigh and steeling myself, I walk forward.

"Elle!" she exclaims when she sees me. Her eyes widen slightly, and I know she must think I look like absolute shit.

"What are you doing here?" I ask.

"Can we talk inside?" She rubs her gloved hands together. "It's freezing out here."

"It's not much warmer inside," I say numbly and open the door.

Chloe follows me inside and looks around. "Wow. This place really brings back some memories." She gives me a half-smile. "Remember how we used to jump off the raft and catch turtles?"

I nod. "How did you know I was here?"

She shrugs. "I didn't. But when I really started thinking about where you might be, I remembered this place. I figured I'd drive up and check it out and I'm so glad I did. Do you have any idea how worried everyone is about you?"

"It didn't feel that way when I left," I can't help but say. I walk over and throw another log on the fire. Sparks shoot into the air, and I drop down on the floor and move my cold hands closer to the flames, trying to warm them up.

"Everyone's a wreck," she says and sits down beside me. "Your parents, me, Gray…"

"Why would Gray care? Or you for that matter? Last time I saw the two of you, you had your tongue halfway down his throat."

Chloe looks down and actually has the decency to look ashamed. "Elle, I am so sorry. I understand if you can't ever forgive me, but don't be mad at Gray. It wasn't his fault. I swear he's innocent in all of this."

I don't comment. I just can't find any words because it hurts too much and my heart squeezes painfully.

"I know what I did was selfish and wrong. There's no excuse and I was jealous. I could only see my side of things. I thought that since Gray was my ex, he should be off-limits to you."

"You never loved Gray," I say. "Not like I did."

"I-I know that now. It took me a minute to figure things out. I think a part of me was always a little jealous of you."

"Of *me*?" I ask, completely shocked. "Why?" Gray had said the same thing, but I brushed it off. I never thought someone like Chloe would ever be envious of someone like me.

"Because everyone always loves you, Elle. You are the nice, sweet one and I'm the dramatic, obnoxious one. I know what people say."

"That doesn't change anything," I say. "Do you have any idea what you did when you kissed him? You purposely tried to hurt me and steal him back when you never even wanted him in the first place. I just don't understand how someone who I thought was my best friend could ever do something so manipulative and hurtful."

"I know," she says in a low voice. "And I'm sorry."

"So am I," I tell her. "I'm sorry we ever became friends."

"Don't say that! Please, Elle."

"It finally occurred to me that I have given up so much over the years for our so-called friendship. But what have you sacrificed?"

Chloe doesn't say anything. Just looks down and twists her gloves in her hands.

"It's always been about you and what you want. But I'm not playing that game anymore."

"I don't expect you to, Elle. And I have been a rotten friend. I can see that now."

"It's too late, Chloe. You hurt me too deeply. And now I have a baby to think about. I can't deal with or worry about your constant drama. I have more important things to focus on."

"I can't believe you're pregnant." Her gaze dips to my flat stomach.

"Yeah, well, I am, and the baby's needs are my priority right now. Not listening to you cry about Olivia's wedding and badmouth every single decision she makes from now until next June."

Chloe looks away, chagrined. "I guess I have been a little harsh."

"Nothing anyone does is ever good enough for you, Chloe. Being your friend is exhausting. It's not something I can even do anymore."

"Elle-"

"You crossed a line." I shake my head and look over at her. "I was so in love with Gray and you tried to steal that happiness away. How can you ever call yourself my friend? And how can I ever trust you again?"

Chloe sniffles and tears brighten her blue eyes. At this point, I don't even know if she's being genuine.

"Elle, please. You have to forgive me."

"Do I?" I ask quietly. "I quit a job I loved, lost the love of my life and my best friend. All because of your selfishness. It's not something I can just forgive and forget."

Chloe swipes a tear away. "At least talk to Gray. None of this is his fault. It's all mine. And I'm so, so sorry."

A coolness settles over my heart. "I don't forgive you, Chloe. My entire world has fallen apart and I'm not sure how to put it back together."

For a long moment, neither of us says anything and the fire snaps and sizzles in the brick hearth.

"When are you coming home?" she asks in a quiet voice.

"I don't know. I'm still trying to figure things out."

"You're coming back to the city, though, right?"

I shake my head. "No."

"But, Elle-"

"This isn't about you, Chloe. I need to find a good place where I can raise the baby. You'll have to find someone else to buy your coffee and hang out at Barneys."

I know I'm being cold, but this has been building and Chloe needs to know the world doesn't revolve around her any longer.

"Will you move back to Fairview?" she finally asks.

I shrug a shoulder not ready to share any of my potential plans with her.

"If I can do anything to help, let me know, okay?"

"I think you've done enough," I say and stand up.

Chloe slowly stands up, too. "I know you don't want to hear it, but I'm sorry. Hopefully one day I'll be able to make it up to you, Elle."

"I'm not going to hold my breath." I walk over to the door, open it and an ice-cold breeze blows inside. "Goodbye, Chloe."

With a soft sigh, Chloe walks past me. "Can I tell Gray where you are?" she asks.

"No," I say and shut the door in her face.

It feels good to finally get everything that's been bothering me off my chest, but now I feel so empty and alone. Tears well in my eyes as I lock the door and walk over to the couch. I grab the end of the sofa and drag it closer to the fireplace. Then I lay down on it, wrapping up in a thick blanket.

Gazing into the crackling flames, tears stream down my face, and all I want to do is curl up and disappear.

22

GRAY

After talking to my parents, I know they're right. I need to talk to Elle, but I still have no damn idea where she's hiding. And then Chloe calls. When her name pops up, I swipe the bar over, and I hope to God that she has something good to tell me.

"Chloe?" I answer and pause mid-step. "Did you hear anything from Elle?"

"I just talked to her," she says.

My heart thunders. "You did? Is she okay? Where is she?"

"She's a mess, Gray, and this is all my fault."

"Where the hell is she?" I demand.

"At their old cottage."

I'd only been there once, but I remember it had been about an hour drive from Fairview. "What's the lake again?"

"It's on Pike Lake and it's so cold up there. There's no heat and she has a fire going but...Oh, God, Gray, I'm so worried about her. They're predicting a huge snowstorm and she's all by herself."

"Not for long," I say and jog down to my room. I start throwing things in an overnight bag and glance out the window where snowflakes are already dancing. The whole East coast is supposed to get slammed with a blizzard, but I don't care.

Blizzard or not, I'm going to Elle.

"The roads are going to be terrible," Chloe says. "They're already slippery. By the time you get here, there's no way it's going to be safe to drive on these back country roads."

"I don't care," I say stubbornly. "I'll fly down to New York and then start driving." I figure that's my quickest option. Hopefully, I'll beat the storm because if they start delaying flights then I have a long-ass drive ahead of me.

"She's so angry, Gray. I've never seen her this upset before. She looks like she's lost weight and she has hollows beneath her eyes. I just feel terrible."

You should, I think. My heart twists in my chest. "She's pregnant. She shouldn't be skipping meals. Do you know if she's gone to the doctor yet?" Worry saturates me and the sooner I get to Elle, the better.

"I don't know. I don't think so. All I know is that I've never seen her like this before. She completely closed me out and I told her it was all my fault. But she didn't want to hear it." Chloe starts crying and I try to find some sympathy for her, but it isn't easy.

"Chloe, you gotta give her time."

"She hates me! I messed up so badly and now my best friend hates me!"

I struggle to find something encouraging to say, but it's damn hard. "She's spent her entire life playing second fiddle to you. Maybe she realized that she doesn't want to do it anymore."

"I know it was wrong to keep you two apart. I understand that now. Please, tell her how sorry I am. What I did was wrong, and I hope you'll both be able to forgive me one day."

"I gotta go, Chloe. If I don't leave now, they're going to start delaying flights and I'll be stuck at the airport."

"Please know that you guys have my blessing. You were always meant to be. I can see that now."

"Thanks, Chloe." I hang up, grab my bag and tell my parents I know where Elle is and that I'm going there now.

"But what about this weather?" my mom asks, her brow creasing in worry.

"It's getting worse out there," my dad says, glancing toward the window from his bed.

"That's why I gotta go now. Chloe said Elle's up at her family's old cottage on Pike Lake. It's not going to be a fun drive." I give them both a quick kiss and throw my bag over my shoulder.

"Be careful," my mom says.

"I will."

"If the roads get too bad, pull over and wait it out," my dad advises me.

I nod, but I have no intention of waiting anything out. I'm going to get my girl.

Heading straight to the airport, I manage to get lucky and get on a flight last minute. The snow is still just swirling and light, so my flight takes off and lands without delay. Back in New York, I race out to the curb and catch an Uber to my place. Then I hop in my car and punch in the directions to Pike Lake.

It's been so long since I've been there, and I forgot how the majority of the drive is on deserted country roads. About 15 minutes into the trip, as soon as I get out of the city, the snow starts falling hard.

My windshield wipers fly back and forth and all I can see is white. I flip on my headlights and squint at the road ahead. The snow is accumulating fast, and my stomach drops when I hit a patch of black ice and my SUV fishtails.

"Fuck," I hiss as the car slides toward the right where the road drops into a ditch. I manage to regain control at the last second and get the car back on track again. Luckily, I have an SUV, or I'd be screwed. I ease up off the accelerator and mentally tell myself to slow down.

I want to get to Elle as soon as possible but that won't happen if I kill myself in the process.

A part of me is tempted to text her and tell her that I'm coming, but then what if she gets upset? God forbid, she freaks out and drives off into this storm. If she did that and something happened to her, I would never forgive myself.

No, it's better to just arrive and not give her any kind of heads-up. I am glad that Chloe made sure to let her know exactly how the situation with that goddamn kiss happened and that I had no idea Chloe had set me up. It still pisses me off, but I know that Elle and I can work through it.

I love her. I love Elle Landon so damn much and now I'm going to tell her.

And it's been a long time coming.

The longer I drive, the heavier the snow becomes. It takes me an extra hour to reach Pike Lake and when I finally get there, it's a complete white-out. Thick, heavy snow falls from the darkening sky, and I send up a silent prayer that I made it here in one piece. My car slides up the driveway and skids to a halt next to her car. I turn the engine off and jump out into the raging snowstorm. Head down, overnight bag slung over my shoulder, I hurry up to the door, trying really hard not to fall on my ass.

I knock hard and wait, heart in my throat. "Elle? It's me!" I pound harder.

The door opens and Elle stands there, wrapped up in a lot of layers, a scarf around her neck. "Gray? What're you doing here? There's a blizzard happening."

"Yeah, I'm aware," I say and mouth my edges up. "I've been sliding around on the roads for over two hours."

"Oh, my God, get inside."

I step into the cottage, stomp the snow off my boots and realize it's way too cold in here. Closing the door behind me, I lock it and turn back around. "It's freezing in here."

"I know," she says, shivering. "I was trying to conserve the firewood..."

"And there's no heat?"

She shakes her head.

I march over to the fireplace and throw more logs onto the dying fire. Sparks fly into the air and the heat increases. "You're going to freeze to death if we don't get this thing going."

"But there's no more wood."

"There's a whole forest out there. I'll find some."

"But it's wet."

"Baby, we'll find more wood, okay? Don't worry about it. I'm not going to let you sit here all night with your teeth chattering. Okay?"

She nods. "Okay."

The fire is roaring hot and steady now and she sinks down before it, hands splayed in front of the flames. I sit down beside her and stare at her profile, so thankful that we're together again. That I got here safely.

Chloe was right, though. Elle looks thinner and so very sad. All I want to do is pull her into my arms and hold her tightly. Promise her that everything is going to be alright from here on out. But I don't want to scare her. I need to earn her trust back. One word at a time.

"I came here the second I found out where you were. We need to talk."

"You shouldn't have driven in this weather."

"I don't care if it was the damn Apocalypse and raining fire and brimstone," I say. "The moment I heard you were here, nothing could've stopped me from getting to you."

Her dark, sad gaze meets mine. "Why?" she asks softly, face lit up with firelight.

"Because I love you, Elle. Don't you know that by now?"

23

ELLE

Gray says he loves me, and I want to believe him so badly. But he hurt me, and I need to guard my heart and not just jump into his arms again. Even though I want to so very much.

"Gray-"

"Just listen for a sec, okay?" he asks, voice low, almost pleading.

I nod and the warmth of the fire feels so good that I pull my scarf off. He's sitting beside me looking so handsome and serious. After shrugging his coat off, he turns to face me.

"Elle, so much has happened since we reconnected, and I just want you to know that you mean everything to me. I know that I messed up after Boston by taking off and not reaching out that whole week. Yeah, I was busy, but a part of me was scared, too. Because what happened that night between us wasn't something I've ever experienced with another woman. I felt myself falling hard and fast and that's never happened before. At least not since the first time we met."

His words are like a balm over my wounded heart and when he reaches out and takes my hands into his, I squeeze his encouragingly. "Same," I whisper.

"I need you to know that my heart has always been with you since the beginning. When Chloe kissed me that day in my loft, I was shocked. I had no idea she planned to do it the moment you walked in and I'm so sorry. When you ran away, I was so pissed at her. And when you refused to talk to me, I didn't know what to think or what to do. Don't ever run away like that again. Do you have any idea how worried I was?"

"I'm sorry. I know I should've at least let you know I was alright, but I didn't think you cared. I thought you'd chosen to go back to Chloe, and I was so hurt."

"Elle, baby, don't you get it?" His metallic eyes lock hold of mine. "It's always been you."

His words make my heart swell.

"There's, um, something else, too. Something that I found out that day," I say carefully. I suck in a deep breath and prepare myself for his reaction that I'm pregnant.

"The baby?" he asks gently.

I look into his silvery-blue eyes, completely taken off-guard. "You know? How?"

"Your parents told me. They thought I already knew."

"Oh. I'm sure you were just as surprised as I was," I say, trying to read his expression.

"I definitely didn't see that coming. But, I guess, there was that one moment…"

"Yeah. Those 3-5 seconds. Guess that's all it took."

He smiles. "For what it's worth, those 3-5 seconds were some of the best moments of my life."

I pull a hand away and swat at his arm. "You're crazy."

"Crazy about you." He stares at me thoughtfully.

I chew on the inside of my lower lip. "So where do we go from here? Because the last thing I want to do is force you to do anything you don't want to do."

Gray turns, reaches into his jacket pocket and pulls something out. It's hard to tell at first, but when he faces me again, he lifts a small velvet box. "Elle, since the moment we met, I fell a little in love with you. Then every moment since, I fell more and more. I'm so deep in love now, baby, that there's only one thing I want. And that's a life with you."

My heart stutters when Gray opens the box to reveal a diamond solitaire set in a gorgeous antique setting. He pulls it free, reaches for my hand and gives me a nervous, adorable half-smile.

"Elle Marie Landon, you are everything to me. The reason I breathe. All I want is to spend every single day with you and every night to be able to hold you in my arms. I want to raise our baby together and grow old together."

He pauses and my eyes fill with tears.

"Will you marry me?" he asks. Outside, the wind whips the snow around and heavy flakes hit the window. "For real this time?"

I try hard not to cry as I nod, and he slips the ring on my finger. "It's so beautiful."

"Not even half as beautiful as you," he says, pulling me closer. "Is that a yes?"

"Yes!" I exclaim.

Then I'm on his lap, wrapped in his arms, and our lips meet. My mouth opens to him, and he slides his tongue against mine. He's being so soft, so gentle, and I wiggle in his lap, yearning for more.

It's been far too long and I'm dying for him.

I pull back and lick my lips. "I need you, Gray. All of you. *Now.*" Desperation fills me and I can't wait a moment more.

When I reach for his shirt, he's reaching for mine, too. We quickly strip out of our clothes and then he's spreading the blanket out that I'd been wrapped up in. We move onto it and then he's on top of me, kissing me hard. There's no hesitation and our mouths meld, the kiss so very deep and thorough. My toes curl and the fire beside us crackles.

The room is so hot right now and our naked bodies sliding against each other only add to the increasing temperature. Being skin to skin with Gray, feels like heaven. He's hard and firm and I arch beneath him when his hand slides between my legs.

He knows exactly how to touch me and in moments I'm wet and writhing as his fingers sink into me. "Gray," I hiss, hips twisting.

"Hold still, baby," he rasps.

Those long fingers touch and tease every secret place and when I come, stars burst around me. With a cry, I arch against his hand and waves of pleasure rack through my body. As good as it feels, I need him inside me. "Please," I murmur and reach down to stroke him.

With a growl, Gray moves between my legs, spreads them further apart and fists his cock. It's engorged, pulsating and hot. I lift my hips, dying for him to take me. When he begins to push inside of me, I relish the feel of him stretching me, sliding deeper, filling me up completely.

"Oh, God," I whimper. Then he begins to rock his hips in a slow, steady rhythm. I know he's taking it easy on me, but I need more. "Faster," I urge him and squeeze his ass.

He hesitates. "Are you sure?"

"God, yes."

Gray picks up the pace and the friction between our bodies grows. "If it's too much-" he grunts.

"It's not," I rasp and arch up, meeting his thrusts. "I need all of you, hard and fast."

He doesn't need any more encouragement and pumps into me so hard that I'm sliding across the blanket. I lock my legs around his waist as he pounds into me and grip his arms tightly, my nails digging into his rock-hard biceps.

"Gray!" I shout as my orgasm slams into me, knocking the wind from my lungs. My lower body clenches tightly around his cock, milking it hard. Gray follows me right over the edge and his entire body tenses and then shudders above me. He groans long and hard through his release, emptying his hot seed inside me.

Since I'm already pregnant, it hardly matters that we didn't use protection. We're both clean and I love being even closer to Gray. As close as possible.

He drops down next to me, breathing hard. For a long moment, we just stare at each other, so damn grateful for this moment. When he lifts a hand and tucks a strand of hair behind my ear, I turn my face into his palm and sigh.

I've never been happier in my life. Gray wants to marry me and raise our baby together. Our future is one that's bright and happy. And no one will ever take it away from us again.

"What're you thinking?" he asks softly and cups my face, fingers lightly stroking my cheek.

"About how very much I love you," I whisper.

His mouth edges up. "Good. Because I love you so much, baby." He reaches for my left hand and lifts it, turning it so the firelight catches the facets of the diamond. It sparkles brilliantly.

"It's so stunning," I whisper.

"I just remembered what my mom told me when she gave me the ring."

"What?" I ask.

"She said it belonged to my great-grandma, Margot. She and my great-grandpa, Sébastien, came over from France. He bought the ring in Paris and then proposed to her on the middle of a bridge during a snowstorm."

We both look over where snowflakes dance outside.

"I love that," I say and snuggle up against him. "It's like their love story and ours are similar."

He nods and kisses my temple.

"How's your dad doing?" I ask.

"Doing better every day. I think he's finally on the road to recovery."

"I'm so glad."

"Just so you know, he's very Team Elle," he adds.

"Really?"

"We've talked about you a lot and he adores you. Same with my mom."

That makes me so happy. I lay a hand over his warm skin, right above his heart, and relish the feel of its strong, steady beat. "We're going to have to work on my parents a little," I admit.

"They've never liked me, and I don't think getting you pregnant helped my case much," he says with a mischievous smile.

"Probably not, but I'm going to make sure that they realize just how amazing you are."

"What was it about me that turned them off?" he asks. "When I came here that one summer and first met them, they seemed to have already decided they didn't like me."

I let out a sigh and splay my hand on his chest, studying the way the firelight hits the diamond and makes it sparkle outrageously. "My parents think people should work hard for a living and for the good things they receive in life. They don't believe in hand-outs."

"Neither do I. My dad and I worked our asses off, building our businesses from nothing."

"I know. And I'm sorry they were so dismissive of all the amazing things you've accomplished. The thing is..." My fingers curl up into a fist against his chest and he grabs my hand, sliding his fingers through mine.

"What?"

"Chloe kept talking about how rich you were and how your dad managed millions of dollars for his clients. I think her bragging left a bad taste in their mouths."

Gray releases a breath. "That best friend of yours is going to drive me to murder," he grits out, sounding frustrated.

"She's not my best friend anymore," I say softly.

His blue-gray eyes lock with mine. "Just to be clear, I am not on Chloe's side. But as annoying and obnoxious as she can be, I think, for once in her life, she's truly sorry for what she did."

"Maybe. But I kind of feel like it's too little, too late. She tried to keep us apart, Gray, and I don't think I can forgive that."

Gray leans closer and kisses my forehead. "I know, baby. You don't need to forgive her today or tomorrow. Just take it one day at a time. Maybe you'll get there, maybe you won't. But whatever happens, remember that I'm here, supporting you. I've got your back. Always."

"I know," I whisper. "And I love you so much for it."

"C'mere," he says, turning me around and dragging me against his chest. His hand drops and covers my stomach. "I feel like the luckiest man in the world."

A smile curves my mouth and I place my hand over his. "I know we didn't plan this," I say, voice trailing off. "And having a child is a huge, life-changing thing…"

"The little nugget in here," he says, lips touching my ear, hand caressing my belly, "is half you and half me. And because of that, I already love him or her fiercely."

My fingers twine through his and a calm, happy sensation flows through me. I haven't felt this good in weeks and I can't wait for all the amazing things to come. "Would you rather have a boy or a girl?" I ask.

"Doesn't matter," he murmurs, kissing along my throat. "Either way, I'm going to spoil them rotten."

I chuckle. "You're also going to teach them how to work hard for things, too, right?"

"I'll teach them the value of hard work, but I have a feeling that I'm going to turn into an old softie. You're probably going to have to wear the pants around here."

"Or we could just have my dad give them a lecture on how hard work is important."

We both laugh. "Works for me. He'll scare the crap out of them, and we can be the good guys."

As the snow continues to fall outside, I curl up into Gray's arms with a little sigh. *My fiancé's arms.* I've never felt so loved, so safe and so protected. All of the doubts and exhaustion melt away and we both fall asleep as the fire crackles bright and warm.

Beautiful dreams of our future fill my head.

24

GRAY

Now that the air has been cleared, Elle and I have never been so close. We've become this united front, and no one is ever going to get between us again. Not Chloe, not her parents, no one.

I keep the fire going all night and Elle snuggles against me. Everything in the world is right once again. Even better than it was because now the woman I love is going to marry me.

We make love again at some point during the night and when morning comes, the room is toasty warm. I burned up all the wood, but it's okay. I can go out and find more today. We're going to be stuck here for at least a few more days, until they get the roads cleared up, and that's fine with me.

Neither of us is in any hurry to get up this morning, but the fire is getting low now. That glow isn't going to keep us warm for long and I need to gather up some more wood. I kiss Elle's head and sit up.

"Mmm," she murmurs and stretches like a cat. "You're leaving me?"

"Never," I say and grab her hand, kissing her knuckles. "But I do need to get out there and get us more firewood. Do you have food for breakfast? Because you look way too thin."

"I can make us pancakes while you find firewood. There's some orange juice, too."

"Perfect." I grab my pants. "Get ready because I'm going to fatten you up."

"You can do anything you want to me, Gray," she purrs. "Especially if it involves feeding me since I am kind of hungry."

"Get dressed, baby. I'm going to have a roaring fire going again soon and then I'll feed you some pancakes."

I slap her ass as she gets up and she squeals. After I'm dressed and all bundled up, I face the cold, snowy outside and set off to find some dry wood. Of course, that's pretty much impossible since the ground is covered with almost four feet of snow. But I do catch a glimpse of a shed and decide to check it out for an ax or something.

After digging through the snow drift, I manage to pry the frozen shed door open, and a huge smile lights my face. The entire shed is filled with dry logs. "Score," I say and start loading up the wheelbarrow in the corner.

After a few trips back and forth, the cottage is loaded with enough wood to last for another week at least. It's a good thing, too, because the snow starts falling and blowing like crazy again outside.

But inside is warm and cozy. True to my word, I fill Elle with pancakes and make sure she drinks two full glasses of orange juice. "You need your vitamin C," I tell her.

"You know what else I need?" she asks, voice dropping.

"To schedule a doctor's appointment," I say, pretending not to notice her husky tone and the slow, sexy blink of her lashes.

Elle sidles around the table, moving up behind me, and wraps her arms around my waist. "Mmm-hmm," she murmurs, pressing her cheek against my back. "And there's something else, too."

Her hands lower and cover the front of my jeans, cupping the erection that soars to life. A low groan rips from my throat. "Take whatever you want, baby," I rasp. "I'm all yours."

The rest of our week plays out much the same way. For the most part, we eat a lot– I hike down to the party store and load up on groceries– and then we laze in front of the fire talking or making love. I get to know this amazing woman on a level that I've never known another soul. We share all of our hopes, dreams, fears and desires. Nothing is off-limits and by the time Saturday rolls around and the roads are clear enough to travel on, I know that Elle Landon is not only the love of my life, but also my soulmate. And now she's going to be the mother of my child. I feel very, very blessed and truly like the luckiest man in the world.

We're almost reluctant to leave the cozy, little routine we've established here at the cottage, but I know it's time to get back to reality and figure our lives together out. We decide that Elle is moving into the loft with me as soon as possible and I can't wait.

Luckily the roads are pretty good, and we make it back to the city much more quickly than it took me to get out here a week ago. We drive my SUV and will return later to get her car. I head straight to her apartment first, but I'm reluctant to let her go.

"I'm just going to freshen up," she reassures me. "I'll be over in a couple of hours."

"I don't like you leaving my sight," I tell her. Then, with a low growl, I pull her closer and kiss the hell out of her. Give her something to remember.

When we finally pull apart, we're both panting. "Oh, wow," she says and cups my face. "How I can still want you so much after our very, um, busy week, I don't know. But I do. I want you so damn much, Gray."

"Hold that thought," I say and drop a kiss on her nose.

"See you soon," she says, a little breathlessly.

"I'll be waiting."

Later that evening, we share a pizza at my place as we figure out exactly how to proceed with Chloe and Elle's parents. My parents already love her, but I'm going to need to do some convincing and impressing when it comes to Steve and Jill Landon. We have some very big announcements to make, and I want her parents to support our engagement and the fact that we're moving in together. We also want our parents to meet and hopefully that'll dispel some of the preconceived notions Elle's dad has about my family being wealthy.

My dad is going stir-crazy since he's been in bedridden state for so long, but he's finally allowed to get up and start moving around. Despite that, we plan to have the dinner at my parents' house in Newport and invite Elle's mom and dad to come up this weekend. We can drop the bombs on everyone then.

I also try to coax Elle into returning to C.T. International. She tells me that she would enjoy helping me run the business but probably remotely due to her pregnancy and the fact that she doesn't feel comfortable announcing it to the other employees yet.

"You don't have to worry about telling anyone because I'm going to be bragging about it to every single person I know," I warn her.

"Gray!"

"You're carrying my baby and it's something I'm so damn excited about. Not some shameful secret so just be prepared because the entire world is going to know by tomorrow probably."

Elle laughs. "I'm glad you're so happy about it."

I brush a kiss across her lips. "I've never been happier."

"Same," she whispers.

The pizza is quickly forgotten as we fall back on the couch, mouths melding, bodies entwining. Every time with Elle is passionate and I don't think my desire for her will ever be fully quenched. Her flowery vanilla scent drives me wild and being inside her, being as close as we can possibly be, is the most fulfilling and thrilling thing in the world.

When the night of the big dinner arrives, I'm nervous as hell. I know my parents' house is really nice and though it doesn't necessarily wreak of wealth, it's pretty clear that my family is extremely well-off. Just when I'm thinking that we should've postponed this until my dad was ready to go to a restaurant, Elle's parents arrive.

Elle and I exchange a look. Then she reaches over and takes my hand. "We got this," she whispers. "But I apologize in advance if they say anything rude."

"Not your fault," I say and drop a kiss on her lips. "Ready?"

"Ready as I'll ever be."

I open the door and invite Elle's mom and dad inside. Elle hugs them both and I'm glad that they've had time to talk and maybe I'm imagining things, but they seem more open to us being together than they were before. Maybe it's because they know a baby is on the way and that helped to change their outlook.

Reaching out, I shake her dad's hand and motion for them to come in and hang up their coats. Then we head straight to the dining room where my dad already sits. He still has to take it slow and easy so, despite his arguing about wanting to meet them standing up, I made him stay seated.

"Mom, Dad, this is Gray's dad," Elle says.

"Jonathan Carter," he says and extends a hand. "I would get up, but my son has strictly forbidden me to get out of this seat due to a few rather bad coronary incidents in the last couple of months."

They exchange pleasantries as my mom walks out of the kitchen.

"Hi, I'm Amelia," she says. "It's so nice to meet you. Thank you for driving up here to have dinner with us."

"Thank you for inviting us," Mrs. Landon says. "And, please, call me Jill. And this is my husband, Steve."

So far, so good.

After the introductions and everyone is seated and served the delicious dinner my mom and Elle prepared, Elle and I decide it's best to bring them all up to date. Hopefully, no one chokes on their chicken.

"We're so happy for you guys to meet each other," Elle says. "We also wanted to catch you up on what's going on with us after this past week."

I reach over and take her hand, noticing how everyone's gaze dips to our interlaced fingers. To the sparkling diamond on her finger.

"I asked Elle to marry me," I tell them. "And I couldn't be happier that she said yes."

"Because I love you. So much." She tosses me a brilliant smile and my heart catches. "I'm also moving in with Gray this week," she announces.

"Congratulations!" my mom exclaims.

"Your ring is beautiful," Mrs. Landon says and smiles.

Elle lifts her left hand and flashes the engagement ring. "It belonged to Gray's great-grandmother. He told me it's from Paris. Isn't it lovely?"

"So lovely," Mrs. Landon says.

My gaze drifts over to Mr. Landon to gauge his reaction.

"You both think this is the right decision?" her dad finally asks.

"Without a doubt," Elle says.

"I love your daughter, Mr. Landon. More than words could ever say. Your blessing means everything to us." I look at our moms and my dad. "All of your blessings."

"Well, you certainly have mine," my mom says.

"And mine," my dad chimes in. "Gray and Elle, I wish you nothing but a lifetime of happiness. I also think you're going to make a perfect team and I don't know about the rest of you, but I can't wait for that little one to call me 'grandpa'."

"Oh, me, too," her mom gushes, getting emotional. "If you both are happy then I'm so happy for you. And I will always be available to babysit."

"Me, too," my mom adds and the grandmas-to-be exchange smiles.

"I have a feeling this little one is going to be a little spoiled," Elle says.

"But he or she is also going to learn the value of hard work," I add. "Just like you and I both did."

Elle nods and we glance over at her dad.

Steve Landon clears his throat and lays his fork down. "I'm not going to lie. I'm a little concerned with how fast things are moving with you two."

I feel Elle tense beside me.

"If it makes you feel any better, don't forget we've known each other for seven years," I say, keeping my voice light. But then I turn serious. I need him to know how important this woman is to me. "I care about your daughter more than anything. Whatever she needs, I'll give her. Loving her and providing for her and our baby is the most important thing and I'll do everything in my power to make sure she's happy every single day."

Elle squeezes my hand, and we share a look that conveys everything I just said is mutual.

It's pretty clear that we love each other, and no one is going to stop us from being together and making a life together.

"You have my blessing," her father finally says in a low voice.

Relief floods through me, lightening the weight on my chest. "Thank you, sir," I tell him. Everyone smiles and breathes out a collective sigh.

Elle and I couldn't be happier, and the rest of the evening goes off without a hitch. Our parents have so much in common and it's nice to see them begin to bond. I have a feeling that we're going to be spending a lot of time together and that's not even including vacations and holidays.

The future has never looked so promising and after driving back to the city the next morning, Elle and I start moving her in right away. I've spent the last seven years without this woman and now I refuse to waste another second without her.

A moving company helps transport all the boxes and some furniture over to my loft. Elle tells me she doesn't need a lot of her bigger pieces and we put them up for sale online. Apparently, she likes the way my place is decorated which makes me happy.

"You can change anything you want," I tell her.

"Maybe some fresh flowers would be nice," she says.

I cock my head, remembering our conversation about her favorite flower. "Maybe some daisies?"

Elle smiles. "I would love that."

"I'm going to make sure every vase you put out is filled with fresh daisies for the rest of our lives."

Elle's eyes shimmer with unshed tears. "Do you have any idea how much I love you?"

I pull her into my arms. "If it's even half as much as I love you then I will be a very happy man."

"It's more than that," she says and winks at me.

"That makes me very happy," I tell her and lower my mouth to hers. "Very happy and very lucky." My lips capture hers and we kiss passionately.

25

EPILOGUE

ELLE

Life with Gray couldn't get any better. When he asks me when I want to get married, I tell him yesterday. I seriously don't need a big ceremony with endless guests, especially since Chloe and I still haven't made up. The smaller and more intimate, the better.

"Honestly, all I need is you," I tell him.

"Are you sure you don't want anything fancy?"

"Positive. The day we get married, it's all about us, right?" He nods. "So, let's just make it the two of us. And then we can have a little dinner with our family and a few friends to celebrate."

"Sounds perfect," Gray agrees.

The following week, we stand before a minister in a small chapel and exchange wedding vows. It's the happiest day of my life.

Right before slipping the platinum band on my finger, Gray holds my hands and we're both shaking a little. Squeezing tight, I look up into his shining blue-gray eyes and smile.

"Elle, I can't tell you how happy I am to be standing with you here, right now, just the two of us. It took us a while to get to this point, far longer than it should have, but we made it. From the moment I saw you at that party our junior year, you made my heart stop. It's always been you, Elle."

Tears fill my eyes and I do my best to hold them back and not let them fall and ruin my makeup. But his words touch my heart and soul and soon the tears are slipping down my cheeks and I'm sniffling like a baby.

"And now I can't wait to make up for lost time and spend the rest of my life with you. Love you, baby."

After putting the ring on my finger and repeating the vows the minister guides him through saying, Gray holds my gaze and says, "I do."

Then it's my turn and I have to blow my nose first. "Sorry," I say and he and the minister chuckle.

"Take your time," Gray murmurs and reaches for my hands again.

"Grayson…" We squeeze hands and I take a deep, steadying breath. "From the moment I saw you, it's like you were a thief in the night. First you stole my interest then my breath then my heart. There's no one else I've ever wanted or loved as much as you. You've given me so many beautiful firsts. And I know there will be many more."

His mouth edges up and I can only imagine where that naughty mind of his is going. *Oh, my man.*

"And you're right," I continue. "It has taken us far too long to get here, but now that we've made it, we have to make up for lost time. And there's nothing I look forward to more because you're my everything– my past, my present and my future. And I love you forever."

I slip the platinum band on his ring finger. On the inside of both our bands, we had that quote engraved: "My past, my present and my future."

The moment the minister declares us husband and wife, Gray swoops in and kisses me. Love explodes in my chest and tingles erupt all over my body. I think he's going to have that effect on me until the day we die.

The following weekend, after announcing our elopement, our parents organize a dinner celebration at a fancy restaurant located high up on a sea cliff in Newport. At first, I'm a little surprised that my dad didn't balk, but when I find out how much he loves their seafood platter, I can only shake my head. Liam also comes and my parents asked if they should invite Chloe.

I tell them no.

I know we still have things to work through and I didn't want that negative, uncomfortable energy present. Eventually, hopefully, I will make my peace with Chloe. However, I'm not quite there yet.

We have a wonderful, cozy dinner and I love how well everyone is getting along.

The weeks and months seem to be falling away and before long, the holidays are over and I'm showing. It's strange having a baby bump, but Gray loves it. He's always touching my stomach, laying possessive hands over our little one. He goes to all of my doctor appointments with me and makes sure I'm taking my vitamins, exercising lightly and eating healthy. I never realized that he was such an amazing cook. It's a good thing because I burn toast.

Even though we're both dying to find out the baby's sex, we decide to wait and be surprised. Gray is convinced we're having a girl and I keep thinking it's going to be a boy. It's a running joke between us that maybe there are twins in there, but the doctor assures us that there's only one bun in the oven.

Since we don't know exactly what to expect, a boy or a girl, we paint the nursery a light, lemon yellow and buy a white crib and matching furniture. There's so much to do to prepare– things I've never even considered– and I'm so grateful to have my mom and Amelia, Gray's mom, to help me get organized.

I'm due in June and every day I'm beginning to feel more and more like a beached whale. I'm gaining weight like crazy, but the doctor assures me everything is perfect, and the munchkin is healthy and growing like a weed.

Everything is going well, but one day while I'm waiting outside for Gray to come back from the office and pick me up for a doctor appointment, I see two girls walking down the sidewalk. Their arms are linked and they're laughing and whispering secrets as they pass by. With their heads bowed together, their giggles float through the air, and my heart constricts painfully because all I can see is me and Chloe. That's how we used to be and, right as Gray pulls up, I burst into tears.

Granted, my hormones are all over the place. But the truth is, I miss Chloe. I miss our chats, I miss her whining and complaining about everything under the sun, I miss her smiling face, I miss our secrets, I miss it all.

"Baby, what's wrong?" Gray asks, jogging up to me. "What happened? Are you okay?"

"I'm f-fine," I sniffle.

He pulls a tissue from his pocket and wipes my tears away. I don't think he ever carried tissues until I got pregnant. Most anything can make me cry nowadays. Sometimes it's just a silly movie or even a commercial on TV that can set me off. I'm kind of an emotional basket case.

"Do you want to reschedule your appointment?" he asks.

I shake my head. "No. I just-" My voice trails off and I swallow my sadness down. Gray waits patiently for me to continue, rubbing a hand up and down my back. "I miss Chloe," I say and burst into tears all over again.

"Aww, baby." He pulls me into his arms and presses a kiss in my hair.

Even though she hurt me, I can't help it. Not having Chloe to talk to and hang out with for so long now makes me sad. Despite everything that happened, I am finally in the right space to talk to her. I've never felt more secure with myself and in my relationship with Gray.

After I'm done crying, he cups my face and kisses me softly. "You should call her. Why don't you invite her over– whenever you're ready– and you two can talk and I'll cook dinner for you. Whatever you want or need, just let me know, okay?"

Fresh, hot tears slide down my cheeks. "Do you know how freaking wonderful you are?" I kiss him hard.

After thinking about it long and hard, I send a text to Chloe later that night and ask if she'd like to come over the next evening.

I'd really like that; she responds back a moment later.

Gray tells me he's going to go out with Liam after work so Chloe and I can have some privacy. He's seriously the best. But he does pop home quickly and makes us dinner just like he promised.

I'm nervous to see her, but also excited. We haven't seen each other my entire pregnancy and I look like a damn blimp. When I hear a knock at the door later that evening, I take a deep breath and waddle over to answer it.

Chloe looks gorgeous as always and her blue eyes widen when she sees my huge belly.

"Oh, Elle!" she exclaims. "You look wonderful!"

"Hardly," I say with a chuckle. "My feet are swollen, and I look like a float from the Macy's Day Parade."

But she shakes her head. "No. You have that radiant pregnancy glow. If someone could ever figure out how to bottle it up, I'd buy a ton of it."

I motion for her to come inside. "Thanks for coming over. Gray made us homemade pizzas and they're just about done cooking."

"Thanks for inviting me," she says. "I was so happy to hear from you."

I nod, guide her over to the kitchen and flip the oven off. I'm not sure how this conversation is going to go, but so far so good. It's clear that we've both missed each other. A lot. Life without your best friend gets lonely fast. Truthfully, I probably would've caved much sooner and talked to her, but with Gray in my life, I have another best friend.

"What can I do to help?" Chloe asks.

I toss her the hot mitt. "Why don't you get the pizzas out and I'll get us something to drink."

"Great," she says and opens the oven.

While I fill two glasses with ice and grab a couple of sodas, Chloe carefully pulls the pizzas out and sets them on the kitchen table.

"These look delish," she says.

"Gray is a great cook. I'm not, so it's nice that he always insists on cooking for me."

We both sit down, and Chloe gives me a tentative smile. "I'm so glad things are going well between you two."

"We got married," I say and hold up my finger.

A flash of sadness passes through her eyes. "I heard. Congratulations."

"Technically, we eloped. Just the two of us."

"No big wedding then?"

"No. After hearing about all the craziness your sister was dealing with, I had no interest. And since we weren't talking...well, it didn't feel right to have a big celebration like that without you being there."

"Oh, Elle, I've missed you so much. I was such a jerk and I really deserved to be shut out. After what I did, I'm surprised you ever want to talk to me again."

"I missed you, too," I admit. "Although it took me some time to forgive you."

"You forgive me?" she asks, hope filling her face.

"What you did was terrible," I say, and she bows her head and nods. "But after thinking about what you said up at the cottage and how you came out looking for me, I know you didn't mean it. Not really."

"I didn't. I swear I never wanted Gray back. Hell, you know we were a horrible mismatch, and he should've always been with you. But I was a jealous, nasty asshole and I will always regret what I did."

"You really hurt me and Gray."

"I've had time to think about my actions and I think I was so unhappy with my life that I wanted to bring everyone down with me. It was selfish and I'm so sorry."

"We forgive you."

"Can I ask you something?"

"Sure."

"What made you finally text me?"

I sigh. "I think it was a combination of things. The other day I saw these two girls walking down the street, talking and laughing. They reminded me so much of us. I burst into tears because I realized how very much, I missed you."

"Oh, Elle."

"And my hormones are all over the place, too," I add, and she laughs.

"Well, whatever the reason, I'm really glad that you did."

"Me, too," I say. "Especially because I'm due next week and this munchkin is really going to need their Aunt Chloe around."

This time, it's Chloe's eyes that fill with tears. "Oh, damn, Elle. You're making me cry on my pizza."

We both laugh and then she gets up and walks over to my side of the table, leans down and wraps her arms around me. I hug her back, so grateful that we're going to be okay.

A comforting relief fills the air, and we dig into our pizzas.

"So, is it going to be a boy or a girl? Have you picked a name yet?"

"We decided to wait and not find out the baby's sex early."

"What?" she exclaims, mouth full of food. "Oh, I'd be dying. Nine months of not knowing would drive me bananas."

"I know. I'm so excited to find out and meet this little one that's been keeping me up all night and kicking the crap out of me."

"I bet Gray is thrilled."

"He is. He's been so supportive since the beginning. God, I love him, Chloe. So damn much."

She nods. "You guys are perfect together. I see that now and I'm so freaking happy for you."

"What about you? Are you seeing anyone?"

Chloe nibbles on a slice of pepperoni and gives me a coy smile.

"Who?" I ask.

"His name is Mario, and he works in the Financial District."

Sounds about right. "A stock broker or portfolio manager?" I ask teasingly. Chloe has always had one type– wealthy.

She chews on her lower lip. "Neither. He owns a little Italian bakery over there. Nothing big. Just lots of cannoli and wedding cake cookies, but it's delish."

"Really?" I've never heard of Chloe dating anyone who wasn't loaded.

"He's really different from anyone else I've ever dated, and I think that's one of the reasons it works so well. He's been really good for me. And he's not afraid to call me out on my bullshit."

"That's great. I'm really happy for you."

Chloe and I spend the next few hours catching up and when Gray gets home, we're on the couch, laughing over an old inside joke. He takes one look at us and shakes his head.

"Glad to see the best friends are laughing together again."

"I'd get up and kiss you," I say, rolling sideways. "But I can't."

We all laugh and Gray leans in, straightens me and plants a leisurely kiss on my lips, his hand sliding over my stomach.

"I think that's my cue to go," Chloe says and pops up. "I had a great time tonight, Elle. Maybe next time, you and Gray can go get some dinner with me and Mario."

"That would be great."

After saying goodbye, Gray sits down on the couch next to me and smiles. "It looks like that went well."

"So well," I gush. "Everything feels right in the world again, you know?"

"I'm glad, baby."

When he leans in and starts kissing me, I pull back with a gasp.

"What's wrong?" he asks.

I look down. "I think my water just broke."

"What?" Gray pops up and all his cool goes flying out the window. "We need to get you to the hospital. Are you having contractions? Shit. Let me get your bag. Where are your shoes?"

I laugh and reach for his hand. "Slow down, breathe…"

"I think I'm supposed to be saying that to you."

"We have time," I remind him.

The crazy thing is we don't have quite as much time as I think, though. By the time we reach the hospital, I'm in labor and this baby wants out. Everyone told me the first baby takes its time and that I could be in labor for up to 24 hours. But, nope, not me.

An hour after arriving, I give birth to a healthy, screaming, beautiful bundle of joy. Gray holds my hand and when the doctor lifts the little one, he declares, "It's a boy!"

Gray smiles. "You were right."

"And you're sure there's only one in there?" I ask.

"Quite sure," the doctor says.

Gray and I chuckle as the nurse cleans and bundles our little man up. Then she lays him on my chest and Gray and I just look at him, too amazed to speak. Finally, Gray nuzzles his face against the top of my head and whispers, "I love you so damn much, Elle."

"I love you, too, Gray."

After a brief stay, we're allowed to leave the hospital the next day and I'm looking forward to getting back to the loft and resting. At least, resting as much as a newborn will allow you to– which I soon find out isn't much. But Gray is fantastic and lets me get extra sleep while he takes care of the baby.

Neither of us has any idea what we're doing, but we're bungling our way through it with a lot of advice from our parents.

When I open my eyes and see sun streaming through the window a couple of weeks later, I sit up and yawn. Gray lets me sleep in again and after washing up in the bathroom, I wander down the spiral staircase, ready for a cup of juice and to see what's going on since it's so quiet.

Halfway down, I pause, eyes going wide. There are probably 20 vases all over the room, each overflowing with daisies. I drop a hand over my heart and feel my eyes prick with tears.

I find Gray in the nursery, rocking Aric, and I pause in the doorway and watch them for a moment. We chose the name Aric because it means forgiveness and that seems to be an important theme over the past year. It's the whole reason we're together now.

When Gray looks up with a sleepy smile, I wander over, wrap my arms around his neck and kiss his stubbled cheek. "The daisies are beautiful," I whisper.

"Not half as beautiful as you," he murmurs.

"Thank you for letting me sleep."

"Thank you for carrying this little one for nine months and being such an amazing wife and mother."

"You're doing pretty good yourself, Daddy."

His mouth edges up. "If I weren't so tired that would almost sound kinky."

I chuckle. "Don't worry, I'm going to take over while you get some rest. I promise I'll find a way to thank you later."

His brow arches. "But we can't do anything for what? Four to six weeks, right?"

"Hmmm, I'm sure there's something I can do for you."

"Really?"

"Oh, yeah. So, you better rest up because I have plans for you later," I tell him.

Gray carefully stands up and our gazes lock. "Promise?" he whispers.

"Promise," I say and stand up on my tiptoes as his mouth connects with mine. We share a long, leisurely kiss, mindful, of course, of Aric, and then I pull away with a sigh.

"You're the love of my life, Elle Carter."

"And you're the love of mine, Grayson Carter. My past..."

"My present..." he murmurs.

"And my future," I finish.

We share a smile and look down at our son. And I have no doubt that our future will be very bright indeed.

FORBIDDEN
LOVE

Office Mischief

A FORBIDDEN OFFICE ROMANCE

KELLY MYERS

BLURB

It's hard to keep your hands off your boss when you catch him naked inside the office... ***and like what you see.***

It's harder when you end up accidentally touching him in a spot that you weren't even supposed to look at.

Awkward.

Wrong.

Everything in between.

The rational part of me wanted to run away, to look for a new job.

But the crazy Lucy in me accepted another position that Caleb offered me.

I'm now his secretary – working way more closely with him.

So *close* that we're no longer just professional.

The lines were already blurred when I saw two pink lines on a stick and found out that I was pregnant.

Until then, Caleb's playboy reputation had started to annoy me.

This time, I actually wanted to run away.

With a baby inside my belly… and love in my heart.

Would that be a bigger mistake than giving him my heart in the first place?

1

LUCY

The sights and sounds of San Francisco surround me as I walk down the street and I think again about how much I love this city by the bay. Breathing deeply, I inhale the scent of freshly baked bread as I pass Boudin Bakery. Fisherman's Wharf is packed with tourists and it's the height of travel season.

While some natives might be annoyed by the crowded trolleys, shops and restaurants, I love it. I enjoy it so much that I'm making a career out of it. Hospitality is something I'm good at, and I'm the girl everyone always labels as "sweet." Maybe because by nature, I'm a people-pleaser. All I know is ever since I was little, I strived to be a good hostess whether I was setting up a tea party for my mom and dolls or organizing a birthday party for my best friend Hannah.

It's important to me that people enjoy the experience, whatever that may be. I suppose I could've been an event organizer or party planner, but I want to affect more people. Hundreds every day, thousands every week. I figure the easiest way to accomplish that is to work for a hotel. But I don't want to work for just any hotel chain.

I want to work for the best.

A month or so ago, I applied to be an intern at The Pink Carnation Hotel Collection. The internship lasts three months and would be a great way to get hired on permanently. PCH owns 20 boutique hotels located throughout the United States and generous hospitality is key and at the heart of each hotel experience. Their motto is "No request is too large, no detail too small."

Talk about right about my alley. The more I researched and read about PCH, the more I fell in love. Everything about their philosophy and beliefs appeals to me. So when I found out last week that I was picked for their internship, I was thrilled.

Now that I'm starting tomorrow, I'm terrified.

As excited as I am, I know there are going to be other interns and I'm hoping to make new friends despite it being somewhat competitive. I suppose if management likes us then they can always hire us all. There are only seven of us and I'm ready to absorb everything they throw at us.

I know that I'm going to have to prove myself, though. For 24 years, it hasn't always been easy being a clumsy, blonde-haired, blue-eyed girl who has a bit of a ditzy side. Despite that, I'm fiercely intelligent and book smart. I graduated at the top of my class from San Francisco State University and always strive to make my parents proud. I guess I'm what you would consider a good girl.

It's extremely important to me not to be labeled the "ditzy blonde" when I show up tomorrow. I'm so much more than that and I really want to make a good impression on my new boss. Caleb Miles started with one hotel and now he has 20. I'm in awe of what he's accomplished in less than 15 years. He's such an inspiration and I look forward to meeting him and picking his brain. He's older, 40 years old to be exact, and I read that he has a good work ethic which is something I can relate to and that I admire. I agree with his hotel standards and philosophy. Something tells me we're going to get along extremely well since we share similar views.

Little do I know just how well we're going to get along.

My whole goal is to get hired after my internship ends and I think I have a very good chance. As long as I work hard and impress Mr. Miles and his colleagues, I should be a full-time employee of PCH in several short months. But everything is riding on this internship, and I need to impress the pants off them.

Hospitality has always been my strongpoint and when I interviewed for the internship, I easily rattled off the key components necessary to have a successful hotel: teamwork, attention to detail, time management skills and the ability to multitask. I possess all those qualities in spades and I'm hoping Mr. Miles will recognize that.

When I reach the wine bar where I'm meeting Hannah, I spot her bright red head of hair right away on the patio. It's a gorgeous, sunny day and I hurry over and lean down to give my BFF a hug.

"Hey, Luce," Hannah says. She waves me over and her green eyes shine with mischief. Hannah is as Irish as you can get. She can drink anyone under the table and has a fiery personality. "I ordered the sampler so get ready to get blitzed."

I laugh and shake my head. "No way. I'm starting my internship tomorrow and there's no way I'm showing up on my first day with a pounding hangover. I have to make an excellent first impression."

"That's right," she says with a grin. "Tomorrow is the big day! Are you ready?"

I nod and reach for my water. "I've never been so excited for anything," I admit. "You know me. I'm completely focused on my career, and this is the opportunity of a lifetime. I've wanted to work for PCH for as long as I can remember."

"But what if they want to send you to manage one of their hotels far away from here? Like England or something?"

"They only run hotels within the United States," I assure her.

"Okay, so what if they offer you a job in Miami or Boston? You know I can't live with my best friend."

"But then you can visit me," I remind her. "And I'll set you up with all the perks: a gorgeous suite, a spa experience and all the freebies you can imagine."

"You're worth more than a free mini bar of snacks or a massage."

"Aww, thanks, Hannah. You're totally jumping the gun, though. They might not even like me."

"Oh, please. They're going to love you, Luce! Everyone does. You're too sweet and accommodating. Which reminds me– don't let them take advantage of you. Be helpful, but don't let anyone walk all over you."

I know Hannah is right. Sometimes I try too hard to make sure everyone is happy, and everything is running smoothly. To my own detriment. "Are you saying I'm a doormat?"

"I'm saying you're too nice and assholes will take advantage of that fact. So stick up for yourself."

"I will," I promise.

The waiter arrives and places a round tray full of small glasses of all different wines in front of us. There are at least ten samples for each of us to try and just looking at all that wine makes me feel halfway buzzed already.

"Thank you," I say to the waiter and then look over at Hannah with wide eyes. "Are you insane? Who's going to drink all this?"

"We are. So better get started, babe."

I love Hannah dearly, but we couldn't be any more opposite. While I'm more careful and like to plan, she's wild and spontaneous. Give me deadlines, schedules and structure any day. Hannah, on the other hand, prefers change, options and flexibility. Guess that's why she doesn't have a normal 9-5 job.

"How's the world of flying?" I ask and we each take a sip of our first glass of Chardonnay. Hannah is a private helicopter pilot and flies tourists around the Bay area so they can see the city by air. It's wildly popular and she makes great money. She also can set her own schedule and several prominent people hire her privately on the side to transport them around town. All in all, it's a pretty sweet gig.

"Good," she says. "I took today off because I'm mentally preparing myself for tomorrow."

"What's tomorrow?"

"The Miller family from Podunk, Indiana. Mom, Dad and three children under the age of ten who can't wait to see the sights have called me 8,000 times since they booked the trip. Kill me now."

I laugh. "Hopefully it's just your 30-minute excursion?"

"I wish," she says and runs a hand through her flaming red hair.

"They booked me for half the day. Apparently, they recently came into an inheritance, and they want to enjoy the money on making memories as a family."

"That's sweet."

"It sure is. Only every time Dad calls, I can barely hear him because the kids are screaming so loudly in the background."

"Uh-oh."

"Exactly. So, I'm going to take 2 aspirin before this memory-making trek and hope my headphones filter out the majority of their squawking." She lifts her fingers, crosses them and takes a long sip of wine. "Ooh, this one's good."

"It's delish," I agree and reach for glass number two. Sometimes I wish I could be more like my carefree friend. She lives life without a care in the world and firmly believes that everything will work out. I'm the complete opposite of that and I'm far too anxious to sit back and hope for the best. I can't wait around. I need to make things happen.

Hannah is also very brave, too. She joined the Air Force straight out of high school and flew all sorts of fancy military aircraft all over the world. A part of me is envious that she's been to so many places and experienced so much in such a short time. She's fearless and that's a quality I admire so much. I wish I could be more fearless.

My motto is work hard, and slow and steady wins the race. Boring, right? Well, I guess we can't all be hotshot fighter pilots. Some of us lead more normal lives and have a tendency to look before we leap. That's probably why my life has been so completely boring. I'm hoping that working at PCH will change all that. Or at least give me a bigger purpose.

I have to admit, I've been floundering a bit. I mean, I've always been on a steady course to a career in hospitality. But when it comes to my personal life, I don't have it quite so figured out. Not even close. My dating life is what you would consider dead in the water. Probably even a lost cause. A spinster at the ripe, old age of 24.

I know I shouldn't be so hard on myself when it comes to dating. But, oh my God, it's the worst. I hate dating more than anything.

Probably because I've never experienced a good date. It's ironic that I go out of my way to make sure people have the best and highest experiences. And then I go out with a guy who can't even hold a door open for me and tells me I should probably just take the cable car home because gas is too expensive.

Um, okay.

Don't even get me started on how my last date conveniently left his wallet at home so I ended up paying the entire bill. That was last year and he ordered so much food off the menu that I was starting to get suspicious. Like it was planned. I haven't been out with a man since and I don't like to think people see me and instantly think "sucker." In my experience, dating is nothing but a hassle. You end up wasting two hours of your life, trying to be entertaining and all for a guy I know I'm not interested in after the first ten minutes. It's rude to leave early and I always suck it up and hope for the best.

It's never happened, though, and that explains why I'm a 24-year-old virgin. If I can't even make it to a second date with a man, how in the world am I supposed to sleep with him?

"How's Jake?" I ask.

"Oh, he's good," Hannah says and we watch the waiter set a charcuterie plate down in front of us. Hannah grabs a piece of toast and spreads brie over it. "Though he did mention moving in together."

My eyes widen. "What?"

She nods and bites into the toast. "It's too soon. Don't you think so?"

Hannah's boyfriend Jake Mullens is one of the nicest guys ever. They met while serving together overseas and she told me he was a cocky flyboy who deserved to get knocked down a few pegs. Which Hannah thoroughly enjoyed doing. They ended up dating and have been together for over three years. I think they're perfect together and so lucky to have found one another.

The way he looks at her...

My chest tightens. No man has ever looked at me with that kind of love in his eyes.

"Well, you've been dating for over three years," I say and swipe a slice of cheese up and pair it with a piece of salami. "You said he's the one."

"I know and he is. It's just...I don't know if I'm ready for things to change. I like my life the way it is right now. I love my apartment and the neighborhood. He wants me to move into his place which makes sense because he owns it, but he didn't mention an engagement. Just living together. It makes me wonder."

"Wonder what? If he wants to get married?"

"Yeah. I don't know. Maybe I'm just being silly."

"No. I think that's a totally legit concern. You should just sit down and talk about it."

"You make it sound so easy."

"It is easy. It's just a conversation about the future."

With hindsight, I could've been talking to myself. *Just a conversation about the future.* It's so easy for a single person to tell someone in a relationship to talk things out. But when you're the one in that confused state and don't know where the other person stands, it's hard as hell.

"What about you?" she asks.

Inwardly, I cringe. "You know how much I hate dating."

"That may be true, but you really need to get out more. I want you to meet someone so we can go on a double date."

I groan. "Honestly, Hannah, I don't think the man I want even exists." I pluck a grape off the bunch and pop it into my mouth.

"What exactly are you looking for? Perfection? Chris Hemsworth? Maybe your standards are too high?"

"I just want someone who puts me first."

"Okay, well that's not asking too much. We can find you a man like that."

I arch a brow. "It doesn't seem like a lot, but it's everything. The thing is I spend so much time taking care of others that it would be nice to have someone take care of me, too."

Hannah nods and reaches for another glass of wine. "What about looks?"

"You know I love tall men since I'm 5'8" but I'm pretty open. I want chemistry, though. That knock-you-on-your-butt spark that makes your heart pound so hard that it feels like it's going to burst right through your chest."

"That spark you're referring to doesn't knock you on your butt, babe. It gets you knocked up."

We both laugh and clink our glasses.

2

CALEB

With an annoyed sigh, I lean back in the large, leather chair and contemplate sneaking out of the office and hopping on a plane. At this moment, I'd rather be anywhere than here. But running away from my problems isn't a viable option or solution. When the going gets tough, I hang around and figure shit out.

There's no other alternative when you're the CEO of a large, successful company. I own and oversee 20 boutique hotels located throughout the United States. Lately I've had my eye on a location overseas and I'm ready to take The Pink Carnation Hotel Collection global. But the news that another company just swooped in and made a bigger offer on the property I want is going to stall my plans.

Fucking Theo Alemaine. He owns Alemaine Properties and lately, he's been popping up at the last minute and screwing up my deals. I thought I had this handled. The signatures were practically on the dotted line, but then he strikes right before we sign and now if I want to proceed, I'm going to have to make a counter offer. The annoying part is the old hotel in London isn't worth more than what I originally offered.

Do I spend more than I want– more than the damn place is even worth– just to stick it to Alemaine?

I run a hand through my light brown hair and frown. Sometimes I enjoy playing games with my competitors, especially a pain in the ass like Alemaine, but this time it isn't worth it. I offered an extremely fair price for the London property. If Alemaine wants to piss his money away, then he can be my guest.

I'm too smart of a businessman to do that. Even if it is getting personal. Honestly, if he wants my ex-girlfriend, he can have her with my full blessing. I've heard through the grapevine that he's got his eye on the French model, but she's still trying to rekindle things with me.

Not gonna happen, though.

As beautiful as Genevieve Blanchet may be, we have less than nothing in common and I never cared for how cool she could be.

Spinning my chair around, I look out over the San Francisco skyline and remember when I didn't have two nickels to rub together. I grew up in a small coal town in Kentucky and my parents struggled financially. Dad worked in the mines and my mom was a waitress at the local diner.

I couldn't get away from that place fast enough.

My dad passed away from lung cancer when I was 16. The day after the funeral, I kissed my mom goodbye, promised her I'd return for her and left to find my way in the world. I had one goal and that was to make so much money that we would never have to worry about anything again.

I made my way East, working odd jobs, and ended up getting hired at a fancy hotel in New York City. I spent two years learning and studying how that hotel ran and why it was so successful. John Goldberg, the owner, must've seen something in me– probably a little of himself– because he took me under his wing. It was an incredible learning experience and by the time I was 18, I could've run that hotel with my eyes closed.

That's when I decided I'd get my own hotel.

Even though I'd managed to save some money, I didn't have enough to go to college, much less buy a piece of real estate property.

John offered to give me a loan to help pay for school. That's when I told him I didn't even have a high school diploma. I thought my dreams of owning my own hotel were over, but John encouraged me to get my GED. Then he spoke to a close friend on the Admissions Board at Columbia University.

For a kid who barely graduated high school, attending Columbia was a pipe dream. It's not only one of the top business schools in NYC, but also one of the best in the country. Even though it took me a hot minute to get my high school diploma, I was a smart kid. I scored high on my entrance exams, and I must've impressed the hell out of John's friend who interviewed me.

I received an acceptance letter to Columbia University and worked my way through the next four years and then continued on to get my MBA. All the while, I still worked at The Carnation Hotel for John and paid him a little each week from my pay check. My tuition was outrageous and every year, I owed him more and more. But the day finally came when I could pull out my check book and pay the entire thing off because a bank loan allowed me to buy my first hotel. And it was making money.

Twenty hotels later, I've got billions in the bank, and I wouldn't be where I am now without the kindness and generosity of John Goldberg. He believed in me when no one else did and encouraged me to pursue my dreams. And he didn't let something as trivial as lack of money hold me back. When my mentor passed away last year, it was like a physical blow.

John was like a second father to me. He continues to inspire me every day and his spirit lives on through every one of my hotels because I implement the same high standards that he did at the original Pink Carnation Hotel.

When no one else believed in my potential, John did. This is one of the reasons it is so important to me to have an internship program here at PCH. Finding young people with promise is a way for me to give back and keep John's memory alive. Twice a year, my company runs a three-month long program where we accept less than ten interns and teach them everything about what it's like running a hotel business. I've met some great kids with huge potential and look forward to seeing what the new group brings.

My phone buzzes and I turn back around and snatch it up. "Yes?"

"I told her you weren't available, but she isn't listening to me and-" Sybil, my very reliable assistant who is normally so calm, sounds panicked and harried. Her voice cuts off as she tries to convince an uninvited visitor to stop. "Wait! Genevieve. I told you he's not-"

Oh, for fuck's sake. The last person I want to see right now is my ex.

The door to my office swings all the way open and Genevieve is standing there with Sybil running up behind her.

"Hi, Caleb," Genevieve says in that low, sultry voice of hers.

"I'm sorry," Sybil mouths over Genevieve's shoulder.

"It's alright," I say and force myself to take a couple of deep breaths. Dealing with my ex is never easy or pleasant. Especially since she hasn't fully accepted our breakup. "Sybil, can you close the door?"

With a nod, Sybil pulls the door shut and I stand up to face the long-legged, French fashion model who can't seem to get it through her thick skull that we're over. Genevieve and I dated for less than a year and most of the time we were traveling for work. As a high-fashion model, she flits around the world from one catwalk to the next and I'm always on a flight, visiting one of my hotels.

It was destined to fail.

We met at a charity benefit and ended up having a quickie in the coat closet. I was stressed out, overworked and needed a release. Genevieve just happened to be there, and she was more than willing. But our relationship wasn't much more than a romp between the sheets here and there. She has no interest in what I do on a day-to-day basis and I don't care an iota about fashion.

Needless to say, we were a complete mismatch and I broke it off with her a couple of weeks ago over a phone call.

And here she is in New York City. *Lovely.*

She walks over and presses a kiss to my cheek. *"Bonjour!"*

My brow furrows. Does she not remember breaking up? I thought I'd been pretty damn clear. "Genevieve, this is a surprise." I try to play it cool, but I'm annoyed.

"I'm only in town for a day, but I wanted to come say hello. I've missed you, *mon amour.*"

I clear my throat. "Okay. But we're not together anymore."

"That's what I wanted to talk to you about. We should try again, don't you think?"

I shake my head. "I don't think anything's changed. We never saw each other, and we never even got to know each other very well." *Hell, at all.*

"Oh, I disagree," she purrs and slides a hand down my arm. "We got to know each other extremely well."

I step back. "Gen, I have a lot going on right now and I'm not looking for a relationship." In my experience, women tend to muddy the waters and they're only good to have around when I want to take them to bed. Casual works best for me, not clingy, and I'm very upfront about that. Serious relationships tend to go bad fast because I don't have the time or energy to invest in them.

I suppose that's how I got my reputation as a player. The Billionaire Bad Boy who won't commit. I think that's what one society column had written. *So fucking stupid.* I'm just a man who's never been in love and doubts in its existence.

"Who said anything about a relationship?" Her hand wanders down and grabs my belt buckle. "How about a blow job? For old times' sake?" She winks at me.

As tempting as that is, I'm not interested. First of all, she wasn't very good at it. Second, I have a gut feeling she's pissed at me for breaking things off with her so the last place I want her teeth is near my dick. Taking a step back, I brush her hand away. "I'll pass. But thanks."

Her dark eyes narrow.

Yeah, she's pissed.

"Maybe if we take a trip together?" she says, pushing like always. "We could go to your hotel in Hawaii. Remember when we talked about going there?"

I struggle not to roll my eyes. She had talked about going there.

Not me. "I'm busy. I don't have time to take a vacation right now or anytime in the near future."

Anger flashes across her face and she crosses her arms. "What's wrong with you? I'm offering myself and you say no?" Those cat-like eyes of hers narrow even further. "Are you seeing someone else?"

"No. It's not really your business, though."

I can tell that she doesn't believe me, but I don't care. I am officially done with Genevieve Blanchet, and I'm allowed to see and screw whoever I want. Glancing down at my watch, I turn away and sit back down at my desk.

"I have a conference call in a couple of minutes," I tell her, hoping she'll get the message and leave.

Instead, Genevieve sashays over and plants her skinny butt on the edge of my desk. I suppress a sigh and do everything in my power to control my temper. I don't want to be rude or say anything I'll regret, but she's testing me.

"We never had one last night together," she says, pushing her full lips out in a pout. "Don't you think we should at least say goodbye properly? One final, hot and steamy-"

"Genevieve," I interrupt, starting to see her as pathetic. "I'm really busy here. I don't have time to-"

"What is wrong with you?" she snaps.

"Me? We broke up and you're here trying to fuck me. I've politely declined– several times– and you're still throwing yourself at me. I don't think I'm the one with the problem." *So much for trying to be nice.*

She eyes me furiously for a moment then pushes off my desk and smoothes her skirt down. "How dare you? I'm fucking famous, a top model in high demand. Who are you? Nobody."

"Get out," I manage to say between gritted teeth. Now she's more than pissed me off. "Before I call the security."

"Ha! Go ahead and try. I'll sue you so fast your head will spin."

That's it. I'm done. I stand up, walk over to my door and open it. I cross my arms and wait for her to step past me and head out. I'm beyond tempted to slam the door and hit her on the ass. But I control myself, a muscle twitching in my cheek.

"Your loss," she simply says and walks away, hips swinging. She also mutters something in French, but I have no idea what. I never learned the language, but I'm guessing whatever she said wasn't very nice.

"Jesus," I hiss and run a hand through my hair.

Sybil hurries over, spewing apologies. "She ran past me so quickly, Caleb. I'm so sorry."

"It's fine. After what just went down, I'd be shocked if she ever shows up here again."

With a nod, Sybil follows me back into my office. "Your conference call got pushed back and if you have a sec, I wanted to talk to you. Oh, and don't forget the interns are starting tomorrow."

"Right," I say with a nod and walk around my desk. Sitting back down, I notice Sybil seems a little hesitant. We have a great relationship and, as my assistant, she's the most important woman in my life. She keeps my schedule, makes sure I eat, arranges my travel and basically keeps my entire life organized and running smoothly. I don't know what I would do without her and the funny look on her face makes me nervous. If she ever quit, I'd be lost.

"So, I wanted to talk to you about my duties," she begins.

"You wanna raise?" I immediately ask. "You got it." *Please, don't leave me.* I am not above begging and will offer her a hefty pay increase if she tells me she's moving on from PCH.

"Um, thanks," she says and chuckles. "But I was thinking more along the lines of some help."

I arch a brow. "Go on."

"You know how much I do around here, and I love it. But lately Matthew has been complaining that I spend too much time working and not enough time at home. He wants to take me on a vacation. If I say no, I think he's going to leave me."

"Matthew would never leave you. You two are the only happily married couple I know."

"He's also talking about starting a family," she says and eyes me closely.

Fuck. That would definitely tie her up and I hate thinking about it.

I know I'm being selfish but if Sybil had a baby, then I'd definitely need to find a new assistant. At least while she was on maternity leave.

"That's...nice," I manage to say, but it's hardly how I feel.

"So what I'm thinking is we find you a second assistant."

"Second assistant?" I repeat.

"Yes. Someone who can help me with everything and also back you up if I'm not here."

"Do you have anyone in mind? Because I'd want someone just as dependable and hard-working as you."

"Well, I was thinking about that and maybe you can hire one of the interns."

I frown. "One of the interns? I don't know. They're so green and we're going to need someone competent and who will be an asset. Someone with experience."

"Why don't we see how they are? Someone might be terrific and if not then I can reach out to the staffing service we use."

I'm not thrilled about the idea, but I understand that Sybil needs help. When she started five years ago, I only had 10 hotels. Our property and the work have doubled since then. "Sure," I finally relent, but it's clear I'm not overly happy. "But whoever it is needs to be good. Damn good."

"You might be pleasantly surprised," she says with a little grin. "We might find someone even better than me."

"I highly doubt that's even possible," I comment in a dry voice. "You're my number one girl."

Sybil grins and shakes her head. "Leave it to me. I will find someone so amazing that you'll be ready to offer me an extra two weeks of paid vacation a year."

"Ha! Nice try," I say. There's no way anyone could be more competent than my current assistant.

3

LUCY

The next morning comes so fast and when I arrive at the building where the Pink Carnation Hotel Collection headquarters is located, I pause before going inside. For an appreciative moment, I stand there in the middle of the sidewalk and look up at the tall skyscraper.

I can't believe I'm here and about to start working at my dream job.

Well, technically, I'm still only an intern, but I plan to work so hard that the right people will notice me. After the three-month long internship, they'll have no choice but to hire me because I'm going to be such an asset to PCH.

That's my plan and nothing will deter me.

Little do I know that I am about to meet a man who will make me start questioning everything. Too bad for me, he's also the CEO of this company and, of course, that complicates my plans thoroughly.

Walking into PCH, my heart thumps with excitement. I feel like my new life begins here. I open the small notebook in my hands and double check the instructions emailed to me a few days ago. I'm supposed to report to the 45th floor and tell the receptionist I'm one of the new interns.

I pull in a deep breath, walk over to security and wait for the guard to find my name on the guest list. After he gives me the okay, I walk over to the elevator bank that will take me up to floor 45. I'm not going to lie. As I step into the elevator with a few other people, for the first time in my life I feel like a young professional making her way in the world. The men all wear suits and the women wear skirts, nylons and heels.

I feel like I fit in and that's not a feeling that comes easily to me. It usually takes me a minute to find my place and my people. I can be a little awkward and a lot clumsy when I'm nervous. Although I always end up making friends, I've never been the most popular or prettiest. But I'm smart and kind so I think that takes me far when it comes to people liking me and wanting to work with me.

The elevator dings and I step out and look at the double doors where the words Pink Carnation Hotel Collection, along with the carnation flower logo, are etched in the glass. *It's so pretty*, I think, as I push the door open and smile at the receptionist who instantly greets me.

"Hi. I'm one of the interns starting today," I tell her, sounding so bright and cheery that I hope she doesn't think I'm being fake. I really am just too excited.

"Fantastic!" she exclaims, matching my enthusiasm.

Ooh, I like her already.

"What's your name?"

"Lucy Everett."

"I'm Malia. It's so nice to meet you."

"You, too." I check out the huge bunch of pink carnations in a vase and I love it. It's the little, extra touches that can take a business to the next level.

Yep, Mr. Miles and I think along the same lines.

Malia pulls up a list on her computer screen and finds my name. Then she stands up and walks around the desk. "Follow me. The interns are all in the conference room. There's juice, coffee and donuts so help yourself. Lisa is the head of the program and she'll be in to talk to you all in a minute."

Malia escorts me down the hall and into a large conference room with floor-to-ceiling glass windows. A big, dark wood table lined with chairs dominates the space. "Have fun," Malia says and disappears with a wave.

I look at the other interns who are already sitting and smile. "Hi," I say with a big, friendly grin. "I'm Lucy." They all greet me, and I sit down next to a guy who looks about my age. There are seven of us– three girls and four guys– and I know we all have the same end goal.

We want to work here.

I have no idea how they decide who to hire and maybe they won't like any of us. But I'm going to do my best to stand out and prove my worth. When I glance over at the guy beside me, his mouth curves up in a half-smile.

"Hey," he says. "I'm Troy."

"Hi," I say and fiddle with the edge of my notebook. "I'm-"

"Lucy," he finishes, and his grin widens.

"Yeah, right," I say with a nervous laugh, forgetting I already introduced myself right before I sat down.

"Nice to meet you."

"You, too." His smile is genuine, and his brown eyes have a warmth that's sincere. I decide I like Troy and have a feeling we're going to be friends.

A petite brunette wearing a tailored pantsuit and high heels walks into the room and we all focus our attention on her. "Hi, I'm Lisa Wilkes," she says, moving to stand at the head of the table. "We're excited to have you with us for the next few months and hope this internship will help prepare you for a career in hospitality whether that's here at PCH or somewhere else."

Oh, it'll be here, I think, leaning forward and listening to her closely. I'm set on it, and nothing is going to distract me.

As Lisa starts talking about the company's history and how Caleb Miles, the CEO, built it from nothing, I become more and more impressed. I've read about Mr. Miles' background but hearing it now from Lisa makes it so much more real. By the end of her spiel, I learn more than I knew before and I'm in awe. I look forward to meeting Mr. Miles and will have to remember to keep my cool. He's definitely a huge inspiration and I open my notebook and start jotting down questions that I plan to ask him later.

Apparently, that will be tonight at a mixer. Lisa tells us Mr. Miles will be there, along with a lot of other employees, to welcome us. Nervous energy fills me as I imagine walking up and introducing myself to him. I have a feeling that I'll learn a lot from him during the next few months.

Lisa talks about herself and her journey to PCH and then asks to go around the table and introduce ourselves. "And tell us why you're interested in a career in hospitality," she adds.

I listen to the others and I'm last. When all eyes turn to me, I pray my voice doesn't tremble. I've never been very good at public speaking, and I pick at the edge of my notebook. "Hi, I'm Lucy Everett," I begin and swallow hard. "I graduated from San Francisco State University and just finished up my MBA there. Hospitality has always appealed to me because I'm a people-pleaser. But more than that, I love the fact that no day is the same and it's a job that involves teamwork."

"Those are excellent points, Lucy," Lisa says. "Teamwork is a huge part of this industry. For example, if you're a Restaurant Manager, you have to work with your Front of House staff to ensure your customers remain happy and also make sure that the Chefs are preparing the food on time and to perfection. Without effective teamwork, customers won't experience the quality service that they expect."

We spend the next hour discussing why excellent customer service is so important and then Lisa glances down at her watch. "Why don't we go on a tour?" she says. "Then we'll break for lunch."

Everyone stands up and we follow Lisa out into the hallway. "PCH starts here on the 45th floor and our offices go up to the top. So six floors total. Each floor has around 25 employees, so here at HQ that's around 150 total. Of course, each hotel has its own employees and managers who run the day-to-day operations."

Lisa escorts us through the office, floor by floor, and introduces us to other employees. Everyone seems friendly and helpful which I really love. The atmosphere is so welcoming, and I feel so comfortable. Like I'm home.

It's a strange sensation, but I'm going to take it as a good sign.

By the time we reach the top floor, it's over an hour later and we're getting ready to break for lunch. Troy turns to me and invites me to go down to the cafeteria with him. "I mean, if you don't have other plans," he inserts quickly.

"Oh, um, sure," I say. "Let me run down to the bathroom and I'll meet you back here in a few minutes."

"Great," he says.

I'm pretty sure that I remember seeing a restroom around the corner and I head back in that direction. As I come around the bend, I instantly see a woman carrying a stack of folders and trying to open an office door. The stack tips precariously and then the top half slides sideways and drops to the floor. Papers scatter everywhere and I hurry over, kneel down and start to help her pick them up.

The brunette looks up with a grateful smile. "Thanks," she says. "I'm such an idiot. I had a feeling I was going to drop everything, and the stupid thing is the papers were all in alphabetical order."

"Oh no!" I exclaim.

"I should know by now to stop trying to do more than I can handle. I'm only one person, but sometimes I try to take on the work of three." As we gather all the files and endless paperwork up, she sighs. "I'm Sybil, by the way."

"Nice to meet you. I'm Lucy, one of the new interns." Sybil seems nice, but a little stressed out.

Her eyebrow lifts. "Really? How are things going?"

"So far, so good. We just broke for lunch, but I had a great morning getting to learn more about the company and how Mr. Miles started it all from scratch. That's very admirable."

Sybil smirks. "He does work way too hard and that's why I'm always swamped."

I merely blink, waiting for her to continue.

"I'm his assistant," she explains.

"Oh, really? Wow, I bet you've learned so much working with him."

She looks around and drops her voice. "More than I'd care to know actually."

When she chuckles, I laugh with her, though I'm not exactly sure what's so funny. Maybe the job is more than she bargained for or too overwhelming. For the first time, I consider that Mr. Miles might not be as easy to work with as I'd like to think.

"Is he nice?" I ask.

"You haven't met him yet?"

I shake my head. "I figured we'll all meet him tonight at the mixer."

Sybil doesn't answer my question and instead stands up, arms loaded, and nods to the pile in front of me. "Would you mind helping me?"

"Of course not," I say and gather the folders up. I follow her over to the door and she manages to open it much easier now that her arms aren't as full.

We walk into a really nice and spacious corner office.

"Wow," I say under my breath, eyeing the huge, spotless windows, built-in bookshelves and massive oak desk.

"This is Caleb's office."

I notice how she calls him by his first name and that tells me they have a good relationship. Sybil moves over to a side credenza and deposits the paperwork there.

"You can put that down over here," she tells me, and I follow suit.

I can't stop looking around the office and then take a step closer to the windows. The view of the San Francisco skyline is breath-taking and I can see everything down to the bay. Sybil moves up beside me.

"It's a fantastic view," she says.

"Gorgeous," I murmur.

We admire the bird's eye view for another moment and then I hear a throat clear behind us. I spin around and see an extremely handsome man wearing a dark suit standing there holding a couple of brown bags.

Oh, my goodness freaking gracious. I don't think I've ever seen such a gorgeous man in all my life. Maybe in the movies but not in person. He has burnished, golden-brown hair, blue-gray eyes and a killer smile. I swear, I completely lost all sense of time for a moment and I don't think I could speak a coherent sentence if my life depended on it.

"Lucy, this is your new boss, Caleb Miles. Caleb, this is Lucy, one of your new interns."

Try as I might, I can't string two words together. Caleb steps closer, sets the brown bags on the edge of his desk and offers his hand. "Nice to meet you, Lucy," he says in a deep voice that's so smooth it reminds me of the shot of whiskey I did on my last birthday.

"Nice to meet you, too," I say and, as I step forward to shake his hand, my heel snags on the carpet and my ankle twists up beneath me. *Oh, God. My hot-as-sin boss is about to see Lucy the Klutz in full effect.* Embarrassment hits me hard, and my cheeks flame bright red as I stumble forward. Caleb reaches out and grabs me, stopping what would've been a humiliating fall at his feet.

"Are you okay?" he asks, brows drawn together in concern.

I nod and straighten back up. "Um, yeah. Sorry," I mumble.

He's still holding my arm with his right hand and our gazes meet. His blue-gray eyes remind me of steel and my stomach does a series of flip-flops. As I'm imagining what it would be like to be with a man this good-looking, he releases my arm and clears his throat again. "Sybil, did you get those, ah, reports I asked for earlier?"

Maybe I'm imagining things, but he seems a little disconcerted, too. Not embarrassingly so like me, but a bit off-balance. Or maybe I'm crazy.

"Over there," Sybil says and points to the credenza. I could be wrong, but she looks amused. "Remember, I said I had to pull the files out of storage and look. It's going to take a while."

"Oh, right," he says and tugs at the tie around his neck.

"Maybe Lucy can help me with that?"

"What?" Caleb and I say at the same time.

"I mean, sure, of course," I amend. "Whatever I can do to help you and Mr. Miles."

"Great! After lunch, come back up here. Lisa was going to separate you guys and send you to different departments anyway, so I'll let her know we need you here. It'll be nice to have some much-needed help. Right, Caleb?"

For a moment too long, he doesn't respond. "Right," he finally says and turns back to the bags on his desk. "I grabbed you a salad."

"Thanks," she says. "See you soon, Lucy!"

With a nod, I walk out, doing my best not to trip again. I can feel them watching me leave and the sooner I'm out of there, the better. Something about Caleb Miles makes me extremely nervous. He radiates an intense energy and he's hard to read. Nevertheless, I'm happy to be here and hurry over to the bathroom to freshen up. Then I go back down the hallway where Troy waits to go to lunch.

I'm not sure how I'm going to spend the rest of the day working near Mr. Miles and not stare at him like an infatuated schoolgirl. He's too easy on the eyes. Like some kind of model or movie star. Luckily, I don't have to worry about it. By the time I return to help Sybil, she mentions that Caleb has off-site meetings for the rest of the day and won't be back until the mixer tonight.

The day flies by and at 6pm, the other interns and I walk into the bar/restaurant across the street where PCH is throwing a little welcome party for us. They reserved the whole place and it's already packed. Everyone has been so friendly, and we all order a drink from the bartender.

I've never been much of a wine drinker, but I decide that's going to change right now. I order a glass of fancy red wine and glance over at Troy who hasn't left my side since I returned from helping Sybil. He sips a beer and asks me if I met Caleb.

"Um, just really quickly," I say vaguely. "He was at meetings all afternoon."

"What's he like?"

All of the other interns gather round and listen. Suddenly uncomfortable, I shift from one foot to the other. "He was, um, nice. I don't know. We just shook hands and that was it." I'm not sure if they were expecting some kind of juicy gossip or what, but they all look a little disappointed.

"I heard he's absolutely gorgeous and a total ladies' man," Shelly says.

"Isn't he dating some model?" Marie asks.

"I'm sure he's a hot commodity," Troy says blandly. "He's a billionaire."

"Probably an asshole, too," Seth adds.

"No, I don't think so," I say, instantly defending him. "He seemed nice. Kind of quiet." They all look at me and I shut up and take a long sip of wine.

As the evening progresses, everyone loosens up and we start having fun. The other interns are nice and I'm starting on my second glass of wine when I feel a tap on my shoulder. Turning around, I almost choke when I see it's Caleb. He looks even more handsome than he did this morning, and I look up into his slate blue eyes before my gaze dips to the five o'clock shadow on his jaw.

My boss is ridiculously hot and it's starting to have a serious effect on me.

"Hello, Lucy," he says in that deep, velvety voice of his. "And you must all be my new interns."

Everyone goes out of their way to introduce themself and shake Caleb's hand. I slink back, suddenly shy, and not sure what to say. I'd rather admire him from afar. Besides, I don't want the other interns to think I was schmoozing with the boss and trying to one-up them somehow.

Besides, the man makes me incredibly nervous. There's just too much hotness happening.

After greeting everyone else, Caleb turns his attention on me. "How did things go today with Sybil?" he asks.

"Oh, fine. Good actually. She's really nice and I like working up there. The view from your office is amazing and, um, I'm just really grateful for this opportunity." I realize I'm babbling and force myself to stop talking before I humiliate myself further.

But I do. In fact, I manage to mortify myself so thoroughly that it's horrifying. I'm talking with my hands, waving them around like some kind of mime, when my left hand hits the plate of hor d'oeuvres in

Troy's hand. The food goes flying and when Caleb reaches out to grab the falling plate, I do the same and accidentally spill my wine all over the front of his pants.

Yep. Not just on his shirt or jacket. I dump my entire glass of red wine on his crotch and my first instinct is to dab it with my napkin and apologize profusely. "I'm so sorry, Ca-, um, Mr. Miles."

Oops. I yank my hand back after getting a pretty good feel of what lies beneath his zipper. And it's rather impressive.

Oh, God.

Yeah, I just touched my hot boss's dick in front of everyone. *Kill me now.*

4

CALEB

"It's okay," I say for the third time to Lucy who's profusely apologizing. "It's no big deal." Her pretty face is crimson. "I'm just going to wash up."

After excusing myself, I head to the back of the restaurant where the bathrooms are located. Even though I said it wasn't a big deal that couldn't be any further from the truth. I don't give a shit about the red wine on my pants. I'm referring to the fact that I liked her hands on my dick.

And that's a big, fucking deal.

When I think about them down there again, I start getting hard. *Shit. She's your much-younger intern,* I remind myself. I shouldn't be thinking sexual thoughts about her. I grab a paper towel, splash some water on it and wipe the front of my pants.

I don't know what it is about Lucy, but she's managed to snag my attention. And that's not an easy feat. Sure, she's pretty but I've been with women who are drop dead gorgeous who I didn't feel a fraction of what I'm feeling around Lucy. Maybe it's the cute way she blushes and how she's so artless and innocent.

I've spent my entire dating life around fast, experienced women. But Lucy is the complete opposite. And that makes her incredibly fascinating in my eyes. I wonder how many boyfriends she's had and if they were passionate relationships. Is she single now? My mind is swirling with questions.

Her personal life is certainly none of my business. But I'm damn curious. I want to get to know her better even though that would be a huge mistake. If I was smart, I'd stay far away from the tempting, new intern with the bright blue eyes. Something about those pretty eyes draws me in and doesn't want to let go. I love how they seem to sparkle and the way they're edged in a darker shade of navy.

I toss the paper towel in the trash. My pants are ruined but I could care less. Against my better judgement, I'm thinking about how I can get Lucy's hands on my dick again. *Pathetic.* Am I just in the mood and want to get laid? *Hmm.* I wasn't until I saw Lucy and she touched me.

Wondering what the hell I should do; I study my reflection in the mirror. I can't help but wonder if she's attracted to me, too? Even though I'm 40 and probably almost double her age, I still work out almost every day and watch what I eat. There's the lightest touch of silver at my temples and the lines around my eyes are usually only visible when I smile.

I'd like to think I'm a catch. Of course, being a billionaire never hurt anything. I don't like it when women are only attracted to me because I'm wealthy, but it comes with the territory. There's really no hiding it. Even if they don't know at first, they quickly find out after seeing my home on Billionaire's Row or hearing about my hotels. I own a couple of damn expensive cars, some overpriced artwork and a walk-in closet full of custom-tailored, designer suits. I'm not afraid to spend and I enjoy splurging on the people in my life.

I think I'd enjoy spending money on Lucy. I wonder what she likes? Flowers, clothes, candy, trips? Jesus, I'm getting ahead of myself. This isn't like me. I enjoy pursuing women, but usually I'm the one being pursued. Chasing after Lucy would be a refreshing change of pace.

Maybe I need some advice. I pull my phone out and text my best friend, Brady Carmichael, and ask what he's doing this weekend. I've been so busy and haven't seen him in a couple of weeks. Normally, we get together once a week, catch up and drink some beers over a game of pool at my place.

Brady tells me he can be over tomorrow by 7pm. Perfect. I'm curious to hear what my friend thinks about the situation. Hell, maybe I'm jumping the gun.

Suddenly, it occurs to me that Lucy might not even be interested. I suppose it's possible, but I guess that's where the chase comes in. If she's shy or unsure, it's going to be up to me to convince her to take a chance.

Then a terrible thought occurs to me: what if she refuses to mix business with pleasure?

I've never dated an employee. Technically, she's not even an employee; she's an intern. Does that make me a creep? I hope not. With a sigh, I shove a hand through my hair and decide to save all the angst-filled questions for Brady.

In the meantime, it's time for me to leave. One, I have a big, wet, red stain on the front of my pants. And two, if I stay, I'm going to be tempted to go talk to Lucy again and that probably isn't a good idea since a part of me wants to drag her into a dark corner and find out what those pretty, glossy pink lips of hers taste like.

After tossing and turning all night, I wake up grumpy and horny. Lucy filled my dreams, and I can't stop thinking about her. I did come to one conclusion, though– I'm hiring her as my second assistant. Forget the internship program. I'm bringing her onboard with me and Sybil. I'm also going to offer her a very good salary, so she doesn't turn the job down.

I take a cold shower, pull on my Armani suit and swallow down a glass of orange juice before heading out the door. It's still early and I should probably go to the gym, but my thoughts are on the day ahead and seeing Lucy again. Slipping into my Maserati, I open the garage door and roll out.

My house sits atop the hills of the Pacific Heights neighborhood. The prestigious area from Lyons Street to Divisadero Street on Broadway has been coined Billionaire's Row and for good reason. The homes here are large mansions mostly owned by business moguls.

A little pretentious? Maybe, but I love my house and the neighborhood. Parts of San Francisco get sketchy fast, and I have the money to avoid that. I do feel for the less fortunate, though. Wealth shouldn't determine how far one gets in life. Ability and hard work should. It's why I'm willing to help out kids who I see potential in– just like I was helped.

When I arrive at the office, I park my car in the garage and head up in the elevator that takes me to the lobby. Instead of going straight up to the PCH office, I walk out the front, revolving doors and wander down to the cafe on the corner. They have the best croissants, and their coffee is so much better than the nearby chain. The barista greets me by name, and I get in line. As I'm waiting, the door opens, and Sybil appears.

"Hey, I thought my job was to bring you breakfast."

"I got in early, so I figured I'd get it for us. And, no, that isn't your job," I say. "Though I do appreciate it when you run out and grab us food."

"I like getting out," she says as we move forward in line.

"So, I was thinking about what you said the other day. About hiring a second assistant."

Sybil arches a brow.

"And Lucy seemed to get along pretty well the other day."

A smile curves her mouth. "She did."

"So, what do you think about it?"

"About bringing Lucy into our crazy orbit? I think it's a fantastic idea. Besides, she mentioned how much she wanted to work at PCH after the internship was over. I think she'll be very happy to jump in with a full-time position."

I nod then turn to order a couple of croissants and black coffees. After paying, Sybil and I move over to wait for the order.

"Do you think she'll accept the offer?" I ask.

"I don't see why she wouldn't," Sybil says and reaches for her coffee. She adds sugar and cream while I grab mine and the bag of hot croissants.

We walk back over to our building and take the elevator up to the office. I sit down at my desk and bite into the croissant. My attention moves over to the stunning view out the window and I'm not going to lie. It feels damn good to be the boss.

After checking my email and making a few phone calls, I decide to stop delaying the inevitable. I call Sybil into my office and ask her to go get Lucy.

Even though I'm only going to offer her a job as my second assistant, I feel like it's more than that. A part of me has this gut feeling that everything is on the verge of changing. Maybe I'm just being dramatic.

The rational part of my brain tells me to fire Lucy and go get laid. The irrational part is picturing her bright blue eyes, plump pink lips and wondering what kind of mischief we could get into. Fantasies start torturing me, filling my head with all kinds of naughty scenarios: bending her over my desk and taking her from behind, showering with her in my private bathroom, fucking her on the conference room table, getting a blow job while sitting here in my leather chair, facing the San Francisco skyline.

Fuck. I need to get my head in the game. The last thing I want is to have a raging hard-on when Lucy arrives. At this point, though, it's probably inevitable.

5

LUCY

The interns and I are listening to Lisa talk about time management and attention to detail, two very important qualities to possess when you work in hospitality. We go around the table and have a discussion about why it's necessary. When it's my turn, I tilt my head and share my thoughts.

"In hospitality, everything is judged by your customers. That means everything you do needs to be of the highest standard. To provide excellent customer service, you need to pay attention to the little things because that's what makes someone's experience special and more meaningful. Remembering details shows that you care." I pause and gather my thoughts. "And time management is just as essential because it helps things run smoothly. For example, you can't make a customer wait for their hotel room to be cleaned after the previous person checked out. You need to keep things moving and running efficiently or you'll probably end up with a bad review."

"Those are excellent points, Lucy," Lisa says.

There's a small knock on the door and we all glance over to see Sybil standing there. "Sorry to interrupt," she says. "But can I steal Lucy?"

Everyone looks at me and I can feel my face flush.

"Sure," Lisa says. "I was just about to send everyone to their assigned department for the day so it's perfect timing."

I grab my notebook and pen then get up and go out into the hallway where Sybil waits.

"Hi, Lucy," Sybil says. "How are you?"

"Good," I say, clutching my notebook to my chest. "Do you have more sorting for me to do?"

"Um, no. Caleb would like to speak with you."

My heart drops. *Caleb Miles wants to talk to me. About what?* I wonder. *Oh, no.* It suddenly occurs to me that he might be angry about me spilling my drink on him last night. Or maybe he's mad because I basically groped him in front of everyone.

"Oh, okay," I say in a lacklustre voice and follow her to the elevator. Every bad thought of what he could possibly say fills my head and dread makes my stomach hurt. I wanted this internship so badly and I messed it up royally. On day one. God, why do I have to be such a klutz?

He's going to tell me to leave. I just know it.

I guess it's my own fault for being such an idiot. But I had such big plans for my future and working here at PCH was my ultimate goal. And then I go and screw it up with the CEO. I am so mad at myself right now that my eyes blur with tears.

Don't cry. Don't cry. Don't cry.

The mantra repeats through my head as the elevator stops and we get off on the 50th floor. As I follow Sybil down to Mr. Miles' office, it feels like I'm walking up to the guillotine. And my hot, pissed-off boss is about to chop my head off.

"Go on in," Sybil says with a wave of her hand. She sits down at her desk and starts typing away on her keyboard.

Sure, why not? What does she care? It's not her future hanging by a thread.

It's mine.

Tentative feet take me into Mr. Miles' office, and I squeeze my notebook, crushing it against my breasts. He looks up from his computer monitor and his blue-gray eyes study me closely.

C'mon in," Caleb says. "And close the door behind you."

I reach for the handle and feel like I'm laying my neck in the rounded curve of the guillotine. *Yeah, close the door so Sybil doesn't hear why you're letting me go.* I pull in a deep, unsteady breath and turn to face him, not sure what to do.

"Have a seat," he says and nods to the chair on the other side of his desk.

As I walk over and lower myself into the chair, it occurs to me that I might have a fighting chance here. "Um, Mr. Miles," I say and clear my throat. "Do you mind if I talk first?"

His brows lift in surprise. Then he leans back in his chair, lips twitching. "Go right ahead."

"I want to make it clear that what happened last night was an accident and I didn't mean to ruin your pants or touch...ah, touch you inappropriately," I manage to say, cheeks flaming. "I'm a little bit accident-prone, especially when I'm nervous, and I'm asking you to please not hold that against me. And here's why."

I pause, waiting for him to tell me to get out. Instead, it looks like he's trying not to smile.

"Please, tell me why, Miss-"

"Everett," I say.

"Miss Everett," he echoes.

"Yes, well, the thing is I graduated at the top of my class from SFSU, and I know I have a lot to offer PCH when it comes to important things like excellent customer service and attention to details." I figure I may as well borrow from the conversation we just had downstairs with Lisa and the other interns. "So, while I may not have a lot of experience yet in the real world, I'm book smart and a quick learner. I've always been a people-pleaser and I learn fast."

Shit. I cringe because I already mentioned being a fast learner.

"And I'm good when it comes to time-management," I add because that was a key point we also discussed. "So, in summation, I think you should keep me as an intern because with me, you'd get book smart, a quick learner, a people-pleaser..." I hesitate, ticking off each quality as

I go. "Um, fast learner. I know I mentioned it twice, but I think it's a very important quality to have in hospitality, don't you?"

He nods his head, and something sparkles in the depths of his steel gaze. *Humor? Is he laughing at me?*

"And, finally, I'd like to pay for your dry-cleaning, Mr. Miles." Okay, that was a lot of babbling and I hope to God he doesn't drop the blade on my neck. Heart in my throat, I wait for his reaction and, ultimately, his decision which will affect the rest of my life.

"First, please call me Caleb," he says, sitting up straight. He places his elbows on the desk, steepling his fingers. "Second, there's no need to pay for anything, but I appreciate it. And third, I'm not sure what all that was about, but the reason I called you in here is because I'd like to offer you a permanent position."

I open my mouth with a rebuttal, but then pause when what he just said fully registers. *Did I hear him right?* "Wait. You want to offer me a job? *Here?*"

Caleb chuckles. "No, at the cafe on the corner."

I frown. "Um..."

"Apparently, I'm overworking Sybil and she's been very vocal about it lately. She's starting to threaten me," he adds with a charming smile. "So, if I don't find someone to be my second assistant, I think she's done with me. Any interest? We could really use your help up here."

I can't believe he's offering me a job. "Yes, I'm extremely interested," I finally say.

"You seem surprised," he says. "Why?"

"More like stunned," I admit. "I thought after my clumsiness yesterday afternoon and then again last night, you were going to fire me."

"Fire you for tripping and then accidentally spilling a drink? I know I have a reputation among some as being cutthroat, but I'm not that heartless. In fact, I'd like to believe I treat my employees more than fairly."

I watch him grab a pad of post-its, jot something down and then slide it across the desk to me. Confused, I look down at the high figure, unable to believe it could possibly be a salary. I arch a brow.

"That's my offer. What do you think?"

I nearly choke and quickly compose myself. *Is he kidding?* I look from the generous number up to his charming smile.

"Is that a yes?" he asks.

"That's a hell yes," I say and then flush again. "Sorry, Mr. Mi-"

"Caleb," he interrupts. "As my assistant, I prefer you use my first name."

"Okay. Caleb."

His eyes darken when I say his name and I finally loosen my grip on the notebook, letting it slide down to my lap.

"I'll have Sybil inform Lisa that you'll be working for me from now on," he says.

With a nod, I slowly stand up, unable to believe my good luck. "Thank you so much, Mr.- I mean, Caleb. I won't let you down."

He nods. "That's what I like to hear. Sybil has all the new employee paperwork at her desk so go on out there and she'll show you what to fill out."

"Okay." I start to turn around when his deep voice stops me.

"Oh, and Lucy?"

I glance over my shoulder. "Yes?"

"I'm happy to have you."

Something in the way he says those words– so low and almost husky– has my pulse racing. I force a smile and hurry out of his office. I walk over to Sybil's desk, and she looks up and smiles.

"Well?"

"I said yes," I tell her.

"Yay!" Sybil jumps up and gives me a hug. "I'm so happy you're going to be working with us. When you helped me the other day, I really appreciated it. I think having you onboard is going to be great and make both our lives easier."

Sybil picks up some forms and hands them to me.

"Can you fill these out for HR? I'm going to have them move another desk next to mine for you."

"Sure. Thanks."

"In the meantime, you can pull up a chair and sit with me."

Once I'm seated and begin filling out the new-hire paperwork, it suddenly occurs to me that maybe Caleb Miles didn't hire me for the right reasons.

Oh, my God. What if he thinks I'm easy?

Maybe I'm just making silly assumptions, but Sybil is married and I'm single and also the girl who pawed his crotch last night. Did I inadvertently give him the wrong impression? My eyes slide shut as I consider the situation from every angle.

No, don't be silly or flatter yourself. Caleb is a hot billionaire who probably has no shortage of women chasing him. It wouldn't surprise me if he slept with a different woman every weekend. There's no way he'd be interested in a nobody like me.

Even so, the thought remains at the edge of my mind, and I know I need advice, so I ask Hannah if she wants to come over tonight and share a pizza. She agrees and by 7:00 p.m. we're sitting on my couch and swapping stories about our week.

The pepperoni pizza and bottle of wine hit the spot. After listening to Hannah talk about her flights this past week and sharing a funny story about the visiting family from Indiana, she tosses her napkin on the coffee table.

"Okay, what's up?" she asks, studying me over the rim of her wine glass.

"Well, you know I started my new job."

"I thought it was an internship?"

"It was and then I got offered a permanent position."

"Already? That's fantastic! What did you do? Blow the boss man?" She laughs, clearly intending for it to be a joke, but I frown the moment the words are out of her mouth.

"Well, um…"

For a stunned moment, Hannah stares at me. Then she sits up straighter, eyes wide, and says, "Lucille Marie Everett, that was supposed to be a joke, but you didn't even crack a smile. What the hell is going on?"

I sigh, take a fortifying drink of wine and launch into my dilemma. Hannah listens closely, offering a word here or there. By the time I get to the embarrassing moment when I spilled my drink on Caleb's crotch at the mixer, she's completely absorbed.

"So, you think…"

"He only hired me because he thinks I'm easy," I finish.

"Is he a sleaze bucket?"

"No," I say and vehemently shake my head. "He seems very nice actually."

"No weird vibes?"

I shake my head. "Not weird…" My voice trails off.

"What aren't you telling me?"

I'm not sure how to say this and I scratch my temple, stalling for time. "I might have a small– and I'm talking miniscule– crush on my boss."

With a whoop, Hannah pops up off the couch and nearly spills her wine in excitement. "Holy shit!" she exclaims. "My sweet, little, virgin of a best friend accidentally touched her hot boss's goods and now she wants him. I love it!"

I can feel my face flame. "It's not like that. I wish I could take that mortifying moment back."

Hannah drops back down on the couch next to me and grins. "Tell me about him. What's he look like?"

I mentally picture Caleb Miles and can't help but smile. "He's tall, which you know I love. At least 6'2" and he has these amazing steel-blue eyes and dirty blond hair. He looks like a movie star or something."

"Hmm." Hannah eyes me closely until I squirm.

"What?"

"Well, if you like him and he likes you that's bound to get sticky fast. In more ways than one," she adds with a chuckle.

"Oh, my God," I say, completely embarrassed. "Isn't sleeping with your boss a terrible thing to do?'

"It could be. But in your case, let's face it, you could use a little office mischief in your life."

"I don't know. Just because I think he's attractive doesn't mean the feeling is mutual. I'm sure he has his pick of women and I'm nothing special."

"That is not true, Lucy Everett! You're one of the most special people ever. You're kind and sweet and gorgeous. Don't let anyone tell you differently."

"Thanks," I say. "But you're my best friend. You're supposed to say things like that."

"I'm saying them because they're true. Don't short-change yourself. You're a catch and any billionaire would be lucky to have you."

I chuckle and finish my wine. "I'm probably getting all worked up over nothing. For all I know, the man could be married."

"Is there a ring on his finger?"

"No."

"No wife then. So, see where things go and don't worry so much. If he actually makes a move on you then you can start worrying. And I'm going to need to know immediately!"

Hannah laughs and I turn my wine glass around in my hand, thinking how I wouldn't mind if Caleb made a move on me. In fact, a part of me kind of hopes that he does. My life could use a little excitement and who better to spice it up than Caleb Miles?

6

CALEB

My best friend Brady Carmichael and I are drinking beer and in the middle of a pool game in the recreation room at my house when I decide to ask the question that's been lingering in my thoughts all week.

"How do you feel about office romances?" I ask carefully, keeping my voice neutral.

His gaze narrows. "Never ends well. Why?"

I frown and pause before I shoot. "Damn. You didn't give that much thought. Are you speaking from experience?"

Brady shrugs a shoulder. "Before I met Liz, I dated Jenny for a hot minute."

"I remember her."

"She was a client and when we broke up, she took her business elsewhere."

My buddy runs a graphic design company, and I never knew that little tidbit about him and Jenny. "To be fair, Jenny was a bit of a..."

"Bitch?"

I laugh. "Yeah." I hit the ball and it slams into the other ball, knocking it into the side pocket. "But I've got my eye on someone who is incredibly sweet."

"Sweet? That's not your usual type."

"I know. Weird, right?"

"What about Genevieve? Is she still trying to get back together with you?" He chuckles.

At the mention of Genevieve's name, I miss my next shot and curse under my breath. "She stopped by the office last week and suggested I take her to Hawaii. Can you believe that shit?"

"Are you serious? I told you she was a gold-digger."

"She also offered to give me a blow job."

"I told you she was whore, too."

I can't help but laugh. "Brady the Omnipotent. What do you see in my future with someone named Lucy?"

"This is your employee you wanna fuck?"

"Don't be crude," I say, instantly coming to her defense. "I don't think she's like that. I told you, she's really-"

"Sweet, yeah. They all are until they're not. Know what I mean?"

He sinks another ball and I tap my stick against the edge of the table, contemplating his words. "There's something else. I probably shouldn't mention it, but she's younger."

"How young?"

"Her paperwork said 24."

"Aww, shit, Miles. So, she not only works for you, but also, she could be your daughter?"

"Don't say it like that. Hell, it makes me sound like a cradle-robbing pervert."

"Sorry. I think the sleeping-with-your-employee part is worse than the age difference."

"It can work, though. Right? I mean, I know it can."

"How do you know? You never dated an employee before. That's why this whole conversation is surprising to me. What department is she in?"

I take a long swig of beer and then clear my throat. "She was an intern and Sybil needed help, so I hired her as my second assistant."

"Oh, man. I have a feeling that's going to lead to all kinds of... interesting situations."

"How so?"

Brady sinks another ball. "She's going to be around you all the time. At least eight or more hours a day. You're going to be smelling her perfume, seeing her bend over, listening to her voice, talking to her while picturing all sorts of filthy scenarios."

"I have some self-control, you know," I say in a dry voice.

"Yeah, we all do until she reaches down to pick up something she dropped on the floor, and you see straight down her shirt. She'll be wearing some sexy lace bra and-"

"Okay, okay," I interrupt and raise my beer. "I get it."

"I am willing to bet that this lovely, sweet Lucy is going to have you so sexually frustrated that you're going to be taking cold showers in the middle of the day in that fancy-ass bathroom of yours."

"There won't be any sexual frustration if she's on the same page as me," I say with a smirk. I'm not exactly as confident as I sound because truthfully, I have no idea what Lucy thinks of me.

"Don't do it, man. Getting involved with your assistant is going to be a first-rate disaster. Trust me."

As I mull over Brady's words, I know he's probably right and the best thing to do would be to remain professional. But something is magnetic about Lucy, and I'm drawn to her. I'm insanely curious and wonder what would happen if I made a move on her. Would she reciprocate?

By the time Monday morning rolls around, I'm looking forward to seeing Lucy so much that it's like I'm some schoolboy with a crush. I'm also feeling something I've never felt before when I decide to focus my attention on a particular woman: I feel nervous. And that's completely out of character for me.

As I ride the elevator up, I wipe my hands down my thighs. They're sweaty. I'm not sure I've ever had sweaty palms like this before over a woman. *You're being ridiculous,* I think, as I step out of the elevator. My feet seem to speed up of their own accord and I realize I'm excited to see her. When I reach my office, I pause where my assistants' desks are and frown.

Sybil types away on her computer, but the desk next to her is empty.

"Where's Lucy?" I ask.

"Good morning to you, too," she says in an amused voice.

Shit. Could I be any more obvious? *Get it together.* "Good morning, Sybil. How was your weekend?"

"It was good, thank you for asking. And Lucy ran down to get us coffee. It's kind of nice to pass that job on."

I let out a relieved breath. A crazy part of me thought she already quit. "Oh, okay. Well, I have some calls to make." I head into my office, toss my briefcase on a chair and sigh. Maybe Brady is right. Being attracted to my assistant might end up causing all sorts of problems.

It also might be a lot of fun, a wicked voice in my head whispers.

Okay, the logical part of my brain warns me to keep things professional. And that makes complete sense. I sit down and flip my computer on while thinking with a different part of my body. The truth is I haven't had sex in a while and now I'm focusing all my pent-up desire on Lucy.

Hell, maybe I should've let Genevieve blow me.

No. That wouldn't have solved anything. I want more than that.

I want Lucy.

As the thought runs through my head, I get a whiff of soft vanilla and look up to see her standing in the doorway.

"Good morning," she says tentatively.

I sit up straight, unable to stop my gaze from sliding down her figure. From her prim, buttoned-up blouse to her skirt which reaches just above her knees to her slim ankles encased in a pair of sexy heels. Her dark blonde hair has a slightly tousled look and her glossy, pink lips curve up in a shy smile.

"Good morning, Lucy."

"I got you a coffee. Black, right?"

I nod as she walks in and hands it to me. Our fingers brush and I feel a tingle. It shoots through my hand and runs all the way down to my dick. "Thank you," I say and clear my throat.

"You're welcome." She hesitates. "Is there anything you need?"

My head snaps up from the coffee. I can think of so many inappropriate ways to answer her question. Instead, I swallow the vulgar words back and smile. "I'm okay. Thanks."

With a nod, Lucy turns and walks out. My gaze dips to check out her ass and that's all it takes. My twitching dick swells, and I curse myself for being so easily affected. With a frustrated sigh, I stalk over to my door and close it. Blocking her from my mind and focusing on work is the only way I'm going to make it through this day.

For the next few hours, I go through emails, return phone calls and keep myself busy, refusing to let my mind wander to the temptress sitting just outside my office. It's probably best if I spend my lunch down in the gym. I could really use a good, thorough workout and exercising hard will help me burn off some of this sexual frustration.

As I'm finishing my last conference call before lunch, Donald Graham, who I'm speaking with, invites me to a formal dinner party tonight. Even though I don't really want to go, he's a business associate that I'd like to stay on good terms with and it would be rude for me to decline. Even though it's a last-minute deal.

"I'll be there," I say, flipping through my calendar.

"Good. Bring a guest, too."

"A guest?" I echo.

"We're going to be discussing business most of the evening, so most people are bringing their assistants. A significant other might get bored," he adds with a chuckle.

"Right. Well, see you tonight." After hanging up, I know that I want Lucy to accompany me to Donald's house. Sybil will be relieved to dodge that bullet. She's never been overly keen on doing anything outside of regular office hours.

A whole evening with Lucy.

I hope she doesn't already have plans. If so, then she's just going to have to cancel them. After all, this is work-related. I stand up, stretch and wander over to my bathroom. No one else has a fancy bathroom like this attached to their office and I love it.

I spared no expense when I had it remodeled. It's large with marble floors, an upright shower complete with jets and a fancy waterfall showerhead, a roomy closet where I keep extra clothes and a huge mirror on the back wall. There's also a big sink and medicine chest above it filled with everything I might need: shaving cream, razor, aspirin, band aids and so much more.

After slipping on a pair of shorts, t-shirt and sneakers, I throw my office door open and come face to face with Lucy. She's sitting at her desk, eating a brown bag lunch. Damn, she's adorable.

"You have an hour for lunch, and you're allowed to leave your desk," I say in a teasing voice.

Her cheeks turn pink, and she swallows the bite of the sandwich she's chewing on. "Oh, I know. Sybil told me, but I figured I should be here in case you needed something. Since she had to run out and do some errands. I really don't mind," she adds.

"I appreciate it," I tell her and step closer. "By the way, I have a business dinner tonight and I was hoping you could accompany me."

"Me?" Her blue eyes widen.

"Sybil doesn't like to do many things after regular work hours, so I thought you-"

"Of course," she says quickly.

"It's formal. Do you have a nice dress to wear?"

"Um, I can find something in my closet." Then she frowns. "Like an evening dress?"

"Just a regular dress," I say. *What the hell do I know about dresses? Aren't they all the same?*

"Super fancy or just really nice?"

I frown. "I'm going to be honest, Lucy. Dresses all look the same to me. So whatever you think is appropriate for a business dinner should work fine."

"Okay," she says, not sounding sure at all.

"Why don't you ask Sybil? Tell her it's over at Donald Graham's house and I'm sure she can point you in the right direction."

Lucy nods and jots a note down in that little notebook she carries everywhere with her. "What is that? Like a journal or something?" I ask.

She closes it. "Just where I write all my notes and things I don't want to forget."

"Okay, well I'm off to the gym. Be back in an hour."

"Have a good workout," she says and bites into her sandwich.

"Thanks," I mumble and head toward the elevator. *If it weren't for you, I wouldn't need to go burn off all this tension right now.*

Down in the gym, it's relatively quiet so I run on the treadmill first and work up a good sweat. I'm trying to run the lust right out of me, but it's not working like I hoped it would. Instead, my mind is wandering and I'm picturing Lucy bending over to pick up that notebook and imagining what color her bra is.

Fuck. Brady was right. I'm in dangerous territory right now. I should be keeping things professional, not mentally undressing my new, second assistant. But I can't help it. The attraction is killing me. Making me hard all the time. After I hop off the treadmill, I start using the machines. I increase the weight, pushing each one to the max, and hope for blessed relief.

But it doesn't fucking come. No matter how hard I work out, tempting thoughts of Lucy still fill my head, taunting me to no end. *What the hell am I thinking?* I should be taking Sybil tonight, not Lucy.

Oh, well. It's too late now.

Guess the only thing left to do to ease the ache in my shorts is go take an ice-cold shower.

I just hope it works.

7

LUCY

After finishing my lunch, I check my social media, and then grab my purse and notebook. I open it and look down at the address Sybil gave me. It's a quick walk down to pick up Caleb's dry-cleaning and I'm off. Sybil came back from her lunch break and asked me to do this task while she went downstairs to have a meeting.

It's a gorgeous day and I don't mind taking a walk. I also get a chance to sneak a call in to Hannah. "Hey! Are you busy?"

"Nope. Just finished my last flight for the day. What's up?"

"Caleb needs me to attend some fancy work dinner tonight with him and I have nothing to wear," I explain, panic lacing my voice. "I need help."

"Okay, calm down. Fancy, huh?"

"He said to wear a dress. When I asked Sybil, she said a cocktail dress is fine. I don't own anything like that!"

"I might have a couple things that would work."

"Really?"

"Yeah, back from when I was working that hostess job. Remember?"

"That's right." For a short time, Sybil was a hostess at a fancy restaurant downtown here. "That would be terrific," I say, relief pouring through me. I tell her I may be able to sneak out a bit early so I can run home first and get ready.

"Keep me posted," Hannah says and then we say goodbye.

I tuck my phone back in my purse and pull-out Caleb's dry-cleaning ticket. The bell rings above my head and I walk up to the counter. It's quiet and I came at a good time. The man behind the counter takes the ticket and goes in search of the three suits I'm picking up.

When he returns and rings me up, I hand him the credit card that Sybil gave me. It's the Centurion Card from American Express, aka the Amex Black Card, and I know it has no limit. It's the exact kind of credit card a billionaire would have since it's so exclusive.

Billionaire...

I have no idea exactly how much Caleb Miles is worth, but he's definitely a part of the elite group of moguls with endless zeroes behind their names.

After tucking the card back in my wallet, I grab the suits and head back down to the office. Sybil won't be back for another couple of hours, but she left me a list of things to do to keep me busy.

The more I think about tonight, the more nervous I get. I know I'm probably just being silly, but I don't want to mess anything up. I'm going to be representing PCH and around a lot of bigwigs. If I let my nerves get the best of me, I could end up tripping or spilling something again.

No, Lucy. You are going to leave the klutz at home and come off as a poised, young professional who is an asset to Caleb Miles as his second assistant.

Not knowing what I'm going to wear makes me anxious and I'm going to have to ask Caleb if I can jet early. If Hannah's dresses don't work, I'm going to have to run out and buy something fast. Hopefully, he won't mind.

Back up on the 50th floor, I drop my purse under my desk and remember Sybil's instructions about hanging Caleb's dry-cleaning in the closet in his private bathroom. After taking a deep breath, I walk over to his office and push the partially closed door open.

It's empty. *He must have run out,* I decide, and head straight to the closed bathroom door, his dry-cleaning hanging over my shoulder. Without thinking, I throw the door open and my entire world freezes as I see Caleb stepping out of the shower.

Water droplets slide down his naked chest as he reaches for a towel. My gaze automatically dips, gliding down his taut abs and lands on his most masculine area. Eyes bugging, I actually gasp and my gaze shoots back up to see his surprised look.

That look of genuine surprise suddenly morphs into something else. *Heat? Do I see an invitation in his hooded eyes?*

Oh, God. "I'm so sorry," I splutter, throwing a hand over my eyes. Utter humiliation fills me and I race out, toss his dry-cleaning over a chair and slam his office door shut behind me.

Breathing hard, I sink down in the chair behind my desk and cover my mouth with my hands. I can't believe I just waltzed into his private bathroom without so much as a tap on the door. *Why wasn't it locked?* I wonder. *Why didn't I knock?*

My mind was so wrapped up in what I'm going to wear tonight that I wasn't paying attention. I assumed he was out and now I feel like the biggest fool. I hope he doesn't fire me. That look in his eye...

He's not going to fire me. I'd bet my life on it. In fact, the more I think about it, he really didn't seem all that embarrassed. More like proud of his body. The image of him standing there, reaching for a towel in all his naked glory has burned itself into my mind. *No doubt about it,* I think, remembering his muscled chest, ridged abs and very impressive cock.

God. I just saw my hot-as-sin boss naked. Gahhhh!

Why did I look down? I should've been less obvious about it. Instead of blatantly checking out his goods, why didn't I just take a quick peek?

He's so damn perfect and he must know it. Any number of women would die to get with that man-God. As embarrassed as I am, I'm also absolutely fascinated by him. I've never slept with a man or seen one standing stark-naked in front of me like that before. But I'm damn curious and now Caleb has me thinking all sorts of naughty things. Like how much I'd like to take another, more leisurely look of his naked body. A slow perusal…

Lucy, stop. I shake my hands out and wonder how awkward things are going to be between us now when my intercom buzzes.

It's Caleb calling me from his office.

Shit. I swallow back my lust and nerves, then swipe the receiver up. "Hi," I murmur. I can feel my cheeks heat up and know they must be fire-engine red.

"Can you come in here?" he asks, voice low.

Unable to read the tone in his voice, my heart slams against my ribcage and my stomach flutters. "Sure," I whisper and hang up. I suck in a few deep breaths, smooth my skirt down and walk over to his office. I reach out for the handle and my hand shakes. I squeeze it into a fist then open the door.

Caleb sits on the edge of his desk looking extremely relaxed. His damp hair reminds me that he recently showered and trust me, I need no reminding. I'm on the verge of apologizing again, but I don't want to draw more attention to what happened.

When I meet his blue-gray gaze, I swear his eyes dance with mirth. The seconds stretch out and then he finally speaks.

"If you need to leave early to get ready for tonight's dinner, that's fine."

"Um, okay. Thanks."

He's studying me closely and I shift under the weight of his steel gaze.

"Lucy?"

"Hmm?"

"I need your address."

"What?"

"I'm picking you up."

"Oh, you don't have to-"

"But I'm going to," he interrupts. "Write it down for me." He nods to a pad of paper lying next to him.

"Sure," I say slowly and walk over where he's perched on the edge of the desk. My pulse thunders as I reach for the pen and lean forward to jot my address down. I get a whiff of his cologne or maybe it's aftershave. I'm not sure. But I like the woody scent with a hint of spice.

Standing back up straight, I look over at him and it occurs to me that we're far too close. My hip nearly touches his thigh and I instantly take a step back, gaze once again moving to the front of his pants and clearly remembering what lays just beneath his zipper.

Flushing, I glance up and see he's watching me closely. And he knows I was just checking out his package. Again.

Oh, God.

"I have some emails to, ah, send. So, if you don't need anything else…" I let my words drift off and his eyes darken.

"Maybe later," he murmurs.

I swallow hard and spin around, nearly colliding with a chair. Hurrying toward the exit as though my ass is on fire, I think I hear his low chuckle behind me. I can only imagine how awkward it's going to be tonight when he comes to pick me up.

Suddenly, I'm dreading this evening.

Managing to slip out and leave for the day before seeing Caleb again, I figure luck is a little on my side. Then when Hannah comes over with two pretty dresses and the black, slinky one fits me like a glove, I know it must be.

"Oh, Luce, you look amazing. Like a model," she gushes.

I slip my heels on and turn around in front of the mirror. My long, dark blonde hair hangs in loose waves down my back, and I actually feel really pretty. Hannah helped me touch up my makeup and the more dramatic look is stunning. For a tough chick who spent her time flying helicopters in the military like a badass, Hannah has a surprisingly feminine side and she's a genius when it comes to fashion and makeup.

"Thanks to you," I say. "Thank you for helping me get ready."

"Of course. We have to make sure you look smoking for your sexy, new boss."

"Speaking of which," I say. I haven't told her about walking in on Caleb stepping out of the shower yet and decide to keep it to myself for now. Instead, I glance down at the slim, gold watch on my wrist. "He should be here any minute now."

As if on cue, my phone rings and I look down to see Caleb's name on the caller I.D. I bite my lower lip and turn it around to show Hannah. "Hi, Caleb," I answer.

Hannah pokes her tongue out of her mouth and suggestively drags it over her lips and teeth, making low moaning sounds.

I spin around and walk further away from her so Caleb doesn't hear.

"Hi, Lucy. I'm downstairs. Are you ready?"

"Yes. I'll be right down."

"Great. I'm at the curb."

After I disconnect the call, I turn back around and slug my friend's arm. "Do you think he heard?"

"Oh, who cares? My advice is to go to dinner, have a couple of drinks to loosen up and then get a little frisky. See what happens."

"That is the worst advice I've ever heard."

"Okay, sorry. But I'm just so excited that you're interested in a man. This never happens!"

Tell me about it. "I have to go."

She grabs her bag and I pick up my small clutch. I lock up my small apartment and we head out the building's front door. "Behave," I hiss, nervous that she's going to do something silly and embarrass me in front of Caleb.

The moment we walk outside, my gaze moves to the black Maserati idling at the curb.

"Nice car." Hannah whistles under her breath and I elbow her.

The driver's side door opens and Caleb steps out. He rounds the back corner of the car and holy wow. He looks so handsome in his dark suit, and I may have stopped breathing for a moment.

"Good God," Hannah mutters.

A bright, white smile curves his mouth. "Hi, Lucy."

"Hi," I manage to spit out. I've never seen anyone so good-looking in my life. Hannah elbows me and I remember my manners. "Caleb, this is my best friend, Hannah. Hannah, this is Caleb. My boss."

"Nice to meet you, Hannah," he says, and they shake hands. Then he turns his full attention on me. "Ready?"

"She's ready," Hannah says with a dazzling smile. "Have fun you two!"

I follow Caleb over to his Maserati and he opens the passenger door for me. After sliding inside, he shuts it and I look through the window where Hannah gives me a thumbs-up. I wave and then Caleb slips into the driver's seat. We pull into traffic, and he adjusts the rear-view mirror.

"This is a nice car," I say and instantly regret opening my mouth to say such a lame comment. He probably thinks I'm an artless idiot.

"I like it," he says.

My hands are clasped in my lap, and I don't even realize my knee is bouncing with nerves until Caleb covers it with his large hand.

"Relax, Lucy," he says.

The feel of his warm hand on my knee makes me suck in a low breath. "Sorry," I say. "I guess I'm just, ah, nervous."

His long fingers squeeze my knee and then they move back to the steering wheel. "Why?"

"Isn't it obvious?"

Caleb glances over at me. "Because you saw me naked earlier?" he asks, completely nonchalant.

I cough, unable to believe he's confronting the issue with such a blasé attitude. "For starters," I manage to finally say. "Wow, you're not shy, are you?"

"No, I'm not."

"Well, I'm not exactly used to seeing my boss stepping out of the shower and..." My voice trails off and I look over to see his lips twitching. "You think it's funny?"

"Actually, yeah, I do."

"And what exactly amuses you?"

"You act like you've never seen a naked man before."

Instead of answering, I turn and look out the window. *I haven't.*

"Lucy?"

I don't say anything. My cheeks are burning, though, and when I glance down, I see my traitorous knee bouncing again. I force myself to stop and then raise a brow. "What?"

"It's fine. I don't want things awkward between us. What happened, happened." He hesitates, on the verge of saying more.

"What?" I ask softly.

"To be honest, I didn't really mind."

Well, what the hell am I supposed to say to that? He basically just told me he likes me seeing him naked. Didn't he?

"You're very bold, you know that?"

He sends a disarming smile my way. "Do you like bold men?"

"I suppose it keeps things interesting."

"Are you dating anyone?" he abruptly asks.

"Damn bold," I say, and he chuckles. "Is this an appropriate conversation to be having, Mr. Miles?" My flirt is turned all the way up and I don't even care. Suddenly, I'm being bold, too. This man has me all kinds of interested.

"I simply asked if you're seeing anyone. Not what color your panties are, Ms. Everett."

Oh, my God. Somehow, I manage to maintain my composure at his comment. I'm getting used to his curveballs and I'm ready to throw some his way tonight, too.

The rest of the ride over to Donald Graham's house is weird and exhilarating because I get the distinct impression that Caleb might be interested in me. As more than just his assistant. Maybe I'm jumping to conclusions, but he seems to be sending me all kinds of subliminal messages and sexy vibes.

Messages that say he'd like to see me naked, too.

By the time we pull into Donald's driveway, I swear the windows are steaming up. I get out of the car and pull in a deep, cleansing breath.

Tonight, is going to be damn interesting.

8

CALEB

The situation is spiralling out of control, thanks to my lack of self-control. I can't help it, though. Lucy is bringing out my wicked side and I'm on the verge of cornering her, hiking up that dress and finding out what color panties she's wearing. Why ask when I'd rather just check it out myself?

This dinner is supposed to be strictly business, but all-night Lucy and I flirt up a storm. She has my full attention and by dessert, I'm not sure what anyone else here really said to me. I've been too busy sharing sultry looks with Lucy, touching her lightly whenever the opportunity presents itself and exchanging whispers and little jokes about the other guests.

Leaning back in my chair, I watch her eat a spoonful of whipped cream off the top of her chocolate mousse. All the while, I'm imagining other uses for the cream and those full lips of hers. I'm grateful we're sitting down, and the evidence of my growing desire is hidden by the tabletop.

It's becoming clear how much I want this woman.

It's interesting because she's so unlike anyone else I've ever dated. Normally, I choose sophisticated, worldly women and Lucy couldn't be any further from that. She has such an innocent air that I find so attractive. She's also charming, intelligent and her klutziness is endearing.

The question is does she find me attractive, too?

I think so because she's flirting right back. She's even touching my arm when she leans over and whispers in my ear. It's not just a meaningless flirtation, either. We had an interesting conversation about the hospitality business, and I picked her brain about what she thinks about how to successfully operate a hotel.

Her answers impressed the hell out of me.

This woman is all kinds of smart and has some phenomenal ideas that I'm now deciding on how to implement. I'm really glad she's at PCH because she's turning out to be a huge asset. Extremely bright and lovely. Not many women have both qualities and Lucy possesses them in spades.

She must feel me staring, admiring her, because she glances over. Damn, those blue eyes of hers are enough to make a man weak. They have the power to make me do her bidding. Do whatever she asks.

"What?" she asks softly and blinks slowly.

I reach over and wipe some whipped cream off the edge of her mouth. Maybe I should be more concerned about who's watching us, but I don't give a shit. I never introduced Lucy as my employee, and everyone knows Sybil is my assistant. By this point, I'm guessing the other guests assume we're dating.

Hell, let them wonder.

"Did I tell you how nice you look tonight?" I ask.

She instantly flushes and shakes her head.

That little blush that always stains her cheeks makes me smile. "You blush a lot," I say, pointing it out and causing her face to grow redder.

"You're making it worse," she murmurs and touches her cheek.

I wonder if she blushes during sex? Would her face be crimson and flushed when I'm moving deep inside of her? Pulling in a steadying breath, I know I need to cool off.

"Excuse me," Lucy says and stands up. "Be right back."

With lazy, appreciative eyes, I watch her walk away, hips swivelling. I take a bite of my chocolate mousse, savoring the sweetness as I think about all the things, I'd like to do to that ass of hers. Spank it, squeeze it, bite it, slap it, lick it.

I'm wondering what she likes. What turns Lucy on? I plan to find out.

"So, Caleb, I take it you're no longer with Genevieve?"

My gaze snaps over to Henry Lovell, a businessman who owns several restaurants. He's been trying to get one of his steak houses into one of my hotels, but I haven't agreed to it. I don't care for the smirk on his face, and I reach for my wine glass and take a sip.

"Nope," I say. "What about you? Divorce final yet?"

"Next month and not a day too soon," he grunts.

I chuckle. He may not be divorced yet but that hasn't stopped him from dating a string of wealthy widows.

Henry leans closer and motions in the direction Lucy just walked. "So where did you find that nice piece of-"

"Don't," I snap. I refuse to sit here and listen to this idiot insult Lucy. She deserves more than that. Lucy isn't some floozy, and I don't appreciate the snide, sleazy tone in his voice. "Stick to your rich widows, Lovell."

He pulls back with a scoff. "I could handle a young thing like her."

My mouth curves up in a sneer of derision. "No, you couldn't."

His eyes widen in insult as I throw my cloth napkin on the table and stand up. I've had enough of this dinner and the stuffy guests. With one last scathing look in Lovell's direction, I walk down the back hallway where the bathroom is located.

The moment I turn the corner, Lucy steps out.

"Are you ready to go?" I ask.

"Oh, ah, sure," she says, a little surprised. "Is everything okay?"

"I'm bored with those people. I'd rather be alone with you." I walk up to her and brush a strand of blonde hair behind her ear. "I apologize if I'm being too forward."

I can see the pulse quicken in the hollow of her throat and her blue eyes blink, staring at me. "No. You're fine."

My hand lingers near her face and when she leans into it and licks her lips, I'm a goner. Every instinct is screaming at me to kiss her, but anyone could walk around the corner and see us. I'd prefer a more private place for the first time I kiss her. Because it's going to go on for a while and I have a feeling things are going to get super steamy, super-fast.

"Black," she murmurs and looks up at me, mouth curving in a mischievous smile.

"What?" I ask, lost in the depths of her blue eyes.

Lucy tosses me a saucy wink and saunters away. *Oh, for fuck's sake.* She's talking about her panties. I reach down, readjust myself, and follow her.

The ride back to Lucy's apartment doesn't take too long but, damn, the sexual tension between us is scorching. Even though I'm wanting all sorts of things right now, I only plan on kissing her. I don't want to scare her away or make her regret what's about to happen. Because there's no denying or stopping it. In the meantime, making her comfortable is my main priority and if that means moving slowly then that's what I'm going to do.

By the time we reach her place, we're holding hands. And it feels really fucking right.

I turn the car off, open the door and follow her up to her building's front door. "I'm walking you up," I tell her as she unlocks the main door. We walk up to her place, and she slowly turns around to face me. She looks unsure and I don't want her to think we need to rush anything.

And, fuck, I don't want her to invite me inside because then I'll go. Without a doubt. And I can't yet. Despite my dick telling me otherwise.

"Thank you for coming with me tonight," I say in a low voice. "I hope you weren't too bored."

"Oh, no. Not at all. I really enjoy your company," she adds.

"Good because I enjoy yours, too." The moment Lucy tilts her head back, I lower mine and brush my lips across hers. It's light, easy and not invasive. But the moment she melts against me, all that changes. With a low groan, I angle her head back and when she opens her mouth in welcome, I thrust my tongue inside.

And Lucy surrenders to me.

How something can be so hot and sexy yet so sweet and innocent at the same time boggles my brain. But that's my Lucy.

My Lucy.

Shit. I've never called any woman mine before. I've never wanted to. Things have shifted and we're heading into dangerous territory fast. And a part of me doesn't even care.

By the time I pull my lips away, I've tasted every corner of her mouth. "You taste like chocolate," I murmur, tracing my tongue across her plump lower lip. I've kissed all the gloss away.

"So do you," she whispers.

"I really like you, Lucy." My hand slides through her long hair and it feels so thick and soft. I pull slightly and her blue eyes widen.

"You do?"

I can hear the disbelief in her voice. "You have doubts?" I ask, kneading the back of her neck beneath that waterfall of gorgeous hair.

"A few," she admits.

My eyes narrow. Not what I want to hear.

"Fuck your doubts," I hiss and crush my mouth against hers. The kiss goes on and on. I force her back into the door and take until there's nothing left to take. Lucy sags against me with a soft whimper and I still kiss her. I'm probably being too rough, but I don't care. I want it to be very clear how much I want her. *No more doubts.*

When we finally come up for air, she's panting hard and I'm on the verge of screwing her against the wall. *Christ.* My hands are on her ass, and I squeeze. "Still having doubts?"

She shakes her head and I smile.

"Good girl. Now I'm leaving before I do something I shouldn't." I take a step back, straightening my suit jacket. "Have a good night."

"You, too," she manages to say and unlocks her door with a hand that trembles.

Good. I hope her whole world just tilted.

I know mine sure just did.

Hot dreams of Lucy taunt me all night and the next morning, I'm sitting at my desk and staring at her through the open door to my office. She keeps throwing me sexy smiles and shifting in her seat. It's driving me insane and I'm hard as steel. *Little tease.*

But I love this playful side of her. She's using her feminine powers to stoke my desire and it's working. I've never wanted anyone as much as I want her. I pick up my phone and call her. Lucy looks down, sees my extension and slowly brings the receiver up to her ear.

"Is there something you need, Mr. Miles?" she asks in a low, husky voice.

Fuck.

"Desperately," I admit. My voice is far too raspy with need and her mouth curves as we continue to stare at each other.

"What can I do for you?"

I watch her lick her lips and my hand drops below my desk, out of sight, and covers my aching erection. "I seem to have a bit of a problem."

"And what would that be?"

I lightly massage my straining dick, wishing it was her hand on me. "Maybe you should come in here and I can show you the… pressing problem."

"Pressing?"

"Yeah. Pressing right against my zipper."

Before she can respond, Sybil appears and sits down at her desk. *Dammit.*

"I'll have to check on that for you," Lucy says and hangs up.

With a grimace, I hang up. After a deep breath, I take the uncomfortable walk over to my bathroom, fully intending to relieve this overwhelming ache.

Lucy Everett is going to be mine soon. No doubt about it.

9

LUCY

I can't believe I'm playing these sexy, little games with Caleb. *Your boss,* I mentally correct myself and inwardly cringe. I've never done anything like this before, but I really like him. Maybe it's the fact that I've been a good girl for so long and now I'm wanting more.

I'm wanting Caleb.

It's a dangerous situation, though, especially with Sybil and so many other employees always coming and going. I think that's what makes it so exciting, though.

The chance of being caught.

After Caleb kissed me last night, the spice keeps kicking up between us. The heated looks, sexual innuendoes, lingering touches…

At this point, I feel like we're being too obvious.

As the week passes, we get more daring. One morning, I'm in the kitchen, grabbing a granola bar when Caleb sneaks up behind me and wraps his arms around my waist. He starts kissing my neck and I drop my head to the side to allow him better access.

After a moment, I pull away and he groans. Before either of us can say a word, someone walks into the kitchen and offers us a cheery good morning. That was freaking close. Later that afternoon while

Sybil is out to lunch, I walk up to Caleb's office and stand in the doorway, watching him talk on the phone.

He abruptly looks up. "Let me call you back," he says and hangs up. "Where's Sybil?"

"Lunch."

"Come in here," he orders, voice low. "And close the door behind you."

I do as he says, and he motions for me to come closer. Walking over to his desk, I hesitate.

"Closer," he says, turning his chair to face me. "Don't be shy."

Feeling bold, I walk right between his legs and wait to see what he does. I don't have to wait long, and I gasp when his long fingers wrap around my wrist and he yanks me onto his lap. When I wiggle, adjusting my position to get comfortable, he groans.

"Careful," he murmurs in my ear.

I can't help but chuckle.

"Oh, you think it's funny?" he asks, steel eyes flashing.

"A little," I admit.

Caleb slides his hands up my arms and then cups my face. "Nothing is funny about what I plan to do to you, my Lucy."

My stomach drops and a fire begins to burn low in my belly. When his mouth captures mine, I melt. The kiss is steamy and wet. The kind of kiss with one intention– seduction. All rational thought disintegrates as he holds my face and thoroughly explores my mouth. I've never been kissed like this. It's like he's making love to my mouth and it's the most erotic thing I've ever experienced.

I suppose that's not saying much since I'm a virgin. But I have a feeling even the most experienced woman's knees would buckle under Caleb's commanding and completely scorching kiss. My hands slide over his shoulders and wrap around his neck. A soft whimper escapes me, and I shift on his lap again. The moment I do, I feel his hard bulge against my thigh. Things are heating up really fast between us and I break my mouth away, panting.

We're in his office in the middle of the day. This can't go much further. Caleb finally releases my face, and I can see the need and desire in his smoking, blue-gray gaze. When his hand slides up beneath my skirt and touches the edge of my panties, I freeze.

"What color today, my little tease?" he asks and nips my bottom lip.

"Um..." I think for a moment, but I'm having trouble remembering with his finger playing with the elastic edge. Slipping beneath it just a bit. "Blue," I finally say, suddenly terrified he's going to want me to show him.

But he just keeps sliding his finger back and forth, gaze locked on mine. Finally, his mouth edges up in a wicked smirk. "Tomorrow... don't wear any."

Squeezing my legs together, I'm not sure what to say. All I know is my current panties are getting wetter and wetter. If he moved his finger over a little more, he'd find that out. *Oh, God.*

But he sticks to only caressing near my thigh. I'm not sure what I would do if he touched me between my legs. Just thinking about it makes my face flame. It also makes me grow more wet. My body might be ready for this man, but my mind is still hung up on the fact that he's, my boss.

Office romances never end well, right?

Every day that passes, my desire for Caleb increases. It's getting harder and harder to resist him. We're constantly finding ways to sneak off and be alone. And every time we're together, things get steamier and steamier. We're also getting more daring and less careful when it comes to people walking in on us.

I guess that's what passion can do to people– makes them reckless. But I'm having nagging doubts. I'm not sure why, but I think it's because we're reaching that next level. It's clear he wants to sleep with me and I'm wondering why. I can't help it.

Caleb Miles is a hot billionaire who has his choice of women. I'm an insecure klutz. *What could he possibly see in me?* I wonder.

One Friday morning, I'm in the smaller conference room, reorganizing some files when I hear the door close. I look up and Caleb stands there, no jacket and sleeves rolled up. There's a gleam in his bluish eyes and he looks like a man on a mission. He stalks over and the next thing I know, he's lifting me up onto the table and laying me back. His mouth latches onto mine and his tongue thrusts past my lips as his hand slides my skirt up.

We've been flirty and sucking faces for weeks, but Caleb hasn't tried to take it further in the office. He's asked me out to dinner a few times, but I keep putting it off. I'm comfortable with the level of intimacy we're sharing, but I know he wants more.

It makes me nervous, though. I've never been completely comfortable with my body and always shy about it. He's definitely pulling me out of my shell, but I don't think I'm ready for that next step yet.

I'm just not sure how to tell him. It will break my heart if he gets mad because then I'd know he wasn't as good of a guy as I think. Maybe I'm just too much in my head and being an insecure virgin.

That's not the only thing, though. A few nights ago, I typed Caleb's name into a search engine, and I couldn't believe all the images that popped up of him with women. The man has a string of ex's that would probably rival the circumference of the Earth.

And I'm talking about beautiful, successful, worldly women. He's dated models, actresses, artists, musicians and even a princess. In all of the pictures and articles, they look so glamorous, sexy and confident. They're everything I'm not and my anxiety is running on high.

What in the world can I offer a man like Caleb Miles? The better question is why the hell is he interested in little 'ol me? *I'm nobody.*

That's when it occurred to me that maybe he only views me as another notch on his bedpost. The thought makes my heart clench.

Now, lying beneath him on top of the conference room table, his fingers hook the top of my panties, and he starts pulling them down. I suck in a sharp breath and bolt up. He pulls back, surprised by my reaction, and frowns.

"What's wrong?" he murmurs, gaze searching mine.

"Oh, God." I drop my head back on the table, on the verge of dying from embarrassment.

"Lucy?"

Swallowing hard, I sit up, pushing my skirt back down. "There's something you should probably know about me," I say tentatively.

"Okaaay," he says slowly.

Releasing a shaky breath, I blurt the embarrassing truth out. "I'm a virgin."

Something flares in the depths of his eyes. I think it's approval. Maybe even excitement?

"My Lucy," he whispers. "That's a good thing."

It is? "I have no idea what I'm doing," I admit, feeling a little frazzled. "And the last thing I want to do is disappoint you."

"Your sincerity is a turn-on," he comments and caresses a hand up and down my thigh. "You should be thinking about yourself, and you're worried about me. Trust me when I say you have nothing to worry about. You being a virgin does nothing to diminish my desire. In fact, it makes me want you more."

"I'm just…nervous."

"About what?"

Is he serious? "Sex. With you. Have you looked in a mirror lately?"

He chuckles. "Have you?"

I frown.

"You're a beautiful woman, Lucy. Don't you dare think otherwise."

"But you date models and actresses," I say, finally getting to the root of my insecurity. *Most recently, the breath-taking Genevieve Blanchet.*

"Oh, for fuck's sake," he grumbles. "I take it you're referring to Genevieve?"

I nod slowly. "She's so pretty-"

"Lucy, let's be clear about my ex. She was a cold woman who I barely knew because we both worked so much while we dated that we barely saw each other. And she was only interested in my money. I'd like to think I'm worth more than the zeroes in my bank account."

Hearing him say that infuriates me. "Of course, you are!" I clamp my jaw together, angry for him. "That makes me so mad. You're sweet and considerate and thoughtful and a gentleman and-"

A loud laugh erupts from his throat. "Wow. If I ever need an ego boost, I know who to come to."

With a small smile, I reach out and grab his tie, playing with it. He reaches down, takes my hands in his larger ones and squeezes.

"Lucy, I need you to know how very much I like you. I like everything about you, and I want to keep getting to know you better. If you need to go slow, we can go slow. It'll probably kill me, but I understand and want you to be comfortable."

"Thank you," I whisper. Hearing him say that means so much to me. It tells me he wants more than just sex and that was one of my biggest fears. "And just so you know, I really like you, too."

"Good," he says. "Now come over here like a good girl and kiss me like you mean it."

"Yes, Mr. Miles," I purr and slide closer. Wrapping my hands around his neck, I pull him in for a toe-curling kiss.

A knock on the door makes us pull apart fast and I hop off the table as Caleb stands up. He looks over at me and once I'm situated, he clears his throat. "Come in," he says in an authoritative voice.

The door opens and it's Sybil.

"There you two are," she says.

When Sybil looks my way, I glance down at the folders laying on the table and pretend to look through some papers. Guilt washes through me. I really like Sybil and I feel like I'm lying to her by sneaking around with Caleb.

"I just got a call from my mom, and she said my grandma is in the hospital. I need to go home, Caleb," she says.

"Of course," he instantly replies. "I'm so sorry, Sybil. Take as much time as you need."

"Thanks. I appreciate it." Her gaze lands on me. "At least you have Lucy here to help you with whatever you need."

My traitorous cheeks flush at her choice of words.

"Yes, good thing," he says in a low voice.

I have a feeling that without Sybil around things are going to get even spicier between Caleb and I. The question is am I ready for it?

10

CALEB

The next morning, I'm on a call with one of the managers from my hotel in Hawaii and I'm pissed. Apparently, two of the other managers were poached by Theo Alemaine, my rival, and they quit without even giving two weeks' notice.

Rivals try to swoop in and recruit your best employees every so often. I just didn't expect two of my top managers to walk out without even trying to negotiate. That tells me something is going on over there. Clearly, they're having internal problems and I can't have that. Especially when I'm based over 2,000 miles away. I need to be able to trust that my people are running things smoothly and keeping everyone satisfied.

It's important to me that my employees are happy– whether it's the manager, chef, bellman, bartender or hostess. Happy employees make a successful environment. That's why I pay well and make sure no one is overworked, and everyone receives proper time off with perks.

I pull up the financial numbers for the Plumeria Inn and study them for a while. They're not great and lower than usual. Every hotel has its ups and downs depending on the season, but we're currently in the prime resort season and the hotel isn't sold out. That concerns me. I need to go over there and see what's going on.

I pick up my phone and dial Lucy's extension. When she picks up, the sound of her voice sends a warm sensation through my chest. "Can you come in here?" I ask.

"Sure."

Ever since our heated encounter in the conference room, I've been on my best behavior. Not because I haven't wanted to fuck her seven ways to heaven, but more so because I've been insanely busy. But I plan to remedy that right now.

When Lucy walks in, I take a moment to admire how pretty she looks today. Her blonde hair is in a high ponytail, and she wears a short swing dress and heels. *Mmm.* It would be so easy to lift that skirt.

I clear my throat and force myself to focus. "I need to go to Hawaii asap," I tell her.

She nods. "Okay. Do you want me to make plane reservations?"

"Yes. For two."

"Two?" she asks, brow furrowing.

"I'd like you to come with me." Surprise flits across her lovely face. "Can you get away?"

"Uh, yeah. It shouldn't be a problem."

"Okay, good, because I'm going to need your help." My voice drops as I say, "We can also stay an extra couple of days after business is taken care of. If you'd like."

"That sounds nice," she murmurs shyly.

"Have you ever been to Hawaii?"

"No. But I'm sure it's beautiful."

"It is," I say. Suddenly I'm excited to take Lucy and show her around the island. "The Plumeria Inn is located on Oahu. There's a lot to do and see there."

A bright smile lifts her mouth. That same mouth that I've been kissing every night in my dreams. I have plans for my Lucy, and I think Hawaii is the perfect place to take our relationship to the next level.

We fly out the next morning and on the long flight, I explain to her what's happening at the hotel. She listens closely and then starts offering advice and, to my complete surprise, shares some very good suggestions and a game plan to improve hotel morale. Her solution is the same thing I came up with the night before.

I'm impressed as hell with her quick thinking and practical solutions.

We talk over several other options and ideas, too. The more we discuss it, the more I realize how intelligent she is and that I really value her opinion. We start bouncing ideas back and forth about other aspects of the hotel business and I'm discovering that I agree with all of her ideas. She and I have a similar view when it comes to running a business. And when it comes to the hospitality industry and PCH, we're on exactly the same page.

Lucy Everett is a huge asset and I'm grateful Sybil told me to hire her on as a full-time employee. I recognized from the beginning that she had a good head on her shoulders, but I didn't know how many great ideas were percolating in there.

I also love how excited she is about it. Her enthusiasm is contagious and suddenly I want to implement all these new ideas. *Slow down,* I tell myself. *One thing at a time.* First, I have to talk to my last manager standing at the Plumeria Inn and hire some help for him fast.

After the business problems are cleared up and fixed, Lucy and I can spend some quality time together. Whenever I visit any of my hotels, they put me up in the best room there. Lyle, the manager I'm going to meet, has me in the Leilani Suite. I told him I'd be bringing a guest and to give her the attached room.

Although, I'm hoping Lucy will forgo her own room and choose to stay in mine.

Despite how badly I want her in my bed, I'm not going to push her. It's going to be damn frustrating, though, if she doesn't want to be with me.

I'm going to do my best to seduce her, though.

We land at Honolulu International Airport mid-afternoon and Lucy is delighted when we're greeted with leis around our necks.

"Oh, my gosh. I love it," she gushes, lifting the fresh flower necklace up and inhaling its sweet scent.

"Get used to it," I say. "The Hawaiian people are very friendly and welcoming."

"I already love it here," she says and smiles at me, blue eyes glowing. "Thank you for inviting me, Caleb."

A warmth spreads through my chest. Because I have so much money, women I've dated in the past usually expect gifts and trips. But Lucy doesn't and she seems genuinely grateful. "You're welcome."

Seeing such happiness on her face makes me grin from ear to ear.

We take a taxi over to the Plumeria Inn and I'm guessing the entire staff knows the "Big Boss" is coming because everything looks perfect. Not one thing appears out of place and every employee greets me with enthusiasm. Nigel shakes my hand and I introduce him to Lucy. Then he personally escorts us up to our suite of rooms.

Everything about the hotel is special and unique in some way. It's styled to perfection and has been called an Instagrammer's Dream because of all the fun photo opportunities. There are one-of-a-kind art pieces, antique tables, denim sofas and it possesses an overall trendy, retro vibe. One of the most photographed spots is the swimming pool which has a stylized "Aloha" written across the bottom with plumeria flowers.

We decide to have a meeting right away so I can hear more details about what exactly is going on here. Nigel tells me to get settled in and that he'll be waiting for me down in the lounge. After he leaves, I change into fresh clothes and then poke my head through the connecting door to Lucy's room.

"Hey," I say.

She's at the window looking out at the stunning ocean view. At the sound of my voice, she turns around. "It's so beautiful here, Caleb."

I walk over and take a quick look at the blue water. "Isn't it?" My hand slides up her back and I squeeze the back of her neck. "Not even half as pretty as you, though."

"I feel so lucky to be here...with you."

"I was thinking," I say, massaging her neck and shoulder. "You've never been here, and I want to give you a taste of Hawaii." *Among other things.* "What do you think about playing tourist? We could go to a luau tonight for dinner?"

"Oh, I'd love that!" she exclaims and turns to face me.

I chuckle. "Alright." I glance down at my watch. "I'm going down to meet Nigel. There's no need for you to come, so why don't you unpack and relax. Explore the hotel a little. I'll be back in a couple of hours, and we'll go to dinner."

"Are you sure you don't need me?"

"Not yet," I assure her. "He's going to fill me in on what's going on, but you're off the hook. For now, anyway," I add.

Lucy nods and I can't wait to get this meeting over with so I can come back and spend time with her. I love that she's never been to Hawaii before, and I can show her around. Her innocence and sweetness is refreshing and so unlike the worldly women I usually date.

"C'mere," I whisper and pull her into my arms. I capture her lips in a kiss that starts turning too hot, too fast. After indulging myself for a moment, I pull back and set her away from me. The temptation to do more takes hold and I need to stop this before I give in. Letting out a shaky breath, I press a quick kiss to her forehead. "Be back soon."

"Can't wait," she says with a small smile.

My meeting seems to drag on and on even though it's not even two hours. Nigel informs me about what's been going on with some of the employees and how Theo Alemaine lured them over to his company with promises of stock, raises and timeshare incentives.

Hmm. Sounds like bullshit to me, but he's the kind of asshole who will promise someone the sun and stars. Then not deliver.

The grass isn't always greener.

But those managers are gone now, and we talk about a couple of potential new hires to take their place. I also share the plan Lucy and I discussed about how we can help rebuild the employee morale. Nigel looks thrilled with my suggestions and tells me the employees would be very excited to have fun incentives, especially ones that are monetary and include paid time off.

After our meeting, I jog back up to the suite and throw the door open. When I mentioned going to a luau, Nigel told me there's a great one nearby and he called the manager over there and secured us two seats at a table in front of the stage.

I hope Lucy enjoys it.

"Lucy?" I wander over to her room and don't see her. There's a note on the bed and I go over and pick it up. *Down at the pool,* it reads. Picturing Lucy in a bathing suit instantly makes my blood heat. I'd love to slip my suit on and join her, but we need to leave for the luau soon, so I head down to the iconic crystal blue pool.

My gaze scans the pool area and instantly spots Lucy lying on a lounge chair. She's wearing a red two-piece and my mouth goes dry. Her body is perfect. But I'd been pretty sure of that even before now. The bathing suit isn't overly tiny or revealing, but it teases and enhances enough that I'm on the verge of salivating.

I release a low, pent-up breath and walk over to sit on the chair beside her. "Hey, good-lookin'."

Lucy turns her head in my direction and smiles. "Hey, handsome," she says and straightens up, leaning on her elbows. "How'd your meeting go?"

"It was productive. I shared some of your ideas and Nigel loved them."

"Really?"

She looks so happy and I'm really proud of her. "I want you to sit in with us tomorrow and help strategize a few things out."

Her head bobs enthusiastically. "Okay. Sounds good."

"Nigel hooked us up with a luau and it starts in an hour."

"Oh, I need to get ready," she says and pops up.

With a chuckle, I help her gather her towel, book and suntan lotion. I'm really looking forward to this evening and whatever it may bring.

The luau begins at sunset and Lucy, and I sit at a long table with other guests. She looks beautiful in a flowy, floral sundress and sandals with a plumeria flower tucked behind her ear. It's a casual party, so I'm wearing a button-down, collared shirt and khaki shorts.

They welcome us with leis made from kukui nuts and Lucy absolutely adores the tradition.

"It's a sign of friendship," I tell her. Then I reach over and touch the flower at her ear. "Do you know what this means?"

Her eyes flutter slightly at my touch, and I caress her cheek as I pull my hand back. "A plumeria flower tucked behind the right ear means you're single and behind the left ear means you're taken."

Lucy smiles mysteriously and takes a sip of her fruity, rum-infused mai tai. I'm not sure what she's thinking, but the plumeria is behind her right ear. My fingers itch to move it over to the other side, but I just follow her lead and take another drink.

When dinner arrives, I explain what everything on her plate is and we try the different foods together. There are tender chunks of slow-roasted pig, *poi* which is steamed, mashed taro root, chicken long rice, Hawaiian rolls and pineapple. Dessert is *haupia* and when Lucy eyes it warily, I laugh.

"What is it?" she asks.

"Try it," I encourage her. "It's called *haupia.*"

"Tastes like coconuts."

I nod and bite into mine. "It's coconut milk, sugar, water and cornstarch. After blending it, it's chilled and served in squares."

"It's pretty good."

When the entertainment begins, Lucy is enthralled. Polynesian musicians play while grass-wearing hula dancers and bare-chested fire dancers show off their moves. I sit back, sipping on another mai tai, and spend more time watching her than the show happening on the stage.

Eventually, they get to the part of the show when some of the dancers come down into the audience and invite guests to learn some hula moves. I'm not surprised when a good-looking, young guy comes over and whisks Lucy up onto the platform with him. After a few mai tais, she's out there swiveling her hips and hula dancing with her partner.

Am I jealous? A little. But she's having so much fun and when she waves at me and begins dancing, I feel like it's just for me. A private show. *Hmm.* Maybe she can do a repeat performance later tonight when we're all alone.

After the luau ends, I can tell she's a little tipsy. She's giggling and grabs my hand, tugging me down toward the dark beach. "C'mon, I want to see the ocean."

"It's too dark to see anything," I say, but she's not listening.

"That's not true." She cocks her head. "Listen. You can hear the waves."

"Yeah, hear them. You said you wanted to see them."

"Oh, don't be a grump."

Am I being grumpy? I don't think so. I mean, I'm still a little annoyed at the way that guy had his hands all over her hips, guiding her in the hula dance. I'm even more bothered that he was whispering in her ear. "What was he saying?" I suddenly ask her.

"Who?" she asks breezily as our feet hit the sand.

"The guy on stage."

"He just told me to let go and not worry about the audience because I wasn't ever going to see any of those people ever again." She laughs. "Except you, of course. Oh, and he may have asked me out on a date."

"*What?*" I thunder in disbelief.

"I'm kidding," she says.

We're standing beneath a palm tree and my second assistant is being sassy as hell. And she's enjoying every minute of it. *Time to remind her who's in charge.* Closing in, I walk her backwards until she's up against the trunk of the tree. My mouth slants down and captures hers, taking, probing, exploring the depths of her mouth. Our tongues duel and I grind my pelvis against hers.

I want her to know what she's doing to me. How hard she's making me. Lucy shifts against my lower body then she lifts a leg and hooks it around my calf. She presses her breasts against my chest and just sort of melts into me. *Fuck.* I reach down and start pulling up her dress, sliding my hands up her silky thighs, searching for the edge of her panties. *No panties,* I realize in shock, as my hands curve around her bare ass. I groan into her mouth. Talk about a pleasant surprise.

She gyrates her hips and I'm not sure how much more of her teasing I can stand. "We should go," I rasp. "Before I fuck you against this palm tree."

"Maybe I'd like that," she boldly says.

Whoa. My Lucy is in a sultry mood tonight. *May as well enjoy it,* I think, and move my hand over between her thighs. My fingers slide through her wet folds then move up to find her clit. I caress and stroke the taut, little bud until she's panting, nails digging into my shoulders.

"You like that?" I whisper and she whimpers an incoherent answer. "How about this?" I slide a finger inside her and, shit, she's tight. But the more I work her and pleasure her, the more relaxed she becomes. It's not long before I have two fingers inside her and my thumb is swirling her clit, teasing, and she's riding my hand.

"Caleb," she cries.

"That's right. Just like that. You're almost there." Encouraging her on, I figure out just the right amount of pressure to apply to make her break in my arms. Her hips buck, her body clenches around my fingers and then she collapses. I catch her, gathering her against me. "You, okay?"

Lucy nods and pulls back to look up at me. Moonlight shimmers across her face. "Take me back to your room, Caleb," she whispers.

I don't need her to ask twice.

11

LUCY

What can I say? After Caleb gives me my first orgasm, I'm shaken. And I want more.

When we get back up to his suite, a part of me thinks it's probably not the wisest decision to sleep with my boss. But, hell, he just pleasured me up against a palm tree. At this point, we've crossed that line. Hell, the line has been left in the dust and it's now full steam ahead.

I don't know if it's Caleb or this tropical paradise or too many mai tais, but I'm determined to sleep with Caleb tonight. It's like a spell has been cast over me and all I want to do is be as close to this man as possible. We've been working up to tonight for weeks and he's been so patient. A complete gentleman who's respected my decision to go slower than he normally does.

That makes me like him even more. The truth is, I'm developing feelings for him. Images of a future together are fluttering through my head, teasing me. I have no idea what his intentions are when it comes to me. Does he just want to deflower his virgin assistant and play sexy office games? Is he looking for a fling to get over Genevieve? Or is he open to a relationship?

Questions make me nervous, so I shut them all out and instead focus on the sexy-as-sin man standing in front of me who is stripping his clothes off.

Mmm. Delish. My gaze wanders down his bare chest, soaking in each ripple of muscle. When his shorts drop, all of my attention moves to the extremely large bulge threatening to tear out of his boxer briefs. A wave of nervousness flutters through me, but I tell myself I'm going to do this. Hawaii is magical, the perfect place to lose my virginity, and this man is the only person I've ever wanted. I'm burning for him, and desire is making me bold.

I drag my dress up, baring my legs, and saunter over to him. A fire simmers in Caleb's eyes and I reach over and run my hand down the front of his boxer briefs, pausing to take in the feel of him. "So big," I murmur. A groan erupts from his throat, and he grabs the edges of my dress, pulling it up and over my head. He tosses it and the soft cotton flutters to the floor.

Caleb's eyes skate down my naked body, absorbing every curve and detail. I swallow hard and bite my lip. When I attempt to cover myself, he snatches my hands and drags me closer.

"Don't you dare," he breathes. "You're gorgeous. Every inch of you."

Goosebumps break out over my skin, and I run my hands over his chest and around his neck. "I'm a little nervous," I admit.

"Don't be. I'm going to take really good care of you."

When his mouth covers mine, it feels so right, and my nerves begin to evaporate.

"You taste like pineapple," he murmurs between kisses.

"Do you like pineapple?" I ask, running my fingers through the hair at the nape of his neck.

"It's my favorite fruit," he says, his tongue tracing my lips. "Let's find out what you taste like in other places."

My heart kicks against my chest and Caleb sweeps me up into his arms. He gently lowers me onto the king-sized bed and begins dropping kisses all over my body. My breathing increases and he's working me into a frenzy of need. When his head dips between my legs, my mouth drops open and I freeze in anticipation.

Oh. God.

The feel of his soft tongue stroking up my folds is nearly my undoing. I let my head drop back and legs fall open. It's clear he knows exactly what he's doing because he has me writhing in moments.

"That's right," he encourages me, blowing lightly. "Spread those thighs more so I can take care of you."

"Ohh, Caleb," I moan, not sure how much more of this I can take. It's too delicious. The moment he sucks my clit into his mouth, I am done. His sucking and licking drives me right over the edge. I cry out as my release hits me, clutching the blankets in my fists and twisting against his face.

Breathing hard, I can only lay there and stare up at the ceiling. *What in God's name did he just do to me down there?* I release a shaky breath and he's sliding up my body, a smirk on his face.

"You're so fucking responsive," he murmurs, licking circles on my quivering breasts. He moves from one to the other and then pulls a nipple into his mouth, sucking.

"Caleb!" I gasp.

He releases it and looks up at me, steel eyes glimmering hotly. "What, baby girl?"

"Are you trying to kill me?" I rasp.

He chokes back a laugh. "Oh, my Lucy," he whispers. "Do you know how badly I want to be inside of you?" He lowers his hand and cups me. "As deeply as possible."

When his fingers slide inside me and begin to move, I whimper. He kisses me and our tongues swirl.

"You're so wet, baby girl."

"You make me wet," I say, rocking my hips. I can feel the pressure building again and I'm panting when he pulls away, sitting back. "Nooo," I cry. "Where are you going?"

He chuckles at my disappointed tone. "Hold on."

I watch him get up and rummage around in his suitcase. When he returns, he has a small packet. I'm glad he brought protection because it's not like I'm on birth control or carrying condoms around with me. Caleb shoves his boxer briefs down, tears the package open and slides the latex on.

I can't help but watch. *Good God, he's big.* I'm not sure if he's going to be able to fit. As he settles between my legs, my body tenses up.

"Relax, Lucy," he says, coaxing my legs further apart.

When he presses the tip of his cock between my folds, I clamp my legs around his waist and lift my hips. *I'm ready. Nervous, but ready.*

Caleb takes his time, not in any hurry even though he must be aching. His arm muscles strain as he pushes forward, and then retreats little by little burying himself deeper. My body stretches, trying to accommodate him, and I cry out when he thrusts all the way inside.

Hovering above me, he pauses. "Okay?"

I nod and try to relax. It's the strangest sensation and I'm not sure what to do until he drops his head and kisses me deeply. I kiss him back and sink deeper into the mattress.

"Move with me, Lucy," he urges, rocking against me.

Following his lead, I meet his slow, steady thrusts. He's so controlled and he maintains a strong, steady rhythm. His hand drops between our bodies and his fingers work magic on my most sensitive spot. It doesn't take long for my body to respond and a cry tears from my throat as everything around me seems to explode. I scratch my nails down his back and vibrations pulse through my lower body. I've lost count of how many orgasms he's given me tonight.

I had no idea how good sex with Caleb Miles would be and my mind is a little blown right now. Above me, Caleb is moving harder, faster, and a moment later, his loud groan echoes through the room as he climaxes.

"Christ," he hisses and collapses beside me.

We're both breathing hard and I'm not sure what to do or say. My thoughts and body are still recovering when he slips out of bed, disappears into the bathroom and returns. Slipping back into bed, he pulls the sheet up over us and lays on the pillow beside me. Silence fills the space between us and he reaches over to brush a strand of my hair back.

"Talk to me, Lucy," he whispers.

"That's not what I expected," I admit.

He props himself up on an elbow, gazing at me. "What did you expect?" His eyes narrow slightly. "Are you disappointed?"

"God, no. You rocked my world, Caleb Miles."

He chuckles. "Good because I wouldn't have it any other way."

"I'm just stuck in my head," I say softly. "It's not every day a girl loses her virginity."

He caresses my cheek with the back of his fingers and my eyes slide shut. "I'm honored you chose me."

"Me, too," I whisper. Caleb is my first lover and a really big part of me is hoping he'll be my last one, too. I can feel myself falling for this man and it's scary. I know he has a playboy reputation and I'm nothing like his previous girlfriends. But a part of me wants to believe that I can trust him. Regardless, I'm so glad I waited and that my first time was with Caleb. He blew my mind in every possible way.

We stay in Hawaii two more days and Caleb treats me like a princess. He spoils me rotten, buying me endless souvenirs and taking me to all the touristy places. We rent a car and drive all over the island. Each day is an adventure and I'm not only falling in love with Hawaii, I'm falling hard for Caleb.

I adore everything about him. From the way he feeds me pineapple slices at the Dole Pineapple Farm to the way he kisses me in the mist of a waterfall. We can't keep our hands off each other all day and end up having a romantic dinner on the beach followed by another mind-blowing night in his bed.

Early the next morning, just as the sun is breaking over the horizon, casting our room in shades of golden yellow light, I wake up and it hits me that we're leaving today. I don't want to go back home yet, and I turn my head to stare at the man who is making me feel things that I've never felt before.

After such an amazing trip– one that I will certainly never forget– all I want to do is please him. I duck beneath the covers with the intention of waking Caleb up in the most delicious of ways. My hand circles his cock and I tease and caress him until he's groaning.

"Lucy," he moans.

Crawling up his body, I straddle him and then slowly lower myself down, pulling that hard, throbbing length inside me. I've learned a lot the last few days and right now all I want to do is satisfy him.

Caleb rolls, pinning me beneath him. He withdraws then slams deep. I arch up, meeting each one of his thrusts, and it doesn't take long for my body to tighten and spasm around him. He follows me right over the edge and erupts as the sun rises, filling the room with a beautiful, warm glow.

The moment is stunning; one that I'll never forget.

Suddenly, he curses under his breath and pulls out. I feel the sticky wetness between my thighs, and it hits me what just happened. I jumped him without even thinking about protection. *Oh, shit.*

It all happened so fast, though. There's no way I could get pregnant. *Right?*

"I'm sorry, Lucy," he rasps. "I wasn't thinking clearly."

"It's okay," I assure him. "It was my fault."

"No," he insists. "It wasn't. I should've stopped you and grabbed a condom."

"I'm sure it's fine."

He stares at me for a moment then nods.

Little did I know at the time, it was so far from fine.

The flight back to San Francisco goes far too fast because I know that once we land, Caleb goes his way and I go mine. For now, anyway. Thoughts flutter through my head about what is happening between us and I can't help it– I begin picturing a future with him. I hope he's on the same page. I think he is, but it's hard to read him sometimes.

Once we land, we get our luggage and hop in the back of an Uber. Caleb is quiet and I'm dying to know what he's thinking. The inevitable doubts start plaguing me and by the time we reach my apartment, I'm a wreck and convinced he's done with me.

Caleb walks me to my door, pulling my suitcase behind him, still quiet. When we get to the door, I look up into his unreadable, blue-gray eyes and fight the urge to throw myself into his arms and burst into tears.

Why am I being such a psycho?

"Happy to be home?" he asks.

"No," I burst out.

His brows shoot upward. "So, you don't regret what happened in Hawaii?"

"Regret?" I repeat in disbelief. "Are you kidding me? Going to Oahu with you was the best time I've ever had. Thank you…for everything."

His shoulders sag a little and he pulls me into his arms. "You've been so quiet. I was scared you were sorry for what happened between us."

"I was only being quiet because you were being quiet," I exclaim.

"Because I was thinking over everything that happened between us. That was the best trip I think I've ever had, Lucy."

My heart soars at his words. "Me, too," I whisper.

Caleb smiles and leans down to capture my mouth in a thorough kiss. We say goodbye and I watch him walk away, grinning like a fool.

After I unpack, I'm starving and realize I haven't eaten all day. Except for a coffee earlier before we got on the airplane. It's Sunday night so that means a family dinner over at my parents' house. I call my mom and tell her I'm back. We talk for a few minutes and then I grab my purse and keys and head over for dinner.

My parents live in a nice suburb not too far outside of the city called Sunnyvale. I spot my brother's Jeep at the curb and pull up into the driveway and park behind my dad's SUV. My family is close and Sunday night dinners have been a tradition ever since my older brother Hunter and I moved out.

The moment I step inside the foyer, my mom appears and hugs me hard. "How was Hawaii?" she asks.

My dad and Hunter walk over, and more hugs are exchanged. "I hope that new boss of yours gave you a little time off in Hawaii," my dad says with a grin.

My face flushes and I smile. "He did. We actually did some touristy stuff, so it was a lot of fun. Not just work."

Hunter is six years older than me and thinks he knows everything.

He's also protective, generous and the kind of big brother that any girl would be lucky to have. I love how he always looks out for me even though it can drive me crazy at times, too. But I know he means well.

As we walk over to the dining room and sit down at the table, Hunter frowns. "You hung out with your boss? Isn't that a little inappropriate?"

I'm in the middle of sipping my water and choke as it goes down the wrong pipe. *No, what was inappropriate was all the sex we had.* "I don't think so," I say carefully, setting my glass down. "It was nice to get to know him better."

"Just don't do anything stupid," Hunter says, blunt as ever, and eyeing me closely. "Caleb Miles has a reputation."

I pause while scooping potatoes on my plate. "What kind of reputation?" I ask, playing dumb. I know his track record for dating women, but I'm curious about what my brother has heard.

"The kind that leaves a trail of broken hearts in his wake. Can you pass me the chicken?'

With a frown, I hand him the plate of poultry. "Have you met Caleb?" I ask.

"I've seen him around," my brother replies vaguely.

Hunter works for a law firm so I'm not sure how their paths would've crossed. They move in entirely different circles. Or at least I'd thought so.

"He belongs to the same club as Joe, right?" my dad asks.

Joe Maloney is my brother's best friend. He's involved in real estate and suddenly the connection is clear.

"Like I said, I've seen him around town, and he always has a different woman on his arm."

My heart sinks. This isn't new information, but I don't like thinking about Caleb's past and all of the women he's slept with. A part of me wants to think that I'm special.

But maybe I'm just one in a long line of conquests.

With a sigh, I chew food that suddenly tastes bland. I care about Caleb a lot and the past few days with him were the best of my life. I just pray that I'm not alone in my feelings. I hope Caleb is thinking about me as much as I'm thinking about him.

But Hunter's words haunt me all through dinner.

12

CALEB

After we return from Hawaii, I'm standing on the patio, sipping a glass of whiskey and looking out over the incredible view as night falls over the San Francisco skyline.

I've never felt lonelier.

It occurs to me that I miss Lucy. I heave out a sigh, lean my elbows on the railing and decide to call her. We haven't even been back home for four hours yet. Is that too desperate? Aww, hell, I don't even care.

Dropping down on the large, comfy couch, I reach for my phone and hope she picks up. After a couple of rings, my Lucy answers.

"Hi," she says.

"Hi. What're you doing?" I take a sip of my drink.

"I just got back from my parents' house. We get together every Sunday night for dinner. What are you doing?"

"Just sitting outside on my patio and wishing you were here."

"Really?" she whispers.

I lean back against a pile of pillows. "Guess I got kind of used to your company," I admit.

"Well, I'll see you bright and early in the office tomorrow."

I'm on the verge of inviting her over, but then decide against it. Neither of us got much sleep the last few nights and I should give her some space and let her get a good night's sleep tonight. Even though I'd much rather have her in my bed tonight.

Instead of hot sex, I settle for stimulating conversation. And it's funny because we talk for the next two hours with barely a pause. Even though I'm older than her by a few too many years, we have so much in common when it comes to our love for the hospitality industry. More than that, though, Lucy listens when I speak.

Lucy is the first woman who intrigues me on every level. Usually, I'll start dating someone because there's a physical attraction and then it inevitably fades. We usually never go deeper than that. But with Lucy, it's different. I want to know everything about her, and she seems equally as interested in me.

It's refreshing.

By the time we finally say goodnight, I'm in a good mood and can't wait to see her at the office. Sybil touched base earlier with a text and she plans to be gone all week.

Fine by me. That gives Lucy and I more time together without the stress or worry of being caught. We haven't done anything more than kiss at the office but that was before Hawaii. Now that we've slept together and I know how damn well it is between us, I'm not sure how I'm going to be able to keep my hands off her.

And it proves damn difficult.

By 10am the next morning, I have Lucy sprawled across my desk, hand beneath her skirt, and the moment I'm pushing her panties aside, there's a sharp knock at my door.

"Shit," I hiss and shove her skirt back down.

Lucy quickly smoothes her hair and buttons her shirt, but there's no doubt that she looks like she just got interrupted in the middle of making out with the boss.

"Caleb?"

Fuck. It's Jasper Reynolds, one of my managers. Before I can suggest Lucy to go into the bathroom to hide out for a few minutes, my door starts to open. Lucy drops to the floor, hiding beneath my desk, and I'm not sure whether to laugh or pretend everything is fine.

Jasper marches toward me, spouting off about a problem at the

Boston hotel. He hates one of the managers there and they're always bickering about something stupid and irrelevant. I sink down into my large, leather chair and scoot closer because it would look strange sitting so far away from my desk. At the same time, I make sure my legs are far enough apart, so I don't squish Lucy under there.

"I'm so goddamn sick of this asshole, Caleb," Jasper yells.

While he launches into a tirade, I feel Lucy's hands slide up my legs. My breath catches as they slowly move up my calves and then boldly curve, gliding up my thighs. *Ahhh, hell.* What is she up to? I have a feeling it's going to be sheer torture and I have to keep a straight face in front of Jasper. I'm sitting ramrod straight, not even daring to breathe, wondering what she's going to do next while pretending to listen to Jasper ramble on and on about nothing important.

I can't see her but the touch of her hands, laying on the tops of my thighs, is electric. She squeezes lightly and then the minx drags her hand over the front of my pants. *Oh, fuck.* I glance down, jaw clamped tightly shut, and watch as she silently tugs my zipper down.

Is she insane? If Jasper catches her under my desk giving me a hand job, how is that going to look?

Aww, hell, who am I kidding? I'm the fucking boss here.

I lean forward, nostrils flaring, and place my elbows on the desk, hiding my lower face behind my hands as best as I can. Digging deep, I try to keep my expression neutral and act like I'm paying attention to Jasper's bitching when in reality I'm hard as hell and dying with each stroke of Lucy's wicked fingers.

My breathing is getting heavier and I'm not sure how much more of this I can take. I'm getting really fucking fidgety and stifle back a groan that's threatening to rip from my throat.

Jasper pauses mid-sentence and gives me a strange look. "Are you alright?" he asks.

"No!" I practically shout. "I mean, I think I might've had some bad sushi the other night. Gimme a minute?"

"Oh, sure, sorry. Come find me later."

As Jasper walks out, eyeing me a little strangely as he shuts the door behind him, I drop back against my chair, eyes rolling back in my head. Lucy's just getting started under there, but I've had enough. I push back, reach beneath my desk and pull her out. She gives me a mischievous smile.

"I wasn't finished," she says with a sassy, little wink.

"Oh, you're finished alright," I say and pull her up onto my lap, spreading her legs so she's straddling me. I reach under her skirt and rip her panties off. Lucy gasps and I nuzzle the side of her neck as I reach into my desk for a condom.

"You keep condoms in your desk?" she asks, arching a brow.

"I do with you around," I say and tear it open. After rolling it on, I lift Lucy and she reaches down to guide me home.

"Ohhh," she murmurs, situating herself.

I push up, relishing the hot, wet feel of her tight pussy. "Take me, Lucy. Take all of me."

"I'm trying," she says, pulling me deeper.

With a groan, I kiss her hard and guide her hips as I thrust up into her heat. She's got me so worked up that I'm not sure how long I can last.

"Touch yourself, baby girl. Let's both make you come."

Lucy hesitates, hands on my shoulders.

"Do it. Touch that sweet, little clit of yours," I encourage her.

She lowers her hand, hesitant, and I grind up, losing my shit fast. "I'd rather touch you," she murmurs.

But I shake my head. "I want to see what you like. How you like to be touched," I rasp. "Show me, baby girl."

When she finally gives in, it's hot as hell. Her eyes close, mouth opens, and she circles her index finger around that sensitive nub until she's writhing.

"That's right," I say, on the verge of blowing. "You're almost there."

I'm trying hard not to come before her, but it's taking every ounce of strength to hold back and hang onto my control. When Lucy breaks, I immediately follow her right over the edge and into the abyss of absolute pleasure. We can't exactly scream out in the throes of passion, so I bury my face in her hair and bite down on the side of her neck. My body shudders and I groan, doing my best to keep it as low as possible.

Fuuuck. The release is too good. Too sweet. Too satisfying.

Too everything.

A moment later, I lift Lucy up and help her off my lap so I can get rid of the condom in my bathroom. I catch a glimpse of myself in the mirror and straighten my tie. I'm not sure I've ever looked or felt so satisfied in my life. Something about that little girl is blowing my mind. And no matter how many times I have her, I can't seem to get enough.

It's like she's cast a spell over me.

I can't help but wonder why Lucy Everett is so different from all of the other women that I've dated in the past. Because let's face it– there have been a lot. Maybe it's because we're keeping our relationship a secret from everyone else so there's a very forbidden feel to it. Or maybe because she's so much younger? I've never dated anyone her age. At least not since I was 24 myself.

No. None of that can be right. The truth is more than all of that. It's deeper. Lucy was so innocent when we first met and I'm the only man she's ever been with. That makes me feel protective over her, for sure. But again, it's more than that.

I run a frustrated hand through my hair, unable to figure out what the answer is, the reason for my insane attraction to her.

Yes, she's beautiful. Yes, she's intelligent. Yes, she drives me crazy in bed.

The perfect trifecta? I wonder.

Thinking back over my dating life, I'm sure other women I've been with had all three of those qualities. But I still grew bored, pulled away and broke it off.

Would I eventually do the same thing with Lucy?

I guess only time will tell. But in the meantime, I plan to enjoy our time together thoroughly. After the little stunt she pulled under my desk, I can't focus on work. I walk out of my bathroom and see she's already back at her desk.

Well, we're leaving, I decide. Taking the rest of the day off.

I grab my briefcase, walk out of my office and pause beside her desk. Lucy looks up at me, big blue eyes shining. "Is there something you needed, Mr. Miles?" She flutters her sooty lashes at me and I go hard all over again.

"Get your purse," I growl. "We're leaving."

Her eyes widen in surprise, but she doesn't hesitate and scurries after me.

When she catches up to me, she asks, "Do you have a meeting?"

The elevator door opens, and we step inside. Once they close, I yank her up against me and kiss her ravenously. Like a starving man. When I finally release her, she steps back on wobbly legs. "We have a meeting," I say, voice husky. "Back at my house, in my bed and plan for it to go all night."

Her mouth edges up. "Yes, sir. Whatever you need."

I cock a brow. "You like playing games, don't you?"

"With you."

"Good. Because I have a couple in mind that involve you being naked."

Lucy swallows hard and when the elevator cab reaches the underground parking garage, I can't drag her over to my Maserati fast enough. I peel out of the garage and make excellent timing back to my Pacific Heights home.

Yes, I have plans for Miss Lucy Everett and they may just involve calling out tomorrow, too.

It's good to be the man in charge.

13

LUCY

My eyes must be as wide as saucers when Caleb opens the door to his home. Billionaire's Row in Pacific Heights is an exclusive neighborhood and beyond amazing. And now that I'm here and actually in one of its swank houses, it's a little overwhelming.

I always knew Caleb had a lot of money, but now it's clear just how much. This place is easily worth $15-$20 million. Probably more. It sits at the top of the hill, and I pause at a window, amazed by the view which extends all the way to the bay.

Caleb moves up behind me, wrapping his arms around my waist and drawing closer. As he begins kissing the side of my neck, a disconcerting thought fills my head: why am I here?

Caleb's lifestyle is so different from mine. Does he want someone like me in his life permanently? Is this just a fling? The more I think about it, the more my head starts to hurt.

Am I being used? Or does he have a long-term plan? The last thing I want to do is ruin the mood or cause a fight. But I can't help and wonder where we're headed.

I feel like I've gotten to know him very well, especially this past week. But my brother's words keep reminding me that I'm just one of many. Another notch on the bedpost. I hate thinking that way, but isn't it the truth? Caleb must feel me tense up because he pulls away.

"What's wrong?" he asks, brushing my hair back.

"Nothing," I instantly reply. Pushing my concerns aside, I turn around in his arms and lift up on my tiptoes to kiss him. He takes control of the kiss after a moment, deepening it, and I gladly give myself up to him.

Because I'm falling in love with him.

The realization hits me hard, but there's no denying it. My heart and emotions are involved and I'm feeling things for this man that I've never felt before. He's all I can think about and the only person I want to spend all of my time with. I want to talk to him, laugh with him and experience life with him.

I have no idea what he's feeling, though, and that's the scary part. When he looks at me, does he see a fling or forever?

Even though I want to know, I'm scared to find out. So, I decide to be a coward and not bring it up. Not now, anyway. Now, I plan to spend the rest of the day and night in his arms, in his bed.

Tomorrow, I'll worry. Tonight, I'm going to shut the world out and spend it with the man who's making my heart do somersaults.

As the weeks go by, Caleb and I are ablaze. The physical connection between us is powerful and, even though we should be professional in the office, it's impossible. We can't keep our hands off each other. Being his assistant makes it extremely convenient, though, and so easy for me to disappear into his office and shut the door. Especially with Sybil gone. But she'll be back at some point and then we're going to have to be more careful.

Or let the world know we're together.

Is that what Caleb wants? Neither of us has made any declarations of love. A part of me wants to tell him how much I care for him, but the more logical part of my brain thinks it might scare him off.

Oh, God. The situation is making me all kinds of crazy, and I call Hannah.

"I'm getting in my head," I confide to her later that evening. We're sitting on my couch and Caleb had a late meeting so that's why I'm not currently in his bed. Lately, we've become worse than bunnies. I have no idea what's going on in his head regarding the future, but there's no doubt that our sex life is outstanding.

"There's nothing wrong with needing answers," Hannah says and grabs a handful of popcorn.

I invited her over here under the pretense of watching a movie, but really, I am freaking out and need my best friend so I can vent. The whole thing is making me sick. Emotionally and physically. Earlier today, I actually threw up in the bathroom at work because I felt so nauseous about the possibility of Caleb dumping me.

My knee is bouncing, and I scoop up a handful of popcorn. "I'm not sure how much more of this I can take. We've been carrying on in secret for months."

"Is his other assistant still gone?"

I nod. "She said she has a bunch of family issues going on so she took a leave of absence. But you know what that means. Without Sybil right there, we're like two unsupervised, extremely horny teenagers."

Hannah laughs. "I can't believe my sweet, little Lucy is all grown up and a woman."

I smack her arm and sigh dramatically. "I'm serious, Hannah. I know I'm being a Drama Queen, but every time I see my brother, he makes sure to remind me what a playboy Caleb is. It's almost like he subconsciously knows we're sleeping together and he's trying to warn me."

"Technically, this is none of Hunter's business. You're a big girl, Luce, and can make your own decisions."

"But am I making the right decision by allowing this to stay casual?"

"Considering the way you're acting right now, I'd say no. It's clear you want and need more from Caleb. I hate to say it, but you're going to have to break down and have an adult conversation with him."

I groan and flop back against a pillow. "I know," I grumble. "My insecurities are kicking in right now, though. I'm so scared he's going to walk away, Hannah."

"Then he'd be an idiot and you're better off without him."

I let out a pained sigh. Even though I know she's right, it's hard to hear. "I'm in love with him," I whisper.

"Oh, Luce," she says softly and lays a hand on my arm. "You need to tell him."

"I know," I answer miserably. "Maybe I'm just being an idiot."

A sudden wave of nausea washes over me and my stomach roils. Pushing the bowl of popcorn away, I jump up and race down to the bathroom. As I hurl up everything, I've eaten the last couple of hours, I can hear Hannah move up behind me.

Hannah hands me a towel and I sit back on my heels and wipe my face.

"Are you sick?"

"I guess so," I say with a sigh. "I thought it was just stress but now I'm thinking I may have a touch of the flu."

Hannah arches a brow. "Lucy?"

I look up and notice the strange look on her face. "What?"

"Could it be something else?"

"What do you mean?"

Hannah kneels down beside me. "Could you be pregnant?"

My eyes bug and I shake my head hard. "No! There's no way. We've used protection every time."

"Sometimes condoms fail. They're only like 98 percent effective."

"They are?" I ask, completely flabbergasted.

"Sweetie, when's the last time you had your period?"

I think back over my cycle and realize that it's been a while. But I just chalked it up to stress and anxiety. *Oh, shit.* My heart drops into my ass when I remember Hawaii. When I jumped on Caleb, the desire and inexperience had me climbing on top of him without a care in the world.

Our encounter plays back, and I remember every detail with complete clarity: the warm morning sun was rising, filling our room with a brilliant orange glow. I ducked under the covers and woke him up with a hand job. He grabbed me, rolled us and filled me up.

Shit. Shit. Shit.

It all happened so fast, and I remember brushing it aside. I thought there was no way I could get pregnant.

What the hell was I thinking?

Apparently, I wasn't thinking. At least not with my head. He hadn't been either but, in his defense, he was still half asleep when I started things up.

"I'm sorry, Lucy. I wasn't thinking clearly."

"It's okay. It was my fault."

"No. It wasn't. I should've stopped you and grabbed a condom."

"I'm sure it's fine."

It's so not fine.

"Oh, my God," I whisper. "There's a chance. When we were in Hawaii…" I can't even finish my sentence.

Hannah stands up and crosses her arms. "Okay, no need to freak out just yet. We're going to go down to the pharmacy on the corner and buy a pregnancy test. You might not even be pregnant, and this is all just a false alarm."

She's right. There's no need to panic until I have a good reason and know for sure.

We walk down to the drugstore and I'm so glad Hannah is with me because I have no idea what I'm doing. When we get to the aisle with pregnancy tests, there have to be at least 20 choices. I'm about ready to burst into tears so she takes over and chooses one that's supposed to be reliable.

After paying, we walk back and head straight into my bathroom. Hannah reads through the directions and tells me to basically pee on the stick. Two lines means positive. She hands me the test and slips out of the bathroom. I'm on the verge of hyperventilating and I have to force myself to calm down.

Deep breaths. You don't know anything for sure yet, I remind myself.

After taking the test, I call Hannah back in and we wait.

It is the longest ten minutes of my life.

Hannah hops up on the counter and I sit on the toilet lid, test in my hand, but facedown. As the seconds tick by, I try to convince myself that this is all a bad dream and that I'll be waking up soon.

No such luck.

Hannah tries to keep my spirits up and after ten minutes, I look up at my best friend. She nods and I slowly turn the stick over.

Two little lines.

"Oh, God," I whisper.

Hannah jumps off the counter and looks down at the results. Our gazes meet and for a moment I have no words.

I'm pregnant. I'm pregnant with Caleb Miles' baby.

"It's going to be okay," Hannah says reassuringly and kneels down in front of me. "I know you're scared right now, but you have options. And whatever you decide, I'll be with you every step of the way."

"Options?" I repeat. I really hadn't given my options any thought.

"If you aren't ready to be a mother-"

I shake my head. "I could never terminate this pregnancy." My hands drop and cover my flat stomach. I won't let anyone hurt the tiny baby growing inside me. It's half me and half Caleb. And even though I have no idea where he stands when it comes to me, I love him.

And that means I love our baby.

"A part of me is completely freaked out and ready to run for the hills," I say. "The other part of me knows that there's only one real option for me and that is to have this baby."

"Are you sure?" she asks. "That's what you want?"

I nod. "You know me, and I'd never be able to hurt the little baby inside me."

"I know," she whispers.

"But that doesn't make it any less scary." I shake my head. "God, and I thought I was freaked out before. It's like everything just got a million times more intense."

"I'm here for you, Luce. Whatever I can do to help, just let me know."

“Thanks, Hannah. You’re the best. I couldn’t get through this without you.”

“Love you, sweetie.”

“Love you, too,” I say and hug her.

My mind goes straight to Caleb, and I wonder how I’m going to tell him my news. *Our news*. God, and I was terrified before to tell him how I was feeling. Now, I need to tell him he’s going to be a father.

My stomach starts to hurt all over again.

14

CALEB

When Lucy texts me early the next morning and says she's not feeling well, I tell her to take the day off. I figure without her constantly tempting me all day, I'll actually get some work done. By noon, I'm lost without her.

I miss her smiling face and sweet attitude. I also miss our playful banter and steamy encounters throughout the office. Sneaking around with Lucy has been fun, but I'm beginning to realize something: it's become more than that.

And, dammit, I'm falling for her.

I've never had any problem walking away from a woman. After all the sexy fun, I can cut ties and not look back like a pro. Does that make me an asshole? A playboy? Maybe. Or maybe it just makes me a man who hasn't found the right woman yet.

Until now.

I think I may have found her. She's much younger and she works for me so that's potentially two big problems. But I don't care. Today is the first day I haven't seen her since she started working here and it feels so empty. I think things have progressed to the point where it's time to make a decision– either break it off with her or introduce her to the world as my girlfriend.

I toss my pen aside and look out my open doorway at her empty desk. Lucy isn't here for four hours, and it feels like it's been forever. Sybil's been gone for a month, and I've barely noticed. The significance of that hits me hard.

I'm catching feelings for my second assistant. In a really big fucking way.

Heaving out a sigh, I grab my phone and text her: *how are you feeling?*

Those three little bubbles float on my screen as I wait for her to reply. She's probably resting, and my dumb ass might've just woken her up. But a moment later she responds - *tired but better, thanks...sorry if you needed me today...*

Don't worry about me. Just take care of yourself, I type and hit send. I want to tell her I miss her and how empty the office feels without her. Instead, I send some dumb emoji with a sick face.

What is wrong with me? So, lame.

The more I think about it, the more I realize that I've never been in a serious relationship with a woman that I've actually cared about. And I've certainly never been in love. What I'm feeling right now is completely foreign and I have nothing to compare it to so I'm not sure how to process what's happening.

I need advice. Normally, I go to Brady for women troubles, but this is serious and not some silly discussion about random musings like does she only like me because I have a shitload of money. That leaves me with one possibility: my mom. She knows me better than anyone in the world and she doesn't bullshit me. We're extremely close and she will keep things real and tell me what I might not want to hear or be able to see for myself.

And that's what I need right now.

I call my mom and smile when her voice comes over the line. Other than John Goldberg, Marsha Miles has been my champion and biggest supporter since I can remember. All I ever wanted to do was make sure she was taken care of and I'm happy to say I've been able to spoil her rotten. I set her up in a beautiful brownstone a few neighborhoods away from me and she spends her days with friends from her senior group. They play cards, have a book club and knit.

They're also rowdy as hell and it's beyond entertaining.

"Hi, sweetheart," she says.

"Hi, Mom. What're you doing?"

"I'm hosting the gin rummy tournament tonight, so Betty and I are making mint juleps for the ladies."

I chuckle. My mom and her ladies are a bunch of gossipy, old hens who love to mother everyone, including me. Last Christmas, the ladies knitted me a sweater, matching scarf and gave me a coupon book for Subway. In return, I gave each of them a ticket for a cruise to Alaska. My mom said they had a "rip-roaring good time" and she told me she "danced with a former Air Force pilot who shot down Nazis during the second world war."

"That sounds fun," I comment and turn my chair around to gaze out at the skyline.

"What's going on, Caleb James? You sound off."

Leave it to my mom to notice something is wrong. She's the most perceptive person I've ever met. "I guess I'm just trying to figure some personal things out."

"Relationship stuff?"

"Yeah."

"Please tell me you aren't thinking about getting back together with that awful French woman. She wore so much perfume I could barely breathe."

I burst out laughing. My mother doesn't mince words and she never cared for Genevieve. "No, not Genevieve. I'm actually seeing someone new." I don't elaborate and wait for her reaction. My mom is used to all of the endless women and dead-end relationships that never go anywhere. She gave up on grandchildren years ago. A part of me feels like I failed her in that regard and another part of me wouldn't know how to be a father. Mine died when I was only 16 and the only other man I had as a role model was John.

"Well, bring her over. I'd like to meet her."

"To your gin rummy night?" I ask. "I don't want to crash your party." Lucy wasn't feeling well earlier but maybe she'd be up for meeting my mom. I do want them to meet, and this is as good an opportunity as any.

"Sure. Why not?"

"Alright, I'll ask her."

After talking with my mom for a few more minutes, we say goodbye and I call Lucy. She answers right away and I get the feeling she missed me today just as much as I missed her.

"Hello, my Lucy," I say in a low voice. "How are you feeling?"

"Hi. Much better. I was just a little, um, nauseous this morning."

"I miss you. It's awfully quiet around here without you."

"Really? I miss you, too."

"Any chance I can swing by after work and pick you up? My mom invited us over for some gin rummy and mint juleps."

"Your mom?" she asks, sounding thoroughly shocked.

Even though we talked about our families, we never specifically talked about introducing each other to them. "Yeah. She and her friends are a lot of fun. You'll love them."

"I'd like that," she says in a soft voice.

"Great. Pick you up at 5? They start playing at 6."

"Okay. See you then."

I'm so stupidly excited to see Lucy that by the time 4:30pm rolls around, I'm ready to jet. I shut my computer down and race out of the office. I think some of the employees are noticing that I'm not staying late anymore and that I seem to have better things to do. Which is completely true.

It's not long before I'm idling at the curb in front of Lucy's building, waiting for her to come down. When she appears, my heart stutters in my chest. One day of not seeing her feels like a year. She slips into the passenger seat, and I lean over and plant a kiss on her lips.

"I missed you today," I say, after finally pulling back.

"I missed you, too," she says with a smile. "I'm excited to meet your mom."

"Fair warning– she tells you exactly what's on her mind. She and her friends don't have filters."

Lucy chuckles and in less than 20 minutes, I'm parking near my mom's brownstone. It's four levels and I installed an elevator in it, so she doesn't have to use the stairs. She claims it's far too big for her, but I don't care. I love spoiling her.

I open the door for Lucy, and we head toward the chaos. My mom has five of her friends over and when we appear, they all look up and grin.

"Marsha, Caleb is here with his much younger, very pretty girlfriend!" Elsie calls out.

I glance over at Lucy who turns beet red. "I'm going to apologize in advance for anything they may say," I whisper to her, reaching for her hand and guiding her toward the table. I pull a chair out for her, and she sits.

My mom appears carrying a tray of snacks and I take it from her and set it on the table. "Looking good, ladies," I say and place a kiss on her cheek. "How're the mint juleps?"

"Splendid," Barbara says and giggles. "I think I may be a little tipsy."

"Oh, Barbie, you always indulge too much," Mary scoffs. "Slow down or Caleb will have to drive you home."

I toss a wink at Barbara. "It would be my pleasure."

"Marsha, your son is an outrageous flirt," Elsie declares and shuffles a deck of cards.

I turn to my mom and introduce Lucy. "Mom, this is Lucy Everett. Lucy, my mother Marsha."

My mom hands Lucy a mint julep and shakes her hand. "Welcome to the party, Lucy. I hear you work with Caleb."

"Yes, that's right."

"She helps Sybil and I out," I quickly say, trying to avoid labeling her as my assistant. I don't want them to get the impression this is just an office affair. It's become so much more than that.

"So she's your assistant?" Mary asks.

Sly old broad. "She's one of my assistants," I admit.

"Is that smart?" Betty asks. "Mixing business with pleasure? It rarely ends well."

They all look at us and I start second-guessing bringing Lucy here. The last thing I want is for her to be uncomfortable or like she's under a magnifying glass. When Lucy looks over at me, uncertainty in her gaze, my chest tightens. I reach for her hand and squeeze it.

"That's because you were shacking up with the wrong boss, Betty," I say.

All the women cackle and Elsie deals us all in.

"Do you know how to play gin rummy?" my mom asks Lucy.

To my surprise, Lucy nods. "My grandma taught me. We used to play all the time."

"How wonderful," Ruby exclaims.

I reach for a tiny cucumber rye sandwich and take a bite, watching Lucy from the corner of my eye. She seems comfortable and she engages easily with the other women. I wasn't sure how she'd react to their prying and if they'd overwhelm her because they're all so outgoing and blunt. But my shy Lucy is engaging and laughing as we play.

It isn't long before we're several hands in and I notice Lucy hasn't touched her mint julep. "Not a fan?" I ask and nod toward the drink.

"Oh, I, ah, still feel a little nauseous from earlier. Probably best if I don't drink any alcohol. But it looks delicious."

"Caleb, why don't you get Lucy some iced tea or lemonade? I made some earlier," my mom says.

I glance over at Lucy, and she smiles. "Iced tea would be nice, thank you."

"Sure," I say and stand up. As I walk to the kitchen, I hear the women start asking Lucy questions about me. I pause inside the doorway and listen to the old bird's pounce. They really are too much and some of the nosiest women I've ever had the good fortune of meeting. Even if they can be pushy and somewhat obnoxious, I still adore them.

"How serious are you?" Mary asks. "You do know Caleb is a serial dater."

I grit my teeth. *Thanks a lot.*

"Caleb is very special," Lucy says, gracefully skirting around the question. "I have such a good time with him, and I feel very fortunate to work with him at PCH."

"That's the PC answer," Betty comments. "Now let's hear the juicy answer."

Aw, shit. I warned her. They're relentless.

But Lucy more than holds her own and I'm damn proud of her.

"Marsha– if I may call you by your first name– I just want you to know that you raised an incredible son," Lucy says. "He's kind, considerate and the kind of man any girl would be lucky to have."

My chest constricts. It's nice hearing those words come out of her mouth. No one has ever said that about me before.

"Thank you, Lucy," my mom says. "That's very sweet of you to say. Caleb is a good boy and I think once he finds someone he cares about, he's loyal as the day is long."

She's right. Loyalty is important to me, and I take care of the people I love. I fill a glass with iced tea and return to the table. "Here you go," I say and set it down in front of Lucy.

"Thank you," she says and takes a sip.

The rest of the evening goes off without a hitch. The ladies entertain the hell out of us, and I can't remember the last time I laughed so much. Lucy, too. She's smiling and full of witty banter all night. As I watch her deal the final hand, I admire her profile and the way she laughs at something Elsie says.

I can't look away. The curve of her face is mesmerizing, and I study her delicate cheekbones, small, straight nose and full mouth. My gaze dips to the slope of her breasts beneath her shirt and I start thinking about tonight. Suddenly, I'm really looking forward to whisking her out of here and getting her alone and all to myself.

There's something about Lucy Everett that has me all in and looking forward to the future. I want her in my life and I'm ready to tell the world. I'm done sneaking around and I have the urge to show her off. To claim her as mine. It's something I've never wanted before, and it scares me.

Lucy has the power to hurt me. I don't think she ever would, at least not on purpose, but it's still something I don't like thinking about.

The truth is, she's got me wrapped around her finger. But I've decided that being with her is a risk worth taking.

I throw my cards down as Betty wins the final hand and decide that for the first time in my life, I'm all in.

I'm all in with Lucy Everett.

15

LUCY

I'm feeling bittersweet after I leave from my doctor's appointment and plan to head straight over to the office. My OBGYN confirmed my pregnancy and I'm doing my best not to panic. After meeting Caleb's mother and her quirky friends a few nights ago, I can see myself fitting in with his family. But does he want me?

I have no idea. The moment I think of Caleb, it's like he subconsciously knows and my phone rings. I pull it out of my purse and see his name on the screen. *Hi, Caleb. Congratulations, you're going to be a dad.*

Can you imagine?

Instead, I swipe the bar over and say, "Good morning, Mr. Miles."

His deep chuckle reverberates over the line. "Morning, baby girl. What's going on?"

"Just left my appointment and I'm on my way in as we speak." When I told Caleb I had a personal appointment this morning, I kept it vague. No need to tell him yet that I was at the doctor's office. But now that my pregnancy is confirmed, I know the next step is telling him. And I'm not ready to do that quite yet. It makes me nervous as hell. "Do you want a coffee or anything?"

"No, thank you. I wanted to let you know that I'm leaving."

Leaving? My mind instantly goes to the darkest place possible, and I assume he's talking about me.

"Last-minute business trip to Boston, so I'm flying out now."

I breathe out a sigh of relief and mentally chastise myself for jumping to the worst-case scenario. I need to relax and not always assume Caleb is on the verge of leaving me. But this pregnancy is making me extremely emotional– more so than usual, if that's even possible.

"Is everything okay?" I ask. After the problems in Hawaii, it seems like more have been springing up. Just little things, but if I can come up with some solutions to help make Caleb's life easier, I'd be more than willing.

"Nothing I can't handle," he informs me. "How'd your appointment go?"

"Oh, fine," I answer vaguely and immediately go silent. *Damn, that sounds suspicious.*

"What was it again?" he asks.

I can hear the curiosity in his voice but now isn't the time to get into it. "Just a, ah, teeth cleaning," I lie. God, I am the world's worst liar.

"Okaaay," he says. "Well, I'm off to the airport."

"Have a safe trip," I tell him, and we say goodbye. I don't think he believes my lame excuse and why would he?

I'm going to tell him. But it's something I can't just blurt out over the phone. It needs to be face to face and he should probably be sitting down just in case the shock threatens to knock him over.

Oh, God. I shake my hands out and try not to let anxiety take over. If I think about it logically, Caleb is a 40-year-old man who is extremely wealthy and quite capable of taking care of a child financially. It's not like he's struggling or in a bad position. He's single and there's no past complications with someone he's had a relationship with or still seeing.

So why am I so scared to tell him?

Maybe because I have absolutely no idea how he feels about having a baby. He's never mentioned wanting a wife, children or a family. It makes me think he doesn't want any of it. If he did, he could have already had it all years ago. Caleb Miles is a damn catch and he's had plenty of women waltzing through his life that he could've settled down with.

But he's chosen to focus on work.

The idea that I could make him feel trapped hits me hard. Caleb enjoys his freedom and now here I am about to announce we're going to have a kid. *Jesus.* He's going to run for the hills. I just know it.

I'm so in my head that I can't see straight as I make my way up to the PCH office. I walk down the hall, trying to figure out the easiest way to break my news to the daddy-to-be and nearly bump right into someone standing by my desk.

And just when I think my life can't get any worse, it turns into a complete shit-show.

Super tall and slim, the woman turns to me and she's so chic. She's wearing what looks like a Chanel suit and pumps with the double "C" logo on them. Her makeup is flawless, and she has long, straight, jet black hair. Whoever she is, she looks like she just stepped off a runway and she smells strongly of flowers. "*Bonjour,*" she says. "Where is Caleb?"

I frown and drop my purse down on my desk. "He had a business trip and flew out a little bit ago," I say, feeling like a dumpy munchkin beside her. I run a self-conscious hand through my wind-blown hair and find a knot.

"Hmm, really?" she asks.

Without another word to me, she saunters right into his office like she doesn't believe me. Like she owns the damn place.

"Um, excuse me?" I follow her into his office. "Can I help you?"

She gives me a world-weary sigh. "I doubt it." Her dark gaze rakes down on me and I can feel her judging me with that one, scathing look. "I suppose I can call him."

"Was he expecting you?" I ask and cross my arms.

"You're not the one who's usually here and acting as gatekeeper," she comments and flips her ebony hair, ignoring my question.

"You must mean Sybil," I say. "I'm Lucy."

She shrugs. "I don't remember her name. Only that she wears those drab sweaters. Like something my grand-mère wears, no?" she asks with a nasty smirk.

Whoever this woman is, I decide that I do not like her. Not at all. It's clear she thinks she's better than everyone else and I also get the impression she can be very mean. Cold, too. I wonder how she and Caleb know each other and it occurs to me that he may have dated her.

I purposely avoided digging into Caleb's past for that very reason. I don't want to know specifics about his string of women. I know there have been a lot and learning details of his affairs would hurt me too much. I'd always assumed that once he moves on, it's over.

But now I'm beginning to second-guess that assumption.

"Would you like to leave a message?" I ask, trying to be patient.

"I'll just call him myself," she purrs. "If you don't know yet, I'm Genevieve Blanchet. Caleb and I dated for about a year and then went our separate ways, but I'm happy to say we're getting back together."

My mouth drops open as I try to absorb her words. "What?" I finally manage to splutter.

She smiles at me and it possesses a devious edge that instantly puts me on my guard. "I'm a fashion model, you see, so I travel a lot. I have a very busy, successful career. Caleb was upset because he couldn't see me as often as he wanted. I suggested we take some time apart and well, what can I say? You can't keep two people in love apart for long."

Two people in love? My stomach sours and I bite my lip to keep from hurling. What is this woman talking about? She's been seeing Caleb, too? At the same time, we've been sleeping together.

Oh. God.

How naive have I been? Was I simply so blinded by his charm that I ignored the signs? I press my fingers against my temple and feel a raging headache erupt, nearly splitting my skull.

"Well, I'm sorry I missed him," Genevieve says, a pouty little look on her face. "I just wanted to show him this." She reaches into her huge designer handbag and pulls out a folded newspaper. "We made the society column."

"Society column?" I repeat blankly.

"That's right. When we attended the Grammerly's soiree. Doesn't he look handsome?"

She tilts the paper toward me and there's no doubt about it– it's a picture of Caleb in a suit standing beside this woman. And they look phenomenal together. Like some kind of stunningly gorgeous, super luxurious, high-power couple. They remind me of an A-List celebrity couple who would have some kind of combined nickname and a social media following in the millions. Like "Ca-Gen" or something equally on par with Bennifer.

It feels like cement is stuck in my throat. "Yes. He looks very handsome," I agree, my heart shattering into a million and one little pieces. And I can't deny it– they look perfect together. Like they were made for one another.

When I glance up, she's studying me closely and I wonder what she sees. Probably just a frumpy-looking, little girl who's trying so hard to make it in the real world but who's nothing more than a fraud.

Genevieve looks at the slim, diamond-encrusted watch on her equally slim wrist and frowns. "I'm late for a luncheon over at the Plaza. Au revoir." She turns on her heel and sashays out of Caleb's office.

My eyes slide shut, and I drop down into the chair opposite Caleb's desk.

What the hell just happened? I feel like I got completely blindsided, clobbered upside the head and then sucker-punched in the gut. Now I have no idea what to think or how to feel.

Other than completely betrayed.

I'm sitting here pregnant with Caleb's baby and he's taking Genevieve Blanchet to parties? My stomach roils and I jump up and race into Caleb's bathroom and puke into his toilet. After eliminating what little is in my stomach, I hug the porcelain bowl and feel tears burn my eyes.

What am I going to do?

I'd been on the verge of sharing my news with him and this changes everything.

He's seeing another woman. *Ugh.* I can't believe this. I know we never promised we'd be exclusive, but I really believed that it was just him and me. We spent so much time together and he introduced me to his mom.

Why? What am I missing?

Pushing up off the floor, I wander over to the sink and rinse my mouth out. Then I open the medicine cabinet and look for some mouthwash or toothpaste. My gaze immediately lands on a pack of condoms. *Asshole.* He sure has enough of those laying around and ready to grab.

Feeling sick to my stomach, I reach for the little bottle of minty freshness and swish some around in my mouth. After spitting it out, I glare at the condoms and slam the cabinet shut.

I am officially devastated.

I'm also confused and suddenly feel lonelier than I've ever felt in my life. A few months ago, my life was on track for success. I got the internship here and was ready to start my dream job. Then I was stupid enough to get involved with my boss.

And now I'm head over heels for a man who's seeing someone else. Oh, God, it hurts.

With a grimace, I walk back over to my desk and sit down, staring at my blank computer screen for God knows how long. An image of perfect Genevieve Blanchet fills my head, torturing me with her complete and utter perfection.

Deciding to torture myself, I open my internet browser and type her name in a search. *Kill me now.* Originally born in Paris, France, Genevieve Blanchet is a world-renowned supermodel and has been a spokesperson for Gucci, Prada and Yves Saint-Laurent. Currently, she's the face of Chanel. She was discovered by Calvin Klein when she was 14 and has walked the runways ever since.

Rolling my eyes, I'm really not surprised. Genevieve is sophisticated, graceful and beautiful. Everything that I'm not.

Deciding to torment myself further, I do a new search and this time I type in both of their names: Caleb Miles and Genevieve Blanchet. A hundred different images pop up with them together and my jaw drops. They always seem to be dressed up and at some fancy event like a gallery opening or dinner party with royalty or someone equally rich and famous. I even stumble across a picture of them on the red carpet at the Met Gala.

Swallowing back more tears, doubt floods me and there's no way Caleb would ever choose me over her. I realize it's game over for me.

It's probably best if I bow out gracefully, quit PCH even though it's going to kill me, and move to an entirely new city where I can raise our baby in peace and quiet. Far away from Caleb and his glamorous girlfriend.

He's going to marry Genevieve and I'm going to have his baby. I have no doubt that they'll start their own perfectly beautiful family together and my son or daughter will never know his or her father.

The thought makes me incredibly sad, but I don't think there's anything I can do about it. At this point, maybe I shouldn't even tell him I'm pregnant. All it's going to do is cause drama, guilt and bad feelings between us. If I'm smart, I should just disappear and start over somewhere far, far away.

Slamming my mouse down, I drop my head back against my seat and close my eyes. I don't want to look at all those perfect photos and read one more nauseating word about what an amazing couple Billionaire Caleb Miles and Supermodel Genevieve Blanchet make.

It's enough to make me vomit again.

16

CALEB

The meeting in Boston took more time than I originally anticipated, and I ended up staying a few days more than I wanted. But what can I do? My work takes me all over the country and I have to be ready to travel when problems come up. Luckily, I always manage to figure out a solution.

I've been so busy that I haven't had any time to talk to anyone back home. By the time I return to my hotel room at night, I collapse and fall asleep. The time difference has me all fucked up. Lucy has been emailing me work updates and helping with tasks, but we haven't been able to discuss anything but business. I miss our personal chats and look forward to picking up where we left off.

My mom adores her. I wasn't sure if bringing her to the gin rummy night was the best thing to do, but I'm really glad I did. Lucy seemed to fit right in and according to my mom, all of her friends loved Lucy, too. They said she "rang true" and was much more interesting than the "snobby French model."

I can't help but chuckle. Those old birds always think they know best, especially when it comes to everyone else's personal life. But I can't disagree with them. Meeting Lucy has been refreshing, one of the best things that has ever happened to me. It's strange to think I was living my life without her for so long and now I can't imagine her not being in it.

Without Lucy in my life, I'm not sure what I would do. She's a breath of fresh air. There's a sweetness about her that women I've dated before usually didn't possess. My experience has been with more worldly, selfish women who are most likely attracted to me because of my money.

Lucy never talks about money. She doesn't expect gifts or to be wined and dined at fancy places. I actually went out with a woman once who, after three dates, asked me to set her up in a penthouse downtown. Needless to say, we didn't last because the moment I said no, she jetted so fast my head spun.

For the first time in my life, I feel like I'm with a woman who wants to be with me. The real me. Not Caleb Miles, billionaire titan, bachelor extraordinaire and CEO of PCH. She sees past the bullshit, to the core of who I really am, and that feels good.

Because under all the gloss and shine, I'm just a guy who didn't have two nickels to rub together when I was growing up. I'm a guy who loves his mom and would do anything for her. I'm a guy who wouldn't be anywhere near where he is professionally if it wasn't for someone else believing in me and helping me.

Lucy also has me thinking about things that I've never thought about before. Things like my emotions and feelings. Every time I see her, my heart kicks against my ribs and my stomach flips. I've never believed in love. Never had time for it.

Now I'm reconsidering.

Because I'm sure as hell feeling something. And every time I'm with Lucy, it seems to be growing stronger.

Is it love? Hell, I don't know for sure. All I do know is I enjoy spending time with her, talking to her and sleeping with her. I always want to be around her and when I'm not, I miss her.

After landing at the airport, I catch an Uber and get back to my house later in the evening. Even though it's only 8pm here, I'm still on East coast time which means it's 11pm for me. I'm tired, but I still plan on seeing Lucy. Wild horses couldn't keep me away. She's all I can think about, and I want to drive over to her place and make up for lost time. It's also Saturday night so we can stay in bed all day tomorrow if we want.

The moment I drag my small roller suitcase into the foyer, I exhale a sigh of relief. Damn, it feels good to be home. I've never had that feeling before. Normally, I could travel for long periods of time and be perfectly fine. But now that I have something– someone– to come home to, everything changes.

Maybe I should hire a couple more people and their sole job could be traveling from hotel to hotel. They could check in on the staff and make sure everything is up to operating standards. That way, I can remain here and handle things on the home front. I wouldn't have to deal with the airport and hotels any longer. Sure, I'd still visit my hotels but not at such a crazy, fast pace. They could be more leisurely visits.

The more I think about it, the more appealing it sounds.

Maybe I'm just getting old. Having a midlife crisis? Or maybe Lucy makes me want to slow down and plant some roots. I scratch my head and jog up the steps, heading down to my bathroom. Whatever is going on with me, it's throwing me for a loop.

Before I drop in at Lucy's, I need a quick shower. Then I plan to grab a bite to eat and go over to her apartment. Pulling off my shirt and tossing it on the counter, I'm kind of surprised she hasn't texted me. She's usually so thoughtful like that and whenever I travel, the moment I turn my phone's airplane mode off, a welcome back message usually pops up from her.

Not tonight, though.

Hmm. I hope everything's okay. The last time I heard from her was early this morning and she sent me an update from the office. It was short, business-like and to the point. Since it came through the company email, she kept it professional. I get it. But I miss her flirty banter and little innuendos.

Deciding to text her before my shower, I grab my phone and pull up her name. The moment I start to type a message, the doorbell rings. I toss my phone on the bathroom counter and wonder if it's her.

Probably, I think, and turn, heading out of the bathroom and down the steps at a fast-paced clip. God, I've missed her.

I open the door with a huge, goofy grin on my face and freeze. It isn't Lucy. It's Genevieve.

Dammit. All of the excitement in me deflates and I frown. "What're you doing here?" I ask, not even trying to hide my disappointment.

"Well, hello to you, too, *mon amour,*" she says and sweeps past me.

I grit my teeth and shut the door. Steeling myself for whatever is coming, I slowly turn around. All of my good energy is gone and suddenly I want to crawl into bed and sleep for a week. Genevieve is beyond a buzz kill. With one look, she destroyed all my enthusiasm.

"I have plans, Gen."

Her dark gaze slides downward and I forget I'm shirtless.

With a sly smile, she caresses a hand along my chest as she walks by me and heads further into the house. "Plans to stay in?" she asks in that sultry voice of hers.

"No. I'm leaving shortly."

"Looks like you just got in," she comments and nods to my suitcase. She continues walking and sits on the couch in the living room, making herself at home. "Where were you?"

"I had a business trip. Why?"

She shrugs. "Well, welcome back."

I'm not in the mood for her games and don't bother sitting down. Crossing my arms, I wait, trying to find patience, but it's hard. "What do you want?" I made it perfectly clear that we were over, so I have no idea why she's here.

Genevieve pulls her skirt higher, crosses her long legs and licks her lips. "There's only one thing I want, Caleb. And that's you."

I sigh and run a hand through my hair. "C'mon, Gen. We ended things. A while ago. Why are we having this discussion again? There is no you and me. It's done."

"Is it?" she asks, batting her lashes.

Shit. She's not hearing one word I'm saying. I don't want to be cruel but she's leaving me with no choice. "I'm seeing someone else."

A slim, dark brow arches and she smiles. Her calm reaction surprises me.

"Are you referring to that dumpy, fashionably challenged blonde at your office? What was her name?" Genevieve tilts her head, pretending to think. "Lori, is it?"

"Lucy," I correct her between gritted teeth. A strange feeling fills me, and I eye her warily. "When did you meet Lucy?"

Genevieve waves a dismissive hand through the air. "The other day. But, really, Caleb. I'm quite disappointed. After being with me, you turn to her? Are you that desperate? Poor thing," she adds in a low, bitchy voice.

Anger flares up inside me and I stalk closer. Things with Lucy felt a little off the last couple of days and now I suddenly know why. *Fuck.* "What did you say to her?" I demand.

"Nothing!"

"Genevieve, I swear to God-"

"Oh, calm down. Just that we used to be a couple." She gives me wide, innocent doe-eyes. "What? It's true."

"What else?" I hiss.

Genevieve stands up and sashays over to me. A devious smile curves her lips, and she drags her hands up my chest. "I don't want to talk about that little nothing, Caleb. Why don't I use my mouth for something more enjoyable?"

When her hands dip to unbutton my pants, I step back and brush them away. "Don't," I snap. Her seductive, little tricks are pathetic, and I'm not interested or stupid enough to fall for them.

"What's wrong with you?" she asks, dark eyes flashing.

"Nothing's wrong with me, Genevieve. For the first time, I'm seeing you for who you really are and it's sad and ugly."

Her eyes narrow.

"This is the last time I'm going to tell you this– I am not interested in rekindling anything with you. We are completely over, and I need you to understand that."

"Do you have any idea what you're saying?" She flips her straight, black hair off her shoulder.

"I know exactly what I'm saying. I don't want you and the sooner you understand that the sooner you'll be able to move on."

"Me move on? Are you kidding me right now?" Genevieve throws her head back and laughs. "I'm doing you a favor by coming back."

"I don't want you to come back. How can I make that any more clearer?"

"You're an asshole," she hisses. Her black gaze studies me closely, shooting daggers. "You're such a fool. You actually think you're in love, don't you?"

I don't say anything because truthfully, I don't know what being in love feels like.

Genevieve laughs again and it's a horrible sound, reminding me of nails scratching down a chalkboard.

"Such a joke. Love is for suckers and dreamers, Caleb. I thought you of all people were smart enough to know that."

"Maybe I met someone who makes me see things differently."

She shakes her head. "Idiot," she mumbles and marches past me. When she reaches the door, Genevieve spins around. "That young, inexperienced slip of a girl is going to leave you, Caleb. There's no doubt about it. And when she does, I'm going to laugh. Opening your heart up to her is the worst thing you could do. Other than turning me down, of course. So, when you're down on your knees, picking up your broken pieces, I hope it hurts like hell. And don't you dare call me."

Her nasty words only confirm the fact that breaking up with her was the right choice. "Have a nice life, Genevieve," I say and slam the door shut behind her. "What a bitch," I grumble and sigh.

I'm not sure what she said to Lucy, but I need to make sure we're okay. Genevieve is good at spewing poison and twisting the situation to suit her. Suddenly, fear snakes through my gut and it occurs to me that she may have tried to sabotage everything.

"Fuck," I groan. I need to talk to Lucy now and make sure no permanent damage was done while I was gone. If Genevieve planted seeds of doubts or fed Lucy a bunch of bullshit lies…

Not fucking good, I think, and go to grab my shirt, phone and car keys. That sick, cold fear slithers through me as I hurry down to the garage.

On the way over to Lucy's, I debate whether I should call or not and decide against it. It might be better if she's not expecting me. Once I reach her building, I park, try to gather my thoughts, and jog up to the front door. Someone is walking out, and I grab the door as it's closing and walk inside. When I reach her door, I knock hard and wait. I hear her moving around inside and when she opens the door, it's like seeing sunshine after the rain.

Lucy looks so pretty and refreshingly innocent. My heart speeds up and I smile. "Hey," I say softly, warmth coursing through me. She's a sight for sore eyes.

"Hi," she says, clearly surprised to see me. "What're you doing here?"

"I missed you. Can I come in?"

Lucy steps back, opening the door, and I walk into her place. It's so small compared to my huge house, but it's cozy and it smells amazing because she's always burning candles. When she doesn't say anything, I wonder what's going through her head. What the hell did Genevieve tell her?

"I take it everything went well in Boston?" she asks coolly.

"Fine," I say. "But I'm not here to talk about business."

Her pretty blue eyes narrow. "It's getting late, Caleb. I'm tired and wasn't expecting you."

Ouch. "Lucy, I know Genevieve came by the office and I don't know what she said, but don't believe her."

Lucy doesn't comment, merely stares at me. And her expression is so distant. *Shit.* The first wave of panic hits me. Normally she would've been in my arms by now, welcoming me back with a hug and endless kisses.

But no. Something happened and I want to know what.

"What's wrong?" I ask.

A frown mars Lucy's forehead. "Nothing. I told you– I'm tired. It's been a long week."

I'm not buying it and when I reach for her arm, Lucy pulls away. And it's like a knife in my heart. "Lucy-"

"I can't do this right now, Caleb," she says wearily.

"Do what?" I ask, confused by her icy tone. "Before I left for Boston everything was fine but that clearly is not the case now. You're pissed off so just tell me why and stop playing games."

Lucy's blue eyes narrow into slits. "Me? I'm not the one playing games, Caleb. You are!"

"What the hell are you talking about?"

"I shouldn't have to explain the situation."

"Well, I wish you would." *What is wrong with her? Why is she pushing me away?*

"God! Just go!" she yells. "I told you I'm not doing this right now."

Anger flares through me, bright and hot, overtaking the confusion. I grab her arm and want to shake some sense into her. Instead, I glare, getting more pissed at the closed-off look in her eyes. "You'll damn well do it right now," I grit out.

Lucy yanks her arm out of my grasp. "Don't you dare tell me what to do. I want you to leave!"

Whatever bullshit Genevieve told her; Lucy clearly believed. Without even consulting me, she accepted it and that hurts. It more than hurts. It makes me really fucking mad.

"Go, Caleb," Lucy says. "I can't do this right now."

"Do what? Have an adult conversation?"

Her eyes narrow. "Get out!"

"Fuck!" I roar and spin around. Fine, if she wants to act like a baby then so be it. I'm done. I storm over to the door and yank it open. Right before I walk out, I throw a parting shot over my shoulder. "Thanks for reminding me why I don't date 20-somethings. So goddamn immature. Call me when you grow up."

17

LUCY

Oh, God. What did I do? A sick feeling sweeps over me, and I clutch the edge of the sofa. Caleb just stormed out, completely furious, but what choice did I have? He's the one who has been seeing Genevieve behind my back. He ultimately made this decision. Not me.

I have to protect my heart and a confrontation with him right now is the last thing I want. I've felt like shit all day and all I wanted was for him to leave after showing up so unexpectedly. After everything I read online and seeing Genevieve's smug face, I could barely look at him.

Lies. Everything between us is based on lies. I don't have the strength to deal with any of this, I think, and drop down onto the couch. His parting words twist me up inside: *Thanks for reminding me why I don't date 20-somethings. So goddamn immature. Call me when you grow up.*

Asshole. I might be younger but I'm smart enough to end things now. I refuse to let him make me look like a fool for one minute longer. Did he really think he could get away with seeing me and Genevieve at the same time?

To be honest, I'm surprised I was in the mix for so long. It's clear that Genevieve is perfect and I'm…not. While she's worldly, rich and gorgeous, I'm the complete opposite. Why did Caleb waste his time with me? Was it the lure of fucking a virgin and making me his and his alone? Did he merely enjoy the sexy office shenanigans?

God, I feel so stupid. So utterly used.

It's one thing if it was just me. But it's not. I was so infatuated with Caleb Miles that I made the biggest mistake of my life and now I'm pregnant. What the hell was I thinking? Sex without protection? Even though sleeping with a man was new at the time, I should've known better.

Now the rest of my life is up in the air. I've never given too much thought to kids. I figured I'd have one or two one day after I got married and had an amazing career established. I never pictured my life going off the rails like this, though. Alone, knocked up and on the verge of quitting my job because I can't face my boss.

My dream job is going up in smoke right before my eyes. I'm going to have no source of income which is a really scary thought. What am I going to do? My experience is extremely limited and short-lived. I've learned a ton working at PCH, but I've been there less than three months. How's that going to look on a resume? And what is my reason for leaving?

My boss knocked me up while dating another woman. I couldn't face him any longer, much less run his errands each day.

So, depressing. I curl up into a ball and the tears begin to flow. I've never felt so lost or sad in my life.

The next day, I mope around and continue to feel sorry for myself. I need advice so I call Hannah. I'm really lucky to have such a good friend and she arrives at my place armed with a box of a dozen donuts.

We're sitting on the couch, and I reach into the pink bakery box and pull out a big jelly donut covered in sugary glaze. Exactly what I need. I take a huge bite and tears start sliding down my face.

"Oh, Luce. What's wrong?" Hannah asks. "Did you tell Caleb?"

"Thank you for bringing donuts," I mumble, trying not to sob. "No. I didn't even get the chance." Suddenly everything inside me breaks and comes pouring out like water from behind a collapsing dam. "He had a girlfriend on the side, Hannah!"

"What?" She pauses, eyes wide, a glazed donut halfway to her mouth.

"Apparently, he's also dating a French supermodel. And she's exotic and gorgeous and I feel like a troll next to her."

"Oh, no. Are you sure?"

I nod miserably. "She showed up at the office looking for him."

"Oh, Luce. That's awful."

"Genevieve is the one he took to formal parties and soirees," I say, wiping snot from my dripping nose. "I'm the one he screwed around with at the office."

"What an asshole!" Hannah hands me a napkin and I blow my nose into it.

"I just feel so stupid. I thought he cared about me, Hannah. It never crossed my mind that he was seeing someone else. What did I expect, though? That's what I get for believing a charming billionaire playboy could change his ways."

"You're positive he was with her, too?"

I nod and take another big bite of my donut. Jelly squeezes out the back and drops on my shirt. *Figures.* When I start crying harder, Hannah grabs another napkin and hands it to me. I wipe the red mess off my t-shirt and start telling Hannah how Genevieve showed up at PCH.

"She told me they dated for about a year and then went their separate ways," I say. "She said Caleb was upset because he never saw her. So, they took some time apart. Then she said she was happy because they were getting back together and that you can't keep two people in love apart for long." Dammit, the tears start spilling all over again. I'm an absolute wreck.

Hannah's face screws up. "Could she be lying? Purposely trying to sabotage your relationship with Caleb?"

"Why would she lie? She even showed me a picture of them in the society column at some fancy party," I tell her. "Besides, she has no idea we've been seeing each other because we've been so quiet about it. Other than you and his mom, no one knows."

"You met his mom?"

I sniff and toss the wet napkin aside. "Yes, and I love her. She's an absolute riot. He took me over to her house and we played gin rummy with her and her friends. He said she adored me, but he probably meant Genevieve."

"If he said you, he meant you," she tells me.

"At this point, I have no idea. I just feel so betrayed, so utterly naive." I squeeze my eyes shut and drop a hand over my stomach. "And now I'm going to have his baby." My voice cracks and Hannah scoots over and hugs me.

When she pulls back, she studies me closely. "You're in love with him, aren't you?" she asks softly.

I take a moment to consider her words. Up until now, I've only allowed myself to say I'm falling for him. But when I think of all the good times we've had and how much I look forward to being with him, I know it's more than that.

The idea of not being with him anymore, of him choosing another woman over me, feels like someone is stabbing me in the chest. Over and over again.

Shit. I'm in love with Caleb. Head over heels, can't live without him, over the moon in love.

"Yes," I finally whisper. "I love him."

Hannah nods and gives me a sad smile. "And he doesn't know about the baby yet?"

I shake my head. "God, no. I couldn't even look at him, much less tell him I'm pregnant. The idea of him with Genevieve makes me physically ill. I told him to leave."

"What did he say? Did he seem upset?"

"He got mad because I wouldn't talk to him. But I couldn't! I was so upset, and I figured he'd just try to sweet talk me with lies and bullshit. I refuse to fall for it again. I can't. It's not just about me anymore."

"How are you going to raise a baby by yourself?" Hannah asks gently.

"I don't know but lots of women do it every day. I'm going to have to figure it out." I rub my temples, dreading the time when I start to show. Right now, the pregnancy is nothing more than a dirty little secret. But it won't be long before everyone knows and the poor-you looks start coming my way.

"You know I'll help you. Your family will, too."

"Oh, God," I mumble. "I haven't even thought about how they're going to react to the news."

"I'm sure they'll be very supportive," Hannah reassures me. "Just a little shocked at first, but they'll get over it."

"Hunter might take a little longer to warm up," I predict. "He warned me about Caleb when I first started at PCH. Basically, he told me Caleb was a womanizer and to stay far away from him. Glad I listened." I drop my face into my hands.

"He'll probably go into overprotective brother mode at first but that's only because he loves you. Once he warms up to the idea of being an uncle, everything will be fine."

Lifting my head, I think over her words, and they make sense. "I hope you're right."

"When do you think you'll tell them?"

"Probably next Sunday at dinner. I can't deal with it today. I already told my mom I wasn't coming over because I felt sick."

For a moment she doesn't say anything, but I know what she's thinking. "I have no idea when I'm going to tell Caleb," I say before she asks. "At this point, he probably won't even care."

"He's going to be a father. That's life-changing, so he should care."

"He has Genevieve. Me and the baby are going to be nothing but a permanent reminder of a fling he had. I hardly think he's going to be excited about it."

"I haven't met Caleb, but maybe you're being too doom and gloom," Hannah says carefully. "Did it ever occur to you that-"

"Don't!" I interrupt and hold a hand up. "Please don't try to make me feel better and get my hopes up. It is what it is. Caleb doesn't want me, and I have to accept that. Living in a dream world and pretending things are okay between us isn't going to solve anything. It's just going to make me sadder."

"I understand that Luce. But, at the same time, you can't jump to conclusions. You're going to need to sit down with him and have an open and honest conversation. No matter how much you're hurting and how bad the situation seems."

I know she's right, but I can't think about that right now. I'm just too fucking sad. "Yeah, one of these days," I murmur vaguely.

For a long moment neither of us says anything.

"You know I'm here for you, Luce."

"I know," I whisper. "Thank you. I don't know what I would do without you."

I have a lot to sort through and my emotions are all over the place. I tell Hannah that it's best if I spend some time alone so I can figure things out. She gives me another big hug and reminds me that she's here for me.

After saying goodbye to Hannah, I lock the door and I don't know what to do. All I know is I have no intention of going back to work tomorrow. I suppose I could address that issue first. With a sigh, I pull my laptop out and compose my resignation letter.

Ten minutes later, eyes full of tears, I read through it. The last thing I want to do is leave PCH, but what option do I have? Facing Caleb every day would be a nightmare. Seeing Genevieve parading in and out, kissing him and flaunting herself as his girlfriend in front me? *Devastating.*

I hit send and off my email goes to the Human Resources Department.

At least one difficult thing is done, I think, and I let out a shaky sigh. I suppose all I can do is face one thing at a time and hope for the best. I've never been in this kind of situation before. I'd never even had a serious boyfriend, so this is all very scary, new territory for me, and I'm trying to figure out the best way to navigate my broken heart and unplanned pregnancy.

It's not an easy situation and things are going to get harder before they get better.

I'm curious how Caleb is going to react when he finds out that I quit. With a scoff, I drop back down on the couch and grab a pillow, hugging it to my chest. He'll probably be relieved.

Me, though? Not so much.

An image of his blue-gray eyes and adorable smile fills my head. For a while, he was so incredibly sweet, and we had such a good time together. I actually began to believe that he cared for me. Then Genevieve forced me to look at the situation clearly and not through the lovey-dovey, rose-tinted glasses I'd been wearing.

Caleb sure put on a good show. *He should win a damn Oscar,* I think sourly.

The problem is no matter how much I'm missing that jerk, there's a baby in the mix now and I have to be strong and figure things out.

How did my life go from nearly perfect with so much potential to an absolute train wreck and heartbreak in a matter of months? I probably shouldn't be surprised because I've always been somewhat of a hot mess. I just never imagined things could derail this fast.

It takes me a moment to realize that hot tears are streaming down my face once again. *Dammit.* I swipe them away. This pregnancy is making me all kinds of emotional. Wishing I could disappear and not deal with my life for the next seven months or so, I curl up into a tight, little ball and weep.

18

CALEB

After I've had time to think all night, I arrive at work the next morning, determined to drag Lucy into my office and make her talk to me. I'm going to force her stubborn, tight little ass right in there and not allow her to leave until I'm good and ready.

But when I get into the office, I see Sybil instead of Lucy.

"Surprise!" Sybil says and grins. "I got back a little earlier than I thought. I figured you were dying without me because I'm the most fabulous first assistant in the world."

I force a smile and glance over at Lucy's empty desk. "Where's Lucy?" I immediately ask. A strange feeling makes my gut churn.

"I don't know," Sybil says. "You didn't chase her away while I was gone, did you?" she teases.

I suck in a sharp breath. "I hope not," I mutter. "When she gets in, can you tell her I want to talk to her?"

Sybil frowns. "Sure."

I turn on my heel and shut my office door behind me. If she's still upset with me– and she probably is– Lucy might not come into work today. I should've tried harder to get her to talk to me, but it got so frustrating because she refused. I'm figuring out that sweet Lucy

Everett is stubborn as hell. Once she makes up her mind about something, she sticks with it.

I spent the weekend confused, racking my brain about what Genevieve could've said. But even more so than that, why did Lucy believe my ex-girlfriend? She wouldn't even listen to my side of the story and completely shut down on me.

It's frustrating as hell. I know I shouldn't have left angry, especially after that snide parting comment. Lucy might be younger than me, but she deserves more respect than I gave her.

With a sigh, I pull my emails up and force myself to focus on work. I've spent way too much time wondering about Lucy and I need to take a break and let work absorb me for a while. At least until Lucy gets in here and we can talk things out.

But Lucy isn't coming in, I realize, after opening the email message from HR and seeing her attached resignation letter.

"What the fuck?" I hiss and stand up. *She quit? Without even talking to me?* Anger and frustration roll through me, threatening to blow, and I get the sudden urge to punch someone.

There's a knock on my door and I stride over and throw it open. Sybil stands there looking unsure.

"What happened?" she asks. "I just saw the email from HR."

I roll my eyes and I am so fucking mad. Storming back into my office, I swipe my telephone up and throw it across the room. It smashes against the wall, and I look around for something else to hurl.

"Caleb!" Sybil cries.

With a huff, I spin around and glare out the window at the city beyond, trying to get my temper under control. "Just go. Please."

For a moment, I think Sybil is going to stay and start asking me a million questions that I don't have the answers to. But she quietly slips out, shutting the door behind her. If Lucy thinks she can hide and ignore me, she has another thing coming.

I grab my cell and call her. It rings and rings, finally dropping me into her voicemail. I hang up and try again. Same damn thing. "Fuck," I hiss between gritted teeth.

My mind is swirling with disbelief; I can't believe she resigned. What can I do about it, though? I can't force her to work here. I inhale a few deep breaths, trying to calm down and clear my head. I need a distraction and to stay busy. I'm the CEO of this company and I can't stop working and running shit because Lucy is having a temper tantrum.

Pushing the infuriating little blonde out of my head, I force myself to sit down at my desk and do what I'm here to do– run my company. I make several calls, go over cost reports and study daily reports from each of my hotels.

I work through lunch, but I'm not hungry, anyway. At 2pm, Sybil knocks and I tell her to come in.

"I have some mail and faxes for you," she says and sets them on my desk. "I also need your signature on a few things." She presents several pages and I scrawl my signature across each one.

This is Sybil's first day back and I've been nothing but a grumpy asshole. "Sorry about earlier," I apologize. "And thanks for getting me a new phone."

"No problem. Luckily there was one in the supply room." She hesitates. "So, since Lucy left, should I talk to HR about getting a new second assistant?"

Replacing Lucy is the last thing I want to do. But I know that Sybil needs backup and help with all of her work. "Can we talk about it later?"

"I guess. It's just..." Her voice trails off.

"I know it's a lot and you need help."

"Well, yeah, but that's not what I was going to say."

I sit back in my chair and arch a brow.

"All I know is right before I left, Lucy was doing so well. She kept telling me how much she loved the job. Like every other minute."

I clamp my jaw tightly shut and don't comment.

"I guess I'm just wondering what happened?"

"It didn't work out," I finally say.

"You had no idea she quit. So, she didn't even talk to you? I'm so confused."

"Sometimes things just don't go the way you plan. All you can do is move on, right?"

"I guess, but-"

"I'm going to go get something to eat," I abruptly say and stand up. Sybil frowns. "Do you need anything?"

"No," she murmurs.

It's clear I'm done talking about Lucy. Conversation over. As I walk out of the office, I know Sybil isn't stupid. Neither are the rest of my employees. By the time I return, she's probably going to talk to other people and the rumors are going to swirl.

The last week or two, Lucy and I weren't very discreet. We disappeared together for long periods of time whether in a conference room or for lunch. We left early together; we took days off together. Anyone with half a brain must've figured out we were seeing each other. Sybil's going to find out but not from me. I don't want to talk about Lucy.

Her complete dismissal hurts.

Stepping outside, the day fits my mood. It's cloudy, cool and looks on the verge of raining. As I walk down to the corner cafe, I'm struck with a paralyzing thought: Is Lucy the right woman for me? I thought so, but if she was, she'd talk to me and not run away.

At the corner cafe, I order a black coffee. My appetite is gone and now that I'm not at my desk, forcing myself to work, all I can do is think about Lucy. I pull my phone out and try calling her again. She doesn't pick up, so I decide to leave a message this time.

"Lucy, we need to talk. Call me. Okay?" I hang up, starting to get annoyed all over again.

Back in my office, I sip the hot coffee and the acid congregates in my stomach. Tossing it in the trash, I sigh and turn around to look out the window. I can't fuck focus any more today. And, let's face it, I need something a helluva lot stronger than coffee.

Deciding to leave early, I grab my stuff and tell Sybil I'm leaving. She has a funny look on her face, and I assume she's heard the rumors about Lucy and me. *Fucking hell.* Well, what did I expect? We weren't careful at all and practically flaunted our affair.

Is that all it was? I wonder. An affair destined to end before it even started? Did I put more faith into us than I should have? Did I really expect to have a serious relationship with her?

Yeah, I think. *I did.*

By the time I reach my place in Pacific Heights, I'm so lost in thoughts of where I went wrong and now, I'm convinced I should've done things differently. I was so quick to blame Lucy but look at me. I'm 40 years old and I suck at relationships. All I've ever done is drift from one woman to the next, unable to commit. Saying I love you and settling down never crossed my mind.

Until Lucy.

With a groan, I walk up the garage stairs and let myself into the house. I don't think I've ever felt so miserable, and I need to dull the pain. I drop my briefcase, pull my tie off and walk straight over to the bar in the corner of the living room. I pour some whiskey, take a sip and sigh.

Lucy was one of the best things that ever happened to me, and I lost her. I'm not even exactly sure how I screwed things up so royally. I grab the bottle of whiskey and climb up the stairs to my bedroom. After stripping off my suit, I pull on a pair of worn sweatpants and a t-shirt. Barefoot, I throw the side door open and walk out onto the patio.

There's a chill in the air that's biting, but I don't care. A few more sips of whiskey help warm me up. I lean against the railing's edge, elbows propped on the ledge, and feel completely lost. It occurs to me that I'm pining. *Holy hell.* I've never pined over a woman in my life. Normally, I walk away without so much as a backward glance.

God, I'm a bastard. No wonder I have such a playboy reputation. I suppose this whole situation is Karma coming around to bite me in the ass. And I deserve it.

I'm not sure how to handle these feelings so I'm just going to get good and drunk. I press a hand to my chest, right above my heart, and feel a pain. I think it's my heart breaking.

Somewhere in the house, my phone rings and I snap out of my misery. *Is Lucy calling? Shit.* I turn and jog back inside, trying to remember where I left my stupid phone. But when I finally find it down in the kitchen, I check the missed calls and it's only Brad.

Did we have plans tonight? I can't remember. My brain is fuzzy, and I lift the bottle to my lips only to discover it's empty. I slam it against the counter and go back into the living to get a new bottle.

After cracking it open, I take a long, satisfying swig. My phone rings again and I look down at the caller i.d. Brad again. With a sigh, I swipe the bar over and grunt what sounds like a slurred hello.

"Buddy, open up. I'm out front."

"Huh?" I swing around to face the foyer. "You're here?"

"Yeah. Let me in."

I walk to the front door and tilt sideways, my balance off. *Oh, man. I am shit-faced.* Taking a deep breath, I open the door and see my friend. "Hey. C'mon in."

Brad looks down at the bottle clutched in my hand and frowns. "I thought you sounded three sheets to the wind." He looks around and crosses his arms. "You look like shit, pal."

"Thanks a lot," I say and take a drink.

"Why don't you slow down with that and come on over here and have a seat before you fall down."

He's right. The room is spinning and when I get to the couch, it's a relief to sit down. Brad takes the bottle from me and snags a swig.

"What's going on that you're blitzed at 4pm? Bad day at work?"

"My life fucking sucks," I moan and shove a hand through my hair.

"You're a billionaire who owns 20 hotels, Caleb. Your life doesn't suck. Maybe just your day."

"No," I insist. "My whole fucking life."

"Why do you think that?" Brad asks patiently.

"Because Lucy quit. She's pissed at me, and I don't know why exactly. I think it's something Genevieve must've said but nobody will tell me what that was, and I don't know what the hell to do. I can't lose her, Brad. I swear to God, it's like my goddamn heart is in a vise and someone is squeezing the shit out of it." I drop back against the couch and scrub a hand over my lower face. "I think I'm dying."

"You're not dying," Brad says. "Genevieve talked to Lucy?"

"Yeah."

"I'm sure she put some serious fucking doubts in her ear. That woman was pure poison."

"I know. Fuck, Brad. What should I do? Lucy won't answer my calls or texts."

"Well, it seems pretty clear to me that you care about her. A lot."

"I do.

"You love her?"

Love. It's a word I rarely use. Maybe because along with love comes vulnerability. And I hate being vulnerable. I like to project only strength and competence to others. "It doesn't matter," I finally say.

"Of course, it matters, jackass. Do you love Lucy?"

I scratch at my eyebrow and the words stick in my throat. "She doesn't love me so there's no point. The smartest thing is to let her go. But, goddammit, I can't."

"Alright, buddy, let me clarify the situation for your drunk, incredibly stubborn ass. You're in love with Lucy Everett. So what do you plan to do about it?"

My eyes slide shut and, as much as I want to deny it, I know he's right.

I'm head over heels in love with Lucy. *Fuck me.*

"What can I do?" I ask miserably.

"Well, you can sit here and mope and stay drunk for the next few days. Or you can clean your act up. Try to get some sleep, sober up and go to her place in the morning. Bring some flowers and beg her forgiveness."

"But I didn't do anything!"

"She thinks you did. Explain the situation and get your girl back, Caleb."

He makes it sound so easy. "Lucy wants nothing to do with me," I tell him and grab the whiskey bottle back. I take another swallow then drop back against the pillows stacked in the corner of the couch. "It's over."

The words practically burn my throat as they come out of my

mouth. It's the truth and the sooner I face it, the quicker I'll be able to come to terms with the situation. Crying and pining over a woman who doesn't want me isn't my style.

19

LUCY

I spend the week trying to figure my life out and by the following Sunday, I am no closer to any answers, solutions or peace of mind. If anything, I'm more frazzled than ever because I'm going over to my parents' house for dinner and breaking my news.

Caleb has called and texted nonstop all week and I keep ignoring him because I'm not ready to talk to him yet. It's too painful. Even though I miss him so much and need to tell him about the baby, I'm going to speak to my family first. They might be shocked when I break my news, but I know that I will have their full support.

I'm not so sure about Caleb, though. How is he going to react to my pregnancy? Is he going to take off and not want to be in the baby's life? Or is he going to want to be involved? Maybe he'll offer financial assistance and that's all. My mind is spinning with the possibilities and none of them are appealing.

I want Caleb in my life, but he chose Genevieve. It hurts and sucks, but what can I do?

The truth is I miss him terribly. His rejection hurts more than anything. I have no idea what he wants from me now and I know I need to talk to him. I just can't. Maybe I'm being a baby about it– one of those weak females who can't live without a man. I always looked down on women like that. I believed I was strong, independent and didn't need a man in my life to make me happy.

Guess things change when you fall in love. Lines blur, feelings aren't just black and white, and it's not about wanting a man in my life. It's about needing Caleb Miles with every breath I take. He swept into my life and turned it completely upside-down and inside-out. I gave him my virginity and he stole my heart.

A small part of me wonders if I should've believed everything Genevieve told me so easily. There's always the possibility that she's a jealous ex trying to weasel her way back into Caleb's life. Could she have lied? Sure. But then she showed me that picture of them together. The camera doesn't lie. As badly as I wanted to dismiss her and her claims, that photo told me everything I never wanted to believe: Caleb was still seeing her.

After that, every single one of my insecurities took over. I've never been the most confident person in the world. I know I'm clumsy and even though I do well with what I have, I'm cute, at best. Maybe even pretty with makeup and dressed up. But I'm not a famous and beautiful fashion model. How could I ever compete with someone like Genevieve?

I can't. So instead of fighting for the man I love, I hid away and crumbled to pieces for the last week. *So much for being the strong, independent woman I always thought I was,* I think with disgust. I'm mad at myself more than anyone else. I should never have let things go so far or get emotionally involved with a man who has the reputation for being with a different woman every other month.

And, on top of everything else, he's, my boss. Well, he *was* my boss. I wonder how he took my resignation? That's probably the only reason he's been calling me. He's mad that I didn't talk to him first and give my two weeks' notice like a professional. Instead, I left him high and dry. All he probably wants to do is ream me out.

No thanks. I have bigger things to worry about. *Like now,* I think, as I pull into my parents' driveway. After sucking in a few, deep, steadying breaths, I open my car door and walk up the pathway to the house. I feel like I'm about to face a firing squad.

It'll be okay, I try to convince myself. You're a grown-ass woman, going on 25-years old. You slipped up and now you're pregnant. It could be worse. I could be on drugs or a prostitute. Or, to my father's absolute horror, a Republican.

"Hi," my mom gushes and hurries over to embrace me. I hug her back and we walk into the kitchen where I help her start carrying dishes out to the table. As I set the table, I lean over so I can see into the family room and say hello to my father and Hunter who watch a game on television. My parents have a rule that I've always loved: Mom cooks, Dad cleans up afterward.

Once everything is situated, we sit down and start eating. Well, they eat, and I nervously pick, moving things around on my plate.

"Aren't you hungry?" my mom asks, noticing that I haven't eaten a bite.

I set my fork down and swallow hard. *Here we go.* "I have some, ah, news to share."

"Did you get another promotion at work already, overachiever?" Hunter teases.

"No." I look from my brother to my dad to my mom. "I actually decided to leave PCH. I resigned last Monday."

For a moment no one says anything and then they all start talking at once, asking a million questions and spewing comments.

"Why?" Hunter asks, clearly perplexed.

"But I thought you loved it," my mom says.

"Of all the stupid decisions," my dad grumbles. "You were making great money."

I hold up a hand and wait until they settle down. "Things got…complicated."

"Complicated how?" Hunter asks, eyes narrowing.

I sigh. "Caleb and I started dating."

Hunter rolls his eyes and gives me an "I told you so" look.

"Lucy, did you ever hear the saying don't shit where you eat? There's a good reason for it."

"I know, Dad," I say. "But quitting my job isn't the most important news I need to share." I release a shaky breath and rip the band aid off. "I'm pregnant."

Stunned looks surround me and no one utters a word.

"Caleb is the father," I confirm.

Hunter is the first to recover and he erupts, angrier than I ever would've imagined. "I knew it! So that bastard dumped you and wants nothing to do with you or the baby?"

"No!" I sigh and twist my napkin in my hands. "I haven't told him yet."

"Lucy! Why the hell not?" my dad asks. "What're you waiting for?"

"It's-"

"Complicated. Yeah, okay. Why? What the hell is Caleb's problem?" Hunter demands, voice raising.

I love my big brother but sometimes he can be far too overprotective. "He's with someone else," I admit quietly.

"What?" they all roar at once.

They want details, but this is turning into an exhausting situation and my first instinct is to leave. When I stand up, rubbing my temples, my mom holds up her hands.

"Honey, wait. Please, don't go. We're sorry."

"It's just all a little much," my dad says. "But you know we're here for you, sweetie."

Their words mean everything, and I slowly sit back down again. "Thank you," I whisper.

Hunter still looks angry, but he doesn't say anything. Just nods his support.

"This has been really hard," I say. "I never planned on any of this happening. I started my dream job and had so many plans. Then I met Caleb, and everything just blew up between us. I fell in love with him," I say and sniff. *Dammit, here come the tears again.*

My mom gets up and moves around the table and hugs me. My dad follows a moment later and I cry my eyes out as they wrap their arms around me and tell me everything is going to be fine.

"Whatever you need, honey."

"Move home, sweetie."

Their support means the world to me and I'm so lucky to have such a supportive family. Once the tears stop falling, I wipe my face and tell myself to get a grip.

"When are you going to tell Caleb?" my mom asks gently.

"I don't know. Soon."

"Do you want me to talk to him?" Hunter asks, eyes flashing.

Horror fills me. "No! God, no. I can handle it myself."

But he has that look on his face– the "I'm the big brother and I'm going to kick his ass" look that makes me nervous.

"Hunter, I'm going to handle it. I don't need you playing the big brother card. Okay?"

"You sure?"

"I'm positive," I insist.

He nods but doesn't comment.

For the next hour, my parents give me so much baby advice that my head spins. I had no idea this was going to be so much work. I mean, I knew it wouldn't be easy, but I hadn't thought about how much harder it's going to be doing it all alone. Without a partner to help. Without Caleb. The midnight feedings, getting no sleep, the never-ending expenses.

By the time I'm leaving, I'm so grateful for my family. I can't imagine being one of those poor single moms who has no one to rely on and has to do everything alone. I'm damn lucky.

After hugging my mom and dad goodbye, Hunter and I walk down the driveway together to our cars. He's being very quiet, and I wonder what he's thinking.

"If you need anything just let me know, okay?" he finally says.

"Thanks, Hunter. I appreciate it."

"Everything will be alright," he assures me. "Caleb will support you and the baby, so don't even worry about it."

I nod although I'm not quite as convinced as he is. But I force a nod then we embrace and say goodbye. His final words make me think he's up to something, though.

"Hunter!" I call after him and he turns around, eyebrows raised. "I've got this under control with Caleb, okay?"

"Sure," he says.

He gives me a wave and hops in his car. I watch him drive away and hope to God he doesn't interfere. I love him, but I'd have to murder him if did interfere.

20

CALEB

I'm sitting at my desk, pretending to work, when I'm actually coming up with a plan to see Lucy today. I've stopped at her place twice, but either she wasn't home or pretended she wasn't there. I'm done playing games and I'm going to force her to talk to me.

My head is throbbing from drinking way too much whiskey the other night and I'm debating how I can scale up her fire escape and break in through her window when I hear a commotion outside of my office. I look up and see Sybil chasing after a man who is currently storming toward me.

Who the hell is this guy? I wonder, getting up. As the thought moves through my head, he stalks over and punches me in the face. My head snaps to the side and anger overtakes my confusion.

I'm about to punch the bastard back when he growls, "I'm Lucy's older brother and you have some fucking explaining to do."

Oh, shit.

"Do you want me to call security?" Sybil asks, wringing her hands in the doorway.

"It's okay, Sybil. Can you close the door?"

My assistant nods and disappears. Once the door is closed, I nod to the chair in front of my desk. "Have a seat," I say, eyeing him closely. The man is tall with dirty blond hair. When I look more closely, I see he has the same shade of bright blue eyes as Lucy. His fists are clenched, and I mentally prepare myself for what's to come.

Sitting back down in my chair, I rub my chin. "Nice uppercut."

"You're lucky I didn't bring my gun."

Whoa. "I'm not sure where this hostility is coming from, but I think we can hold a calm discussion like two rational men. Clearly you know me, but who are you exactly?"

"Hunter Everett," he says, blue eyes cold as steel. "Why don't you explain yourself?"

Explain myself? "I hired Lucy a few months ago," I say, not caring for his tone. "She resigned without a reason last week and refuses to talk to me."

His eyes narrow. "Do you make it a habit of fucking all your assistants or was my sister just the unlucky one?"

"No offense, but our relationship is none of your business." My jaw tightens and I'm trying to remain civil, but this asshole is really pissing me off.

"If you don't man up and take responsibility, I'm going to do everything in my power to destroy you. Your reputation, your business, your whole goddamn life," he threatens.

I frown, not sure what he's talking about, and fight to hold myself back from booting his ass out of here. "I didn't do anything. Lucy left of her own accord."

"You knocked my sister up and then dumped her!"

My mouth drops open and it takes me a moment to absorb his words. "Wait, what?"

We stare at each other for a moment.

"You really didn't know?" he asks.

"Lucy is *pregnant?*"

Hunter nods and I fall back in my chair, completely shocked.

"I figured she was lying about not telling you." he says.

I rake a hand through my hair and frown. "She didn't tell me. I had no idea. I've been calling her every day, but she won't pick up." I squeeze my eyes shut. *How could she not tell me?* "I never dumped Lucy. She's the one who left without telling me why."

"Because you're seeing someone else," he snaps.

"No, I'm not! Fuck!" Outrage surges through me and I slam a fist against my desk. "I'm getting really goddamned sick of being accused of shit that isn't fucking true!" I yell, my temper finally snapping.

Hunter considers my words then crosses his arms. "Be straight with me, Miles. How do you feel about my sister? And don't bullshit me."

Being apart from Lucy has been the lowest point of my life. I've never been so miserable or lonely. But I'm also angry that she brushed me off and has been ignoring me. I think about what he just told me, and it hits me that Lucy is probably feeling just as alone and confused as I am right now. Especially if she believes that I'm with Genevieve. I swear to God, I want to wring that woman's neck for spreading lies to Lucy.

Despite everything, the truth is I love Lucy. I'm tired of the miscommunication and games. It's time to be honest and confront my feelings and Lucy herself. "I love her," I say. "I love your stubborn, pain in the ass, best-thing-that's-ever-happened-to-me sister and I'm going to go tell her."

I stand up and Hunter's eyes go wide.

"You do?" he asks. "You're not just saying that?"

"Piss off," I say and push past him. I've wasted enough time talking to him. Lucy is the one I need to clear the air with and there's no better time than the present.

"She is a pain in the ass," he calls after me.

"Huge," I agree. "But she's *my* pain in the ass." As I grab my shit and walk out, I hear Hunter chuckle behind me.

I'm a man on a mission and I'm going to get my woman back. I'm going to do it right, too. I don't plan on losing Lucy ever again and this time around, I'm playing for keeps.

I spend the next couple of hours racing around the city like a complete lunatic, organizing a present that I hope will help soften her up. At the bottom of a bunch of hopefully meaningful things that I collected, sits a single velvet box. My palms start sweating when I think about it.

I'm setting myself up for the biggest potential let-down of my life. But, at this point, it's all or nothing. I'm going for broke and hope to God I can finally and completely win my Lucy over. Otherwise, her rejection is going to be brutal.

When I arrive at her apartment, I grab the gift, manage to get inside her building when someone is leaving, and now I'm standing in front of her door. My pulse roars as I lift a fist and pound on the door. "Open up, Lucy!"

I keep pounding, giving her no choice but to come open the door. She's not going to ignore me a minute longer. When the door finally opens, Lucy looks at me like I'm crazy.

"What is wrong with you?" she asks. "My neighbors are going to call the cops!"

God, she's a sight for sore eyes. A part of my heart melts at seeing her. "We need to talk and you're not going to ignore me any longer," I state firmly.

"Yes, we need to talk," she says, opening the door to allow me inside.

Well, that was easier than scaling up her fire escape. Glad I didn't have to do that. I walk past her and everything I'd planned on saying suddenly flies out of my head. My nerves kick up a notch and as she turns to face me, I have a momentary panic attack.

Right now, Lucy has the power and she could potentially destroy me if she rejects me. Heart in my throat, I hand her the box adorned with a bow and pray this goes well.

21

LUCY

Caleb hands me the box with a big white bow and I take it. "What is this?" I ask and give it a little shake. I was expecting to finally confide in him about being pregnant and not open a gift.

"It's just a little something I put together for you," he says and shoves a hand through his hair. He looks nervous and shifts back and forth. "I don't know. It's stupid."

But I'm touched that he took the time to get me something and I'm dying of curiosity. "Sit," I say and move over to the couch. He follows, dropping down beside me, and I carefully lift the lid off the decorative box. I reach inside and pull out something wrapped in colorful tissue paper.

"There are a few things," he says. "In order."

With a frown, I pull the paper off and look at a cute journal. I raise a quizzical brow, not sure of its significance.

Caleb clears his throat. "So, I, ah, put together a box of things that represents our journey together."

He looks like he's second-guessing what he did, but I think it's sweet. "And this represents what?" I ask.

"When you came into my life at PCH. You always carried that little notebook around wherever you went."

With a smile, I set it aside and reach back into the box. The next thing I unwrap is a bottle of stain remover. I can't help but chuckle. "For when I spilled my wine on you?"

He nods. "I find your klutziness endearing, by the way."

"You just liked that I touched your crotch."

He smirks. "I had no complaints."

My cheeks grow warm as I pull out the next thing– a bottle of shower gel and wash cloth. I frown, trying to figure out what it means. *Oh, right!* My face burns.

Caleb leans closer. "I wasn't expecting you to walk in as I was stepping out," he murmurs.

I lick my lips, remembering the sight of him naked, water dripping down his amazing body. The shocked, yet steamy look on his handsome face. Shifting on the couch, I lay it down beside me. "God, that was humiliating. And very…enlightening."

"I wanted to hop back in and yank you with me," he says in a low voice.

"Maybe you should take a cold shower," I advise him. All these sexy reminders mean nothing if he's with Genevieve, I remind myself.

The next object I unwrap is a can of pineapples. "For Hawaii," I say. My mind wanders back to the beautiful place where I fell head over heels for this man. My heart twists and sadness washes over me. I'd love nothing more than to go back there with him one day, but it's never going to happen.

"After the luau, you tasted so sweet. Just like the pineapple we ate."

"Caleb-"

"There's one more thing in there," he says.

With a sigh, I can only imagine. I lower my hand inside and find the last item. Lifting it out, I pull the tissue paper off. It's a small velvet box and my mouth goes dry. It looks like a ring box. When I hesitate, he nudges me.

"Go on. Open it," he encourages me.

Heart in my throat, I flip the lid up and stare down at a diamond ring. The sheer size and brilliance of the stone makes my mouth drop open. It's the most beautiful thing I've ever seen. As I'm trying to make sense of it, Caleb slides off the couch, dropping onto his knees in front of me.

"Lucy Marie Everett," he says, taking my hands in his, "I think there's been some confusion and I'm going to clear it up right now." His steel-blue eyes lock onto mine. "From the moment you spilled your wine all over the front of my, ahem, pants, you intrigued the hell out of me. I thought you were gorgeous. And then I realized how damn smart you are. Your business mind is savvy, and you proved what an asset you are when we went to Hawaii. I've never slept with an employee but crossing that line with you was the best decision I ever made."

He pauses and I don't say anything. It's all so overwhelming.

"I fell hard for you in Hawaii. But I didn't realize how hard it was until I lost you." His voice catches. "Lucy, I don't know what Genevieve said, but I swear to Christ, we haven't been together since I broke up with her almost four months ago. She's tried everything to get me back, but I don't want her. I want you, baby girl. I've always wanted you. Since the moment you first walked into my office, tripped and fell in my arms. I love you, my Lucy, and now I have a question to ask you."

My eyes fill with tears, and I know he's telling me the truth.

"Will you make me the happiest man in the world? Will you marry me?"

My heart thunders as he plucks the ring out of its velvet bed and slides it onto my finger.

"Oh, Caleb!" I exclaim. I can't believe this is happening. Before I answer him, though, he needs to know about the baby. And that might change everything. *Oh, God.* I suck in a deep, steadying breath. "There's something that I have to tell you," I whisper.

He squeezes my hands. "I know," he whispers back.

"What?" I ask, completely stunned. How could he know about the baby?

"Your brother may have spilled it about you being pregnant."

"Oh, my God. Hunter told you? When?" *I'm going to kill my brother.*

"It was right after he stormed into my office and threatened to murder me this morning," Caleb admits. "But don't worry. I think we're going to get along just fine. As long as you don't throw me out now."

I realize that I haven't answered his proposal. Dropping down on my knees in front of him, I lift his hands up and press a kiss to his knuckles. "I know I'm a hot mess," I say. "An insecure klutz who never had a relationship until you. I freaked out when I found out you were seeing me and her at the same time. And that she was the one you flaunted at fancy parties while I was just the one you screwed around with at the office. Like a dirty, little secret."

"What are you talking about?" he asks, brow furrowing.

"She showed me the picture in the paper."

"What picture?" he asks, looking truly confused.

"From the society column. You guys were at some fancy party, and she told me you were back together and in love."

"Christ," he swears. "I know exactly what picture you're talking about, and it was taken a year ago after we first met."

I blink, suddenly feeling like a complete fool. "You weren't seeing her again?"

"God, no." Caleb grasps my shoulders, dragging me closer. "You're the one I want. I never loved her. I love you, Lucy. *You*," he emphasizes.

"I love you, too," I whisper, my voice breaking. "But with a baby coming-"

"I can't wait," he interrupts.

"Really?"

"Stop trying to complicate the situation. You love me, I love you. Are you going to marry me or what, baby girl?"

A huge smile breaks out across my face, and I nod hard. "Yes! Yes, I want to marry you!" I cry.

"Thank God," he murmurs and captures my lips in a hard kiss.

Knowing that Caleb loves me makes me the happiest girl in the world. It also turns me into a blubbering mess, and I start crying and laughing at the same time.

"Sorry," I say and pull back. "This pregnancy is making me extra emotional."

"It's okay," he says and brushes my hair back.

"Aren't you freaked out?" I ask.

For a long moment he doesn't say anything. Then his hand drops and covers my lower belly. "Actually, I'm not. I'm a little in awe that there's a baby in there, but it's kind of exciting."

"I guess I assumed you didn't want to be a dad."

"I honestly never gave it a lot of thought. I've always been so focused on work. But the same could be said for getting married. I was never against either, but I never thought it would happen for me because I was so busy with PCH."

"And how do you feel now?" I ask.

"So damn good," he says. "You're going to make an amazing mom, too."

"I hope so," I whisper.

"I know so," he answers and wipes the last tear away. Then he pulls me up, sweeping me into his arms and carries me down to the bedroom. "You're also coming back to work at PCH. You'll get a raise; your own office and you're going to help me run the business. Does that work for you?"

"Very much so," I say with a smile.

"Good." He lowers me onto the bed and his gaze heats up, roaming over me. "Now get undressed because we have a lot of time to make up for."

With a smile, I start shimmying out of my clothes.

22

CALEB

Sliding up over Lucy's naked body, leaving a trail of wet kisses, I finally reach her mouth and my lips move against hers. She tastes like sugar, and I've missed her so much. When we were apart, it's like I'd lost a part of myself. But now I feel like I've come home. Settling between her thighs, I lift her hips and plunge deeply inside her wet core.

We both groan. I begin to move faster, harder, setting up a grueling pace. I can't get enough of her, and she wraps her legs around my waist, pulling me even deeper. "Ah, Christ," I hiss, pounding away.

I need this. I need her. Every last bit of her. And I'm going to take until there's nothing left. But I'll never get to that point because Lucy always has something to give me. She's the sweetest woman, always putting others first, and when her mouth opens, I kiss her deeply, savoring each touch of her tongue and lips.

"Caleb!" she cries, writhing beneath me as my finger circles her clit, rubbing just how she likes until she's quivering and in the throes of an orgasm.

Once she breaks, I follow with a loud groan, emptying into her long and hard. My release leaves me shuddering and I fall down beside her. I pull her into my arms and press a kiss in her softly scented hair. I'm never letting her go. "I love you," I rasp.

"I love you, too," she whispers back, curling up against me.

Everything is once again right in my world. *Better than right,* I think. Everything is perfect.

Lucy and I spend the next three days locked up in her apartment. We talk about our future and what we want from each other and married life. We discuss how we're going to raise our baby and how we're going to work together at PCH. I've never been so in tune with anyone in my life. For the most part, we agree on everything and see things the same way.

Life with Lucy is going to be beautiful. A gift that I'm going to get to unwrap every single day. I truly feel like the luckiest man in the whole damn world.

We decide to get married as soon as possible. Just the two of us and we know we want to go back to Hawaii to do it. Then we'll return here and have a party with our family and friends.

The evening we exchange our vows on the beach is breath-taking. It's sunset and the ocean waves roll in and out behind us. Lucy wears a pretty white sundress and a plumeria tucked behind her ear. I have a loose white shirt on and khaki pants that are rolled up around my ankles, so they don't get sandy. We're both barefoot and as the sky explodes in a series of reds, oranges and golds, we promise to love each other forever.

I'll never forget how beautiful she looks with the sun glowing around her dark blonde hair, lighting it up from behind, reminding me of a halo.

After the officiant declares us man and wife, I sweep my bride into my arms and kiss her with all the love in my heart. We spend a week in Hawaii and, of course, return to the Leilani Suite at the Plumeria Inn. I can't get enough of my new bride and she's just as insatiable.

I think we're both glad to have this special time on the island together because the moment we return to San Francisco life becomes an absolute whirlwind. We announce our elopement to family and friends, and they insist on throwing a party the following weekend.

Everyone shows up and the champagne flows. Except not for Lucy. I make sure she has unlimited apple juice for the endless toasts, though.

I'm talking to Brad when Hunter approaches us. I haven't seen or spoken to him since our last encounter at my office. When he walks over, I prepare for the worst, but hope for the best. I just whisked his baby sister to Hawaii and married her without telling anyone so I'm not sure how he's going to feel about it.

Brad excuses himself and I turn to Hunter who has an unreadable expression on his face.

"Congratulations," Hunter says and extends his hand.

I shake it. "I wasn't sure if you were going to congratulate me or punch me," I joke.

"Yeah, sorry about that. I've always been a little overprotective of Lucy. But now that's your job."

We both chuckle. Nearby, Lucy looks radiant as she talks to Hannah. There's a luminosity that surrounds her and I'm not sure if it's the pregnancy that's giving her an extra glow or it's happiness because she's with me. I'd like to think it's a little of both.

"She's never looked so happy," Hunter comments. "And I know it's because of you," he adds gruffly.

"I'm going to treat her like a princess," I assure him.

"I'm sorry about storming into your office like I did. I hope we can put that in the past."

Hunter gives me a sheepish look and I nod. "You're my brother-in-law now," I say. "So that makes you family. And I think we both agree that Lucy's happiness is most important."

"For sure," he says. Then Hunter slaps me on the back with a grin. "Welcome to the family, Caleb."

"Thanks, man." We shake hands again and I have a feeling that Lucy's brother and I are going to end up good friends. I appreciate his directness and how protective he is of his little sister.

The rest of the night goes by in a blur. We dance, eat cake and kiss constantly. By 9pm, I'm ready to leave and take my bride to bed. Luckily, the party is winding down and Lucy and I are back at my place within the hour.

Lucy still seems a little overwhelmed to be living in my Pacific Heights mansion. I tell her she can change anything she wants so she feels like it's her home, too. So far, she's added candles all over and she also likes fresh flowers. When I found that out, I hired a florist to come every week and make sure all the vases throughout the house are filled with seasonal flowers.

Whatever I can do to make Lucy's life brighter, I'll do. She has become my everything. My reason for breathing. I've never looked forward to anything more than having a life with her. It's strange how someone can sweep into your life and flip your entire world on its head.

That's exactly what my Lucy has done, and I wouldn't change a thing.

23

EPILOGUE

LUCY

Ten Months Later...

A little over a year ago, I began my internship at PCH. Little did I know that my entire world would immediately change. Falling in love with Caleb Miles was something that I never could've prepared myself for and now he's the love of my life.

One month ago, I gave birth to our son, and it only seemed fitting to give him a Hawaiian name. We ended up choosing Kekoa which means "The Warrior." It fits him perfectly. He's Caleb's mini-me in every sense of the word. Same eyes, same hair, same fierce, stubborn, alpha personality.

As much as I adore my son, we found out fast that a new-born is so much more work than either of us had anticipated. Luckily, Caleb is beyond helpful and lets me get some sleep whenever possible. We also have my parents and his mother constantly volunteering to babysit.

This weekend, we're taking my mom and dad up on that offer. Caleb said I need some uninterrupted time to rest, and he booked us a weekend getaway at a fancy hotel renowned for their spa. I'm booked for two straight days of pampering– from massages to a mani/pedi to a facial. He ordered the works and I'm ready to be spoiled.

We're also deciding whether or not we want to buy the hotel. So, there may be a little business happening during all my relaxation.

I've finally found someone who puts me first. After spending so much time taking care of others, I now have someone who takes care of me. And it's wonderful.

Right now, though, I stifle a yawn as I lean over the baby's crib and scoop him up into my arms. His crying woke me up and I check his diaper. Clean. I'm not sure what exactly he's squawking about, and I shift him in my arms. Most likely he's hungry. I have to go down and warm up his bottle.

As I walk out of Kekoa's room, I see Caleb coming up the stairs, a bottle in his hand.

"You're a lifesaver," I say.

Caleb walks over with a sleepy smile. "Want to sit outside?" he asks, and I nod.

The outdoor patio is my favorite place and Kekoa seems to like it, too, because whenever we take him out there, he stops fussing. I'm not sure if it's the cool breeze or the sky above us or the sounds of the city that soothe him.

Caleb set up two comfy rockers near the glass wall and we sit down. It can get chilly late at night, so I pull the blanket down around us and tilt the bottle toward Kekoa. He latches right on, and I watch his little hands grasp it. I can tell he's going to grow up to be smart and determined just like his father.

He's also going to be just as handsome. I'm going to do my absolute best to make sure he knows how to treat women. But with a face like his, it's inevitable that he'll break some hearts.

Rocking back and forth, Kekoa's steel blue eyes finally close and I look over at Caleb. God, they're so similar it's disconcerting. It's also completely adorable.

"Only a couple of more days until your pampering begins," he whispers. "And you can sleep for 12 hours straight if you want."

"Mmm, sounds wonderful," I say softly. Then I give him a sly smile. "You do realize that it'll have been six weeks since I gave birth, right?"

His mouth edges up in a wicked smile. "I didn't want to push you if you weren't ready, but baby girl, I've been counting down the days."

I chuckle softly. "Why am I not surprised?"

"So, what are the chances I'm going to get lucky?" he asks.

I pretend to think. "Oh, I'd say 110 percent."

Caleb drops his head back on the chair and moans. "Two more days, two more days, two more days."

I laugh at his mantra and extend my hand. He instantly threads his fingers through mine and squeezes. "Can you believe this?" I ask, voice barely above a whisper. "When I spilled my wine on you a year ago, I was scared you were going to fire me. Never in a million years did I think we'd end up married with a baby."

"I think you being prone to accidents is what caught my attention. First you tripped and practically fell into my arms and then you were pawing me below my belt. I was a goner. Never stood a chance against your charms."

"Pawing?" I laugh softly. "And speaking of charms, what about me?" I ask. "One look at my new, hot boss and I didn't know my right from my left. I came in so eager to please and learn. I learned a lot more than I ever anticipated."

We share a low laugh. Then Caleb's blue-gray gaze turns serious, and I see so much love shining in his eyes. "All I want to do is make you happy, Lucy."

The way he's looking at me...

My chest tightens. No man has ever looked at me with that kind of love in his eyes...except my husband.

"You do, Caleb." My eyes prick and suddenly they're swimming in tears. "You're my everything, and it doesn't matter if we're sitting here on Billionaire's Row or shoulder to shoulder in some tiny apartment. As long as we're together, I will always be happy."

Caleb stands and moves up behind me. He leans over, hands on my shoulders, and presses his lips to my temple. Then he tilts my head back and kisses me thoroughly. Heat floods through me and I lift a hand, cradling his stubbled cheek.

When we finally break apart, he swipes a tear away with his thumb. "Those are happy tears, right?" he asks.

"The happiest tears in the world," I assure him. "Now kiss your wife again, Mr. Miles."

And that's exactly what he does.

INCLUDES FREE BONUS
BONUS STORY
UNRELEASED STORY

SERIES COLLECTION

Forbidden Love

OFFICE ROMANCE BUNDLE

KELLY MYERS

FRISKY BUSINESS

I was all set to say goodbye to dating drama and focus on my new career...and then I met the boss.

Henry had a magnet under his skin that pulled all my sexy thoughts to the surface.

The catch? He was my boss.

Worse still, that only made him more irresistible.

I'd never forget the amazing night we spent together at his penthouse…

Especially because I left with an unexpected souvenir growing inside me.

Now a spiteful coworker is out to get me.

And Henry has his own controversial past to deal with.

Can we overcome the odds together, or will I have to start my life all over again alone?

1

TORI

The offices were absolutely immaculate—the kind of thing I'd only really seen in the movies. Heck, even the air smelled like money.

"This place is really amazing," I said, meaning every word.

"That's just this floor," Wendy said. "There's a whole other suite down on twelve." She wrinkled her nose at me as if to say, "Isn't it *crazy*?" Wendy Chasen had a fun, slightly wicked streak tucked beneath her round, borderline maternal exterior.

"Wow," I said, nodding as I took it all in. The gleaming mirrors set in exquisite woodwork, the obviously curated art hung in just the right places. It never occurred to me that I'd ever find myself working in a place like this.

"Yeah," she joined me in appraising it all. "Wow is right."

"You know, after so many years working in nonprofits, I feel like Alice Through the Looking Glass stepping into the private sector. Here's hoping I find my footing."

"Pfft," Wendy shook her head and let out a chuckle. "You'll be fine. If anything, you're ahead of the game."

"You think so?" A nagging voice inside me wasn't so sure.

"He's going to be impressed you came in early, believe me." From the look on her face, there wasn't a doubt. I wished I could say the same about myself.

"Well," I said, perching on the corner of my desk, "it's nice to know I'll have at least *one* thing in my favor right off the bat."

"Oh, now." She waved me off. "First-day jitters. Happens to everybody. Let me tell you something." She leaned in, a conspiratorial glint twinkling in the corner of her eye. "Even Henry looked nervous on his first day."

"No."

"Of course he was," she said. "Standing in his office looking like he was wearing a suit for the first time." She put a hand on her chest, shaking her head. "It was adorable." I looked down at my own brand new skirt suit, almost expecting to see the price tag hanging from the cuff.

"So I'm in good company?"

"The best." She winked, every inch the cool aunt. Not the one who winds up sitting next to you in jail—the one who bails you out. The one who bakes all your favorites and knows how to keep a secret. "Alright. Can you think of anything else you need?"

"Not at the moment. I still have to go down and get a few things out of my car."

"Sounds great." She clapped her hands. "If you think of anything at all, just come and find me." She turned to bustle away, and my anxiety got the better of me.

"Hey, Wendy?"

"Yes, honey?" When she saw my expression, she sidled right back next to me. "What is it?" I sat, picking my cuticle and trying to figure out how to put it into words.

"It's just... My last job had me keeping schedules and setting up meetings and everything, but this?" I gestured to the tasteful opulence on every side. "I'm just worried I might not be the right fit."

"Victoria." Her round face held a level of seriousness that surprised me. "Do you know how many applied to be his personal assistant?"

"No."

"Seventy-nine. Six got interviews, and after yours?" She shrugged, her warm smile returning. "It was no contest. If you weren't the right fit, you wouldn't have gotten the job." For the first time all morning, my shoulders dropped.

"Thanks for that. It really helps."

"I'm glad," she said, patting my knee.

"Oh, and everybody calls me Tori."

"Well, alright, Tori. I'm around if you need any little thing." And she was off. Our impromptu little heart-to-heart had settled me down, even if only a bit. Taking a moment to run a hand along the edge of my desk, I took a deep breath and let the reality of it all sink in.

Just two weeks ago, I'd been living thousands of miles away in Topeka, doing grand works on a meagre scale. Now here I was, in easily the biggest city I'd ever lived in, with the rent to prove it. I was going to have to be good at my job if I had any hope of affording to live there.

It was a massive life shift, but I felt like I needed one. Sure, I could have stayed at my small job in that small town, going on dates with the same small-town guys. But it was time for a change, especially after the disastrous end to my first and only serious relationship. Besides, I always felt like I was destined for bigger things, and there I was standing in the middle of it.

Goodbye small-town dating drama, hello big-city career gal.

"Alright," I said, bolstering myself. "When the boss gets here, I'm going to be ready." With that, I squared my shoulders and made for the elevator. Its gentle hum settled my nerves a touch as I descended to the parking garage. Checking my makeup in the spotless, polished door, I couldn't help thinking that the whole situation really was odd.

After all, acting as someone's personal assistant can be an incredibly close working relationship, and yet I'd never actually laid eyes on Henry Weston. I'd read that his father died, leaving him to run the company, but all my googling to find out about my new employer turned up exactly squat.

The doors opened with a ding, and I strode into the cool, dim garage to try to find my car. It was like a maze down there, and despite coming in early, it had been tricky to find a spot for my little Honda among all the luxury models. That had been the first clue that I was in the big leagues now.

Honestly, given how tight the job market was, I felt lucky to have anything. I mean, *seventy-nine*? I knew things were tough out there, but the number seemed crazy to me. If anything, it only made me feel more grateful to have sealed the deal. Maybe this flying leap was going to work out after all.

As if on cue, a Jaguar came ripping around a bend, like it was running from a crime scene. I leaped back, and the tires screeched as it lurched to a stop.

Holy crap, that was close!

For a second I stood absolutely frozen, stunned at how close I'd just come to being flattened. The car sat there idling, like some great, sleek monster. All at once, blinding fury flooded through me, and I started shaking so hard I could barely contain myself.

"Are you fucking insane?" I slammed my ledger on the hood, adrenaline surging through me. Every inch of me tingled, and I felt like my fingers could shoot lightning bolts. The window rolled down, and the driver sat there looking sheepish.

"I didn't see you," was all he seemed able to say. If anything, it only stoked the bonfire raging in my gut.

"I figured that part out," I shouted. "What do you think you're doing, speeding around here like that? You could have killed someone!"

"Look, I..."

"You know what? Save it. God, you rich assholes buy yourselves these hotshot cars, and it's like you expect the entire world to just get out of your way." I gave his tire a solid kick, scuffing the toe of my brand-new pumps. I'd just bought them, so that really sent me over the edge.

"God *dammit*!" All the nerves I'd been working to suppress bubbled to the surface, and I called him every name in the book, and even a few I made up myself. I'd never been much of a swearer, but suddenly

I became the Mount Vesuvius of *fucks*—every single one of them aimed squarely at his bewildered, frat-boy face.

"Are you done?" he asked when my whirlwind of obscenity finally blew itself out.

"With you? Absolutely," I snapped. I turned on my heel, nose in the air, and stormed off to find my car. When I reached it, I looked back and saw the Jag creeping away at a snail's pace.

That's right, I thought. *Maybe you've learned your lesson.*

Popping the trunk, I looked at my trembling hands and took a moment to steady myself. That wasn't like me at all. All the worry and apprehension had gotten the best of me, and while I didn't regret letting him have it, I needed a second to crawl back into my skin.

After a few deep breaths, I grabbed the last box of supplies and mementos and scoured the back seat to make sure I wasn't missing anything. My phone said ten to nine, so once I was up at my little roost, it was going to be off to the races.

Back in the elevator, I studied my reflection again, tucking a few stray hairs behind my ears and patting everything back into place. My tirade had left me a bit disheveled, and I was determined to leave Dragon Tori down in the basement where she belonged. As far as the good people at Weston and Hart were concerned, Victoria Hudson was the picture of poise and grace.

The doors opened, and the once quiet office vibrated with the low hum of an office morning. At least that sound was familiar.

Shoulders back, eyes ahead. You've got this.

Carving my path through a smattering of impeccably tailored suits, I finally came into my office. *My office.* It felt good. I was just tucking away the last of my things when a light knock on the door drew my attention to Wendy's excited grin.

"You ready?" she asked.

"Of course." I got to my feet, smoothing my skirt and giving the hem of my jacket a little tug.

"Tori, this is Henry Weston." I looked up, and my jaw dropped. *It's him.* The guy who almost mowed me down. The guy I'd shouted at until my face turned purple. My knees nearly gave out from under me.

"Oh, we've met," he said. Just the hint of a smirk pulled at his lips, nearly sending me into a full-on tailspin. My cheeks burned, but I couldn't tell if it was from embarrassment or residual anger.

"Is that so?" Wendy raised her eyebrows at me, positively beaming.

"Yes," I mumbled. "Yes, I think we have."

"How nice," Wendy said, "I'll leave you two to get started. If you need anything..."

"Just come find you," Henry said with a warm smile. "You got it." She practically cooed at his ready charm and trotted off. As soon as she was gone, Henry turned to face me.

He looked completely different from the slack-jawed asshole, gawping at me through the window of his flashy car. He was tall, with strong shoulders and a jawline you could cut an apple with. His dark hair set off his startlingly blue eyes. I wondered how I had failed to notice them earlier.

"So," he said, leaning against the door frame, "you took off before I could apologize. Not that you gave me much chance to." Henry smiled at me out of the corner of his eye as if sizing me up.

"First impressions, huh?"

"Oh, I'd say you made one heck of a first impression, Victoria Hudson."

"Tori," I said, feeling more than a little at odds with myself.

"I'm sorry?"

"Everyone calls me Tori, Mr. Weston." He studied me, and to escape his gaze, I scrutinized the scuff on my toe.

"Well, Tori, since we're playing by those rules, I'm Henry. And, I should explain about our brief encounter earlier..."

"You don't have to," I said, desperate to forget everything about it.

"I didn't want to be late," he said with disarming earnestness. "After all, I was meeting my new assistant today. Given what the hiring team had to say about her, I wanted to have myself together when she walked in."

"Oh. I see…" It sure sounded like he meant it. "I did the same thing, actually." Everything about him brightened.

"Is that right?" He let out a quick stab of laughter and asked, "So, what time did you get in?"

"Maybe fifteen after seven?" His jaw dropped.

"Are you serious?" He shook his head, then nodded, as if duly impressed. "I have to hand it to you. I don't think I've seen seven in the morning in years. At least not from this side." That last bit seemed to slip out, and he looked momentarily pained.

"What's that?"

"Nothing." Again, that smile. "Forget I said anything. So, between your early arrival and your display in the parking garage, I've learned something pretty important about you, Miss Hudson."

"What's that?" I asked, half waiting for the hammer to drop.

"You're a very passionate woman." This time, the flush in my cheeks had nothing to do with anger. He stepped towards me, his hands slung loosely in his pockets. "I truly am sorry about what happened down there. I can promise you, I won't be doing that again." The sincerity on his face cut right through me, and a tiny something in my chest prickled up. Henry Weston might have been many things, but it looked like an asshole wasn't as near the top of the list as I'd initially thought.

"Me too."

"Well, alright then," he grinned, extending his hand to me. "What do you say? Think we can make this work?"

"You know what?" I took his hand and gave it my best professional shake. "I think we can."

2

HENRY

A firecracker with a firm handshake? That definitely made me sit up and pay attention. Things might have gotten off to a rocky start, but I was almost glad about it. This woman was formidable, and that's exactly the kind of person I wanted in my corner—because my transition hadn't exactly been smooth. And my number one priority these days was proving I belonged.

"Can I ask you something, Henry?"

"Anything."

"It just seems strange," she said, shaking her head. "If I'm supposed to be your personal assistant, why weren't you part of the hiring process?"

"Oh!" I laughed out loud. "There's a lot of things they've been trying to keep me out of. If I'm being honest," I leaned in close enough to get a whiff of her perfume, "I think the board was essentially looking for a chaperone." Her dark eyes flashed wide, an incredulous smile creeping across her lips.

"Are you serious? Why?"

"Let's just say my dad did things a particular way, and they've got the idea that I may not be as… orthodox." It was a tricky balance—

trying to give her the lay of the land without diming out my party boy reputation. Especially when that life was firmly in the rear-view mirror. "But don't get the idea I was completely shut out," I went on. "I got blind files on all the major candidates. No names, ages, nothing. Just accomplishments and letters of recommendation. It was fascinating."

"So, did you get a vote?"

"Sure," I shrugged. "One. In a hiring team of eight. It's not like I pulled rank or anything. Naturally, you were my pick," I said in answer to her expectant look.

"Oh, good," she said, huffing out a charming little sigh of relief. "I'd hate to think we were starting off with you wishing I was somebody else."

"Hardly." Looking at her, I would have been hard-pressed to wish it was anybody else. There she was, feisty and tenacious—and gorgeous to boot. When she wasn't breathing fire all over my jag, that is.

She was petite, bordering on pint-sized, but her skirt suit did nothing to disguise her curves. Heck, the button on her jacket was working overtime. Her dark, straight hair was pulled back in a professional ponytail, showing off her high cheekbones and fine jaw. She was a beauty by just about any standard.

"Well," she rattled me back to the present, drumming her fingers on her ledger, "how do you want to get started?"

"Good question. We should get our hands on a meeting list and start sorting out my schedule. It's been a tangle playing catch-up around here."

"Knock, knock," came a voice from behind me. I turned to find Richard leaning through Tori's open door. "Hank, Tom Ellsman is waiting for you in the Mansfield Room."

"He is?" That was a surprise.

"Yeah, man." He wrinkled his brow, shaking his head like I was a dope. "This has been on the books for over a week."

"First I've heard of it." I almost succeeded in trying to keep the edge out of my voice. Ever since I landed, I had the feeling he'd been intentionally keeping me off-center. It was tempting to call him on it, but I opted to keep things light.

"See," I turned back to Tori. "Guess this is why I need a personal assistant. You got here just in time." Her face lit up with a modest glow, then she tucked her chin, hugging her ledger to her chest.

"I'm Richard, by the way," he reached past me to offer her his hand. "Richard Kirkland. Since *somebody's* not making introductions." He cut his eyes to me with a playful wink, like he was just kidding, and I was sorely tempted to sock him in the jaw.

"Victoria Hudson." She took his hand, her face a mask of pure professionalism. "Call me Tori."

"Tori?" Richard held onto her hand just a little too long, and her poker face flickered just a bit. "It's good to know you."

"Tori, is there anything you need to take notes from this meeting?" I asked, swooping in to rescue her.

"Just my pen." She leaned across her desk to retrieve it, offering a view of her stunning ass. Trying to be a gentleman, I looked away only to find Richard helping himself to an eyeful. "Anything else?" He started a bit at being caught in full-ogle.

"Oh, uh," he stammered, smoothing his tie. "Nope. But if I were you, I'd get over there."

If you were me? Good luck with that. "Thanks, Richard."

"You got it, Hank." I'd made it clear that I didn't like being called *Hank* anymore, but Richard insisted on doing it, anyway. He cast another hungry look at Tori, adding, "Nice to meet you, Tori. Hope I'll be seeing more of you." The way he eyed her up set off an odd stab of jealousy in my gut. It startled me, and I assured myself that it had nothing really to do with Tori—it was just my distaste for him.

"Shall we?" Tori asked once he was gone.

"Let's." Putting a little extra CEO in my step, I made way for the Mansfield Room. It was our largest conference room, so maybe a touch ostentatious for a one-on-one, but that was Tom all over. He was waiting for us at the far end of the table, arms folded behind him. Clearly a power move, and again—classic Tom.

"I'm sorry to keep you waiting," I said, walking over to take his hand. "Somehow, this wasn't on my schedule. Of course, that kind of thing isn't going to happen from now on. I believe you know Victoria Hudson?"

"I do," he nodded to her, stopping shy of offering to shake. "Glad you've joined the team, Miss Hudson. Ol' Hank here could probably use the help, huh?" He chuckled, but his familiarity left me in no mood to join in.

"What can I do for you, Tom?"

"Ah." He eyed me. "Straight to business, eh? Nice to see you taking the initiative." He gave me a solid pat on the shoulder and headed over to look out the window. "I wanted to talk to you about your acquisition strategy for Briarwood Financial."

"What about it?" I bristled. "I thought I made my stance clear at our first meeting."

"Yes, you did." He clucked out another laugh, looking at me out of the side of his eye. "Don't you think it's a little... *ambitious?*" My chest went hot, and I stole a glance at Tori. Day one, and the first thing she was going to see was some senior board member undermining me. Fantastic.

"It is ambitious, Tom. That's exactly the point. When my father died, he was actively working on expanding our holdings. He always had his eyes on growth, and I think that following in his footsteps would make him proud."

"Yeah, maybe." Again, that condescending chuckle. "But your father was also shrewd in how he wanted that growth to happen, Hank."

"It may surprise you," I said through gritted teeth, "but he and I spoke about it quite a lot, actually. It wasn't all parties and late nights, Tom." That only earned me a patronizing look, as if I was some spoiled child instead of a thirty-seven-year-old man.

"No need to get defensive, Hank..."

"It's Henry, actually. I've said it more than once." That got his attention. "And I imagine you'd be defensive if I came in here and started condescending to you about decisions that are already on the books. I have to ask, are you here on behalf of the rest of the board?"

The crown of his balding head went pink. "No."

"So you've come here on your own to try and sway a decision that has been approved by the board at large? Is that what I'm to understand?" Clearly, he hadn't expected to get called on the carpet.

"Listen, Ha- Henry, I just wanted to be sure of where things were."

"Let me ask you something, Tom. Did you approve of my father's judgment?"

"Absolutely," he said without hesitation.

"So, you'd say his decision-making capacity was what? Above average?"

"Exceptional. I've never known another business mind like his."

"Well then, how about you trust his decision to name me CEO of Weston and Hart. I don't recall ever hearing that you second-guessed him, and I'll thank you to offer me the same courtesy. Now, I'll accept advice and good stewardship as the company transitions to my leadership. What I will *not* accept is undermining, condescension, or to be patronized. Are we clear?" He stood stunned, then nodded slowly, his mouth slightly agape.

"Yes, Mr. Weston."

"Excellent," I said, straightening my cuffs. "If you need to see me again for any reason, please feel free to contact Miss Hudson. Thanks for your visit, Tom." It was my turn for the shoulder pat. "I think we'll keep this one out of the next meeting's minutes."

As I strode for the door, I caught a look from Tori, and her eyes shimmered in a way that caught me in the chest. That little tingle in my gut went off again, only this time I didn't have Richard to blame it on.

* * *

"All in all, I'd say a pretty good first day."

"Thanks," she said, offering me a radiant smile. The office was quiet, and we lingered next to my door, enjoying the stillness of it all.

"Hey, I don't suppose you'd be interested in celebrating it?" I jerked my thumb toward the cabinet behind my desk. "Raise a little glass?" She hesitated for a moment, gears clearly turning. It was crossing a professional bridge, but I could tell she was tempted. In the next instant, she broke into a wicked grin, nodding vigorously. A tiny flare went off in my chest, my attraction to her getting harder to ignore.

"I really like hanging around the office when nobody's here," I said as we made ourselves at home. "I used to come meet my dad after work sometimes. We'd sit around, joking over a glass of good scotch. He always kept his proudly on the shelf, but me?" I pulled open a lower door and fetched the bottle. "Can't give folks any more ammunition."

My party life had come up obliquely all day, and Tori had almost certainly noticed. If she was going to ask about it, now was the time. We were off the clock, after all.

"You must really miss him," she said instead, and my heart went tight. It was the last thing I expected. Her face brimmed with sympathy, and I took a beat before I could finish pouring.

"I do. He was..." How could I possibly sum him up? "What's that line? 'I shall not look upon his like again.' So, there you go."

Her jaw dropped and a sharp laugh flew out. "Wait, did you just quote *Hamlet*?"

"Maybe." I grinned and handed her a glass. "Surprised?"

"I imagine you've got lots of surprises up your sleeve." She immediately blushed and started scrambling. "Oh, wow! I... um... That came out different than it sounded in my head." She put a hand over her face, stifling an outright guffaw.

"I'm impressed," I said. "Not even a sip, and you're already on to the innuendos. Bravo."

"Oh, my gosh, don't!" She blushed even harder, waving her free hand as if to erase the embarrassment. It was impossibly cute. I felt myself start to stiffen and sat on my desk to keep my arousal hidden.

"Alright," I got myself together and raised my glass towards her. "Hey." She peeked out from behind her hand, shook herself together, and raised hers. "To a great first day. And to greater things to come."

"Cheers to that." Our glasses clinked, and a faintly charged silence lingered over our first sips. "Holy smoke," she said after her first swallow, "what is this?"

"Glenlivet Archive 21. Not bad, right?"

"Not bad?" Another bark of laughter blew past her lips. "Henry *this*? This is the next level."

"I'm pleased you're pleased," I almost purred, and those luminous eyes flashed up to me, her look startlingly open. Easy, Henry. "How do you like your new apartment?" I asked to break the tension.

"It's good! I've never lived in a city this size before, so I was surprised at, um..."

"How expensive everything is?"

"Yes," she practically shouted, slapping her knee. "It's like a cliché that rents are high here, but *oh, my God*!" We both fell apart laughing. It felt strange somehow because I never really had to worry about money. Even less so now that I had stepped firmly into my father's shoes.

When we'd finished our drinks, I tucked everything away and escorted her to the elevator. It's hard to say why, but elevators almost demand silence. Thankfully, the lull in our conversation felt easy. At every opportunity, I stole glimpses at her reflection in the doors. Her lips carried just the trace of a smile, and I was transfixed. Did she catch me looking?

The doors opened, and I walked her to her car without asking. It was the gentlemanly thing to do, after all, and I was determined to be the perfect gentleman.

"I'll make you a promise," I said when we reached her little Honda. She turned to face me, almost startled.

"What?" Her voice was impossibly soft, eyes shining in the dim hush of the garage.

"I'll try not to hit you next time."

With a wink, I leaned down to open the door for her, and suddenly we were incredibly close - my face mere inches from hers. Instinct took over, and I leaned in—stopping just shy of her lips. We hung suspended there for an eternity. Just the tiniest push from either of us and...

My brain shouted, *this can't happen! You're her boss, asshole,* but my other brain wanted something else entirely. Her eyes were closed, and her expectant mouth beckoned me. She wanted this every bit as much as I did, but I couldn't let it happen. I had to pull myself together.

"Goodnight," I whispered against her lips. "Drive safely, alright?" She opened her eyes, searching into mine, then settled back on her heels, never breaking her gaze.

"Goodnight, Henry. I'll see you in the morning."

"I look forward to it."

She got into her car, and I stood to watch her drive up the ramp and out of sight. Even after she was gone, I stayed there, hundreds of different thoughts whistling through my veins.

3

TORI

My stomach was twisty when I arrived at work, but I told myself it was impossible that we came so close to kissing. Henry had just leaned in to open my door like a gentleman, and I dreamed up the rest. A misunderstanding—chalk it up to world-class scotch.

"Good morning, Tori." Henry arrived at my door, every inch my employer and nothing more. My stomach settled immediately.

"Good morning, Mr. Weston." Bright, friendly, efficient. Well done.

"Mr. Weston?" His eyebrows shot up, and he rested his hip against my door frame. "I thought we'd established 'Henry.' Don't tell me we're back to titles?" A good-humored smile tickled across his lips, but the hint of something unreadable left me off-center.

"Alright, Henry it is."

"That's better." He ambled over to perch on the corner of my desk. "So, what are we getting up to today?" A completely normal question, but the way he said it sent a shiver through me. My imagination had spent the entire previous night finding us getting up to all kinds of things. He was just so close, I felt flushed, unable to concentrate. Was I going crazy?

"Hey," he said, drawing my eyes up to his. "Are you okay?"

“Fine,” I lied. “I just didn’t sleep well last night.”

“That’s a shame.” He kept his attention fixed on my face. “Neither did I.” A glint in his eyes unleashed a beehive in my chest. I hadn’t imagined it—and he felt it too. His whole demeanor was a tease, and a warmth spread through my core.

This is dangerous, I told myself. Dangerous, and exciting in a way that I’d never felt before. It may have been the whole ‘Forbidden Fruit’ thing, but there had to be more to it than that. Henry had a magnet under his skin that pulled all my sexy thoughts to the surface. The catch? He was my boss.

Worse still, that catch only made it more enticing.

“Well,” I said, getting to my feet and facing him directly. “Sleep or not, you’ve got a big day.”

“Is that right?”

“Uh-huh.” I trotted past him through my door. If I didn’t get some space between us, I’d burst into flames. “You have a meeting with the legal team of Cardew Associates in the Langworthy at ten. Why don’t we go over there and review the materials until they get here?”

He sat on my desk grinning at my poise and control. Back straight, outfit just so. I was the picture of the studious personal assistant. Henry looked at his watch, then got to his feet.

“Yeah,” he smirked, “why not?” As he passed, his sleeve brushed mine, and I’m surprised sparks didn’t fly off. In the conference room, we lingered over the materials, shoulders almost touching—all under the guise of examining our documentation.

We must have been speaking, but my ears rang too loudly for me to remember any bit of it. My imagination was fixated on our near kiss. A little devil inside me wished it had actually happened, but the more rational part of me kept firing off warnings.

Things were complicated enough already—an actual kiss would really put us in the soup. Everything about our flirtation was positively perilous, and yet I was powerless to stop myself. It was like someone else was driving, and I sat in the passenger seat of my body, shivering over every tiny moment. Whether out of anxiety or excitement, it was impossible to say.

By the time the Cardew lawyers arrived, I'd managed to paint the veneer of calm back over the tingling mess I was rapidly becoming. A trio of middle-aged men in expensive suits filtered into the Langworthy Room, and Henry straightened to greet them.

"Gentlemen, thank you for taking the time to meet with me."

"Not at all," the oldest of the men said. "Thanks for expediting things. Please accept our sympathies for the loss of your father." Henry's expression flickered the tiniest bit, making my throat go tight.

"Thank you." After a heartbeat, he brightened and said, "I'd like to introduce you to my new assistant, Victoria Hudson." He placed his hand on the small of my back, setting off an explosion in my chest. It was a casual, ordinary gesture, but my bones rattled with it.

Pleasantries done, everybody sat and got down to business. Regardless of the difference in age or career experience between him and these other men, Henry radiated self-possessed authority. He was magnificent—clearly born to sit at the head of a table. Even so, I caught glance after stolen glance. Henry's ability to retain control of the meeting while still darting hungry looks at me was equally exhilarating and unsettling.

Be careful, I reminded myself. It's all fun and games now, but it can't be anything more. There's too much at stake—for both of us.

What if someone else noticed? Henry was deliciously subtle about it, but every look felt like a spotlight with me right in the middle. My knee bounced under the table so hard, I thought it might jackhammer through the floor.

At last, everyone rose to their feet, and the handshake party broke out. Looking at the pad in front of me, I was astounded to find that I had actually taken meticulous notes. Must have been some kind of fugue state, because my mind was in one place, and one place only. The lawyers shuffled out, each bobbing his grinning head at me. I smiled as best I could, my whole body threatening to vibrate to pieces.

"Tori?" Henry was right beside me, and I almost jumped out of my skin.

"Hm?" Again, his hand just dusted the small of my back, and he brought his head so close to mine I could smell his aftershave.

"Would you please type up those notes, then forward everything to Cardew Associates?" His palm pressed a touch more firmly. "Cc me, and include all their upper staff."

"Yes, sir," I whispered.

"Sir, again?" He patted my back, chuckling softly. Walking past me, his fingertips trailed across my shoulder until the thread between us broke. I watched his wide, confident shoulders as he moved, the cut of his jacket hugging his trim waist. My knees turned to jelly, and my head whirled.

What kind of game was he playing? So many emotions spilled through me, and it felt impossible to grab onto one long enough to examine it. It was all such a transgression, and yet I almost glowed from the inside out. Somehow I made my way back to my office, only to find Richard loitering by the door.

"Everything go alright in there?" he asked.

"Very well, I think. Everyone seemed pleased." I opened my door and entered, hoping that would be it. Instead, Richard rested his back against the door jamb, making himself right at home.

"How about that?" He batted lazily at the knot of his tie. "Some of the boys were laying bets on whether those lawyers would eat him alive."

"Nobody seemed intent on eating anybody," I countered, laying out my notes in an effort to dismiss him.

"You really think so? That's not how it looked to me." Something in his tone rattled me, and I looked up from my notes.

"What?"

"Oh, I don't know," he shrugged. "I thought it looked like someone was very interested in eating someone." The innuendo was so overt, my jaw dropped at it. My blood rose immediately, and I flattened my hands on my desk.

"Excuse me?" Fixing him with the hardest look I could muster, I dared him, "Say that again." Visions of HR danced in my head. He put up his hands, laughing in mock surrender.

"Woah, hey," he inched closer, "I'm not saying anything. Just observing. Still," he put his palms on my desk and grinned at me, "it's not like I blame him. Or you, even." Rocking back on his heels, he stuffed his hands in his pockets and looked around my office. "There's no denying Hank has a way about him. Lots of women have fallen into that trap."

My stomach shrank at the thought of other women.

"It's understandable." His face dripped with phony pity.

"Richard," I clutched my desk hard, struggling not to let my temper flare, "is there something specific you wanted?"

"Funny you should ask." He settled himself on my desk in exactly the same spot Henry had occupied earlier, though his presence was far less welcome.

What was it with these men and sitting on desks?

"I was wondering if maybe I could take you for a drink one of these evenings. Purely professional, of course. I could bring you up to speed on how things work around here."

The audacity of this man! Still, I did everything I could to meet the offer at face value.

"It's a really busy first week, I'm afraid. In fact, I should really get to typing these notes from the meeting..."

"Oh, come on." He flicked at my pages. "Everybody needs to blow off a little steam. My treat."

"Richard, I appreciate your generosity, but I really don't have the time."

"Well, it looks like you've got plenty of time to flirt with the boss." I froze solid, and he let out a low laugh. "Little touches, and cutesy glances? Not too professional, I'd say. Office romances are one thing, but with your actual boss?" He hissed in through his teeth, folding his arms with a wry face. "Sounds messy."

My jaw clenched until my teeth threatened to crack. Just breathe, I told myself. You haven't done anything wrong. Just breathe.

Where did he get off coming in to torment me about Henry? I didn't even know what was happening with Henry if anything! My cheeks burned to think that our—whatever it was—had been so overt that someone like Richard could see it through the conference room windows.

"Take it easy," Richard said with an oily smile. "I'm not saying anything to anybody. In fact, I think it could all just be a misunderstanding on my part. We could probably sort out all these mixed messages over a drink, yeah?"

"She said no, Richard." Henry stood in the doorway, and I flinched at the sound of his voice. Richard was so startled, he damn near did a backflip.

"Hey, Hank. Tori and I were just getting more acquainted."

"I heard." He stepped in, shutting the door behind him. "I'm not sure how our harassment policies worked under my father, but I can assure you that under my watch, when a woman refuses a drink, that's the end of the discussion."

"Listen, Hank, I wasn't..."

"My name is *Henry.*" Even with the door closed, it was a safe bet people heard that. "Richard, I know you feel pretty at home around here, but there's a difference between being comfortable and being unprofessional. I'd advise you to take a hard look at which side of that line you fall on, and adjust accordingly. Do we understand each other?"

"Yes, sir." Richard looked like he could spit nails, but Henry had him dead to rights. For my part, my heart was so high in my throat that it threatened to bounce out onto the desk. Without another word, Henry opened the door and Richard left.

"You," Henry said, turning his attention to me. "My office." My insides withered.

"The notes...?" I gestured weakly to the papers in front of me.

"They can wait." He turned and left, and I stood to follow, tingling all over. My second day, and I already had visions of packing my things and being escorted to my car.

"Close the door," Henry said when I stepped into his office.

I did, then perched on the edge of one of his chairs, doing everything I could to avoid his gaze.

"Hell of a day, huh?"

The sudden shift in his manner damn near gave me whiplash. "What's that?"

"Jesus, that Richard, am I right?" He scrubbed his hands over his face, then looked at me with a crooked smile. "Not exactly that he's wrong, though. You and I should probably clear the air."

"You're right, we should."

"So, last night..." he took a deep breath, pulling his lips tight. "I crossed a professional boundary. For that, I'm sorry."

"You didn't," I protested. "Nothing happened."

"Something happened alright. Even if we didn't... you know."

"Kiss?" Saying it out loud felt sinful.

"Yeah." He nodded, keeping his focus entirely on me. "I told myself I wasn't going to linger over it, but when I saw you this morning? Well, I've not been on my best behavior, and I'll try to do better."

"You know," I said, "I think it could be about proximity."

"You do?" His eyebrow went up, and mischief stole over his face. There was that invitation again, calling to everything I fought to suppress.

"Yes." I got to my feet. "We just need to know how close is too close. Once we've established that, everything should fall into place."

What was happening? Again, I found myself watching this other woman steering my body and mind. Henry came to stand directly in front of me. The whole room grew smaller in an instant, tightening around us.

"Alright," he said. "How is this? Too close?"

Yes.

"No."

"I see." He took a half step closer. "Now?" My chest pounded.

"No." The air between us shimmered, and I trembled where I stood. We had gone from zero to a hundred in an instant, but I had no desire to hit the brakes. With another step, we were mere inches from each other. Everything about me quivered, as if alive for the first time.

"Now?" It wasn't even a whisper, and his thick voice poured down on me. I couldn't breathe to speak and shook my head instead. His face tipped down toward mine, stopping exactly where it had the night before. "Now?"

I hit the breaking point and surged up to cover his mouth with mine. His hands caught me by the waist, almost lifting me from the floor. I reached up, entwining my arms around his neck and hanging on for dear life. Our tongues grappled with each other, the ferocity of our kiss deepening as he pulled me tighter to him.

"Fuck," he hissed when his mouth broke free, grazing my jawline to find my ear. "What are we doing?"

"I don't know," I moaned in pure surrender. "But, don't stop."

"I couldn't if I tried." He took my earlobe in his teeth, sending sparks racing under my skin. His breath on my neck sent my mind reeling, and I shook as if I might come apart in his arms. Spinning me around, he planted my ass on his desk, towering over me to take my face in his hands.

"Tori..." He tried to speak, but there were no words. I was past the point of return.

Our lips came together again, and my heart slammed to the top of my chest. I clawed past his jacket, desperate to feel his body. It was taut and muscular, and my hands relished every inch of it.

His palm slid down over the swell of my breast, massaging until a stifled groan caught in my throat. The hand ventured lower, scouring over my ribs down to the corner of my hip. My legs spread of their own volition, and I rocked back into his other arm, starving for his touch.

Henry's lips abandoned mine, burning a path down the side of my throat. As he did, his fingers traced a line along the line of my skirt, raising goosebumps in their wake. Slowly, gingerly, he slid his hand up my thigh until he found my soaking panties. Just the faintest touch and a spasm jolted over me until I had to bite my lip to keep from screaming in pleasure.

"Tori," his voice was hushed and hot on my skin, "I need to feel you." Words were impossible, so I took his hand and pressed it firmly to my crotch. A bare fingertip rode the edge of my panties, driving me into a frenzy. I was wetter than I had ever been in my life.

"Please," I begged again. He hooked his finger and pulled my panties aside. Then, with the deftest press, he parted me. My spine snapped straight, my head back gasping hard. Smashing me to him with his other arm, he ran his finger up through my slippery folds to find my throbbing clit. The barest pressure rolled through me like thunder, and I fought to keep from howling. A few tight circles and the gentlest flick, and he rendered me helpless.

A tongue of pure fire licked up through me, threatening to reduce me to ashes—and then another chased it. I clutched Henry's body, and he shoved a hand over my mouth to muffle the moans threatening to spill out of me. Shock after shock wracked my body as the orgasm intensified. He clamped down harder, sealing my cries in my chest, his other hand continuing his tender assault on my clit, driving me deeper and harder into chaos.

I'd never experienced anything like it before—but it wasn't just his touch. Something far deeper was at work, and when the waves finally broke and I was able to open my eyes, I found Henry looking down at me with pure wonder. How the hell had I let any of this happen?

One thing was certain — I was in serious trouble.

4

HENRY

With anybody else by my side, the week would have been a train wreck, but Tori laid the tracks with remarkable skill. She was on top of absolutely everything - except me, which had been exquisite torture. At first, I had no idea what the fallout would be from our wild, impulsive collapse. How would it be possible for us to move past something like that?

The first morning back saw both of us on tiptoes, which only made things crackle more. Despite my commitment to proving myself as the boss, I had no regrets over our rendezvous. If anything, I wrestled with a powerful desire for more. Tori was irresistible. She seemed anxious, but once it was clear that no shoes were about to drop, we found our rhythm.

Since that magnificent clinch in my office, we had barely touched each other beyond casual, common contact, yet each of those brief interactions sizzled. When Tori retreated behind a façade of respectability, I'd manufacture excuses to get close to her. She might wear the mask of propriety, but the flush in her cheeks was undeniable.

I positively itched to be with her again.

"Where are we with Sanders?"

"We needed to prioritize a few big money clients, so I've pushed him back until Thursday after lunch." A tiny, triumphant smile graced her face.

"I thought we were going to Headlong for a tour Thursday afternoon?"

"Headlong is next Thursday," she tapped a finger on her calendar, her grin widening into something nearly mischievous. "What would you do without me, Mr. Weston?"

I shifted in my seat to hide my arousal. Every time she slipped into formalities was like a siren song to my cock.

"I'd be helpless, Miss Hudson," I replied, hoping to goad her as well. "Absolutely helpless."

"You really think so?" There was something startlingly earnest in her question, but she caught herself and returned to scrutinizing her date book. "Somehow I doubt that." All business again. "By the way, here." Reaching into the back pocket of her ledger, she drew out an envelope and slid it across my desk.

"What's this?"

"Your cousin Nerissa's birthday is coming up. It's already addressed, so you can write a message if you want, or just sign." My mouth fell open, but she didn't even glance up. "I also fielded a call from your tennis partner Clayton Harris and set up a cocktail hour Saturday at five. Your Jaguar will be out of its detailing by then, and I've arranged for it to be brought to you."

"You can't be serious," I goggled at her, thunderstruck. "Is there anything you can't do?"

"Pick up your dry cleaning," she said, drawing a slip from her inexhaustible ledger. "You'll have to manage that one for yourself." Our fingertips touched as she handed me the receipt, and I pinched the ends, holding on for a second. Her breath immediately quickened, as did mine.

"Thank you," I murmured, grateful for so much more than the dry cleaning.

"It's my pleasure." That last word rode heavily on her tongue, and my imagination leaped back to the feel of her incredible body on the very desk that stood between us. Little brushes like this had peppered the last week, and every one had the power to stop me cold. Daring just a bit further, I extended my index finger to rub along the back of her hand. Her eyes locked on the gesture, then floated up to meet mine. How was it possible we hadn't succumbed again? Latent sexual tension fretted beneath everything we did.

This was the first time we had been in the office after hours since her first night, and our every move carried an extra thrill. With no prying eyes to catch us, a full-on tumble felt shockingly inevitable. The question was, should we? Or was the possibility of it enough?

"Listen, Tori…"

My email pinged, and our hands jumped apart like we were teenagers caught making out in the garage. "Saved by the bell," I mumbled with a breathy laugh.

"Shall I?" she asked, gesturing to my computer. "It is my job, after all."

"After hours," I protested.

"Still." Shifting out of her seat, she came to my side of the desk, and I dutifully shifted to give her room. As I rolled my chair back, she bent forward, resting her elbows on my desk to make a show of reading the offending email. The real show was her magnificent ass, poised directly in front of me. There was no way it could have been accidental.

Tori was an expert in picking skirts that were long enough for the workplace and short enough to fire my imagination. Her position was an overt invitation, and I decided to RSVP. After a moment of basking in the view, I inched forward, daring to reach for her.

"Oh, my God," Tori blurted, bolting upright before I could lay a finger on her. I nearly came out of my chair. Shit, had somebody seen us?

"What is it?" I asked, bolting to my feet and tugging at my collar. Tori wheeled around to face me, absolutely beaming.

"Henry." She sparkled, barely able to contain her joy. "You've been nominated for the Forbes 40 under 40!" My heart stopped.

"Wait, are you serious?"

"Take a look." She slid to the side to give me room. This had to be some kind of joke, I told myself as I studied the screen. It had to be from a joke account—a prank like this just stank of Clayton Harris. The address looked legit, as did the layout and sign-off.

"Holy shit," I mumbled. It was real. "How the… Who would… I haven't even done anything!"

"Evidently somebody disagrees." When I turned to face her again, Tori looked absolutely radiant. All I wanted in the world was to scoop her up and kiss the hell out of her.

"We need to celebrate," I exclaimed. "Come on, let's get out of here." She hesitated, the wheels spinning like mad - what was she going to do?

"Just a second." Tori hunkered down again, typing furiously. This was no presentation of her ass for inspection. This girl was on a mission.

"What are you doing?"

"Sending a company-wide email with the announcement, including the board and shareholders." This woman thought of absolutely everything. Even so, I felt slightly queasy at the thought of it all.

"Are you sure we should do that?" Startled, she stopped mid-keystroke and looked up at me.

"Are you kidding me?" she balked. "Henry, this is huge."

"Yeah, I know, but…"

"What?" She shook her head, those doe eyes sparkling with excitement.

"I don't want it to seem like I'm bragging." Admitting it felt oddly confessional. I'd always hated people who went around trumpeting every little accomplishment like they wanted a medal for getting up in the morning.

"Henry?" Tori squared up to me, putting her hands on my chest, inciting a riot in my blood. There was no hiding the bulge in my pants, but she kept her gaze locked on my face. "This isn't bragging. Being nominated is an accomplishment, and everyone here needs to know it. This is proof that you…" She stopped herself, but she didn't need to finish; I knew exactly what she was thinking.

All the people who doubted me, from Tom Ellsman to the shareholders, even a pissant like Richard—this showed them all that I belonged right where I was. And they were just going to have to deal with it.

"Go for it," I said, giving a brief nod to the computer. "Let's let everybody know who's boss." With a quick laugh, Tori dove back at the keyboard, typing so fast I thought it would catch fire. I'd never seen anyone so happy on my behalf, and my breath caught at it.

"Sent!" she exclaimed with a final, deliberate keystroke. Turning back to me with the biggest smile imaginable, she said, suddenly shy, "Now, how about that drink?"

* * *

Washburn's made the best martini in the city, and from its position on the upper terrace of the Xavier Center, it also boasted one of the best skyline views around. Not that I was paying much attention to the view with company as captivating as Victoria Hudson. We were well into our second round, and she was clearly buzzing.

"I didn't even know this place existed," Tori said, gazing out at the city sprawling out around us.

"Well, you haven't lived here that long. There are lots of secrets to explore." I took a long sip of my martini, letting the words hover in the low light between us. Tori's chest rose with a sigh, and she turned to study me with an unreadable expression.

"Secrets?" The word swelled with meaning.

"You could call them that," I nodded. Then, putting my hand on the table quite close to hers, I added, "Secrets are almost always worth exploring, don't you think?" Tori sat still, her eyes fixed on my hand.

"If I have the right guide?" It was barely a whisper, and her face remained impenetrable. With the lightest shift, one of my fingers brushed hers. A light shiver washed over her, and she looked to find my face.

"The right guide—the right company—always makes exploring richer."

She drew her hand away, chilling the heat rising inside me. She took her glass and lifted it almost to her lips.

"I find the present company very agreeable," she whispered, then took a sip.

Fireworks went off in my chest. After a week of teasing uncertainty, the door swung open wide.

"Perhaps a little exploring is in order?" I was riveted to her, blazing with anticipation.

"Perhaps." Her eyes found my face again, brimming with a heady mixture of fear and hunger. I took her hand, intent on stoking the hunger and chasing away the fear.

"Do you like art?" After a beat, she nodded.

"Well," I said, rubbing the back of her hand with my thumb, "I have quite the art collection in my penthouse. Would you like to explore it?"

She took a long breath, and I could feel her trembling across the table.

"Very much, Henry." At that moment, I discovered I'd misread her. This wasn't fear—it was caged desire.

Needless to say, once back at my place, we didn't look at a single painting. We spilled through the door so tangled with each other, it's a wonder we made it past the umbrella stand. My mouth roamed her neck, and she knotted her fingers in my hair as I feasted on her.

"God," she whimpered when I reached the ridge of her collarbone. "Fuck." She hooked her leg around my thigh, imploring me for more. Yanking her skirt up over her hips, I anchored my hands on her ass and lifted her up to me. She grunted with pleasure, and I pinned her to the wall, grinding myself between her legs. She let out an unrestrained cry, and I shoved again to show her how hard it made me.

"Jesus Christ, Tori. You have no idea what you do to me."

I dove back up to find her mouth, claiming it with a savage kiss. Peeling her from the wall, I held her harder and steered us toward the couch. Once there, I tipped on top of her, pressing her down among the cushions. Her mouth answered mine, her eager tongue begging for more.

Prying myself away from her, I snatched at my buttons, finally tossing my shirt aside and whipping my undershirt over my head. A fresh hunger spilled across her face, and she leaped forward to pull at my belt. As she did, I set to work, freeing her from her top, relishing each fresh inch of exposed skin.

My belt slipped free just as I spread her blouse open to expose her ivory breasts, barely contained by her lacy bra. Unable to resist, I plunged my face into her cleavage, lashing my tongue along the supple expanse of her. Her head tipped back, shoving deeper into the cushions, a groan rumbling up from her core.

"Henry, yes." I dragged my ravenous mouth across the lace, seeking out the hard nipple straining against her bra. Somehow, I managed to free myself from my trousers, kicking them aside on the rug. My cock strained with need, impatient to plunge inside her, but I had other plans.

Abandoning her glorious breasts, I kissed a trail down along the plane of her stomach. Her breath came in sharp stabs as I drew lower, and she rocked her hips up in anticipation. Hooking my thumbs through the edge of her panties, I drew them down to expose her to me.

"Fuck," she howled as I teased a finger along her glistening slit, savoring the silky feel of her. Once free of her panties, I nibbled along the inside of her thigh, growing ever closer to her pussy.

"God, Tori," I mumbled when I faced it at last. "You are just..." No words came, so I surrendered and slipped my tongue between her succulent lips. At the taste of her, my hard-on throbbed, aching for her.

Tori went taut as I licked up to find her clit, a steady stream of quick, high breaths panting out of her. Raking my tongue across her swollen nub, I worked her to a fever pitch. Her thighs locked around me, and she clutched at my head as I lapped at her with lingering strokes.

"Henry," she gasped, "Henry, I'm..." I licked harder, long caresses giving way to fast, hard flutters. My mouth closed around her, every ounce of my being centered on driving her over the edge. "Oh, shit!"

Her hips bucked up, and she screamed in pure ecstasy. Flailing for anything to steady herself, she seized the couch as her body shuddered and jerked. Her thighs clamped together so hard it would have been impossible to break free. Not that I wanted to.

Even as she came, I kept at her, a demon inside me furious to give her more. My tongue had a mind of its own, following every shift in her body and change in her breath. Her skin was hot and damp, electric to the touch.

"Oh, my God," she sighed as the last swell broke over her. Relinquishing, at last, I peered up to find her looking at me in almost bewildering satisfaction. "Henry, that was... Fuck." She heaved herself towards me, pulling me up to meet her in a deep, passionate kiss. It grew hungrier, and I pulled her back with me until I lay prostrate beneath her on the floor.

Her hand closed around my cock, the sensation sending a current surging through my veins. "Jesus," she whispered as she ran her palm along the entire length of my shaft, "I knew it." Straddling my hips, she angled my cock to meet her and settled over me. The aching head prickled like fire at the first touch, and I clenched my eyes shut to hold on.

"Do we need protection?" I whispered. She froze for a moment, and my heart raced—desperate with the fear of losing this moment.

"I'm on the pill," she said after what felt like an eternity, then settled just enough for the crown of my cock to slip past her entrance.

"Shit," I hissed, gripping her thighs and hanging on for dear life. All I wanted was to drive into her with all my strength, but I could tell that would be too much.

With tortuous slowness, she lowered herself onto me. She was impossibly tight, and it took all my willpower not to thrust my hips up and have her all at once. My hands rose to her hips, and together we pressed until I was finally buried inside her. Tori gripped my shoulders hard, and I opened my eyes to find her staring into my face, her brow furrowed and mouth locked open.

"Fuck," she mouthed, and her hips rolled against mine. When we found the spot of maximum pleasure, we both knew it. Everything about us synced up, and we rode into each other in complete harmony. Slowly at first, but with increasing intensity as she ground her clit against my body.

The faster we went, the tighter she became, until a low fire kindled in my abdomen. Her nails dug into my shoulders, desperation rising as I shoved up into her. Cry after cry rattled out of her chest, and her spine coiled like a spring.

"You like that," I grunted after one particularly powerful thrust earned a scream.

"Yes," she wailed. "God, Henry, yes!" I rewarded her by hammering up into her, the heat inside me rising to a fever pitch. The inevitable was approaching fast, and I dug my fingers into her soft, grinding hips.

"Tori, you're gonna make me cum." She convulsed, teetering at her own brink. "Come with me," I hissed. "I need it."

"Fuck, Henry!" She broke over, clenching down on me until it was impossible not to join her. We thundered into each other, and I could feel the moment she lost control and descended into madness. She tipped forward, giving me all her weight as spasms took control. The spinning top inside me reached its peak, and I exploded inside her. Pulse after pulse quaked through me as I spilled everything I had.

Tori's name blew over my lips again and again as I crushed her to me, digging as deep as I could. No climax I'd ever had could touch the intensity of what coursed through me as we lay there.

When I could breathe again, I blinked at the ceiling and planted a row of tiny kisses across Tori's forehead. She groaned lazily, and I could feel her smile on my chest. There was no telling what would happen from here, but I knew for a fact that I would not trade this moment for anything.

5

TORI

"Well, if you ask me, you're off to a banner start." Janet popped the cork on the wine she brought over, sloshing out a pair of generous servings. "I don't know what's got you so nervous; you've been absolutely killing it at the office."

"Thanks." She passed me a glass and flopped onto my couch, raising hers in a toast.

"So, I say, here's to killing it!" She took a healthy sip, but I just sat staring into the deep ruby liquid as if it held the answer to all life's mysteries—which I was absolutely certain it did not.

"Hey," Janet said, "what's up?"

"I don't know."

The thing was, I did know. Janet and I had been out for drinks once before, and we spent the entire night laughing. Not only was she quick with a witty turn of phrase, but her reputation as the Queen of the Water Cooler was also sterling. Not that she was a mean girl in any way, but she had the pulse of the place better than a doctor. She was excellent company in any weather, and I was in serious need of cheering up.

"Come on," she teased. "You didn't call me to come watch you mope around in your socks. What's the scoop? Don't tell me things are on the outs with Henry?" His name wriggled into me, and I tucked my knees up to my chest.

"I don't know what you mean—what about Henry?"

"Really?" She let out a massive belt of laughter. "You're not gonna play that with *me*, are you? I mean, the chemistry's obvious."

Obvious? The word burned like acid in my stomach.

"What I want to know is," she said with a grin, "are you guys actually... you know?"

If anybody else was asking, I'd have been mortified, but Janet was well on her way to becoming a true friend—and I was desperate for someone to confide in.

"Fine," I caved, forcing a smile. "Yeah, there's a *thing* there." Janet let out an enormous whoop, pumping her fists in the air, very nearly spilling all of her wine.

"I knew it! I totally knew it!" She settled back again, glowing like she'd just won the lottery. I'd have joined in the fun if my nerves weren't eating me alive. "So, is that what's got you all down in the mouth? Trouble in paradise?"

"No, he's been great," I admit. "Wonderful, actually."

"Oh, thank God," she sighed, putting a hand on her chest. "I mean, that's how it looked from the outside, but you never know what happens behind closed doors." She put a little extra spin on the last bit, and I flashed back to the first time Henry and I were behind closed doors. I'd worked like hell to keep quiet, but maybe we'd failed.

The idea that he and I were that obvious left me queasy. People were bound to pick things up along the way, but I'd been so at odds with myself at the very beginning, I'd made a point of doubling down on decorum. Now that Henry and I had actually slept together, we were both minding our Ps and Qs.

"What are people saying about us?"

Janet nearly choked. "About you?"

I nodded, fearing the worst.

"Nothing."

"Pfft! You don't expect me to believe that, do you? Come on, you know everything," I pleaded. She rolled her eyes, then looked at me for a long second before flashing into her signature grin and huddling up to spill the tea.

"Look, anybody can see there's an attraction there. Even when you're not looking at each other, sparks are flying all over the place. One or two folks think you're fucking—Richard *definitely* thinks you're fucking—but apart from that?" She shrugs, "As long as you're not boning in the foyer at lunchtime, nobody cares. You're great at your job, so nobody can say you sucked his dick to get it."

"Alright." That was a relief. "Thanks for telling me."

"That being said," her eyes twinkled, "if this couch is Vegas, and what happens in Vegas stays in Vegas, you gotta tell me. You guys are totally fucking, right?"

I laughed in spite of myself. Her glee was infectious, with just a whiff of a desire to live vicariously through my trysts with the boss. But could I really tell her? Vegas or not, keeping secrets wasn't exactly her claim to fame.

"Janet, really."

"Don't play fake-scandalized with me. You knew we were going to talk about this." She had a point there. It's not like I asked her over to start a book club. "You can tell me," she sparkled with lascivious giddiness, "his dick is huge, right?" As edgy as I was, she still had the knack for making me laugh.

"Oh, my God, Janet," I guffawed, tickled by her shamelessness. She wagged her eyebrows, certain she was winning the battle. One thing about Janet, she was irresistible. That's how she got all the gossip in the first place.

"He's very well endowed," I deadpanned, sending her into a swooning mass of giggles. It would have felt so good to join her, but remembering our tempestuous night in Henry's penthouse cut right to the heart of my unease. We'd spent the entire night having each other again and again, but I'd made a mistake that had the potential of swelling into a massive issue.

"Again," Janet said, wiping away tears, "I don't see what you've got to be down about. Especially if things are going well enough for you to know *that*."

"I think I might be pregnant." The confession fell out of me before I had a second to catch it. All the air went out of the room, and Janet sat straight upright, deadly serious.

"You *what?* How did… What makes you think that? You've been using protection, haven't you?"

"I told him I'm on the pill."

"And you are, right?" At my silence, she put her wine down and scooted closer. "Tori. You are on the pill?" I thought I was going to cry. My throat constricted, and my chest burned.

"I had been but… After coming out here, everything's been so hectic, and I've been so nervous…"

"And you forgot." Her voice was even, as if she knew exactly how it could happen. I nodded, unable to look up from my ragged cuticles. When Henry asked about protection, I didn't know about the missed days. After that, the rest of the night just tumbled after.

"I don't know what I was thinking," I mumbled. "I guess the problem was, I wasn't thinking."

"Hey," Janet put a hand on my arm. "Don't beat yourself up. Heat of the moment. It can happen to anybody. Have you taken a pregnancy test?"

"Not yet, I just…" I shrugged. In a flash, Janet was on her feet, rummaging through her bag. After a quick paw-through, she came up with a test, and I shook my head in disbelief.

"What? I was a Girl Scout. Be prepared." The old motto almost sounded like an admonition. If I'd been a little more prepared, I wouldn't be sitting there, in this situation.

Janet stuffed the test in my hands and ushered me to the bathroom to take it. When I came out again, we both sat in hushed suspense.

"Who'd have thought staring at a piece of plastic would be so nerve-wracking?" She was right there. I was so tense I almost had to remind myself to breathe.

I'd only had one other pregnancy scare. My long-term boyfriend back in Topeka handled it all really poorly, which was probably the first crack in our crumbling relationship. Aside from some dating in high school, Cody was pretty much it for me in terms of romance. To have him bungle a potential pregnancy so hard was pretty damaging.

When things went full-on sour with him, I'd made up my mind to steer clear of men in general. My heart was bruised, and the breakup was one of the major reasons I shook my life up in the first place. Getting out of Kansas felt like the only option, and my own personal tornado had blown me to the couch I sat on, tying myself in knots waiting for the news.

Things started to come into focus. My mouth went dry as a plus sign faded into view. I slumped back on the couch, an ice block dropping into my gut.

"I don't know what to do," I muttered.

"Well, first of all," Janet scooped up my wine glass and dumped it into hers, "no more of this for you. Second, my sister just made me an aunt, so the doctor situation is locked down."

"What should I do about Henry? I have to tell him, right?"

"Err." Janet wrinkled up her nose and winced.

Fuck. The icy boulder inside me just kept growing.

"What?"

"I really shouldn't say." Her resistance made me bristle.

"Janet, you just declared this couch Vegas, so if you know anything shady about Henry, it's time to fess up."

"Okay," she said, folding her legs up onto the couch to face me. "So, the good news is, it's not exactly shady. It's just... Look, before his dad died, Henry was pretty much a full-time party boy."

"Really?" My heart wilted. "How bad?"

"I don't know the particulars, but in his Hank days, Henry was all about fast cars and faster women." The image of him racing into the parking garage in a gleaming Jaguar lodged like a bullet in my brain. The fast cars were definitely still around.

I must have looked terrible, because Janet fell all over herself to add, "But, he's been working real hard to change all that."

"Maybe," I mumbled.

"You should call him," she said. I folded myself up as small as I could, but she put a hand on my knee. "Hey, I'm not saying you need to tell him. Just give him a call and see how you feel when you hear his voice. Trust me, it's better to do this litmus test now instead of seeing him in the morning after what's bound to be a sleepless night."

"Yeah." She was right. I reached numbly for my phone, and Janet sprang off the couch.

"Let me get out of here. The last thing you need is an eavesdropper. But I'm just going to a bar around the corner, so text me when you're done. If you need me to come back up, can do." With that, she collected her bag and pointed to her wine glass. "Save this for now—if you want me again, I'll need it."

"Alright."

She shot me a thumbs up and was gone. Henry's contact was right at the top, and I sat staring at his name. Was I really going to do this? My entire life had been turned on its head in the last ten minutes, and here I was about to drag somebody else into the scrum.

With a deep breath, I hit the call button and sat prickling as it rang.

"Hey," Henry answered, voice raised above a jumble of others. "Gimme a sec, I'm gonna step outside."

He was at a party. My hand started to shake, and I shoved myself deeper into the couch.

"That's better," he said when things quieted down. "I'm so glad you called—what's up?"

"Oh, um." I was at a complete loss. "Do you want me to move your first phone meeting until after lunch?"

"What?" He sounded thrown, and I squeezed my eyes shut.

"It's just, you know, I thought you said something about wanting to keep your morning clear tomorrow. Clearly, you're out, so maybe it's a good idea?" My stomach seethed so hard I had to press a hand into it to keep it from grumbling.

"Look at you." His voice was warm and fond, and I wondered how much of that was liquid affection. "Always looking out for me. Sounds great—let's do it."

"Okay." The line went quiet, but the silence lacked the charge that usually ran between us.

"Anything else?"

"Nope. Have fun out there tonight?" My effort to sound chipper tasted sour.

"Thanks," he barely seemed to notice, which only made me feel worse. "Have a good night!"

With a click, he was gone. I tossed my phone on the cushion next to me and hugged my knees to my chest. Everything felt awful. To keep from falling apart completely, I got up, took Janet's brimming wine glass into the kitchen, and poured it down the sink.

6

HENRY

I walked into my office feeling fantastic. There'd been times in my life when a night out with friends would have left me too hung over to be much use to anybody, but those days were solidly in the rear-view mirror. That fact alone might have been part of why I was feeling so good.

My itinerary for the day was on my desk, as well as bullet pointed notes to prepare me for my upcoming meetings. Just like she'd suggested, Tori had moved my phone call with Carmine Analytics until 1:30, so things were relatively loose until my 10 a.m. Just thinking about her made me smile, and I decided to duck over and say good morning. After a day apart, I was eager to see her.

"Hey," I said, leaning through her door. She stood behind her desk, oddly stiff.

"Good morning," she replied without moving. I stepped closer, hoping a bit of proximity might loosen things up a bit. When it came to composure around others, she was an expert—but there was nobody watching us. Why not flirt a tiny bit?

"I saw that you moved that phone thing." I flashed her my most winning smile. "As usual, you're on top of things." It was tempting to wink, but there was enough sauce on the double entendre as it was. Instead of the coy grin I expected, she pulled her lips into a taut smile.

"Glad to see you ready to go this morning. How was last night?"

"It was good." I sidled over to sit on the corner of her desk. As I did, she darted out a hand to pull a folder out of the way. The action seemed weird, but I chose to ignore it. "Two of my friends from college are in town for a conference, so we had a couple of drinks and caught up."

"That sounds nice," she said, but it didn't sound like she meant it. "Where did you go?"

"Just over to D'Amico's."

"Huh. Not to Washburn's then?" It felt almost like an accusation, and I blinked to clear it away.

"No," I chuckled lightly, "that's not the kind of thing we were after. Washburn's is high-end cocktails, and we just wanted a few beers. D'Amico's was one of our top hangouts when we all got out of school."

"I see," she nodded. "Old stomping grounds then. I bet you guys really tied one on then?" She was smiling, but there was a sharpness to it that put me on edge.

"Not really," I said, trying to remain casual. "We all had things to do this morning, so we kept things pretty light. Besides, none of us are in our twenties anymore." I laughed a bit, but she just stood there watching me.

"Well, I'm glad you guys had a good time. Anyway, the notes for your ten o'clock with our public relations team are on your desk. I'm going over to pick up the documents from the copy room." She came from behind her desk and headed for the door. Normally, one of her hands or the side of her leg might brush my knee, but this time there was no contact.

"I could come with you," I said as she stepped through her door.

"No need," she answered without looking back. "I've got it."

Well, that was weird.

I'd hoped for... I wasn't sure exactly what I'd hoped for, but being grilled about a night out with my friends wasn't it. Was she upset that

I hadn't spent the evening with her? I certainly would have welcomed it myself, but didn't want to come on too strong.

The last time I'd seen her was putting her into a car the morning after she stayed at my place, and she was glowing. She'd even kissed me in public, which felt positively daring. The woman I'd just talked to felt like an entirely different person.

Was it possible she regretted our night together? The thought stung me, but I had to consider it. After all, while there's no company policy against sleeping with the boss, it's definitely taboo. Covert flirting is one thing, but I could see where she might worry over her job—or at the very least her professional reputation. With that in mind, she had every right to impose a bit of distance.

I could see her through the conference room windows as she laid out the packets in front of each chair, squaring them up with the precision of a surgeon. Tori was fantastic at her job—amazing, really. I'd hate to have any hand in making her fear she was in jeopardy. Still, it's possible I had just misread our conversation. Lord knows I'd never been particularly good at reading women.

My first longtime girlfriend in college left me bewildered more often than not, but what the hell did I know? Guys in their twenties aren't exactly renowned for their intuition. Then there was Beverly, and she really ran me in circles. Hell, I thought we were going to get married. That whole thing coming apart is what tipped me backward into partying all the time. Let's just say I was more of a scribble than a downward spiral.

To make matters worse, when you come from a family with money and a little bit of prestige, a party boy reputation hangs around you like an unpleasant odor. Even now that I was making strides every day, some folks around the office still treated me like they expected me to come tearing through the office on a skateboard or something.

Watching Tori toiling in an empty room to prepare for a meeting made me think I should take a page from her book. After all, the biggest priority in my life was washing my reputation clean again. My father left a huge pair of shoes behind, and I didn't want to just fill them—I wanted to make them mine. This much was certain; if losing Beverly shook me apart, losing my dad pulled me together again. He always wanted the best for me, and now I needed to make good on all of it. It was the least I owed him, and I wanted to honor his memory by becoming the best damn leader I could be.

Thankfully, the PR team had always been in my corner, so the meeting went without a hitch. Though I managed a mellow, professional attitude, my eyes kept flicking over to Tori. She never once returned my glances, keeping her focus locked on her notepad. Not one stolen look? Even if she was worried about how a glance might get taken, it made me queasy.

In truth, I thought things between us had been going well, professionally and otherwise. Add a night spent chasing each other around a mattress, and I felt like there was a genuine connection. Had I rushed things? Tori definitely seemed to be into it at the time, but I couldn't help feeling that something was off.

The meeting wrapped up, and Tori was out of the room like a shot. As much as I wanted to follow her, I hung around with the gang for the customary post-meeting chit chat. By the time I made it to Tori's office, she was buried in work. I stood for a moment, watching her hands race across the keyboard.

"How's it going?" I asked.

"Hm?" Her attention stayed bolted to her screen.

"Hey, Tori?" I waited until she looked at me, "I just… is everything okay?"

"Yeah." A bright phony smile set my stomach twisting. I stepped into her office and closed the door. When I turned back to her, she almost looked afraid.

"Listen, I don't want to seem like I'm reading into things too much, but are you alright? You seem… I don't know, different? I can't help feeling like I've done something wrong."

"No," she said, settling in her chair a bit. There was the Tori I knew. "Everything's fine. I'm stressed a bit over the Briarwood Financial acquisition, that's all. There's a lot of paperwork to catch up on and it's taking a lot out of me."

"Alright." I didn't want to push the point. Neither of us needed that. "So long as you're fine. I just wanted you to know I'm here if you need to talk or anything."

"Thanks, Henry," she said. "Really." She still looked at odds somehow, but I decided to take her at her word. I left her office, determining that what she probably needed was a bit of space. After all, things had moved quickly between us, so wanting breathing room was perfectly natural. I opened my door, and before I went in, I saw Richard coming to hover at Tori's door.

The sight of him set off a little flare in my gut. While he'd never said anything overt about it, I knew he was one of the people who resented that dad had chosen me to succeed him as CEO. As if his snide attitude wasn't bad enough, he'd clearly set his sights on Tori.

After everything with Beverly, I'd made myself a promise never to get too deep into a woman again. Tori was the first one who made me question that—even if only a little. Richard followed her like a hound and seeing him insinuate himself into her presence the second I left had a surprising effect on me. Was it possible that I was questioning the promise I'd made myself more than I thought? It felt dangerously like the answer was yes.

7

TORI

I started to wonder if I would ever get a good night's sleep again. My exhaustion was bound to have an impact on my work eventually, and the thought closed around me like a fist. All of it was going to catch up with me at some point, wasn't it? Once I started showing, no amount of tap dancing would hide what was really going on.

Was I going to have to quit my job? Being pregnant with the boss' baby was going to paint a giant scarlet *A* on my back that nobody could scrub off. Visions of moving back to Topeka sent a shiver through me, but what else could I do? Even if I managed to find a roommate, my little apartment would chew through my savings in a matter of months—even without all the costs of a new baby. A hopeless chill settled over me until I wanted to curl up under my desk and disappear.

"Tori?" Henry's voice made me jump so hard I nearly had a stroke. "Woah," he said, grinning to cover his discomfort. "Sorry, I didn't mean to scare you!"

"It's fine, Mr. Weston. I was just… thinking. What can I do for you?"

"Nothing, really." He stepped into my office, causing the entire room to constrict. "I just wanted to thank you for all the hard work you've been putting in. It's been amazing." Even a little bit of praise blossomed inside my chest—especially as I felt like I managed to fuck up everything I touched.

"Really?"

"Absolutely," he smiled. "In the short time before you came, I could barely get to lunch without feeling completely overwhelmed. My email inbox alone gave me hives. I hate to think that I've just shoved all that stress off on you, and just wanted you to know how much I appreciate it."

I damn near melted. One thing about Henry, there wasn't an ounce of guile in his whole body. The man practically oozed sincerity, and it made my knees buckle. Suddenly I wished for the fun, flirtatious energy I'd spent the last day and a half sprinting from. The tiniest, wicked glance might have melted the enormous glacier lodged between my ribs.

"Thanks," I said. "It really does mean a lot." Our eyes met in a rare moment of connection since I'd gotten my news. My mouth opened, and I had to clap it shut again to keep from spilling everything out on the desk. An ugly little cavern in my gut wasn't ready to share.

"Well," he said after a beat of silence, "I should get back to it. My eleven o'clock phone call is coming up."

"Reavis International." Another shared spark, and then he vanished. As soon as he was gone, I collapsed into my chair. It all felt impossible. He had been nothing but sweet all morning, which only went to make me feel worse. Our subterranean lines of communication had been shut down, and it was clear he missed it all as much as I did.

A week earlier, and I'd have been walking around three inches off the carpet from the attention. The idea of him going out of his way to get close to me had been so thrilling, and I interrogated myself over it. After all, he hadn't changed—I was the one who couldn't settle. And there was a slowly growing reason in my belly that made me all the more squirrely.

That was just it; he hadn't changed. That phrase was a hornet's nest in my brain, stinging me every time I wanted to settle back into our blissful familiarity. Whatever he may have said about his college buddies, I couldn't shake the image of some bacchanalian night out on the town.

I hadn't done myself any favors by Googling Hank Weston, only to find a small brace of tabloid pictures. Every one showed a carefree hedonist, living his life all the way to the edge. There was a version of Victoria Hudson that would have sorely loved to meet him at those limits, but she wasn't the one who was carrying his baby. A baby that felt impossible to mention to a professional partier like Hank.

But was he Hank, or Henry? That was the most pressing question in my life, and I had no idea what the answer was.

"Knock, knock."

Oh, for fuck's sake.

"What is it Richard?" I asked, barely concealing my annoyance at his twentieth visit of the morning.

"Woah, hey," he ambled in with his signature don't-shoot-the-messenger pose. "Easy with the friendly fire. I just wondered if his highness might have some time this afternoon to go over some numbers with me. I'd ask him myself, but then I wouldn't get one of these little moments with you."

All those *little moments* had a way of stacking up into him never leaving me alone. He was a fly buzzing around an ice cream cone dropped on the sidewalk, and I was melting fast. Trying not to show my exasperation and give him an excuse to pester me more, I opened up the afternoon itinerary.

"I'll be honest, Richard, things are tight today."

"I bet they are. Nice and tight." The bare-faced audacity of his leering was staggering.

"I beg your pardon?"

"Oh, come on, Tori," he said as if I was being unreasonable. "It's just a joke."

"Fucking hilarious," I snapped, closing my datebook. "You know what? There's nothing for you this afternoon. Sorry." With that, I stood up and brushed past him.

"Don't be like that, Tori." He poked his head out after me. "Where are you going?"

"I'm taking an early lunch." With that, I inched into Henry's office to find him embroiled in his phone call. He looked up at me, eyes brightening as he covered the receiver. Not wanting to interrupt, I mimed I was going out, and he answered with a smile and a thumbs up.

Richard paralleled me as I carved a path to the elevator, but was intercepted by a colleague long enough for me to slip away. As soon as the doors closed, I started to hyperventilate. Everything had become so claustrophobic, and I had to check myself to keep from running screaming into the street the moment I reached ground level.

With no real appetite, I spent my lunch hour wandering the surrounding blocks, wondering if I'd ever be able to coax myself back into the building. Even if I did, would I make it all the way back up to Weston and Hart without crumbling to dust? The odds seemed dismally slim.

As one o'clock approached, I stood facing the revolving door leading back into the cool foyer. Impossible or not, I had a job to do, and I'd never shirked a day's work in my life. Holding my breath, I plunged back into the lion's den. Doing my best to let the tasteful marble and terrazzo surroundings pull the fever of worry out of me, I waited for the elevator to carry me back up.

The doors opened, and my heart dropped into the frozen pit of my stomach. There, caught in an act of gleeful conspiracy, were Richard and Janet. Their faces were awash with wicked delight, but Janet paled the instant she saw my face. A flash of undeniable guilt betrayed that I was the precise target of all their fun—and they'd been caught red-handed.

My legs turned to water, but my chest was a molten ball of impossible fury. If I could have shot laser beams from my eyes, they both would have dropped dead where they stood.

"Janet," I spat, "how *dare* you?" I was quaking with rage, my hands knotted so tightly my nails cut into my palms. Janet's ashen face turned green, and she fled before I could muster up any of the curses she so richly deserved. I caught myself to keep from calling out after her—the last thing I wanted was a crowd. Instead, I wheeled on Richard to find him leaning back against the lobby wall.

"Don't get mad at her," he sneered. "After all, she's not the one trying to fuck her way to a corner office." All that searing rage curdled to acid in my veins.

"What did you just say?"

"You heard me, *Victoria*." He wielded my name like a scalpel, cutting me to the core. "It's disgusting, really. Besides, it's not just Janet who knows—everybody's talking about it." An involuntary shudder ran over me, and Richard stepped away from the wall, circling me.

"They are not."

"Of course they are. How could they not be? I mean Jesus, Tori, you're not exactly subtle." He closed the distance until my back was flattened in the very spot he'd just emptied. "And when I think about how many times I tried to rescue you—tried to get you to come out with me so you could maybe save a little face? But no." His hands were on either side of my shoulders, penning me in as he leaned closer.

"Richard, let me go." But he was focused as a viper, drawing ever closer, ready to strike.

"There's no saving face now though, is there?"

Something new in his tone hit like an electric shock, and I turned to look him directly in the eye.

"Oh, so it's true? Janet's a great gossip, even if not always accurate, but this? It's too much." He drew back just enough to study me in earnest. "Does ol' Hank know?"

I convulsed, which was all the answer he needed.

"Interesting. I wonder what he'd say if he knew his assistant got herself pregnant to snag a rich husband. It's a hell of a ploy."

It hadn't occurred to me that's how things might look, and it hit like an arrow to the chest. Richard saw it, clearly satisfied.

"See you upstairs," he grinned and dropped the cage of his arms to hit the button. We just stood staring at each other until the chime dinged, and he left me there without a word.

I hugged myself and slid to the floor, staring blindly at the row of glass doors facing me, numb to the point of total insensibility. My ears rang, and my eyes refused to focus. Somehow, I don't know after how long, but I managed to get to my feet and press the button.

When the doors parted onto the main floor of Weston and Hart, I shuffled forward on tingling feet. If I looked as bad as I felt, nobody said anything. In fact, it was like I was invisible, moving in slow motion through the bustling office. A ghost doomed to wander through an impeccably curated purgatory for eternity.

Through the mottled window beside my office door, I could see a shape waiting for me. Nausea rose like a wave at the possibilities. Had Richard let himself in to gloat some more? Or perhaps he was there to offer some Faustian bargain to keep my secret if I let him claim me for himself.

Worse still—was it Henry? I could already see his dark, accusing eyes. Not only had I kept a life-changing secret from him, but I'd dragged his reputation across every bathroom floor in the building. He'd worked so hard to prove he wasn't some wild man fucking his way through the world, and here I'd shown that's exactly what he was.

Steeling myself for the worst, I opened the door, only to hear a stream of clumsily stifled sobs. Janet sat curled in a chair, hair on her face, and streams of black mascara coursing down her cheeks. The clear depths of her misery did exactly nothing to move my sympathy.

"Tori," she whimpered as I halted past her. "Tori, I'm so sorry."

"For what?" I kept my voice flat for fear of descending into tears myself.

"I didn't mean to..." My spine went stiff, and the wildfire that had blown out earlier came surging back.

"Say that again," I said, gripping the edge of my desk until my knuckles whitened. She choked back a sob, but I wasn't letting her off. "Say. That. Again," I insisted.

"Tori, please, I didn't mean to..." I lurched up to tower over her.

"You didn't mean to what, *Janet*? You didn't mean to run your mouth to fucking *Richard*? You didn't mean to betray my friendship—my *trust*—to the worst person you possibly could? You didn't mean to jeopardize Henry and everything he's been working for? You didn't mean to ruin my life? Just what is it you didn't mean to do, *Janet?*"

She looked like I'd slapped her, which I would very much like to have done. My jaw clenched until my temples throbbed, and I glared down at the woman with all the venom I had. She cowered, writhing in agony.

"He... He made me." She whispered.

"He made you," I growled. "How? How did Richard *make* you tell him?"

"He said he already knew," she wailed like a wounded animal, and I knew in an instant she wasn't lying. "I was getting ready for lunch and he came up smiling and dropping all kinds of hints. You know how Richard is." I certainly did.

"And you just told him?"

"Not at first. I really didn't want to—but then you never called me after you said you were calling Henry-"

"So this is my fault," I flared.

"No," she cringed. "But I thought maybe you had told Henry and somehow Henry told Richard. I swear, I thought it was just talk. I didn't know anything."

I was shivering with anger and fought to get myself together. It was clear she was telling the truth, and even clearer how guilty she felt over it. None of that let her off the hook, but it did allow a prickle of sympathy to fill the cracks of my temper. Slumping back into my chair, I pressed my palms flat on the desk and made myself breathe.

"Tori?"

"Don't." The word cracked in the air like a whip, and Janet sat rigid, not knowing what to do. "Get out," I said, freeing her at last. She crept out of her chair and slunk to the doorway, turning back to face me. I couldn't even look at her.

"Tori, please?"

"Janet, get out of here." She squirmed where she stood, wincing like she'd never had to pay the piper in her life.

"Can you forgive me?"

I inhaled hard through my nose and kept my eyes fixed on my desk. After a long beat, I offered the only answer I had.

"I don't know."

Her whole body convulsed, then she opened the door and stepped out, pulling it shut behind her. I sat in the throbbing silence of my office, my brain roiling against the inside of my skull. The secret was out now. And, as happens, shared secrets don't stay secrets for long. If Richard knew, then everybody was going to know. It looked as if my only option was to resign—that was the only way I was going to leave the humiliation behind. Resignation was awful, but somehow it felt better than being fired—at least I'd be in control of something in my life.

8

HENRY

Knock knock.

"Henry?" She didn't say Mr. Weston! We'd come to use it as a game, but in the last few days every time Tori had called me *Mr.* it felt like the spark was gone—and each time my heart ached a little. Who am I kidding? It ached a lot.

"Come in, Tori." She did, shutting the door behind her. My pulse thundered just looking at her, but something seemed off. Even the veneer of formality had slipped, leaving her vulnerable in a way that tugged at my gut.

"Do you mind if I sit down?" Her voice was so thin, I barely heard her.

"Please." I went to hold the chair for her, and could almost swear she flinched. My throat dried out in utter dread. It was impossible to tell what was wrong, but Tori was absolutely ashen, and tiny, as if she had shrunk by a third.

"Listen, Henry—we need to talk." Those dreaded words echoed in my ears, and a bomb detonated inside me.

"You're right," I said. "We do." This time she flinched in earnest, and looked up at me with eyes the size of saucers. She was afraid, and not even trying to hide it. Every protective instinct I'd ever held fused in an instant. The only thing I wanted was for her to never feel that kind of fear again.

I'd spent nearly every moment since I met Tori denying something that was ultimately undeniable. We had chemistry, sure, but I'd had chemistry before. The easy way we could be together, coupled with the fact that there were times I felt like we were damn near reading each other's minds, cinched it. She made me a better man, a better boss. At that moment, there was no doubt as to how I felt, and it was time I did something about it.

"Henry, I—"

"Victoria, I'm in love with you."

As much as I'd feared ever saying those words, they flew off my tongue with remarkable ease, leaving me feeling seventy pounds lighter. Tori sat riveted to her chair, still as a statue.

"What did you say?" she whispered. She was unreadable, making me every bit as afraid as she looked, but now that the words were said, there was no taking them back. The only choice was to soldier forward and take whatever came my way.

"I wish I could say I've known since I first saw you, but... Well, we both know what that was like."

An embarrassed smile stole over her, and the anxious knot in my chest loosened a little.

"Look, I don't know what you have heard about me, but *love* has never really been a word I used. Now I know it's because I had no idea what it meant."

"And now you think you do?"

"Now I *know* I do," I said, holding her gaze. "Tori, it's crazy, but it's more than the fact that you're amazing at your job, or the fact that you come close to making me like mine. I can't stop thinking about you—I don't *want to* stop thinking about you—and I've never felt that before. Now, I know saying this could fuck everything up, but I don't have a choice. If you want to leave, it will break my heart, but I'll understand. If you think you could love me too, people are going to talk about the boss and his assistant, but they can go fuck themselves. None of them matter. Nothing else matters but you."

I was a hollow shell. Everything I had was on the table, and I waited for Tori, tingling in my shoes. Her eyes shone as if she might cry, and my arms begged me to cradle her where she sat—but I couldn't. First, I had to know what my confession meant to her. The silence threatened to strangle me.

"I'm sorry if I said too much," I whispered.

"I'm pregnant."

At first, I wasn't sure I heard her right. Her voice was soft, and she sat like a mouse in a fairytale staring up at me.

"What did you say?"

"Henry," she shivered ever so slightly, then said, "We're pregnant."

For a long moment, I just stared at her, drinking in the enormity of it. With each breath that passed, she withered further into her chair until the room sang with tension. All at once, I turned into a giant, swelling from my feet to the top of my head with pure elation. Letting out something between a whoop and a laugh, I scooped Tori up from her little perch and swirled her around in a massive hug. Then, breathless, I planted her backside square on my desk and crouched in front of her.

"Is that why you've been avoiding me?" I asked. She nodded, and I laughed. "Why were you so afraid? Did you think I'd fire you or something?"

"I didn't know," she said, still fearful. "Henry, everything they say about you—"

"Is true," I cut her off. "Or at least, it was. But not anymore, Tori, I promise." Relief took hold of her, and she looked like herself for the first time in days.

"I was so afraid you'd abandon me," she said.

"Not possible." I reached out and touched the back of her hand with my fingertips. "I would never leave you. Tori…" Here it was—the moment of truth. "Do you think you could love me, too?"

"Henry, I've loved you from day one. That's why I was afraid. Things have been so complicated, and I thought a baby would be the last straw."

"The last straw? Tori, this baby makes everything certain. I want to..."

The words were coming too fast, and this moment couldn't be fumbled in my haste. Stilling myself, I settled from my crouch, dropping one knee to the ground. Then, taking her hands, I looked into her face to take the biggest leap I could imagine.

"Victoria Hudson, I know I don't have a ring, but will you marry me?"

The silence probably only lasted a second, but it might as well have been eons. Tori sprang forward, tackling me backward until we both landed in a laughing heap on the floor. I covered her entire face with kisses, buzzing to the marrow of my bones.

"Is that a yes?"

"Henry," she sat up on her elbows, looking down at me with a level of serenity that seemed impossible for the stricken creature she'd been mere moments before. "If you want to go to the justice of the peace right now, I'm game."

"You deserve so much more than that, Victoria, and I'm going to make sure you have the wedding to end all weddings." She kissed me, and then we settled back to lie on my floor as if it were my penthouse bed. "You know," I said with a light chuckle, "we've got our work cut out for us here. If we've been trying to keep this quiet, this is going to be a complete 180."

"I know," she sighed out a laugh and covered her face with a loose palm. "I'm sure some people are going to have a lot to say about it. Especially if what Richard says is true..." Her voice trailed off as I went rigid at the sound of his name.

"What did Richard say?" She could feel the danger radiating inside me, and when she spoke again, it was hushed.

"Lots of things. God, Henry, it's like he never leaves me alone. And the things he said today were awful. "

"Today?" A low fire started in my core. "What did he say to you today?"

"That everyone said I was using you to get ahead. That I'd gotten pregnant to trap you." I was on my feet so fast I had a head rush. Or maybe that was the boiling rage stealing my balance.

"He said that?" My fingers itched, hungry to be at Richard's hateful throat.

Tori could smell the blood in the air, and nodded.

"When?"

"Just now," she said. "In the lobby downstairs."

"Really? In the lobby?" A tickle settled into the bottom of my stomach.

"Yes," she said, not knowing how fast my mind was racing.

"What did he do? Did he put a hand on you?"

"Not exactly," she admitted. "But he did corner me and trap me against the wall."

"With his arms?" The need for anything physical vibrated with insane urgency.

"Yes."

Gotcha, motherfucker.

I was out of the room like a cannonball, careening through the main office on a collision course with Richard's door. When I hit it, I didn't even knock. Richard looked startled at his desk, probably justly. The maniacal grin on my face must have been terrifying.

"Hey, Richard?"

"Hey, Han- Henry. I'm in the middle of something."

"No, you're not," I said, dripping with giddy malevolence.

"I'm not?" He looked appropriately baffled.

"Nope. Pack your shit."

He lurched forward in his chair. "What?"

"I said, pack your shit. You're fired. You've got one hour."

"You can't do that," he shouted, surging up from his chair.

"The fuck I can't," I said, holding my position.

"On what grounds?"

"Harassment. Victoria Hudson has told you on multiple occasions to leave her alone, yet you insist on invading her personal space. She'll be filing a formal complaint with HR immediately."

"We work together, Hank." He leaned back, shrugging with a wry face, adding, "What am I supposed to do? Get a go-between?"

"You're not getting anything, Rick. You're fired." At the sound of the nickname, he bristled so much I wondered why I hadn't come up with it sooner. "You physically pinned her to the wall and verbally abused her. You're out." He faltered for a second, then folded his arms with a smug grin.

"Is that what she said? Hank, you're asking for one hell of a lawsuit with this he-said-she-said bullshit. I've got a great lawyer."

"That's cute. I've got a video." That got his attention, and he blanched white.

"Nice bluff," he said at last.

"No bluff. This was in the main lobby, which is under 24-hour video surveillance. There are five cameras, and two of them even have audio. With that kind of coverage, we probably have you accosting her from multiple angles, and I'm willing to bet there's a record of every word you said. So," I smiled as brightly as I could and knocked on his door frame, "pack your shit, and get the fuck out of my office."

"You might end up in hot water yourself," he said, his voice trembling despite hinting at a threat. "Office romance? Fucking your secretary? It's not the best look, and you know it."

"I don't give a damn about how it looks, Rick," I answered, working to keep my composure. "What we have is consensual. And at the end of the day, there's no policy against it. On the other hand, there *is* a policy against harassment. Now, for the last time, pack your shit or I'll pack it for you. Security will be up in an hour to walk you out."

With that, I turned and made a beeline back to where I hoped Tori was waiting for me. The rest of my appointments were going to have to wait—the only thing on my agenda was kissing the hell of that woman and going to find us a ring.

9

EPILOGUE: TORI

A YEAR AND A HALF LATER

"Who's my little man? Who is it?" Barrett cooed and sprawled in his crib, gurgling with delight. A yawn stole over him, and he rubbed his tiny fists into his sharp blue eyes—perfect replicas of his father's. "Aw, is somebody tired?" In answer, he stretched hard and grunted a few times, tugging at his onesie.

Fair enough, I thought. He'd had a big day visiting with his auntie Janet and her puppy Tugger. The four of us had spent most of our Friday lunchtimes together since Barrett turned four months, and now that he was pushing the six-month mark, he and Tugger were joined at the hip for their weekly playdates. Not that said playdates were much more than squealing and rolling around in the grass.

"One little butterfly flitted through the meadow, searching for a little flower of the fairest yellow." As I murmured through the little nursery rhyme I invented, my left hand wafted through the air toward one corner of his blanket. Barrett burbled and kicked his feet, alight with our little nighttime ritual. "Another little butterfly sighed as he flew, searching for a flower of the deepest blue."

My butterfly hands fluttered upwards, lifting his blanket high to billow down over him, and every night, he squealed at that precise moment. Then, as I hummed my improvised butterfly tune, I settled the blanket over him and tucked in the edges. That done, he let another yawn, and I bent low to plant a kiss on his tiny, perfect forehead.

"Goodnight, my love." One more nuzzle, then I turned on the wave machine and clicked off the overhead light. He was asleep before the door was closed. What I knew of the typical six-month-old made me feel fortunate in our son—he was good as gold and slept like a college freshman.

Weston and Hart's generous maternity leave made me feel even more fortunate. Some version of it was in place before my pregnancy became company-wide knowledge, but nobody batted an eye when a more robust policy came into play. In fact, I was the recipient of many clandestine high-fives from other women on the staff. That kind of treatment was a far cry from the near pariah status I had feared.

"I suppose he's already down," Henry grinned as I stepped into the kitchen. I hadn't even heard him come in.

"Just missed him," I sighed. He was usually home to see Barrett off to sleep, but the last few nights had seen Henry bustling into the evenings.

"Damn," he said, smiling gently. "Well, I suppose the cat's out of the bag?"

"What cat?"

"No need to pretend, Mrs. Weston," he put on a mock stern tone, playing up being the boss in a way that always makes folks snicker at the office. " You've heard by now, yeah?"

"Heard what?" I asked, surprised by the quietly proud smile he wore.

"Oh!" He looked genuinely surprised. "I thought Fridays were your lunch dates with Janet."

"They are, but she didn't say anything."

"Huh." His expression was equal parts impressed and pleased. "I guess a leopard really can change its spots."

Henry was right on that front. After Janet and I had our run-in over her—shall we say betrayal—it was as if she'd shaken herself into line and become the picture of restraint. In fact, people sought her out for advice, knowing there was nobody safer to confide in. My heart warmed at it, and I was proud to count her among my closest friends.

"So," I said, leaning a hip against the counter and planting a kiss on his shoulder, "what's this mystery I'm already supposed to know?"

"Oh, nothing." A coy smile couched on his lips, and he pulled a magazine from his briefcase to lay it on the counter. "Only this."

I picked up the copy of Forbes. "I thought this wasn't out for another two weeks?"

"Folks who make the list get an advanced copy." For the first time in ages, Henry looked genuinely proud. My heart sparkled with excitement—he must have worked really hard to keep this under wraps.

"Henry," I cried out, flinging my arms around his neck and kissing him hard, "I'm *so* proud of you!"

"You're not going to look?" Something in his voice tickled with mystery, but his expression gave nothing up. Peeling myself off him, I flicked through the pages until I found the stunning portrait of him they'd taken just for the profile. Before I could register what I was reading, my breath came in short, and a fine mist dampened my eyes.

"Are you serious?"

"I like it," he shrugged. "It's a chance for me to stake my claim, don't you think?"

In the picture, Henry sat on a plain stool, leaning forward with his elbows on his knees and his fingers locked. Those blue eyes pierced the viewer, daring them to see him as anything other than the successful man who had fought to earn his place among the forty represented there. And next to his head, the text that took my breath away.

Hank Weston: Bad Boy to Best Boy.

"Hank?" I turned to face him, and he beamed down at me. "You had them call you Hank?"

"I did," he shrugged. "Thought it was time to take it back. If I own it right up front, then nobody can accuse me of keeping secrets." With that, he pulled me in for a kiss that made my bones ache.

"No secrets here, eh?" Our faces were so close that I could read his spirit.

Thank goodness that after those first wild days of glorious flirting, he had never made me his secret. We were always hand in hand in front of the world. It felt glorious to enjoy a love that we didn't have to hide.

"No secrets," he whispered, kissing me again.

"I like that." Then, leaning back, I unfixed his hands from where they had come to rest on my hips and pulled him toward the kitchen door.

"Just where do you think you're taking me?" he smirked.

"To the couch, of course. I'd say we deserve to celebrate."

"The couch?" His eyes burned into me, and I answered every bit of their heat.

"Of course. It's the sexiest spot in the building, in my experience. Don't you agree—*Hank*?"

EXCERPT: MISUNDERSTOOD

I ran into a single dad from hell... and then I made the mistake of accepting his job offer.

Turns out, hell had some scandalous plans for me.

Plan #1: Move into Hunter's house as his live-in nanny.

Plan #2: Fall into Hunter's bed.

Plan #3: Get pregnant with his baby and regret plans #1 and #2.

Living with a snob like Hunter wasn't easy.

But his daughter brought us closer.

The problem, though?

It's not just us three in the house.

Hunter invited his ex to live in his guest bedroom so she could recover from an illness.

My frustration was through the roof.

So, imagine my shock when I realized that I was expecting my snobby boss's baby.

Especially when I felt like he hadn't even given me his heart.

Chapter One: Jane

I turned the page and released a happy sigh. Another inset color plate. These were my favorites. The book was old with the yellowing of age on the edges of the pages. Each page turn revealed another puff of musty old book smell. The black and white illustrations were pretty and informative but they didn't hold the magic of color on glossy paper.

I didn't think anyone had checked this book out of the library for a very long time. I felt like I was discovering a treasure trove of information. This particular image was worth documenting. I felt like a big fat cheater when I focused the image into the rectangle of my phone's camera.

My hat cast an obnoxious shadow that I didn't notice until I scrolled back through the pictures. It was easier to just take the thing off than it would be to find the right angle where it wasn't blocking light. After all, that was the entire point of wearing the hat, to keep the light off my face.

The few freckles I had were bad enough. I didn't need any more sunspots across the bridge of my nose. Sure I could wear more foundation, but in this heat, the last thing I wanted was more of anything on my skin. So big hats were a necessity.

To reclaim any artistic cred I may have temporarily lost by taking pictures with my phone's built-in camera, I copied down the image in my very own scribble scratch attempt at drawing. The image was of a dancer, drawn in long graceful lines by the master of Art Deco himself, Erté. Festoons of pearls dripped from the dancer's arms that were extended away from her body. A broad fan of a headdress looked like some magical combination of a Czarina's crown and a peacock tail on full display.

My drawing looked nothing like the original, but it gave me the visual clues and construction notes that I needed to study the costume. I made more notes about the colors and turned the page.

A little hand reached into my view and flipped the page back. My head shot up and I yanked my earbuds out. Someone small had snuck up on me and I hadn't noticed in my focus. Not cool. My gaze was met by the top of a little head with medium brown hair pulled into two sloppy pigtails.

"I like this one better," the little girl said.

I sat back on my butt a little more from my hunched-over posture.

"Oh yeah?" I said.

I gave the small person a once-over. The pale blue tutu with matching leotard and tights, and hairstyle indicated this mini-person was a girl. The rhinestone-studded cowboy boots, the faded denim jacket, which attempted to have thrift-store styling but was clearly new, and the ice cream cone-shaped purse— that was perfect for a little girl in its style, but I happen to know cost more than two hundred dollars— all said, little rich girl. Somewhere nearby was a frantic nanny, or stay-at-home mother.

"So you like this one? Did you even look at the picture on the other page?" I asked as I scanned around for the missing adult for little miss money bags.

"The other one is not in color. I like the colors." The girl sat down on the opposite side of the book from me.

"She looks like a dancing peacock, don't you think?" I asked.

She nodded, intent on the picture in front of her.

I flipped back a few chapters to the previous color plate. "What do you think of this one?" I asked.

She giggled. "He's silly. He's dressed up like a big cat."

She wasn't wrong. The dancer on this color plate wore another one of Erté's designs for the Russian ballet company the Ballet Russe. The designs were magical, at least in my opinion. And it appeared this kid thought so too.

I picked up my phone and snuck a quick picture of the kid. I paused as I opened a new text, Should this go to non-emergency, or to 911? I gave myself a quick shake and texted 911. A missing kid would be an emergency.

"My name is Jane. What's yours?" I asked.

"Autumn."

I typed a text message to the police and sent the photo I had taken.

"I bet you like to dance. I see you are wearing a tutu." I described her tutu and the rest of her pricey outfit in my text to the police. I described our location the best I could. I was near the reservoir, closer to Fifth Avenue than Central Park West, but well inside the middle of the park on a lovely green grass hill. I snapped another picture and sent that as well.

"I love it," she gushed. Autumn stood. For a second I was afraid she was going to run off. She did a sloppy off-balance pirouette.

When prompted I sent all of my information and a basic description of what I was wearing: big floppy hat, breezy green floral kimono style cover-up, tank top, and jean shorts. My dark hair was up in a scarf, and my pasty white legs were getting their second annual exposure to the elements. I was out for some vitamin D3 absorption, not a tan.

I patted the blanket next to me for Autumn to sit down. My park quilt was a couple of old thrift store sheets I had stitched together so I could go to the park in style. My phone buzzed. I checked my messages.

"Police are coming to your location. Please don't move."

I flipped to a few other pictures and asked Autumn what she thought. Mostly she thought they were all silly. She wanted to go back to the peacock queen image. Her description, not mine, but a more useful description than "Pearls, 1924" that I had put in my notes.

"Are you Jane Hill?" a uniformed officer asked. She approached with the same swagger I saw on every other city cop when approaching a 'situation.'

I wanted to jump up, but then I realized I was the reason for 'the situation.' So I stayed firmly planted on my butt.

"I am, and this is Autumn."

"Miss Hill, can I see a form of identification?"

I handed over my driver's license. It was from Ohio, but it was still valid. I didn't need a New York license because I didn't drive here. I also handed over my student ID, so the officer wouldn't ask why I didn't have a New York ID.

"Autumn!" a loud bark sounded behind me.

I turned to see a red-faced man in a business suit walking toward us with determination. "Autumn, where the he—" he cut himself off.

"Daddy," Autumn said. She didn't sound scared, or surprised, or excited. It was simply a statement. This man was 'Daddy.'

The cop handed my ID cards back to me and approached the businessman. I noticed Autumn didn't seem phased that he was here, and seemed rather upset. She continued to flip the pages of my book.

I stood and brushed the legs of my Bermuda shorts down. I hovered next to Autumn, keeping an eye on the library book– since I couldn't afford to replace it if she decided to start chewing on pages or something– and eavesdropping on the cop and the man.

He was frustrated. There was a vein along the edge of his temple that popped out every time he clenched his jaw. And he was clenching that jaw a lot. I bet his dentist hated how much he ground his teeth.

"She was right behind me. We were getting snow cones from a

vendor." He reached inside the front of his suit jacket and pulled out a slim wallet and removed his ID and handed it to the cop.

She talked into the walkie-talkie clipped to her shoulder. It chirped and beeped. She handed him his card back, stepped back toward me and the girl, who wasn't interested in anything except the dancers in my book. The officer squatted down next to Autumn.

"Is your name Autumn McMillan?"

Autumn nodded and made uh-huh sounds.

"Hey Autumn, why don't you close the book for a minute. Okay. This nice lady needs you to talk to her," I said as I closed the book and moved it away from the little girl.

That's all it took for her to perk up and pay attention.

"Who is this?" the officer asked and pointed to me.

Autumn shrugged. "She's the one with the book with all the dancers in it."

"And him?" When the officer pointed back to the man, I followed her gesture and looked at him for the first time. I had noticed just how square and sharp-edged his jawline had been, but I had been distracted by the teeth clenching.

"That's Daddy," Autumn said.

Daddy was gorgeous for one of those Wall Street business types. His dark hair was perfectly parted and slicked back. A stark contrast to the hapless mess of his daughter's hair. He had a regal nose, with a slight Roman hook to it. His eyes were hidden behind aviators, and expensive ones too. Yeah, Daddy had money, and Autumn was a spoiled princess.

"Okay, you check out. Glad you found her. Next time, maybe pay better attention to the kid. Thank you for letting us know, miss." and with a curt set of nods, the officer left.

"How did you manage to keep her in one place?" Daddy's voice was a nice tenor with undertones of a deep rumble.

I shrugged. "She liked my book." I waved the heavy tome the best I could with one hand.

"Looks like a textbook." He nodded at it.

"Yeah, it's a history of costumes. Autumn seemed to like it."

"Anything Autumn likes will hold her attention. Unfortunately, she seems to not like a whole lot. What do you do for a living? Are you a teacher? You said history."

"Student. I'm studying."

He reached back into his inner jacket pocket, and I couldn't help but notice how broad his shoulders were. He handed me a card. "My name is Hunter McMillan. Autumn seems to like you, she listened to you. Ever consider being a nanny?"

Read the full story here!

INVITATION TO JOIN KELLY'S NEWSLETTER

Kelly Myers writes contemporary romance. She tries to bring that feeling which makes you feel connected to the characters in her books. Her stories have characters that make their partners feel seen, heard, and understood.

Once you've read her book, you won't forget it and you won't stop chasing that feeling again till you grab her next book.

So, she's inviting you here to subscribe to her newsletter and stay updated with latest information on upcoming releases or special price promotions.

Sign up to her Newsletter -> https://landing.mailerlite.com/webforms/landing/m8t0h0

If you want to get in touch with her, drop her an email at:

kellymyers@kellymyerspublishing.com

Made in United States
North Haven, CT
28 February 2023

33355653R00345